Other works by
EDWARD M. ERDELAC

NOVELS:
Buff Tea
Coyote's Trail
Andersonville
Monstrumführer
Mindbreaker (in Bond Unknown)
Perennial (in Humanity 2.0)
The Knight With Two Swords

THE MERKABAH RIDER SERIES:
High Planes Drifter
The Mensch With No Name
Have Glyphs Will Travel
Once Upon A Time In The Weird West

THE VAN HELSING PAPERS:
Terovolas

COLLECTIONS:
With Sword And Pistol
Angler In Darkness

KNIGHT THE
WITH TWO
SWORDS

EDWARD M.
ERDELAC

THE KNIGHT WITH TWO SWORDS
Copyright © 2018 by Edward M. Erdelac. All rights reserved.

Editor: Gwen Nix
Cover Illustration: Chris Yarbrough
Cover Design & Interior Layout: STK•Kreations

Worldwide Rights
Created in the United States of America

To Aunt Vicky,
For always being there and for lending me those Mary Stewart books.

AUTHOR'S NOTE

This is a tale of that long-ago kingdom of faraway Albion which exists only in dreams; of the shining Camelot of Malory, White, and Boorman, which is as far from 6th century England as the Emerald City of Oz is from modern day Topeka. It's a story of the greatest earthly ruler ever known, King Arthur, the magic Isle of Avalon, of Merlin the enchanter, the Holy Grail, and the Lady of The Lake. It is pretense, not historicity. While I find Arthurian scholarship endlessly intriguing, I'm a storyteller, and this is a fantasy, so the reader must expect nothing more...or less.

Special Thanks to Nightbringer and Christopher W. Bruce.

FIRST PART:

THE
ADVENTUROUS
SWORD

CHAPTER
ONE

THE STONE COTTAGE at the edge of the forest had seen the Roman wall that crossed the emerald field in its bare and austere prime, patrolled by grumbling legionaries far from home.

Now, the wall was a gathering place for long grass, leafy Solomon's seal, and sun-yellow cinquefoil blossoms. People came to pick wild chives and spignel from its overgrown base. Dandelions drifted back and forth over its top, as heedless of the boundary it had once stolidly denoted as the idle clouds in the sea-blue sky overhead.

The works of great men rose and fell, except for the cottage, which had been erected long ago by a forgotten woman's hands.

Chickens scratched at the tamped earth surrounding it, and a red-haired woman with callused palms sat on a rude wood bench outside mending a pair of boy's trousers, a nest of brown thread piled in a basket beside her. An old white wolfhound dozed at her feet.

A rough, brown dirt roadpath meandered out to the cottage door from the forest, its wild appearance indicative of the self-reliance of the homestead. There was a cool well, there were chickens, there were bright yellow apples from the tree growing on the hill. What need of travel? Visitors were infrequent.

In the upper reaches of the apple tree, a pied raven alit and preened. It was not wholly black, but splashed with an array of patchwork hues. Its long black beak poked like a scholar's nose, and its black and brown feathers showed as if beneath a threadbare coat of stark white. It was an oddity unnoticed by the two rough-garbed dark-headed boys fighting a ferocious stick duel below. Each boy was the mirror of the other, down to their hands, for one favored the left and the other the right. They disengaged at the sight of a tall woman seated on a long-maned white horse when she appeared at the edge of the wood.

The woman wore a seamless garment of sugar-white samite, and her unbound white-gold hair spilled over the rump of her barebacked mount. The woman sat regal and aright, and though her pale fingers were entwined in the mane of the horse, its mouth bore no bit, its face no bridle. She guided it with her knees alone.

It clopped down the narrow path to the cottage.

The white wolfhound picked up its head, but after focusing its failing eyes on the rider, laid back down, unconcerned.

The two boys raced down the hill, shoving each other the whole way, reaching their mother's side at the same time as the newcomer on the horse.

The fleeter of the two had won the right to speak, and announced breathlessly to their mother, who had not yet raised her attention from her work:

"Mother! A visitor!"

The red-haired woman looked up, unsurprised at the radiant woman towering above her. She nodded her head in greeting.

"Lady Lile," she said.

"Eglante," the woman replied.

"Balin, Brulen," Eglante said to the boys, "go back to your play."

Brulen looked disappointed, and his dark eyes lingered on the Lady Lile, but his brother, Balin, nudged him roughly and stomped off, apparently deciding that if his mother had deemed to exclude them from the visitation, then the visitor was not worth his attention.

"Come on, Brulen," he said, swiping the back of his hand across his nose, a calculated show of dismissal.

Brulen walked in the shadow of his brother, glancing back curiously.

The Lady Lile never looked at them but kept her blue gaze fixed on their mother as they tromped off, finally breaking into a run halfway up the hill. Their makeshift stick swords clacked in the distance.

"Your sons?"

Eglante held up her work to inspect it, then broke off the thread and laid it aside.

"Your nephews," she said. "You might have acknowledged them."

"You endanger them," said the Lady. "King Detors has turned from the old ways. He is ambitious, and sees in the crucified king a means of wresting the hearts of the people from the spirits of tree and stone."

"Detors is a small man," said Eglante, smiling thinly. "Hardly a king at all. Your Uther Pendragon will bring him to heel soon enough."

"Uther is temperamental and a lustful brigand," said the Lady. "He will not be the one to unite the land. Already he has sown his own undoing."

"Has he bucked under your measured guidance, Lile?" Eglante asked with a hint of slyness.

"I am here for your benefit, not to hear your disapproval of my methods," Lile snapped. "How can you remain here? You are a daughter of Avalon. You should pack your things and come with me. It's the only safe haven for our kind. Even those who can find their way through the mists cannot stand against the Red Knight."

"And what of my sons? Shall I leave them to fend for themselves, or has the Isle rescinded its ridiculous prohibition against men?"

"They are boys; they may thrive in this world of men."

"And there is my answer," said Eglante, rising from the bench and picking up her sewing.

"How long can you continue to play the part of a wise woman, doling out love potions and cure-alls to the ignorant?" Lile said, as Eglante went to the cottage door. "Detors' holy men have declared you an outlaw. You are a priestess of Avalon! How long will the love of a dead man keep you from your sacred duties?"

Eglante stood in the doorway and looked back with a kind of pity in her eyes.

"Look at you on your horse. My sister. The Lady of The Lake. Privy to the Great Mystery. No one, perhaps not even the Merlin, is more learned in the magic of the land or versed in the Sight. And yet," she said, her eyes going to the two boys on the hill. "What price have you paid? You are yet a girl. You hold your duty above all else, but you think my duty to my sons is somehow less. How very little you see."

"Shall I tell you what I see, sister?" Lile said, her face coloring. She wheeled the horse about and thrust one finger at the road through the forest. "Shall I tell you what is coming down that path for you?"

"Nothing that does not come for us all, in the end," said Eglante, turning back to the cottage.

"I will have need of a successor someday," Lile called.

Eglante disappeared inside.

"I am sure you will find her, milady."

Lady Lile sat atop her horse, with the foraging chickens orbiting her. As if self-conscious, but more likely in imitation of their industry, the horse pawed the earth with one hoof.

The wolfhound roused itself and followed Eglante inside.

The white rider glanced toward the forest road, then nudged the horse in the opposite direction and loped for the edge of the field.

The pied raven squawked in the tree.

CHAPTER
TWO

THE BROTHERS BALIN and Brulen sat upon the hill, their backs to the trunk of the apple tree between them.

Their boy hearts still thundered from the race, and their lungs burned.

Brulen watched the woman depart from their home. "Do you know who that was?" he asked.

Balin shrugged. He stared up at the sky through the branches at the strangely colored raven near the top. He had been imagining the tall masts of sailing ships until the bird had raised its cry and sunk the imagined vessels in their daydream sea. He had never before seen a raven that was not completely black.

"The Lady Lile," said Brulen. He twisted and looked at his brother.

Balin showed no reaction, but yawned and smacked his lips.

"The Lady of The Lake?" Brulen prodded.

Balin looked after the shrinking woman at that and narrowed his eyes, the raven forgotten. He reached into his tunic, brought out a small wooden cross hanging from a bit of leather, and twisted it between his fingers thoughtfully. The Lady of The Lake, he knew. The mistress of cursed Avalon, that ensorcelled island hidden by shifting mists and infernal guile where witches did secret spells at the behest of their demon patrons.

"The priest in the village says she's the Devil's wife," he muttered.

Brulen scoffed.

"He says that about Mother too."

"He does not!" Balin said, appalled.

"Does," Brulen insisted.

Balin turned toward his brother and knelt on one knee dramatically, striking his chest with his fist.

"Oh Heavenly Father!" he intoned to the sky. "This day let the truth be known! For no knight who is false may stand against one who is true!"

It was an old saying which they had both committed to heart, as their mother had told them their father had often repeated it.

Brulen's face broke into a grin and he picked up a rotten apple and flung it at Balin. It burst on his shoulder.

Balin grimaced and jumped to his feet. He put one boot to Brulen's arm and kicked him over with a laugh, then sprang for the lowest hanging branch and began to scale the tree like a mountaineer.

The first shock of weight on the tree sent the piebald raven flapping away with an annoyed cawing.

Brulen jumped after his brother, at first following his path up the tree, and then leaping for more daring handholds.

It became a vertical race for the highest bough, and the boys interspersed their huffing breaths with agonizing bursts of uncontrollable laughter.

Brulen got a hold of Balin's heel and tried to pull him down but came away with only a boot.

Heavy apples shook free and rained to the ground like conquered defenders plummeting from a high tower besieged.

At last Balin rose triumphant above the leafy corona of the tree and hunkered on the solitary high perch, grinning down. He seized the topmost golden apple as a prize and bit into it loudly.

"Cheat," Brulen grumbled up at him.

Balin let the apple fall. It bounced off Brulen's head and tumbled down beside Balin's discarded boot.

The boys sat quiet as finches in the tree for a while, delighting in their unprecedented vantage of the land. Balin closed his eyes. In his mind, trumpets blared and maidens called out his name.

They were fatherless, but it was the war between King Uther and the Saxons which had made them so. As sons of a martyred knight, they were welcome to bear their father's red boar crest in the service of the High King as knights themselves, should they so choose, but their mother had discouraged their training. She taught them to be peaceful, to take sustenance from the land and thus serve no one, and to respect all life as sacred.

Balin accepted all that his mother taught him, which was practical, but in his heart, he suspected that as a short-sighted woman, she gave herself over to much that was impractical. His father had been a follower of Jesus Christ, he knew, though Balin had no real memory of him. He thought that as his father had been a hero, then there must be something in the faith that had borne him through so many battles. He knew that the Saxons were evil heathens that had slaughtered women, children, and the family of the King, as well as murdered his predecessor and brother King Ambrosius by poison. He felt great pride that Christian men like his father had opposed them.

He talked as much as he could with the village priest about the God of his father and came to understand that the goddess his mother sometimes referred to was a lie; at best a woman's fancy, at worst a fell deity in league with angels cast from heaven and very likely an agent of the Devil, if not the Devil himself in woman-form.

Yet he loved his mother dearly, and as he had no tongue for debate, tolerated her sinful ways. He knew well that some thought her a witch, and she did nothing to disprove them, selling charms and unctions to the peasants that came under cover of night to her door with their heartaches and ailments. He prayed fervently that she should see some bright light and come to Jesus as the Jew killer Saul had on the road to Damascus.

In contrast, Brulen listened rapt to the tales their mother told them of mystic, timeless Avalon and the enchanter, Merlin. His favorite story though, was of old King Llud of the Silver Hand, who had defended Albion against plagues of dwarves and giants, and how he had trapped two dragons beneath Dinas Emrys on Mount Erith in a stone pit full of mead in the very center of the land. Years later, when King Vortigern had tried to build a fort there, he discovered that each night the masonry his builders had erected would shake apart. Young Merlin revealed the dragons to Vortigern, telling him their endless battle was indicative of the clash of the Welsh and the Saxon invaders, and that the Welsh would win.

But, their mother had told them Merlin had misinterpreted the meaning of the two warring beasts. Vortigern had brought the Saxons to Albion as mercenaries to help wipe out the Old People, the Picts, who revered the Goddess, and the dragons were a reminder of the war he had set in motion: the war in the heart of the land, between the Old and the New.

"Because," she had told them, "to every land there is an appointed spirit, a set Way of honoring that spirit. When the Way of another is forcibly brought to a place it does not belong, there is always conflict, until one Way defeats the other. Sometimes the old prevails, sometimes the new. In the meantime, we balance between the shifting meanings of what is sacred and what is profane, like a person standing on a narrow log across a deep ravine."

She talked of lighter things, too, of fairy circles and half-glimpsed unicorns, and of the Lady of The Lake, the queen of the apple orchard isle of hidden Avalon, who granted the chosen rulers of Albion their authority by bestowing upon them the indomitable sword of power, Excalibur, the Steel-Cutter, one of the thirteen sacred treasures.

This was a story that intrigued both boys, though in different ways. At the end of such tales, Balin would say, "I should like to have a sword like that."

And Brulen would say, "I should like to visit Avalon someday."

But Avalon, their mother said, was a hidden place that no man could set foot on, save two: Merlin, who was more than a man; and The Red Knight, the mysterious, ageless, and undefeatable defender of the Lady and her followers. The only man who could reside in Avalon.

"No knight is undefeatable," Balin scoffed.

But Brulen said nothing. He respected the high magic, understood the power of Avalon. He would share a look with his mother and change the subject, knowing his brother's heart better than she.

They were two of a kind, yet different. Born from the same widow's womb at almost the same moment, each had always been the only significant male influence on the other, save for the storied exploits of a phantom father they managed to snatch from passing knights and wring from their mother, who was reluctant to glorify his warrior deeds.

Yet whereas Brulen took his mother's lessons to heart, Balin snuck off to hear the Gospel from the village priest, a soft bellied, hard-hearted hermit named Brother Gallet. Brulen spoke sometimes to the people who came to his mother for help and knew many of them had become Christians. He knew there was good in the way of the crucified king and his teachings.

But the stories Balin brought home secondhand, for he was unwilling to learn to read them himself, were cruel and exclusionary, selected or perhaps concocted by Gallet to stir his aggressive soul with notions of divine righteousness and holiness. Brulen found it hard to reconcile the man who had died on a tree for teaching love with the God of Gallet, who instructed the leaders of His chosen people to show no mercy to captives and to stone women to death.

"Listen," said Balin.

Brulen looked toward the road.

That road wound sleepily through the forest in which they stalked and played, emptying out at last to the village of Belande and the Castle Sewingshields, the stronghold of King Detors. It was through this tunnel in the greenwood that people came now and then to seek their mother's aid.

They always came one or two at a time, usually after nightfall, fearing the edicts of Detors against witchcraft.

But it was only a little after noon. The sun was high and perhaps a dozen people emerged from the forest, the two biggest of their number, the blacksmith and butcher, Balin noted, pulling a squeaking cart piled with unbaled hay. A single stout post rose from the center. The crowd bore an assortment of tools as if bound for some unguessed communal task: knives and hatchets, a scythe and sickles.

At their head was Brother Gallet, bearing his staff of office, a pine pole capped with a simple leather-wrapped cross within a crude willow circle.

Brulen caught his breath and Balin held up his hand.

They would make no move. These were their neighbors. Several of their number had been to the cottage before for succor.

They watched as the priest led the others down the path.

Their old hound, Killhart, bounded from the cottage as he had not done in uncounted summers. Planting his legs apart, he situated himself in the center of the path, laid back his ears, bearing his teeth in a warning snarl. When the people gave no heed, he split the air with a volley of snapping barks, so ferocious it flecked the ground with froth and caused the priest to pause. Several of the villagers recoiled.

Eglante came out of the doorway, wiping her hands on her skirts. She had been preparing their supper.

"Get back, cur of Satan!" Gallet screamed over the dog's incessant barking. He stormed at the dog, raising his staff over his head.

Killhart sprang.

Gallet brought the staff down with a crack on the dog's head that resounded in the clearing.

Killhart fell limp, his old white head red with blood.

The priest fetched him a few heavier clouts to be sure, making Killhart's limp body jump.

Balin cried out in anguish. They had both loved that dog, been carried in its jowls as babes. To Balin especially, Killhart had been more than an animal. He had been Balin's constant companion in his adventures in the forest, running down rabbits and breaking hosts of imagined enemies with a stick of wood. Their mother had told them Killhart followed him around in the woods much as he had their father, and Balin had taken a special pride in that relationship.

His shriek was matched by their mother's own, as she ran forward and fell on her knees next to the faithful old animal, cradling his broken head.

"See?" Gallet called out to the others, beckoning them forward. "What need of a lawful husband has this witch of the wild? She has this hound of hell for a mate. Mark you well her unnatural grief."

The people gathered closer, some of them nodding to themselves, never taking their eyes from Eglante.

"What is the meaning of this?" she wailed. "Who are you?"

"A servant of the Most High," Gallet responded, drawing himself up imperiously as the dog blood ran down his staff and over his pale knuckles. "Who do you say you are?"

Eglante rose from the corpse of Killhart, the front of her skirt stained red. "Ask these people who I am," she said.

"They have told me who you are," Gallet said, gesturing at the people shuffling at his back. "They have told me of your potions and spells. Do you deny brewing them here?"

"I do not," Eglante said, throwing back her head and brushing away her tears with the back of one hand. "I give them whatever they ask of me for a fair price."

Gallet thrust his finger at her like a dagger point, his stained, rotting teeth bared much as Killhart's had been. "What price, vile succubus? Their bodies? Their souls? You lead them down the Devil's road!"

The boys dropped nimbly from the tree, but in the end, Brulen's grip failed him and he crashed unprepared to the ground, twisting his ankle.

Balin landed panther-like beside him and hoisted him up without a word. They limped quickly down the hill, Balin with one foot still bare.

"What gives you the right to murder my pet?" Eglante shrieked, balling her fists.

"The authority of the king and the God that reigns above him," said Gallet, gesturing to the sky as though his deity were looking on them from some celestial pavilion.

At that instant, the pied raven swooped down from atop the cottage thatch and flew in the priest's face, drawing blood with a claw from under his left eye. The priest struck at it with his staff and it wheeled away, gliding into the forest as the villagers gaped after it.

"You see?" Gallet bellowed, dabbing at his bleeding face with his sleeve. "She commands the fell beasts of land and air. Take her!"

The butcher and the blacksmith rushed forward and snatched Eglante's arms.

She tried to tear herself free, but they held her too tightly.

"What have I done?" she demanded, as the crowd parted and they dragged her toward the hay cart.

Balin and Brulen stumbled to the edge of the crowd, breathless.

"Mother?" Balin called.

The closest man to the boys, the miller, Hull, laid hold of Balin's arm as a woman pulled Brulen from his brother's grasp.

Enraged, Balin lashed out and bit the soft part of Hull's hand till his teeth crunched against bone.

Hull shrieked and flung him away. He landed in the grass, sprawling.

Brulen offered no resistance. His wide eyes followed his mother as her hands were bound behind her back. She was carried up into the hay cart and fixed to the pole.

Two other villages hauled Balin to his feet. He thrashed and snarled wordlessly, bucking in their grip, and two more gripped his ankles and hoisted him in the air. They pulled his wiry limbs taut, and still he shook, although it agonized his small muscles.

"Look you, brothers and sisters," Gallet said, pointing to Balin. "This hellspawn Brulen is like a wild animal nursed on black milk! The Devil's own son."

Neither Brulen in his shock nor Balin in his rage bothered to correct Gallet's mistake.

But an old hag of a woman with wild, unbound silver hair in a white robe spoke up.

"No! Their father was Sir Ballantyne, one of King Detors' noble knights."

"This one's savagery is more suited to the nobility of hell than of any knight," Gallet sneered.

"Ballantyne died a hero in service against the Saxons at Cad Hill," she went on.

Gallet stared at the old woman, and she met his gaze with bold blue eyes that made his own narrow.

"Who are you?" he whispered uncertainly, the blood from the raven's claw trickling down his cheek like a demon's tear.

The blacksmith leapt down from the cart, leaving Eglante alone.

She twisted to look at Gallet.

"It will go ill for you, priest," she called, "if you murder the heirs of a noble knight in the name of your god."

Gallet turned from the old woman, oblivious to her as she faded back into the crowd and passed unnoticed to its rear.

"But my god is your God, harridan," he said to Eglante. "You shall learn that presently."

The priest's eyes went to the butcher. He was kneeling, striking flint to tinder, sparking a brand.

Balin stopped thrashing and watched in disbelief as the butcher flung the burning brand into the back of the hay cart.

Every maddened eye turned to the fast rising flames. Only Eglante's saw the old woman who had spoken give a single prim nod. Eglante bobbed her chin in silent recognition and then she turned once more to her sons as the unbearable heat rose and her hair singed. Her dress caught fire and her reddened eyes splashed her cheeks with tears that the thirsty blaze drank up almost immediately.

"Be good boys!" she choked through the flames as her hair blackened. "Be good men!"

Brulen wailed and sagged in the arms of the villagers who held him.

The villagers retreated from the blaze and the human fuel which burned at its center.

Gallet raised his arms and spoke a benediction, which the crackling fire and the screams of Eglante and Brulen drowned out.

Balin made no outcry.

He looked across the torch head of his mother at the place where the old woman who had spoken his father's name had stood.

But she was gone.

In her place was the Lady of The Lake, undimmed by the inky smoke that rose from his burning mother, cold in her glittering white garment atop her spotless white horse, her beautiful face terrible and remote, majestic as a snow-covered peak.

Balin watched her as she turned and rode back up the little path to the forest.

Somewhere the raven called, perhaps in laughter, perhaps in lament.

CHAPTER
THREE

FOR TEN HOURS, the two brothers spent their last night as squires kneeling shoulder to shoulder in silence before the altar in the dim candlelit chapel of Castle Sewingshields. It was the final test of knighthood, the last passion, and for Balin, a reminder of Christ's lonesome vigil in Gethsemane. His legs were numb and stiff, well beyond aching, and the sweat had spoiled his ritual bathing, but he didn't care. The beauty and power of the moment, the culmination of all his boyhood aspirations, almost overcame him.

They were garbed in the ritual black hose and boots of death, the white vestures of purity, and over all, the red robes representing the royal blood to which they would swear fealty. On the altar lay their swords, entwined in belts and frogs, their gilt spurs, and the shields bearing their chosen blazons. *Per pale indented argent and gules, two boars combatant, argent and gules.* It was a special dispensation the College of Heraldry had granted them, two knights bearing the same design with the placements reversed. Twin knights were uncommon. The boars were a tribute to their father's own rampant boar crest.

Already they were the two greatest fighters of Northumberland, unmatched except by each other. King Detors bragged that they would be the finest knights in Albion.

What Brulen prayed for in the stillness, if he prayed at all, Balin could not guess. Brulen still admitted to him a lack of faith in the god of their father. In the intervening years since their mother's death, he had cleaved to her teachings more fervently than ever, though necessarily in secret. Balin prayed to be as good a knight as their father had been, to be truthful and brave, to serve his king well. He prayed for his brother, that he come to know the light of the Lord Jesus Christ before the Devil took his soul.

Long and hard had they trained, orphan brothers wielding dirty spoons and towels in the kitchens of Detors, pitchforks and shovels in the stables, and finally porting lances and swords and securing armor in the pavilions and on the tiltyards. They were no man's sons, and yet every knight had become like a father, eager to teach them all they could, for all knew their circumstance and pitied them. The greater was their achievement for their sad and humble origins.

Balin apprenticed to brawny Sir Claellus, a God-fearing man and an even tempered master, a master swordsman who bragged to the other knights that Balin was the finest fighter he had ever trained. Brulen had fattened Claellus over the years with the abundance of game he had brought to their table.

Claellus had known their father Ballantyne, and presented them both with their father's own swords.

Brulen was the squire of Sir Gernemant, a quiet, lanky fellow, well-traveled, who led his apprentice around King Detors' library almost as much as he did the proving grounds and valued lessons of wisdom over strength at arms.

They shared some of their training with each other, of course. Balin instructed Brulen in the finer points of jousting, and Brulen tutored Balin in heraldry, an aspect of book learning that appealed to Balin for it entailed so many colorful pictures. Brulen got a better education in tilting than he did from Gernemant, and Balin learned the emblems of much of the Albion gentry.

When the morning light shone through the stained-glass window, casting the brothers in deep reds and blazing whites, the prelates entered for the morning mass, along with the sponsor knights, Sir Claellus and Sir Gernemant , old silver bearded King Detors, and his callow son, Prince Clarivaunce, the heir apparent.

The mass began, and the celebrating priest took the lectern to intone the opening prayer in Latin, Balin sensed Brulen stiffen at his side.

The priest was Gallet, the very same who had presided over their mother's execution.

Of course, it would be Gallet. Gallet had been Balin's mentor and confessor. As the man who delivered them to Detors, he had truly put them both on the path to knighthood and had likely requested the honor of presiding over their accolade. It made Balin slightly uncomfortable, but in the years since their mother's execution, he had come to understand Gallet's cruelty. The enemies of Christ must be eradicated without mercy lest the world fall to darkness. His mother, unfortunate fool that she had been, had counted herself against God by indulging in the Devil's teachings. He still grieved for her. She had been a kind woman, and as a son, his heart ached for her, but he bore Gallet no hatred. That, he reserved for the bitch who had led his mother astray. That villainess, the Lady Lile. He could still see her as he had that day, haughty through the flames.

Brulen, however, was another matter. Out of the corner of his eye, Balin could see his brother fixing the priest with a hard gaze.

"Someday I will kill Gallet," Brulen had told him once.

"Why?" Balin had asked.

"How can you ask me that?" Brulen had countered.

"Will you kill Hull the miller and all the villagers who were there that day?"

"If ever they have the misfortune to cross my path," Brulen said.

"That's foolish, brother."

"Don't you hate them for what they did?"

"Who am I, to hate them for doing what the Lord decreed?"

"You think God wanted our mother dead? Burned alive?"

"Not her, but her wickedness, yes. And she wouldn't let go of it. That's what burned her in the end. Gallet did not light *that* fire, Brulen. It was lit in her long ago. A devil's fire. And you know well the hand that lit it."

It had been a point of perennial and heated disagreement between them, and they had not spoken much of it after that. But even though they didn't give it voice, it came out sometimes, in their sparring. The clacking of their practice weapons, struck to shivering, became the harsh words of their unending contention. Every counterattack was a retort, every blow a point. When either fell or was thrown exhausted to the straw, that was an argument won.

No knight who is false can stand against one who is true, their father had said.

But they were too evenly matched. Neither could ultimately ever convince the other. This was a bitter shim between the brothers, who should have loved each other above all others and without condition, but did not. Could not.

The mass progressed to the accolade. As King Detors limped slowly to the other side of the communion rail, assisted by Sir Claellus and Sir Gernemant, Gallet blessed their shields and swords.

Sir Claellus took Balin's shield and spurs and passed him his naked sword.

Taking it point down in his fist, Balin touched his forehead to the pommel and intoned:

"I swear by my faith, by my blood, all loyalty to my lord under God. I shall honor my oath to him against all his enemies, in good faith and free of guile."

He held his sword out and lowered his head.

King Detors took the sword from him and touched the flat of the blade first to one shoulder, then the other, saying, "In the name of God, St. Michael, and St. George, I dub thee, Sir Balin."

Sir Claellus took the sword from the king and handed it once more to Balin. He rose on shaky legs, but did not falter, and accepted his shield. Sir Claellus wrapped his belt twice about him and handed him his chivalric spurs. Balin sank his sword into its scabbard and felt its weight at his side.

It was the happiest moment of his life. His head swam with the great things he would do. He breathed in the incense clouding from the assistant priest's censer the sweet odor of heated tallow, and the candle smoke. These were the smells of the breath of God Himself to Balin, and he felt the approval of the Divine wash over him. He was a knight at last in the eyes of God and man.

Beside him, the ritual was repeated for Brulen. He heard his brother murmur the sacred oath, and prayed it was true.

"I dub thee Sir Brulen."

Brulen accepted his sword and spurs from Sir Gernemant and rose. Balin felt a flush of pride in his brother. He, too, had not stumbled, though his legs were surely as dead as Balin's own, which now prickled as the blood returned. Sir Gernemant affixed Brulen's belt, and Balin looked across at his brother and smiled.

Brulen did not notice. He was staring at Gallet.

The priest smiled placidly beside the king, hands folded before him. He was an old man now, thin and wraith-like, his ears overlarge and strands of white hairs sticking out like unruly cat whiskers.

Sir Gernemant rose and stepped back to King Detors' side.

Brulen took a step toward the altar and thrust the point of his sword into Gallet's belly just above his hands, with a sound like a spade sinking into wet earth.

It was as though Brulen had stabbed the entire congregation, for everyone present let out a collective gasp.

Gallet's smile trembled, but did not fail. He blinked at Brulen. Brulen gripped the front of Gallet's cassock in his fist and pulled the priest forward on the blade, until it burst from his back. The gathered clerics moaned in impotent distress.

His face mere inches from Gallet's, Brulen spit on his cheek. The action was punctuated by another gasp of horror from the audience. The knights nervously, livid in outrage and yet paralyzed by the sacrilegious audacity of the moment, crossed themselves.

Still Gallet's expression did not change. His eyelids fluttered. Blood dribbled down his lips.

"May the fires that burn you burn hotter and slower than those that consumed my mother." Brulen hissed and with the last, he put his hand to Gallet's chest and shoved him off his sword.

Blood cascaded from the priest's wound. He made no outcry as he fell back sprawling over the altar table and lay spread eagled, staring like some ghastly pagan sacrifice.

Brulen held up his red-stained sword and backed away. His eyes darted to the king and his two knights, who appeared stupefied.

Balin drew his sword and stepped in front of the king.

"Brother…" Brulen faltered. There were tears in his eyes.

"Do not call me brother," Balin said through his teeth. In his heart, he prayed a final time that Detors would not order Brulen seized.

Brulen backed away down the aisle, the tears running freely down his cheeks now, blood dripping from his blade. His left hand and his white vestments were spotted with Gallet's blood. He turned to the men at arms in the pews, but although some had risen and put their hands to their hilts, no one moved against him. They all feared his prowess, and knew that even if they managed to best him, the possibility of inciting Balin's wrath might be their only reward. They, too, prayed their king would not order them into action.

Detors was either shocked into silence by the depth of Brulen's sacrilege, or he valued his knights too highly.

Balin watched his brother turn and run from the chapel.

CHAPTER
FOUR

TWO YEARS AFTER Balin's accolade, Old King Detors died in his bed and his son Clarivaunce was crowned.

As a boy, Balin impressed the knights of Belande with his woodcraft and even taught the royal gameskeeper certain tricks of stalking. He soon gained renown as the most skillful hunter in Northumberland. King Clarivaunce selected Balin for the dubious honor of guiding the royal person and the emissaries of neighboring nobility on an endless series of pleasure hunts. These were mere courtly entertainments, unlike the hair-raising boar hunts of his squire days, which he and Sir Claellus had undertaken on foot with spears. The lack of sport bored Balin. Yet, being in such constant close proximity to the new king, he quickly learned what type of ruler Clarivaunce aspired to be.

Clarivaunce began discussing the possibility of war with their neighbor, King Leodegrance of Cameliard, a good Christian and an old ally of Detors. Balin soon realized that Clarivaunce was a Christian only in the chapel. Ambition was his one true god. He wished to expand his lands and wealth and didn't care a whit for honoring his late father's timeworn alliances. He even began negotiating with the pagan King Carados to invade and divide Cameliard between them.

At the same time, word came to Northumberland of the existence of a strange wonder: a sword in a stone had appeared outside a church in Londres. The sword supposedly bore a legend which decreed that whosoever removed it would be crowned high king of all Albion.

Normally, Balin would have dismissed such a thing as deviltry of Avalon, but the Archbishop Dubricius was said to have ratified the sword in the stone as a true miracle, an answer from God to the bickering of petty rulers and the outcry of the people for a benevolent monarch to unify all of Albion in peace. The outer boundaries of Londres swelled with the pavilions of warriors and nobles who came to joust for the right to draw the sword. Everyone expected that the true king would step forward any day now.

Apparently, no one had so far been able to do so.

When Clarivaunce heard that King Leodegrance had traveled to Londres and failed to draw the sword out of the stone, one of the king's counselors asked him if he, too, would make the pilgrimage.

Clarivaunce laughed and said, "Why bother? It doesn't take a single sword to claim this land. It takes ten thousand. And soon I will have them."

Balin saw more and more that he served a king far different from the one to whom he had pledged his heart.

He had prayed long and hard, and contemplated his oath.

Then word came that the sword had been freed, beyond belief, by a boy of seventeen years.

When this news reached Clarivaunce, he dismissed it with another infuriating chuckle.

Balin was unable to remain silent. "But sire, if the sword really was immovable by other men, and the Archbishop identified it as a miraculous test, then…"

"Sir Balin," Clarivaunce had said, smiling like a patronizing father though they were both the same age. "You're the best hunter among my knights and a rare swordsman, but you'd do well to leave the affairs of state to those bred to understand its intricacies. This sword is no miracle from God, it's a scheme to convince the fool peasants to support a puppet ruler. A fatherless boy out of nowhere with no name and no lands claims the high kingship, and we nobles are meant to bow? Preposterous! Dubricius has been bought and paid for, likely by this backcountry Lord Ector of Caer Gai, who I understand was the boy's *foster* father. It's a clever plan to win the loyalty of the poor, but carving knives and pitchforks won't stand long against swords and halberds."

A counselor of Clarivaunce spoke then.

"Sire, King Lot of Orkney has come out against the bastard, as well as Aguysans and a few others. They have pitched their pavilions outside Londres."

Clarivaunce looked thoughtful.

"It may be we situation to our advantage," he mused. "Ready my men and prepare my royal train. We shall travel to Londres to see this great sight. What say you, Sir Balin?"

But Balin was nowhere to be seen.

He had slipped from the throne room, gone straight to his chambers, gotten his armor, sword, and shield.

While Clarivaunce waited for word from Carados and amassed his troops, Balin rode from Belande, never to return.

THE TOURNAMENTS AT Londres had ended now that the sword had been drawn from the marble block, but the kings and nobles had almost unanimously stalled the coronation of the boy, each demanding to see the feat repeated with their own eyes and to have their own respective champions try.

The boy, as a squire, had not participated in the jousting, the nobles argued, and so every knight must now be given the same opportunity. Scheduling a demonstration for the arrival of each dissenting noble and his coterie had dragged the whole affair out for months. Three times now the boy had drawn and replaced the sword before a crowd. Yet still, only a few of the kings and nobles had pledged allegiance to him.

Leodegrance, Balin heard, was one of them.

Balin arrived in time for Pentecost and waited in the packed courtyard with an assortment of curiosity seekers, knights, and rowdy peasants, while the Archbishop held mass inside St. Paul's for the boy and the nobles.

Anyone had free access to the sword now. It took an hour for Balin to get near it as unruly queues of men from every station tried their hand at drawing it and shuffled off in sullen defeat.

It was a four-foot stone of pure white marble with a gleaming new anvil atop it. Sprouting like some metalworker's crafted flower was the golden hilt of a Roman-style sword.

"It's Macsen Wledig's sword," said a regally dressed, white bearded noble at his side, when he noticed Balin staring admiringly at the ancient weapon.

Sir Gernemant had taught him and his brother about Macsen. He had been called Magnus Maximus, a great general in Albion who had taken the Roman Empire from Gratian by force of sword. Macsen had dreamt of a beautiful Welsh woman and gone seeking her. The woman was Elen, a Lady of Avalon, with whom he formed a dynasty and whose father Eudaf he appointed High King, granting him his sword as a ceremonial symbol of authority.

"The sword has been passed down for centuries," the noble intoned reverently. "It hung in Vortigern's hall, and in the hall of Ambrosius, then Uther's. It was thought lost, stolen by the Saxons. All the more reason its reappearance is a miracle."

A burly peasant gripped the handle of the sword with both hands and strained to pull it free, until the tendons stood out on his arms and his face blazed so red it looked about to burst. Though his rowdy friends cheered him on, he released the sword with a gasp and walked off laughing and shaking his head.

"In the annals of the kings," the noble said, smiling, unperturbed by the profane chides of the peasants, "only Excalibur is as highly regarded."

Excalibur. The legendary magic sword.

Balin found himself pushed to the forefront.

"You look like a strong one! Try! Try!" someone hooted.

Embarrassed, he squinted at the letters engraved in gold on the pommel.

The noble was in his ear then, a gentle voice, a calm hand on his shoulder, having seen his difficulty on his face, perhaps.

"Whoso pulleth out this sword of this stone and anvil, is rightwise king born of all Albion," he whispered.

Swallowing, Balin remembered his mother's tales of Excalibur and how he had longed to possess a magic sword. Macsen's blade was a symbol, nothing more. It was not the weapon Excalibur was said to be. But to bear something of such beauty! He had no thoughts of kingship as he tentatively reached out and gripped the handle.

It was like trying to uproot an old tree with his hands.

He strained for all he was worth, but knew it was not to be, and backed away at last with the jibes of the rowdies in his ears.

The noble pulled him close. "Don't be ashamed, sir knight. I tried myself, and I have seen hundreds of men do the same. I have also three times seen the true king pull it forth like a blade of grass from the ground." He glanced up as a cheer made its way through the crowd, and pointed as the doors of the church opened. "And here he is. Here is King Arthur!"

The old man raised his voice with the rest, forgetting ceremony and decorum, as though he were just another boisterous commoner in the throng.

The crowd split before a retinue of seven knights, who gently pushed back the curious for the trio at its center and the line of sour-faced nobility marching behind. Five highborn doubters and their knights, come to scoff at this supposed miracle.

The foremost knight, about Balin's age, a blonde haired, rough looking fellow in a backcountry warrior's armor, shouted loudly:

"Make way for the king!"

Of the three directly behind the knights, the first was an austere looking ecclesiastic with a golden staff, resplendent in the robes and tall, elaborate miter of an Archbishop. This was Dubricius. In contrast, on the other side walked a fearsome, wild looking figure in a barbaric robe of shining black bear skin. This man had a feral head of silver-flecked, black hair and beard, and reminded Balin of John the Baptist in the wilderness. A glittering torc encircled his throat, and he gripped a gnarled ashwood staff in his fist.

"Who is *that*?" Balin asked the nobleman at his side.

"That is Arthur, the rightful High King, chosen of God," the nobleman said.

But the man wasn't talking about the wild man in black fur.

The two impressive robed figures, one like the embodiment of darkness and the other of light, had completely distracted Balin from the slight figure walking between them.

An upright, solemn, bright-eyed boy in a simple tunic and white silk diadem stepped up to the stone.

Balin and the nobleman stood exactly opposite the boy and watched as he gripped the sword of Macsen one-handed and drew it out easily with a resounding ring. He held it above his head and turned in a slow circle, and wherever he faced, the crowd genuflected.

When Arthur looked directly at Balin, it was like facing a terrible angel. Balin's knees buckled unbidden, and he threw himself to the flagstones, the noble doing the same at his side.

"Long live King Arthur!" The black bearded wild man roared, raising his arms. The Archbishop repeated the cry. It burst from the throats of the multitude.

This was God's chosen king. He felt it in his heart. His eyes spilled tears.

"You nobles and kings, do you still doubt?" the blonde knight demanded.

When Balin saw the men in question were still standing aright with expressions of naked doubt, he felt his own anger mount. He wanted to charge among them and force them to their knees.

"Pellinore of the Isles and all his sons, born and unborn, swear fealty to King Arthur!" called an old man in bright armor, and he held aloft a naked sword.

"Cameliard pledges its loyalty to God's king!" The nobleman at Balin's side called out, and he stood and drew the ornamented sword, raising it defiantly to heaven.

Balin realized with a start that this was King Leodegrance.

Several knights did the same, and every peasant gathered. Why Balin did not add his voice to theirs, he didn't know. Something held him back. It was the black garbed man with the golden torc. There was something in that dreadful figure that gave him pause.

Of the five richly attired men who had not bent their knees, one, a thin, black bearded wraith who towered over the rest, called out, "Who is this beardless boy that he should be our king?"

The blonde knight stepped forward, ready to answer, but the man in black touched his shoulder.

"I will tell you," said the man in black. "He is Arthur, the son of Uther, begotten on Igraine!"

"The duke of Tintagel's wife? A bastard, then!" scoffed another one of the kings.

"He was born in wedlock, King Uriens," the Archbishop interrupted. "Conceived after the death of the duke and born thirteen days into the marriage of Uther and Igraine. The church recognizes his parentage. Does the King of Gore refute the Church's authority in these matters?"

Uriens grumbled but said nothing.

"What say you, Lot of Orkney? Your own wife is the duke's daughter. Arthur is her half-brother."

Lot, the tall, hollow-cheeked king, stroked his thick beard.

"Pardon your grace, but *I* rule Orkney, not my wife." He whirled and marched out of the courtyard with his guards, and the other four nobles followed.

Arthur stepped down to confer with Dubricius and the man in black.

Leodegrance rammed his sword back in its scabbard and shook his head. "Those fools! Do they not see? Whether they worship God or not, Arthur is by blood High King. Even the Merlin acknowledges it."

Then Balin knew.

The wild man in black with the golden torc bending to Arthur's ear was the magician, Merlin. Gallet had called him the Cambion; the son of a witch and the Devil himself. He was the antichrist. Brulen had doubted this, and when they had once asked their instructors at Belande about him, Sir Claellus told them it was true his father was a demon, but that a holy man called Blaise had intervened and baptized him on the birthing bed, foiling the Devil's plans for him.

Their mother had told them of Merlin, too, and by her tone he was not quite on the best terms with Avalon. But the Bible spoke against the counsel of magicians and soothsayers. Could God choose a king and allow a son of the Devil to advise him?

Leodegrance moved closer to Arthur. Balin backed away, until he was out of the press of the crowd.

He went back to his tent outside of Londres and knelt there in the grass, praying for some sign. He had come to see this chosen king, felt in his heart this truth. But the Merlin…was this wizard's presence enough to drive him back into the service of an unworthy king like Clarivaunce? Perhaps not. But neither did it win him fully to Arthur's side. Had he been rash in leaving Northumberland? Was he to be a knight errant like his dishonored brother, wandering the countryside, selling his sword and lance to the ambitions of the petty under-kings? The last he had heard, Brulen was in the army of Lot of Orkney. If he joined Arthur, he might very well meet his brother on the battlefield.

Brulen had been excommunicated by the bishop for killing Gallet on the altar, and his shield had been hung upside down in disgrace in the hall at Belande. He hadn't seen his brother in two years, not since the happiest and saddest day of his life.

Balin remained in his camp for weeks, praying and pondering, listening for news, looking for a sign from God.

Then, one June morning, both came at once.

It was known that Arthur and his small body of supporters had retired to Caerleon as guests of Leodegrance, and that the five rebellious kings had mustered their knights and gone there to besiege him. King Clarivaunce had ridden down from Northumberland to partake in the slaughter to follow, no doubt as part of some dark room plan with one of the other kings to seize Leodegrance's territory.

Six armies against Arthur.

Balin had fought his desire to ride out to Caerleon and partake in the battle. He could not. He did not yet know on which side he truly belonged.

Then, while at the well in Londres to draw water for his horse, a yellow-haired barefoot boy leapt upon the rim ringing a cowbell for all he was worth and yelling, "King Arthur has routed the rebels!"

"How?" an old man with a wheelbarrow demanded.

Balin was thunderstruck. Six armies against Arthur and Leodegrance! How could Arthur have triumphed?

"It was the people!" the boy shouted, his voice breaking in his shrill excitement. "The people at Caerleon took up whatever they had and helped him drive them back across the river!"

The people in the square around the well sent up a cheer and leapt about, hugging each other as if a war had ended and not begun.

Balin grabbed the boy by the arm. "Where is the King now?" he asked.

"The rebels are regrouping, and five kings have joined them. Arthur's army is pulling back to Castle Bedegraine to await the arrival of King Pellinore, and Merlin has gone to Gaul to bring back the brother kings, Bors and Ban."

Balin left the revelers of Londres, refusing offers of drinks and celebratory feasting, and even the embrace of women.

He broke camp and rode for Bedegraine.

As his father had said, no man who is false can stand against one who is true.

He had found his king.

CHAPTER
FIVE

BALIN FOLLOWED THE mighty wake of King Arthur's army through Sciryuda Forest, but he did not find the host at Castle Bedegraine. The captain of the garrison there told him that the rebel armies of Orkney and Cornwall had retreated across the River Erewash at word of Arthur's advance and now he, Pellinore, and Leodegrance were headed west across the forest after them.

As he was about to depart, Balin espied a train of three carts piled with high ricks of cut wood parked outside the castle gate. An ancient man sun brown and dry as the wood he shuttled struggled to climb into the seat of the lead cart and nearly tottered to the ground.

Balin could well imagine the old peasant tumbling and snapping in pieces in the road, so he went over and helped the trembling man onto his perch.

"Thankee, sir knight." The old man gasped when he was settled, mopping his wrinkled face with the end of a threadbare black muffler that dangled between his bony knees. He was a scarecrow, all white beard and eyebrows over beady black eyes set deep in parchment skin, dressed in a straw hat and patchy rags. "Wither are ye bound? Across the river?"

"I'm riding to join King Arthur," Balin answered.

"Arthur goes to war," the old man coughed.

"I know."

"Do ye, do ye. Well, ye may as well ride along with us then," said the old woodcutter, "for we're headed to the king's camp. Come and protect an old woodcutter's precious cargo."

Balin eyed the man's cart of wood poles dubiously. The two able-bodied drivers of the other carts, presumably the woodcutter's sons, waited patiently, armed with nothing more than hatchets through their belts.

"I don't believe anyone will accost your goods, old man," said Balin. "I have to make haste."

"Oh, there'll be plenty of blood left for you to spill, Sir...?"

The old man let the sentence trail off expectantly and raised his bushy white eyebrows.

"Balin," said Balin.

"Ah, Balin. But tell me, what do ye want with King Arthur, Sir Balin, for are ye not a knight of Northumberland? And is not yer master King Clarivaunce, one of the rebels?"

"How did you know that?" Balin demanded.

"Oh, my business has taken me to Northumberland now and again, and I hear things wherever I go. But come now," the old woodcutter said in a low tone. "Tell me what ye're after, for it's a loyal king's man I am, and I ain't afraid to cut short my twilight years shoutin' up to the castle guards if it means stoppin' an assassin's sword from strikin' down Good King Arthur."

"I'm no assassin!" Balin said, aghast. "I left Clarivaunce's service to pledge my life to God's one true king."

The old man's dark eye twinkled beneath the curling webs of his eyebrow, and he nodded to himself and smiled.

"Well, then I beg ye, Sir Balin, if it's a true champion ye be, escort us, for Arthur commissioned us personally, and I know the shortest route to the king's camp."

Balin hesitated and looked across the river at the woods beyond. He knew he could find Arthur's army on his own. He knew no wandering enemy patrol would bother with the old woodcutter's kindling, but the old man had requested his help, and believed he needed it, whether he did or not.

Balin sighed. It could heap a full day on his journey, traveling with this slow moving train.

"Why is this wood so important?"

"Why?" the old man exclaimed. "Have ye no knowledge whatever of fightin' tactics? Do ye not know archer's stakes when ye see 'em?"

The old man twisted around in his driver's seat and pulled a slim sharpened wood pole off the stack and thrust it at him.

Balin took the pole and looked it over.

"Ye plant 'em in the ground and angle the points at horse's chest. Good sturdy line of 'em could turn the cavalry of Aguysans' Hundred."

Aguysans' Hundred.

Aguysans was the King With A Hundred Knights. The Hundred Knights were the most feared fighting force in all of Albion following the dissolution of Uther's Table. They had made their name against the Saxons and were the particular bane of their chieftain, Osla Big Knife. Some said that more than a few of Uther's former champions had in fact joined the anonymous esteemed ranks of the Hundred. They only ever numbered a hundred, and competition to join their ranks was fierce.

Balin handed back the stake.

"That's it? Three wagons of archer's stakes?"

"No, the second is replacement lances for the cavalry," said the old man, setting the stake back in the pile and gesturing to the two wagons behind, "and the third is kindling for the cook fires. Can't fight on empty bellies and can't eat raw rabbit, can they?"

Balin wrinkled his nose and looked once more across the river, longing to just bolt across and follow the trail.

"Will ye refuse an old man's call for protection, Sir Balin?" the woodcutter said quietly.

Balin closed his eyes.

"No, of course not, sir," Balin said, though he had to force the words. "But when can we be off?"

"Right now, if ye like," said the old woodcutter, flashing a surprisingly clean grin.

THE MOST ARDUOUS part of the journey came first, fording the Erewash without losing a stick of the woodcutter's coveted goods. Balin had to fight the stubborn old horses more fit to the plough than the harness, and he and the woodcutter's two sons all got a good wetting before they reached the far bank.

Their progress was as slow as Balin feared, and the woodcutter liked to talk.

"Tell me, Sir Balin, do ye know the nature of the rebels' grievance against Arthur?"

"I saw Lot and Uriens call Arthur a bastard in the courtyard of St. Stephen's. As for Clarivaunce and King Carados, they want to annex the land of King Leodegrance. I don't even know who else opposes Arthur."

"There are seven more," the woodcutter chuckled, and he ticked them off on his crooked fingers. "King Aguysans and his Hundred, as you know, King Brandegoris of Stranggore, King Pinel, King Idres of Cornwall, King Cradelment of North Wales, King Nentres, Anguish the High King of Hibernia, and King Rience of Snowdonia. Aye, and many a slaverin' duke or count besides, hopin' to snatch up a crown for themselves if enough go a'rollin." He cracked the reins and urged a little spirit into his team. "Pride and ambition, greed and power lust," said the woodcutter. "That's what drives mighty men to fall, an' sometimes, to act against their own best interest."

"But each of them is a king in his own land," said Balin.

"Aye, each one the biggest frog in their pond, an' none wantin' to hear of anything greater. It hurts their pride to think of bending their knee to a boy. An' some of them, well, a man who's got everything can want for nothin' but more of the same," said the woodcutter. "Now, best to ride on ahead and show your charge, state our business official-like, for here we are."

Balin looked ahead and was stunned to see a pair of armored, bareheaded knights ride into their path and bar their way.

They had only left the river behind a short time ago. Was it possible they had arrived already? Maybe Arthur's pursuit of the rebel kings had slowed.

"Who goes?" called one of the knights.

"Sir Balin of Northumberland," Balin replied without thinking.

At that, the knights drew their swords.

"King Clarivaunce is our enemy!" declared the younger of the two sentries, a grim, sandy haired man with pale skin, who might've been Balin's age or a little older.

"Please sirs, I have foresworn my oath to Northumberland and come to offer my sword to the one true king."

"And who is that?" demanded the other knight, a scowling graybeard.

"King Arthur," said Balin, "whom I saw draw the sword of Macsen with my own eyes at Londres."

"No, who is that with you?" the elder knight said, gesturing to the old man with the point of his sword.

"A woodcutter and his sons, sir," said Balin, "commissioned by the king to provide...wood."

"Hold out your arms, if you speak true," the first knight called.

Balin drew his sword and held it out by the blade.

The younger knight rode up and took it. Up close, his unkempt hair and beard belied the hardship of the campaign. His shield blazon was *Or, a purse, gules.* Balin recalled that charge from his heraldry lessons with Brulen.

"Are you Duke Corneus?" Balin ventured.

The knight started and glared at him sharply.

"Why do you ask that?"

"Your charge," Balin said.

The knight's expression softened and he glanced down at his own shield.

"I'm his son, Bedivere. You have a command of heraldry."

"It's one of the only studies I really took to," Balin admitted.

Bedivere gestured to the older knight.

"This is Sir Ulfius."

Balin had heard of him. He had been a knight of the High King Uther.

"Don't get so friendly," Ulfius warned, eyeing Balin like an unlikely deal in the marketplace.

"We were told to expect a woodcutter," Bedivere said.

"A woodcutter yes, but not in the company of a knight of Northumberland," said Ulfius warily.

"You're right," said Bedivere with an expression so deadpan Balin wasn't wholly sure he was joking. "This woodcutter must *surely* be an imposter."

"What if he is?" Ulfius said ignoring Bedivere's tone. He urged his horse to circle the old woodcutter's load. He poked the pile of stakes with his sword, then glared at the two sons.

"Careful!" begged the woodcutter. "That is my livelihood, sir knight!"

"I say we leave the wood and the wagons," Ulfius declared, "and let's take these men to the king."

"Oh, but sir!" the woodcutter protested. "I was ordered to deliver my product in a timely fashion to the king himself! Say ye won't molest me when I'm so close."

"Show me your order then," Ulfius said, coming back around to the woodcutter.

The woodcutter fished in his rags a bit and came out with a scroll.

Balin stared. The wax seal was imprinted with the crest of Pendragon. Balin looked to the woodcutter, holding it out to Ulfius, apparently innocent of its import. He had thought the old man was putting on heirs. Surely this could be no mere peasant bearing an official order. Some spy of Arthur's with a secret message for him? Or had he been entrusted with an official missive because he was illiterate and truly believed it to be an invoice?

Ulfius' eyes widened at it, and he put away his sword.

"Who gave you that?" demanded Bedivere.

"I was made to swear by the Virgin not to say," the old man said.

"I cannot break the seal of Pendragon," Ulfius said. "Let's escort these men to the king."

The woodcutter put the scroll back in his tunic.

Bedivere shook his head as Ulfius trotted to the lead of the train.

Balin fell in line behind Bedivere and beside the woodcutter once more, as their cart wheels began to squeak and rumble.

"Who are you, sir?" Balin whispered to the woodcutter. "Really."

"Just an old man, doin' his part for king and country," said the woodcutter humbly. "And if I lay down a bit of security to keep me own house an' home in the meantime, who's to say I shouldn't?"

"Not I," said Balin.

They found Arthur's three armies camped in a clearing. The rich smell of the cook fires reminded Balin that he had not eaten since the day before. Knights and men at arms alike looked over at the appearance of the wagons, and Bedivere hailed a skinny young squire leading the finest bit of horseflesh Balin had ever seen, a white stallion whose muscles rippled beneath its hide.

"Griflet!" Bedivere called.

The boy jogged over with the horse behind.

"Where are you taking Hengroen?"

"To Arthur, sir," said the boy. "He expects to ride out soon."

Balin sucked in his breath. Of course the young king would choose such a fine white stallion to ride against his enemies. He admired it as if he were in Arthur's presence already.

"We'll go with you," said Bedivere, and turned in his saddle to gesture to the woodcutter and his sons. "Leave your carts here."

The old man and his sons dismounted and followed, though the woodcutter kept glancing back suspiciously at the carts.

Finally, he croaked loudly so that all the men in camp glanced over.

"Let no man lay a hand on them carts till what's in 'em's been duly paid for!"

There was a bit of laughter, and the carts were ignored.

"Where's Lucan?" Bedivere asked.

"Your brother's in the kings' pavilion," said Griflet.

The place in question was a large purple silk tent, the skirts raised to let in air. The three kings and their numerous attendants and captains stood around a table staring at a map of Bedegraine and Cameliard.

A hulking old shaven-headed knight stepped into their path and held up his hand, regarding Balin and the woodcutters with violent blue eyes.

"Who are these with you, Ulfius?" He growled.

"Let them in, Sir Brastias!" called a young voice behind him. "I've been waiting for them."

Brastias of Tintagel. Another name Balin knew from stories of Uther's knights. Supposedly he had been the most unquestioning, the most loyal to the High King. Balin had no time to marvel at this legend come alive, for Brastias stepped aside dutifully, revealing Arthur, Pellinore, and Leodegrance.

The polished, ornate armor of the two Christian kings, adorned with golden crosses, easily outshone the piecemeal plate harness that had been apparently hastily donated from at least a half a dozen knights to protect the boy king, yet something in Arthur's bearing, the sight of him bedecked for battle, affected Balin, as the sight of the other two ostentatious monarchs did not. He wished he could suddenly contribute a gauntlet or helm to Arthur's costume. There was something innate in the boy king's presence. He commanded all attention, and the knights around the map seemed to lean close to him. His armor was ill-fitting and his face was bare and almost girlish. Any other boy would have been a source of mockery. Instead, Balin thought, this was how young David must have looked trying on King Saul's armor before he dismissed all soldier's arms and went out to meet the Philistine Goliath naked. He almost believed Arthur could do the same, if he wanted. But Arthur had no use for a sling and a shepherd's staff. The sword of Macsen hung from his side in a rich leather scabbard, claimed once and for all.

"Sire, this woodcutter bears an official scroll with your own seal," Ulfius began.

"I know. I've been expecting it," said Arthur.

The old woodcutter took off his straw hat reverently and gestured to his two sons.

"May we approach, yer highness?"

Arthur looked at them and nodded.

The woodcutter handed over the scroll. Arthur broke the seal and scanned the contents. He glanced up at the woodcutter and his sons, then kept reading.

"Is it word from Merlin?" Pellinore asked excitedly.

"Has he secured the alliance of the Gauls?" Leodegrance asked, looking as if he wanted to pull the scroll from Arthur's hands and read it himself.

"Bors and Ban are with us," Arthur announced.

There was a cheer from the men in the pavilion, but Arthur did not smile and held up his hand for silence.

"But there is a storm in the channel, and they may not arrive in time."

He held the woodcutter's message to a candle flame and watched it burn.

"We should wait then, until they arrive," said a graying knight with a fluffy beard.

"No, father, the more we wait, the more troops the rebels will amass," said Arthur. "We have to cross the river and hit them fast."

Balin looked at the pained expression of the man Arthur had called father. King Uther was dead of course, so this must be Sir Ector de Maris, the knight who had raised him, according to Clarivaunce. By the similarity of the arms of the knight at his side, Balin knew him to be Arthur's stepbrother, Sir Kay. Balin recognized him as the same outspoken blonde knight who had loudly proclaimed his younger sibling's kingship at St. Paul's.

"Don't be stupid, Arthur!" Kay snapped, to the chagrin of Ector and the other men in the tent. "You think Lot and Idres abandoned Castle Bedegraine out of fear of you? They want to lure you in. We should wait for reinforcements."

Arthur seemed unfazed by the comment. Probably he had grown up used to an older brother's ill treatment.

"No, we'll ride and take the fight to them. I want to face them before they cross the Trent."

"Oh, but sire," said the woodcutter. "What about my stakes and all this wood?"

"Kay," said Arthur, without looking up from the map. "Pay the man his due price. As for the wood, we'll be moving, so we've no need for fortifications. Spare lances and firewood would only slow us down. Take it and sell it with my blessing."

The woodcutter stood stricken as Kay grumbled and pushed a bag of clinking gold at him and Ulfius took him by the elbow.

"I thankee, sire, but surely ye can't expect me to haul all that back through the woods unguarded! With all them rebel ruffians about!" the woodcutter complained, as Ulfius pulled him and his sons from the pavilion.

"Griflet, saddle Hengroen. My lords, round up your soldiers and prepare them to march," Arthur directed.

Balin watched the growing tumult, felt his own blood begin to course and surge. Battle was coming. Real battle!

As the two old kings went their ways, each sparing the other a worried look, and servants began to break up the pavilion, Balin looked pleadingly at Bedivere.

Bedivere acknowledged the look with a nod.

"Sire!"

"What is it, Bedivere?" Arthur said, rubbing his bare chin and studying the map once more.

"This is Sir Balin, come from Northumberland to pledge his sword to your service."

Arthur straightened and looked into Balin's eyes. Balin held his breath and went to one knee, bowing his head.

He glanced up as Bedivere handed Arthur his sword.

Arthur examined the old weapon, nicked and tarnished by Balin's father on campaign against the Saxons.

"You served King Clarivaunce?" Arthur asked.

"I served his father, Detors, as did my father before me," said Balin, fighting to keep the quiver from his voice. If Arthur rejected him, what then? He kept his head bowed, and stared at the mud on Arthur's armored feet.

"Why did you serve the father but not the son?" Arthur asked.

"Clarivaunce is a greedy, disloyal man," Balin said. "He allied himself with the pagan Carados against his father's friend King Leodegrance, so as to have his lands."

"Do you dislike pagans, Balin?"

Balin wanted to tell Arthur all about his mother, but this was not the place.

"I hate their sin, and those who encourage that sin in them."

"Yet Albion is home to pagan and Christian alike. If I am High King of Albion, I must love and protect all my subjects. Even Carados and Clarivaunce."

"Clarivaunce is not the king I pledged myself to."

"Yet he *is* a king. Is it the right place for a knight to stand in judgment of his king?" Arthur pressed.

Balin swallowed and chose his words carefully, for he felt that he was but a hairsbreadth from having his sword accepted or refused.

"Only God may judge any man," said Balin. "But each must follow God's law first."

Arthur stood a moment.

"You speak true," he said at last, "and by God, after my own heart. I have no need for knights who fulfill unworthy orders without question. I want men with strength of character. Men who can reason for themselves, and who will argue their hearts, that I may understand them."

Arthur held out his sword to him, point down.

Balin straightened, glad his armor masked the nervous trembling of his limbs. He felt his eyes well, even as they had not when he'd sworn his life to Detors. He didn't fully understand all that Arthur said, but he knew somehow that it was wise.

"Take your sword, and swear to obey the High King and defend him against his enemies, to uphold the law of God so long as he does so, and to defend all women against villainy."

Balin gripped the blade and touched his lips to the steel, bowing. "I swear, my King."

"Rise, Sir Balin."

Arthur released the sword and Balin stood and sheathed it, brushing the tears hastily from his cheeks.

"Now," said Arthur, clapping a hand to Balin's shoulder. "I have an important task for you."

Balin nodded, caught up once more in the thrill of looming battle. Where was he to go? In the vanguard, at Arthur's side, he hoped.

"Go to those worthy peasants, the woodcutter and his sons, and escort them safely from here, wherever they wish to go," said Arthur.

Balin felt as if the pavilion collapsed on his head.

"Bedivere, go with him."

"*Me*, sire?" Bedivere exclaimed.

Arthur took note of their grimaces.

"If we can put our wants above the needs of our subjects, we are not fit to rule. Guard those men as you would guard me. Go."

CHAPTER
SIX

BALIN AND BEDIVERE rode with the woodcutter's wagon between them down the Bedegraine Road west, the marshaling trumpets fading far behind them. Even their horses seemed to drag their hooves at the prospect of this mundane duty. Bedivere's squire, Griflet, had been impressed to go along and could hide his disappointment no better. He sagged in his saddle and drew the hood of his cloak up to hide his morose countenance.

Only the woodcutter seemed chipper. Even his silent sons looked dour.

"Not a bad deal by far in the end, eh?" the old woodcutter chuckled, clinking the sack of gold in his palm as he drove the cart with one shaking skeleton fist. "Oh, we lost time and labor sharpenin' stakes and carvin' lances, but we been paid all we was promised plus all this wood to sell again elsewhere at a fair price. God bless King Arthur, says I!"

"Where do you wish to go, sir?" Bedivere mumbled.

"Oh, I'll not keep ye from yer war long," the woodcutter said, stowing his gold beneath his seat. "Just on to Aneblayse Town, in the valley on the edge of Bedegraine, I think. They're always in need of wood, and the good thing about firewood, it don't matter what shape it's in, so long as it can be broken up for the hearth."

He laughed to himself, and that mirthful laughter, combined with the dwindling trumpets, compounded Balin's misery as sure as any ireful taunts.

He had ridden so far, pledged himself to the High King, and now on the eve of battle, to be so soundly discarded!

"I wonder how I have displeased the king," Bedivere grumbled, voicing Balin's own thoughts.

Balin looked across the rump of the old woodcutter's horse at him.

"You mean to say, why have you been shunted off to a duty like this with me, an unproven knight, in the face of a battle?"

"In the face of what will likely be the greatest battle in Albion's history," said Bedivere. "Yes."

"As to that," said the old woodcutter, "if ye'll pardon me interruptin', sirs, I'm no man-at-arms, but it seems like avoidin' head-on bloodshed's a blessing ye ought not to discount, lest the Almighty repay yer ingratitude with tenfold troubles."

"I'd welcome those troubles, old man," said Balin. "I came here to fight."

"Aye," said Bedivere.

"Well, there's many a man comes to fight," said the old woodcutter, "an' none that comes to die, but they does so all the same."

"How is it your sons weren't conscripted?" Bedivere asked. "Every able bodied man in the country's been marshaled for Arthur or one of these rebel kings, it seems."

"My sons *do* fight," the old woodcutter mumbled. "And in these troubled times, not on the same side, I fear."

Balin looked back at the two drivers querulously.

"Oh, *they're* not my sons," said the old woodcutter, with a chuckle and a wave.

His face fell beneath the shade of his straw hat then. He drew the reins back on the old horse, holding up one trembling hand for the others behind to stop.

A phalanx of armored men was riding toward them. It was too late to pull the carts off the road. There was nowhere to hide.

"Oh, God," said Balin at the sight of the three flapping banners, for he recognized two of them. One, the flag of Gore, he had seen with Uriens' attendants at St. Paul's. The other, *sable, a tower argent*, he knew all too well, for it belonged to the pagan King Carados. "It's the enemy!"

He drew his sword, and Bedivere did the same.

"Who are they? I don't know those arms," said Bedivere.

"Uriens of Gore and King Carados." Balin hissed, shaking his head at the irony. Was God punishing him for breaking faith with Northumberland? Maybe he had been wrong to pledge himself to Arthur after all.

"The other is King Aguysans!" Griflet exclaimed. "Look!"

Trotting majestically upon uniformly black destriers came Aguysans' Hundred. The best knights in Albion, all in gleaming black armor, all bearing their master's black mailed fist emblem upon a white field. Alone among all Albion's knights, the Hundred surrendered their lands and their names to devote themselves wholly to the life and service of Aguysans as elite paladins. As part of their induction, they hung their own coats of arms in Aguysans' hall, foregoing personal glory to share the greater honor of the nameless, faceless Hundred.

Aguysans himself rode at their heads, identifiable by the gold circlet and purple plume on his closed great helm. Behind him rode the captain of the Hundred, the renowned Sir Morganore, with his white plume of rank streaming behind.

Balin's heart fluttered. If his service to Arthur were to be cut short here in this road, at least he would die at the hands of heroes.

"Griflet," Bedivere said. "Fetch me my helm."

"Belay that, sir," said the woodcutter pleadingly. "I beg ye. Don't throw all our lives away here."

Balin glanced at the woodcutter. The old man was trembling more than usual.

Griflet, paused in extracting Bedivere's helmet from his saddle.

The column had spotted them now, and some of the knights had drawn arms.

"Who goes there?" someone shouted.

"Answer true, and we all die." The woodcutter hissed. "Please, sirs, Arthur bid ye escort us to Aneblayse in due safety!"

He had, yet here was a chance now to strike a crippling blow against the enemy. In a few hour's march, they would meet Arthur's host in the forest. Perhaps they could weaken them here. He and Bedivere and Griflet.

That did seem foolish, and it would surely end in their death. He hesitated, horse sense stymying his will to act.

"*Please*," the woodcutter said, clasping and wringing his hands now.

"Ho there!" called King Carados. "Sir Brulen! What are you doing out here?"

Balin stiffened in his saddle as Carados and his entourage spurred ahead of the column and came to treat with them.

Balin had guided Carados through the woods of Northumberland on Clarivaunce's hunting excursions. They knew each other. But Carados had never been to Sewingshields in the days of King Detors, when he and Brulen had been squires. Detors and Carados had been enemies. How then, did Carados know Brulen's name, and why would he mistake Balin for his brother?

"I thought you were with King Lot's forces back in Aneblayse," Carados said, leaning from his saddle and knitting his white eyebrows together over his pinched face.

Balin thought hard. Lot of Orkney was the king Brulen served now. Carados must have seen him there. Brulen was at Aneblayse, where they were headed. Now he was conflicted. If he took up arms here, he would die. If he said nothing to correct Carados, he could conceivably escort the woodcutter to Aneblayse and see his brother again.

But Bedivere spoke first.

"Your Highness," said Bedivere. "King Lot sent us to escort these fortifications and lances to Aneblayse."

"Who are you, sir? Do I know you?" Carados said, frowning behind his curling mustaches.

"Sir Amren, sire," Bedivere said, striking his gauntlet to his chest and bowing his head. "And my squire, Pedrawd."

Carados' flinty eyes moved between the knight and his squire, the woodcutters, and finally to Balin, where they rested a long time, before the king shook his head and chuckled.

"Lugh's Hand! But you truly are the mirror image of your brother Balin, Sir Brulen. It is uncanny. Did I tell you I knew him in Northumberland, when I attended Clarivaunce's invitations to hunt? He was a good guide, but a bit of a brute, if you'll pardon me."

Balin could find no words. He only smiled back foolishly and shrugged.

"Well, we shan't detain you," Carados said, waving back to the train. "You must have passed dangerously close to Castle Bedegraine. Any word of the bastard?"

The knights and Griflet shook their heads, but the woodcutter cleared his throat and raised a withered hand.

"*You* have news? What is it, man?" Carados said.

"Gauls, sire," said the woodcutter, bowing his head and averting his eyes.

"Gauls?"

"Aye, from across the channel, Gaulish brothers, they are. King Bors of Gannes and King Ban of Benoic, each with oh, hundreds of men, I should think."

"Reinforcements!" Carados exclaimed, eyes going wild. "Is this true? How many?"

"Oh, I couldn't rightly say, sire," said the woodcutter in sly, mock innocence. "More than Bedegraine Castle can hold. They was camped all about the outside of the walls, chatterin' on in that rascally tongue of theirs, and fellin' trees for their cookin' fires. Fryin' up periwinkles, I shouldn't wonder."

"Halt!" Carados called to the army, and waved Aguysans and Uriens to his side.

The three kings drew their horses together off a ways and conferred hurriedly in fervent whispers, while Balin and Bedivere glared at the woodcutter and each other, unable to speak in earshot.

Why had the woodcutter spoken such wicked deception? What had inspired this sudden act of heroism, such as it was? Gratitude to Arthur, for his generosity? He remembered that the peasants had taken up arms in defense of Arthur at Cameliard. If Carados and the other kings believed this story, they could effectively hinder the rebel advance into Bedegraine without spilling a drop of blood.

The kings finished their discussion. Each withdrew to their respective commands and began shouting orders to turn about.

Carados returned to them.

"Sir Amren, take your squire and these loyal men on to Aneblayse," he said. "Woodcutter, if your intelligence proves true, you shall be paid triple for these carts."

The woodcutter's eyes lit up and he bowed deeply.

"Thankee, sire!"

"Sir Brulen, you will accompany King Aguysans and his Hundred on down the road to Bedegraine and scout ahead. Bring back word of these Gaulish reinforcements, if they are there."

"As you wish, sire," Balin said, glancing at Bedivere in wonderment.

The majority of the column turned, taking the woodcutter's train in. Balin watched Bedivere and Griflet ride away to Aneblayse as around him, the silent black company of Aguysans' Hundred waited.

THOUGH HE WAS ushered to the front of the Hundred beside Aguysans and Morganore, the ride back toward Bedegraine was a quiet one. The king, as mysterious as his silent men, said nothing to him. Sir Morganore and the Hundred rode in utter quiet. There was no idle soldier's chatter, no remarks on the countryside, only precise, unified, Spartan discipline. They had their orders, and nothing else warranted attention.

Balin had dreamt now and again of riding with the Hundred, but never like this.

They came to a shallow tributary crossing, and there, from the woods on the opposite bank, came Arthur, Pellinore, and Leodegrance with their armies. Balin clearly saw Kay and Ector and Ulfius, riding bareheaded. The Pendragon banner hung limp as a hanged man from a gallows pole.

Balin stood up in his stirrups and cupped his hands about his mouth.

"ARTHUR!" he cried, in as loud a voice as he could blow from his lungs.

Beside him, Aguysans and Morganore started.

"My God!" said the captain of the Hundred with a snarl, drawing his sword. "It *is* Arthur!"

"With Pellinore and Leodegrance," said King Aguysans, muffled behind the steel of his great helm. "We are outnumbered."

Across the river, the vanguard of Arthur's host milled in confusion. Then a lone rider broke from the rest and went charging atop his white stallion right for the enemy, lance leveled.

Balin gasped.

It was Arthur himself.

Several knights fell in behind him. Kay, Ector, Ulfius, Brastias. Then Leodegrance and Pellinore were caught up in the surge. A cry rose across the river.

"He is in front," said Morganore, and he kicked his horse. "I will end this villainous bastard myself!"

King Aguysans held back though, drawing up his reins and watching his captain charge to the riverbank. Then he turned in his saddle and raised his hand to the Hundred.

They couched their lances.

Aguysans dropped his hand.

"Attack!" He roared.

The black knights rushed around Balin in the wake of Morganore, a rapid river of dark steel and grunting horses.

Balin held his breath as Arthur's horse Hengroen splashed into the shallow ford. Sir Morganore hit the river at the same instant.

The two horses, white and black as opposing chess pieces, rushed at each other, scattering a silvery burst of water. It was not enough to slow their deadly course. Lances met shields, both shivering to pieces. Arthur rocked in his saddle, but Sir Morganore landed in the water.

The rising cheer from Arthur's army blew into a soul shaking bellow of exultation.

The bright host of the High King, emboldened by their lord and master's audacious success, flung themselves headlong into the black Hundred. There was a shuddering crash as steel met steel and horses collided, and a rapid series of splashes as men fell into the river. These latter rose, shaking their heads, and fell to fighting on foot with swords and maces. Some did not rise at all, but turned and drifted away down to the deep part of the river, where they sank in clouds of scarlet.

Aguysans clapped a hand on Balin's shoulder.

"Ride back to Aneblayse and tell them what you saw!"

To his credit, The King With A Hundred Knights galloped to join the fray.

Balin sat awestruck at the selfless gesture for a moment and entertained thoughts of doing as the forceful commander ordered. But then he spied Arthur turning and slashing with his sword on Hengroen in the center of the river, and shook off the King With A Hundred Knight's authoritative spell. Balin plunged toward his true sovereign and master.

His heart matched the pounding of the great horse's hooves on the ground beneath him, and he drew his sword for the first time in life and death.

His horse broke the surface of the water, and he was in the thick of the fight then, steel ringing all around him. He passed half a dozen combatants before he finally, shakily, drew back his sword and struck a black helm, the shock of his first killing blow vibrating up his arm to his shoulder. He imagined that in the spray of blood from beneath the enemy helmet, the soul of its wearer wheeled and passed like a puff of cold air through his own heart.

Balin felt a moment's ache, a moment's regret. Then he gave himself over to war.

Striking as he had trained his whole life, every thrust at the soft points between the dark steel plates of harness drew blood, every slash of sword and heave of his shield battered a man from his saddle. Men screamed beneath the feet of his horse and disappeared beneath the shallow water.

Then he was near Arthur. The boy king accounted for himself gamely, felling man after man, and never left Hengroen's back, St. Michael beating back the devilish hordes of rebel angels, untouchable. Unassailable. The noon sun cast a corona about his naked head, as though beatifying him. Balin half-expected to see the clouds part and to hear the booming voice of God Himself declare Arthur His son in whom It was well pleased as He had Christ at the River Jordan. Balin feared the stray cut or blow that might bloody that handsome crown, but Arthur fought as though he feared nothing at all.

Balin did not know how long they fought, but as suddenly as it had begun, the clash ended. He had skewered a black knight through the visor of his helmet with his sword and turned to meet the next only to face a riderless black horse wading past him for the bank.

The river ran red with blood and slow turning bodies. Bits of black steel jutted out of the water like stones. Many of Arthur's men lay too.

"God," said Arthur nearby, gasping, wiping the blood from his eyes with the back of his mailed hand. "I've never fought better men."

Balin could not argue that.

"Are you unhurt, my king?"

"Sir Balin!" Arthur said in surprise, straightening in his saddle. "Where are Sir Bedivere and the woodcutters?"

"In Aneblayse, by now," said Balin.

"Good. But why are you here?"

"You don't understand, sire. Aneblayse is occupied by the rebels. We met King Carados and King Uriens on the road. The woodcutter…"

But Arthur had turned away and was shouting.

"Kay! Kay!"

His stepbrother came plodding over. He was soaking wet and had lost his horse. His armor was dented, but when he raised his visor, he looked unhurt.

"It was foolish to charge in like that, Arthur," Kay admonished.

"Spread the word," said Arthur, ignoring him. "We ride double time to Aneblayse. I want to be there by nightfall."

"Ah," said Kay, closing his eyes and smiling. "Soft beds."

"No," said Arthur. "Not yet. The rebels are there."

"We can't fight them in the dark!" Kay protested. "We're outnumbered!"

"The night will be our ally."

"The night can't hold a sword, or break a charge," Kay argued.

"The night won't have to," Arthur smiled. "Spread the word. Devils bite your hide, Kay, hurry now!"

Balin looked around. He did not see Aguysans among the dead, nor Morganore. He said so.

"Good," said Arthur, urging Hengroen for the west bank. "I'm glad. I would not want to be known as the man who ended The King With A Hundred Knights."

"But, they are your enemies, sire," Balin reasoned.

Arthur rested in the saddle for a moment, then reached down and dipped the bloody sword of Macsen in the river, to clean it.

"The High King isn't meant to be a conqueror, Balin," said Arthur. "I don't want to kill these good men. I need to unify the land, heal the wounds my father and Vortigern before him inflicted, or I'm not worthy to be king at all."

Balin stared in wonderment, pondering these strange notions. What was there to be gained in not eradicating an enemy?

"But surely they're racing for Aneblayse now, to warn the other rebel kings."

Arthur frowned at that, but a voice from the shore said:

"You needn't worry about those two."

It was Sir Ulfius, hobbling over, leading his horse.

"Aguysans was wounded, and Morganore lifted him onto his horse and fled south," Ulfius reported. "I tried to run them down but my horse tripped. It was nearly the death of me. Of course, they *could* double back to warn their allies."

"We can't spare knights to go shaking the bushes for two men," Arthur said, as behind him, the army began to gather itself and splash across the river. "Well done, Sir Ulfius."

"And well done, Sir Balin!" said King Leodegrance, riding up with Ector and Kay. "I saw you account for fourteen men in the river."

There were whistles from the others around Balin.

Fourteen! That many? He hadn't counted. He felt a giddy rush of satisfaction, particularly at receiving such appreciative praise in front of Arthur. Fourteen of the best knights in the world. They would ride no more, because they had met him.

"You fight like a wild savage, Sir Balin," Kay said appreciatively.

Arthur nodded to Balin.

"May you fare as well at Aneblayse." He spurred Hengroen to reach the forefront of the army, and Leodegrance and Sir Ector followed.

"Well fought, Sir Balin," said Ulfius, heaving himself up into his saddle. He sat there for a moment looking at the sky and sighing. "I'll sleep well tonight."

"Take care, old man, or Christ himself will be the one to wake you, with angel trumpets," said Kay.

Balin fell into line with the column, and it wasn't long before a thin, dark haired knight had sidled up alongside him. Balin recognized him from Arthur's pavilion as Lucan, Bedivere's brother.

"Sir Balin, what of my brother? Is he well?"

"When I left him, yes," Balin said. "His quick thinking saved us on the road. I owe him my life."

Balin realized this just as he said it. Had they attacked the army alone as had been his own instinct, they would now be dead or captured. He wondered how Bedivere's deception had held up when they reached Aneblayse.

Balin looked at the concern in Lucan's eyes and felt again his own.

Once they reached Aneblayse, he might end up crossing swords with his own brother.

CHAPTER
SEVEN

I T WAS WELL past nightfall and the moon was doused in clouds when they reached the far edge of Bedegraine. Across the trickling river, they saw the lights of the hamlet of Aneblayse down in the valley below, huddled in the center of the black plain of stubble rye and wheat fields, which were dotted with campfires. This was the breadbasket of Leodegrance's realm.

"How many men?" Balin heard Pellinore ask.

"More than enough to crush us," answered Kay. "Unless the night itself decides to take up arms for you, brother."

He was hushed.

If Arthur gave the order to charge into the midst of the huge encampment now, they had a good chance of wreaking havoc. Yet somewhere down there in the dark, his own brother Brulen lay or sat near a fire, to say nothing of Bedivere and the innocent woodcutters.

The clouds shifted in the sky then, and moonlight spilled upon them, arrayed on the crest of the Bedegraine Road like a gleaming wall of steel.

Down below, a horn sounded, followed quickly by another and another.

"The moon at least," said Kay, "has proven unsympathetic to your cause, brother."

All around, Balin heard the rasp of swords clearing their scabbards, orders shouted to squires, and the footmen shuffling into place, their pikes gleaming in the lunar glow.

"Archers!" Arthur called.

The bowmen sent flights of arrows streaking across the face of the warden moon, but after that first flight, an answering volley had them tucking in behind their shields. Most of the enemy arrows went whistling among the trees. Several men cried out. Balin felt one missile go winging off the edge of his shield.

But this was not to be decided by archers shooting blind in the night.

Arthur called for the attack. Balin slammed shut his visor and set his lance, urging his horse down into the valley as the knights of the three kings charged for the campfires and the footmen clanked behind.

The clouds drifted again like the hands of a shrinking spectator shielding the scandalized eye from the bloodshed about to occur. The darkness hid their approach, but it also hid their path, and several knights crashed into unseen hedgerows or flipped over stone field walls. A few plunged into the river, which was too deep to ford.

The obstacles didn't cull enough of the charge to render the attack a disaster, and Balin, like most others, steered for the silhouettes scrambling around the campfires. He found himself at the forefront of a body of chargers, thundering over the wide stone bridge that spanned the river, and rode right through the first of the fires, scattering embers and leaving a man spitted on his lance.

He didn't see the pavilion beyond the firelight until it was too late and crashed right into it, upsetting a support pole in the process and bringing the whole affair down around himself and those who had ridden in his wake. Horses screamed and panicked against the clinging, stifling canvas. There were curses all around him, and he knew the enemy was in here with him. Something struck his horse, a spear or a sword, and the animal shuddered between his legs, giving a heart wrenching cry and fell. Balin actually felt it die.

He managed to land on his feet and swung his sword wild, connecting with the offending horse killer, hearing his edge cut meat and canvas both. The man went down gurgling, but from what kind of death, Balin couldn't guess.

They fought like rats in a sack, and Balin prayed he did not, in his confusion, strike any friend. Finally he found space to split the tent and regain the freedom of the night air.

The moon had forgotten its earlier prudence and now gazed in full morbid fascination upon the carnage in the valley.

Balin saw the lights of the village winking out, the peasants no doubt blowing out candles and huddling in the dark, desperate to discourage the ravenous beast of war rampaging in their fields from turning its attention to their homes. Around the other fires, men fought on horse and foot like intricate shadow puppets enacting some grand performance. Very near, he saw a man-at-arms pinned by a lance like a butterfly in the campfire, screaming.

He managed to pick out Hengroen, unmistakable in the gloom, flitting back and forth like a specter with Arthur dealing death from his back amid a ring of knights.

Balin fought his way closer, contending with men who emerged bellowing from the dark and who returned to it whimpering and clutching at the wounds he ripped in them. Yet every time he neared the young king, Arthur raced off to another end of the battlefield, his bodyguards struggling to keep up with him. It became a distraction to his own livelihood, and when he was nearly decapitated by a blow from behind, he resolved to focus on presently staying alive.

He did not know how many he slew. The battle raged like a night fever, in untold time. He did not know if they were winning or losing. Each death avoided became a small victory, each death inflicted a major gain in the push and pull of the greater fight. He was distracted, though. Worried for Arthur, and worried, too, that Brulen would come at him from the dark. He hesitated too often and allowed many more blows that he would have liked to land on his armor by peering at the arms of each knight he fought. The footmen with their deadly pikes were almost a relief. He slew them without a thought, like offending flies.

He narrowly avoided an unhorsed knight who charged at him with the end of a broken lance. Balin gutted him between the faulds and cuirass almost from instinct. This unknown knight had no charge, and when he sank to the ground bleeding, Balin was almost certain he had slain his brother. He stabbed his sword in the blood soaked earth and caught the knight as he fell forward, turned, and held him for a terrifying moment before he mustered the courage to raise the dead man's visor.

The breath blew from him when he saw a stranger's slack face, and he let the nameless man lie and took up his sword again.

Balin went where the tide of steel and blood buffeted him, and he soon found himself with his back to the dark village, the battlefield spread out before him. He could not tell foe from friend here. Tents burned brightly, contending with the moonlight and casting the sky orange. The cries of men in contention had become one unending wall of roaring sound punctuated by the incessant ring of metal on metal. The smell of blood was thick in the air.

The main road into Aneblayse had been barricaded with wagons. Balin was amazed to see the old woodcutter and his sons standing atop their still laden wood carts, the horses still in the traces, watching the battle, limned by the hellish light of it. They had been the last faces he expected to see this bloody night.

"Sir Balin!" the old woodcutter called down. "Ye live!"

"Thus far! Where is Bedivere?"

"Out in that maelstrom," said the woodcutter, jumping down with surprising agility.

He strode toward Balin, passing from the light into the shadow, his whole bearing strange, not bent and feeble as before. He spoke words Balin didn't understand. They sounded Gaulish.

The woodcutter's two quiet employees answered him in the Gaulish tongue and got down from their respective carts. They went to the traces and began to free the old plough nags from their burdens.

The woodcutter walked past Balin to a nearby abandoned campfire and crouched before it, pulling his black muffler from his neck and wrapping it around a stick of firewood. Something gleamed and glittered around the old man's neck as he leaned forward and held the wood in the fire till it caught.

When he rose and turned, an uncontrollable shudder went through Balin.

The black bearded, black robed wild man of St. Paul's courtyard stood before him, the golden torc shimmering around his throat.

The wizard Merlin, his dark eyes ablaze.

And though Balin was painted red as a devil in blood and gore, the sight of that terrible man made him shrink back, even when he smiled at Balin in passing.

"Sir Balin's horse!" Merlin called into the dark.

Balin was astounded to see his own lost horse step out of the shadows. He had been sure he'd felt the animal die, but there it stood waiting, nothing more than a shallow scratch over its heart where the spearman in the tent had apparently nicked it.

"Mount, Sir Balin," Merlin commanded, raising the burning torch above his head as he walked toward the wood carts. "Arthur has need of you at the bridge."

Balin did not doubt the man's words. He touched the neck of his horse gingerly. It was cool from the night air.

"King Lot's army has him surrounded," Merlin went on. "Hurry!"

Balin climbed into the saddle and peered across the tumult, trying to recall the direction of the bridge. He looked back and wished he hadn't. The two woodcutters had been transformed. They sat resplendent in shining Gaulish armor and ermine capes atop fine fresh warhorses in plate barding.

Merlin thrust the fiery brand into the first of the wood carts. It flared up with a blinding, unearthly white glare. He did not pause, but did the same with the other two. Each emitted the same phosphorescent blaze. Balin had to shield his eyes against it and finally looked away.

That glorious fire lit the entire battlefield as though it were the sun, and Balin saw every man afield turn aghast toward the strange sight. It was as though a fiery seraph had walked out of Aneblayse.

For Balin's part, it lit the path to the bridge over the river where a knot of horsemen and foot soldiers roiled and surged, as sure as if he had been pointed the way on a map.

Then the glow faded.

He feared to look again behind him, but he steeled himself, and did.

The carts and the ricks of wood were gone. Where the stakes had been piled stood hundreds of archers. Where the kindling cart had been, an equal number of Gaulish footmen. And as for the cart that had borne the wooden lances, there was arrayed a hundred mounted armored knights bearing the arms of Benoic and Gannes.

"Balin!" Merlin roared, wheeling fierce and terrible upon him, pointing directly at him with his staff. "Go! *Attaque!*"

Balin could not have been more motivated than if he had seen Satan himself rear up from hell and crack a whip.

He kicked his horse and charged, and behind him, he heard the roar and thunder of the Gaulish army. They were not some illusory phantasms conjured by Merlin. They were the reinforcements the scroll had promised Arthur; not harried by any unfortunate winds in the channel at all, but secreted into the very heart of the enemy encampment in three lowly woodcutter's carts.

He did not need to cleave a path through the battlefield to the river. Men on either side cried out and parted before that supernatural charge. Some threw down their weapons at the sight, thinking them some infernal force mustered from hell itself at the behest of the Merlin.

Balin leaned low over his horse and concentrated only on gaining the bridge where he saw Hengroen pitching and turning, a white mirage in the center of a cluster of cavorting figures.

As he neared the edge of the bridge, his heart stopped dead in his chest. Arthur was pressed between two of the mounted rebel kings. One was an enormous, black bearded man in a fur-trimmed mantle he didn't know. The other was the tall, wraith-like King Lot of Orkney.

Orkney.

Brulen was a knight of Orkney now. His brother could be in this tangle of men somewhere or already floating dead down the river, pitched from the bridge.

Balin crashed into the back of the melee, but his progression was jammed by the sheer number of bodies alive and dead glutting the bridge. He pressed forward, but the horse could make no headway in that tightly packed mob.

The nameless king in the fur mantle wielded a shining, thick bladed sword with both hands. He chopped at Arthur's head, and when the boy raised the sword of Macsen to check it, the sword from the stone snapped at the hilt, broken beneath the titanic blow.

The rebel king laughed at Arthur's understandable look of distress. Momentarily distracted by his own excitement, he missed the knight slipping through the combatants to jump on the back of his horse.

The brute twisted and landed a glancing blow with his weapon. It didn't seem that palpable a hit, but it sent the knight's visor into the river.

It was Bedivere.

Bedivere did not answer the blow, but called out:

"Arthur!"

And threw his own sword to the High King.

The boy plucked it from the air in time to parry a blow from King Lot's battle axe.

The king in the furred robe sheared off Bedivere's outstretched hand with his terrible sword.

Bedivere cried out and the king shoved him from his horse.

Gamely, Bedivere gripped the king's mantle as he fell, and the two men crashed to the bridge.

King Lot landed a heavy blow to Arthur's shoulder and unhorsed him. The High King went down beneath a writhing mass of armor and arms, and Balin shrieked in alarm behind his visor.

He leapt from the saddle, clambering over the heads and shoulders of the fighters until he reached Lot himself. He struck the rebel king upside the head and tackled him from his horse. Lot flipped over the rail of the bridge and fell headlong into the water below.

Balin stabbed desperately down again and again, trying to drive the screaming men from the king, ignoring the upthrust blades and pikes that slashed his cheeks and cut his underarms.

He dove from Lot's horse and punched and kicked madly to clear a space. Somewhere beneath those steel shod feet Arthur was being crushed.

Balin felt the press of bodies all around, a man's head lolled limply against his shoulder, the face slack. He was dead, but there was no room for him to fall.

"Arthur!" Balin called. "Arthur!"

Then, to his right, a single bloody hand, bereft of its gauntlet, burst from the crowd and gripped the pommel of Lot's horse.

Arthur's face appeared, bloodied, battered, but animate. Then his shoulder. He slowly pulled himself up, extricating himself from the press, and gained Lot's saddle.

He still had Bedivere's sword, and he hewed furiously down at the men about him, until they cried and begged for mercy, climbing over each other to escape his fury.

Balin let himself be jostled. He was in awe of the High King. No force in Albion, none on all of the earth could harm the one God had chosen. He was sure of that now. His heart nearly burst in his chest to know that he was counted in the company of such an august and worthy leader, as the hearts of the twelve disciples must have warmed in the reflected light of their Master.

He would live for this boy

He would die for King Arthur.

But not today.

Balin renewed his own attack, and with a mighty bellow sent six men flipping into the river. It was enough to clear an egress for Arthur, and the King took it, urging Lot's horse through the fight to the edge of the bridge.

Balin watched him with pride. Arthur did not race to escape, but turned back and slashed to free his beleaguered men.

Then Balin saw Bedivere struggling to lift himself from the crush and forced his way over. Bedivere's wound was grievous. Blood coursed from the stump of his left wrist. Balin threw that arm over his own neck and pulled him aright for all he was worth. Another knight came to their aid. It was Lucan, Bedivere's brother. His wide, dark eyes said his thanks.

A piercing light shone down on all of them suddenly, as the flare of Merlin's magic had done when he'd revealed the Gaulish army. Enemy and ally alike paused and blinked up at it.

Maybe it *was* Merlin's magic, for the black robed enchanter stood on the rail of the bridge, his arms outstretched, an ashwood staff in his hand like Moses over the Israelites.

"What is this?" someone cried. "The Cambion brings the day!"

"No!" Merlin called in an unnaturally loud, impressive voice, loud enough for the listeners to cease fighting across the valley and fields. "You have been warring all night! Dawn is here! Aguysans and the Hundred are gone! Clairvaunce of Northumberland and King Nentres have fled! The combined forces of Benoic and Gannes are joined against you now. Will you kings who oppose the High King treat now for peace?"

There was silence for a moment, and then, from somewhere upriver, a voice called out.

"This night I have seen, in the mettle of my enemy, the spirit of his father, King Uther, which I cannot deny!" It was Uriens, bloodied and held up by his knights. "As in days of old, Gore pledges its loyalty to Pendragon!"

There were cheers in answer, and Arthur raised his hand in a salute which King Uriens returned.

"Hibernia is for King Arthur!" called another. "So says King Anguish, and bless him!"

"Never!" called a deep voice from the riverbank.

Lot sat there, bleeding and soaked, his squire wrapping a bandage about his head where Balin had struck him.

"Orkney will not surrender to you, Arthur, be you Uther's son or no." He pointed one gloved hand up at Arthur on the bridge.

"Nor will Stranggore!" another called.

"King Carados will not bow to you either!" Carados declared from far afield.

Merlin looked pained, and Balin saw him share a look with Arthur. Then he raised his hands and his voice blared out terrible again:

"Be still! If it's war you want, look to your own lands! Look to Vambieres! Osla Big Knife has landed there, and even now his tribe seeks to penetrate the walls!"

"Saxons, Merlin?" Carados chuckled. "What, have you brought them along in your pockets to frighten us?"

"I tell you, even now the Saxons have their eye on Cornwall," Merlin said. "And you well know it is the backdoor to all your lands."

An older man, bearing the arms of Cornwall, spoke from the opposite bank.

"Merlin! You have been a friend to Cornwall in days past. If you say this is true, and that we are threatened, what must we do?"

"King Idres," said Merlin, leaning on his staff. "Take your men to Nauntes and keep watch over the sea."

Balin watched Lot scoff and shake his head.

King Idres turned and called to the others.

"If this alliance is to hold, we must be prepared to defend each other! I ask your help in defeating these Saxons!"

"You old fool, Idres!" Lot barked, reeling on his heels so that he had to lean on his squire. "You'll listen to that creature?"

"Your wife, Morgause, has the Sight, King Lot," Merlin countered. "Ask her to confirm what I say."

"I will!" Lot said. "Because I am tired of this fight, and I am tired of listening to this black liar! Bring me my horse!"

"I have it here, Uncle!" Arthur called down. He dismounted, and though Balin and several soldiers moved to escort him, he held up his hand and led the horse down to the riverbank.

Lot watched him come, and Balin watched for him to make some violent move.

But when he was near, Lot simply climbed up on his horse's back, Arthur holding the animal still for him the whole time.

"If you are Uther's son, do not share his failure." He pointed again at Merlin, without looking at him. "Do not trust that creature's words or his magic. Do not let him hold your scepter." He held up his hand then and stood in his saddle. "Orkney goes!"

"The Master of Orkney is always welcome to return," Arthur said. "I would like to meet my cousins."

"You will meet them," Lot said. "That I promise. On the battlefield."

He spurred his horse up the slope and went to the road, his men falling in behind, without a look back.

It was the strangest end to a battle Balin had ever imagined. Once again Arthur allowed his enemies to simply depart with their living and their dead.

He could not fathom the breadth of Arthur's mercy in that. King Lot had all but threatened him in parting, yet they were ordered to make no pursuit.

He wondered, too, at Lot's admonition about not trusting Merlin. In that at least, Balin and the King of Orkney were in agreement. Now that he had seen the extent of the wizard's power first hand, he feared it more than ever. Yet he heard some of his fellow Christians praise Merlin's deception as miraculous.

He parted with them at that.

Balin walked alone up and down the battlefield the rest of the day as the remaining rebels left the valley and Arthur took the formal oaths of King Anguish and King Uriens in his pavilion.

Balin poked among the discarded dead, swatting flies and holding a rag to his face against the increasing stench, looking for Brulen.

As the sun set, he knelt in prayer, giving thanks when he didn't find him.

CHAPTER
EIGHT

KING ARTHUR AND nine hunters in creaking leather cuirasses
rustled through the blazing yellow-orange autumn of Sciryuda
Forest. The guide—marked as the most experienced among
them by the set of long tusks and whetters strung about his neck—lifted
his cruciform boar spear with one hand, a signal for the party to stop.

They crouched, listening to the far-off barking of the bay hounds.

"They don't seem to be getting any closer," whispered the king's
yellow-haired young cousin, Culwych. "We shouldn't have left the
horses with Lucan."

"Have patience," Arthur whispered back.

The guide looked sharply over his shoulder down the line of crouching men and hissed disapprovingly. "Quiet!"

Arthur smirked and hunched, a boy chastised. It was a mischie-
vous gesture. He was only a few summers out of his youth, but he had
commanded a victory against thousands of soldiers here in this very
forest only a year ago.

"Here now..." Culwych began "You let this greenwood ruffian..."

Arthur put a firm hand on his cousin's shoulder.

"That ruffian is Sir Balin of Northumberland," Arthur said in in his smallest voice. "One of the best knights in Albion and the finest woodsman I have."

"Balin The Savage?" said the Welshman, peering with new interest at the back of the broad-shouldered fellow at the front.

"That's an unfortunate appellation and not of his choosing," Arthur warned. "He doesn't like it. Sir Balin personally accounted for fourteen of King Aguysans' famed knights at Bedegraine."

"My lords!" Balin said again, wheeling on them with a desperate glare. His bright eyes flashed with annoyance in his ruddy, unshaven face. "You will spoil the hunt! Listen!"

The men listened. Save for the newly dubbed Sir Dagonet of Caerleon, they were all of them veteran warriors, battle-seared and disciplined. They had crept through sleeping enemy camps and themselves foiled ambushes. Old Sir Ulfius and bald pate Sir Brastias were there. So was Arthur's foster father Sir Ector and his foster brother Kay, and of course Bedivere.

But none of their trained ears heard any change in the bay hounds' pitch that signaled their coming.

"Ready your spears!" Balin commanded. "This is a wily one."

They did as they were told, and presently a loud huffing sound came to their ears, and a snapping of the underbrush.

Moments later, an immense boar, something that must have rivaled the Calydonian monster loosed by Artemis, burst through the shrubbery and charged directly into their midst.

Dagonet lost his nerve in the face of that mound of wiry hair and tusks, and rolled aside, clearing the way to Arthur.

The young king, to his credit, stood his ground, but Balin leapt nimbly between them and set his spear against the side of his boot, angling it so the squealing thing took the point down its throat. Balin's back leg furrowed the earth, but he leaned against the charge and twisted his spear, until the boar's eyes glazed and it shuddered and sagged heavily to the ground, its snout nearly touching the knuckles of Balin's lead hand.

The knights leaned on their spears and sighed their relief. Arthur touched Balin's shoulder and smiled.

Ulfius turned and slapped the back of Dagonet's head. "Heart of a lion," he remarked.

"Aye, a lion cub," said Sir Ector, and they broke into nervous chuckles as men who had narrowly avoided the same horrific fate.

"That's a chide against lion cubs," Sir Kay said, and Arthur laughed and shook his head.

Balin failed to see the humor in Dagonet's cowardice. He was as shoddy a specimen of knighthood as ever he had seen, thin and bony. Most disturbing to Balin, he had a more than passing resemblance to images of Jesus Christ, with his long dark hair and sparse beard, and wide, doe eyes. Having observed his irreverent nature, Balin could not help but suspect Dagonet had cultivated his appearance to some ironic, blasphemous purpose, which angered him irrationally. Maybe it was the uncanny resemblance and Balin's knowledge of Christ's renowned instruction to meet a blow with a proffered cheek that made him suspect the man was ill suited to war. He was somewhat new to Arthur's service and did not yet know the intricacies of their camaraderie, so he said nothing. He had heard word the man was not even born to knighthood. He was some sort of entertainer Arthur had elevated.

Culwych jammed his spear point in the ground and put the back of his hand to Balin's arm.

"Sir Balin, why did you not grant your king the honor of the kill?"

Balin looked at the Welshman. What was there to say to such a question? He had seen danger and interposed himself. He looked past the man to Arthur. "Did I do wrong, sire?"

"No, Sir Balin," Arthur smiled. "You probably saved me a bruising."

"Likely a goring," said Dagonet. "That monster must weigh thirty stone."

"More," said Bedivere, pressing the toe of his boot to its thick side.

"It might've swallowed me whole," said Dagonet, with appreciative awe.

"It would've still had plenty of room for Arthur." Kay laughed, shoving the smaller man off his feet.

"You're fortunate it didn't work its way up the shaft and kill you," Bedivere said to Balin.

"That's why we use the cruciform spear," Balin said, pointing out the cross guard at the point where the haft met the steel head of Arthur's spear. Claellus had taught him that.

"So the arms prevent it," said Arthur, looking at the spear admiringly.

"Yes, my king."

"We should forge all our spears thus," said Arthur, "to keep an enemy from doing the same thing on the battlefield."

"A man is not a boar, Arthur," said Bedivere, smirking. "It would take more animal hatred than a man has in him to force his own body down the length of a spear shaft."

"Don't underestimate the hatred of men, for I've seen a Saxon do that very thing," said Brastias grimly.

"I would think a spear through the chest would have a more calming effect on the temperament," said Dagonet. "Even a Saxon's."

"Well, I still say a straight spear point is better," Bedivere went on. "The quicker out, the quicker back in."

"At last you speak of something I know of," Dagonet said, causing the others to laugh heartily.

"Too quick for most ladies' tastes," Kay said, and they roared even louder.

"We'll sup well tonight," said Ulfius, admiring the carcass.

The king's cousin had stared at Balin throughout the exchange, his expression one of disdain. He was a high-born fool, and his father was a devil worshiping pagan who let the witches of Avalon roam free throughout his kingdom, preaching their dark gospel, leading astray the women of the land as the Lady Lile had his mother. Balin didn't care for him, but he turned away, having a more pressing concern.

"Where are the damned hounds?" Sir Brastias said.

"That was my thought, sir," Balin said, stepping away from the group and straining to hear.

It was the middle of the rutting season. Rare to find such a strong male apart from a sow. But the dogs were still barking, and he recognized the catch hounds' call too.

"I think they have cornered the mate," said Balin.

Culwych pulled his spear from the earth.

"Then what are we waiting here for?" he said, and went running off into the brush.

"Hastiness in a knight makes for a swift undoing," Sir Ulfius said.

"He's just eager to prove himself," said Arthur. "Call the hounds back, Sir Balin. We have enough meat here to bear."

"I fear Balin's horn won't bring your cousin back, Arthur," said Ector, watching with amusement the rustling leaves that marked the Welshman's flight.

"It's growing late," said Ulfius, peering up at the descending sun through the canopy. "We should butcher this beast and pack it before the meat spoils."

"I'll fetch him, sire," Balin announced, and ran off into the woods after Culwych, leaving the others to dress the carcass.

BALIN'S YOUTH HAD been spent leaping and running through the tangled woods and peat bogs behind surefooted Killhart, so he traversed the rises and gullies of Sciryuda with relative ease. He soon spied the Welshman bumbling ahead of him.

When he caught up at last, he found Culwych standing on a rise looking down on a squealing hunchbacked sow. She backed into the hollow of a great oak within a cacophonous semicircle of Arthur's dogs. The two catch hounds, Cavall and Drudwyn, pulled at her ears, bearing her great head down, keeping the wildly spinning and bucking swine from breaking away.

Yet by the swell of her flanks, Balin could see the sow was heavy with her litter. She had probably chosen the hollow tree in which to drop her farrow. The boar they had killed had tried to lead the dogs away and failed.

Culwych raised his spear, and Balin called out, "Do not cast, milord!"

Either he had not been heard above the frantic barking of the hounds, or Culwych simply ignored him. Balin was too far to grab the poised haft, so he put his hunting horn to his lips and blew the recall.

The baying hounds pricked up their ears and ceased their noise. They spun almost as one and streamed up the hill past Culwych. Cavall and Drudwyn, each with a jaw full of bleeding ear, released and bounded back to their master, Arthur.

The bay hounds swarmed around Balin, leaping and licking at his hands. The sow swung around and abandoned her would-be nursery, crashing off into the brush.

Culwych flung his spear. It arced down and struck her in the left ham. She shrieked and stumbled, before tearing off into the woods.

"Damn you!" Culwych yelled in frustration as Balin came up beside him. "That's the second boar you've cost me."

Balin furrowed his brow. The last boar had been in no danger from Culwych.

"That sow is ready to drop her litter, sir," said Balin. "If the mothers are killed, the next season's hunt is spoiled."

Culwych waved him off and began to trudge back in the direction of the party.

Balin whistled and set the dogs on the sow's blood trail. He walked off in their wake.

Culwych's hand gripped his elbow and spun him around. "Where are you going?"

"Your cast was sloppy," he said, breaking Culwych's offending grip with a jerk of his arm. "She's only wounded and in pain."

"Now I see your intent." Culwych spat in a rage. "You will kill her and take her back to Arthur as your own prize."

Balin blinked. Was it possible a cousin of the king could be so stupid? "I told you my intent, sir. If you wish, come along and you may kill her yourself. If you can."

That last word, he knew, was hasty. He should have ended his statement a few words early, but the man grated on him.

"You insolent dog! Is that how you address the king's cousin?"

Balin sneered and turned away, but Culwych's hand went to the hilt of his sword and drew it with a rasp.

That sound and the flash of naked steel awakened his reflexes. He spun and set his spear as he had with the boar.

"Put away your sword, sir," Balin said evenly.

"How dare you?" Culwych snarled. "You think you can raise arms against me? I'm a prince of Celyddon!" He advanced toward Balin. "Who are you? Nothing! The brother of a murdering hedge knight, the son of a country footman and a pagan whore…"

The man's chest was inches from the point of Balin's spear. It would be a simple thing to meet his haughty advance with a single step forward, to cut short his imperious tirade. Balin sorely wanted to.

Then Culwych stumbled on the mossy slope and pitched forward.

The next instant, the steel sunk into the center of Culwych's chest to the arms of the cross, and the insult to Balin's mother was choked off in his privileged Welsh throat.

A glittering woman's ring dangling from a silver chain slipped out of the open neck of Culwych's tunic as he sagged forward, gasping. The delicate green stones were capped with silver leaves and stems, and set within a fanciful winding device, so as to give the impression of a pair of green apples huddled on a bough. It was much like a ring his mother had kept in a box on the mantle of their cottage.

Culwych's blue eyes bulged. His breath rattled hoarsely in his throat, and he gripped the haft of the boar spear. With great effort, he tried to pull himself toward Balin, but the cruciform design kept him at bay. Blood dribbled from his lips, and he sagged heavily, his chin dropping at last to his chest.

Balin realized with a burst of cold sweat down the back of his neck that he alone was holding the king's cousin aright.

CHAPTER
NINE

NIMUE WAS LOVELY.

Many men had told her this, from the time she was very young. Too young, really, to be told such things.

Her father had tried to shield her from the world of men. He had sent her to a nunnery as soon as she was of age, to preserve her virtue from the mousy-haired farm boys who followed her home from market and lingered stupidly at the edge of their land.

But the world of men had come smashing into the furtive, hushed prison of the tallow scented cloisters when the round shield Saxons of Osla Big Knife had raided her abbey. They had carried off all the young girls, putting the abbess and the elder sisters to the sword.

For months, she had been passed among the army, subjected to their vile attentions, made to stumble behind their horses and plunder wagons by a tether which had left scars on her wrists she hid to this day with bands of gold and leather.

Of her own craft, she had escaped them, leaving a Saxon soldier lying dead in his tent, his yellow bearded face cleft by his own axe.

She had wandered for a time, skirting like a nervous field mouse near the clanking armies marching cattle-like to their slaughter grounds, until she had come to the forest of Celyddon and met a woman named Gwendydd, who was searching for her twin brother, a wild man called Lailoken Guynglaff. Gwendydd took Nimue back to her mother's cottage, a simple stone affair with a thatch room that stood beside a lake, at the edge of an apple orchard.

Adhan, Gwendydd's old blind mother, had been high priestess of Avalon for a time.

As a nun, Nimue had been taught to fear the magic of Avalon and the witches who called it home, but Adhan and Gwendydd were too kindhearted for her to do anything other than dismiss these misguided teachings and embrace the gentle ways of their ancient sisterhood.

They were the custodians of Albion and the handmaidens of the timeless Goddess whose breath hissed through the trees and whose cool, nourishing blood rushed down the snaking rivers which were her veins. They offered her the peaceful contemplation of the nuns, but with the natural reward of the perennial gardener. Their duty was to honor their Mother by nourishing and defending the Land. It was a fine life.

Then one night, the world of man had once more interrupted her idylls.

Lailoken, the Merlin, returned.

Fittingly, it was in the midst of a torrential storm, and they were finishing up their supper when the door, though barred against the wind howling off the lake, flew open and a terrible blue-painted naked figure of a man, tall and lanky, his black hair and tangled beard adorned with nettles, burst in.

"Who is this woman?" he had demanded, as though he were the master of the house and not its prodigal son. He stepped into the warm light, boldly running his crazed eyes all about her.

Gwendydd had risen and fetched a long mantle of black bear fur from beside the hearth fire and draped it over her brother's shoulders.

"Brother, this is Nimue, a lady of Garadigan."

"She is lovely," he said, as though it were no compliment, but a curse he had lain upon her. He narrowed his eyes. "She will be my downfall."

She had been startled at this and averted her eyes from his, settling on the gleaming double dragon torc of white and red gold in the form of two dragons entwined about his neck.

Nimue was lovely.

The Merlin, as the Cambion, and the only man privy to the same Sight as the Lady of The Lake, was said to let nothing pass unobserved, and he had said she was lovely.

OF THE MEN she had known as lovers, the Saxons had been stinking, rutting boars. Merlin was like a strong but timid stag, insistent and ready always, drawn from the wilderness by her beauty, but ready to bolt back into the trees at the first sign of cruelty.

This strange family had taught her many things; chiefly, they had informed her she was powerful. Adhan and Gwendydd had instructed her in practical power, in scrying rootwork, and small wonders. The Merlin had taught her she could hold sway over men. With but the promise of what the ignorant Saxons had roughly taken from her, she had induced him to teach her things about magic even his mother and sister did not know. Deep, dark ways, the messy blood and entrails magic of men and devils, those things outside the natural order, which his devil father had imparted upon him. For a kiss, he had shown her the secret way to Avalon, and for a few moments of passion, he had vouched for her with the Lady of The Lake herself.

She had studied the mysteries then at Avalon, with the Merlin her constant companion. But after his departure, the sisterhood had proved a stifling arrangement, too similar to the nunnery with its prohibitions against men and the disapproving looks of the other women. She had opted to return to the world of men and live as Adhan and Gwendydd, planting her guardian apple seed beside her cottage, becoming a warden of Albion, practicing her art for the good of its people.

Then, for the third time, a man had changed her life.

This man, a knight and a Welsh prince, a lithe, golden-haired hart of a man, encased in a skin of gleaming steel. Culwych was his name. He was the first beautiful man she had known.

He had ridden to her door one morning, bleeding over his saddle, having fought his way through a tide of King Carados' soldiers. His father, the King of Celyddon, had pledged fealty to the High King Arthur Pendragon, the champion of whom both Merlin and the Lady Lile had spoken, the one who they said would be given the sword Excalibur to unite the Land and its people.

She had treated his wounds, tended him like a helpless but obstinate babe, grown affectionate toward him in his weak repose, and loved him when at last he stirred and regained his strength.

Culwych. He had been strong, arrogant at first, but a tender, ardent lover, haughty and entitled in all things but that which mattered most to him. In her he swore he had found at last something worth humbling himself for. Something he did not feel his birthright alone made him worthy of. He was charmingly desperate to prove to her his gratitude and love.

And she had grown to love him too.

They had pledged themselves to each other. He had given her his princely signet and she to him her priestess' ring. He had promised to return once the rebel kings had been dispatched and he owed no more to Arthur's service. They would exchange their rings for vows. She would bear him knights and priestesses, and he would make her a queen in time.

She had heard the news of the great victory at Bedegraine and of the rout of the rebel kings.

She had expected to see him ride to her door.

Instead, one morning she had woken to find Merlin standing under her tree, noisily eating an apple.

She had seen little of him since she had left Avalon. If the unearthly Merlin harbored any love for her, if he was even capable of such feeling, he had never shown it. She knew he had been consort to Lile and that he passed among the women of Avalon like a satyr. Some whispered that he had even given attention to his own sister and that that was the source of his dark power, though Nimue, knowing Gwendydd, dismissed this as gossip. Even so, he had departed Avalon and gone to the side of King Arthur without even a parting word for her, so she felt no discomfort in asking him if he had news of her Culwych.

He had said nothing, but only took her hand and pressed the green stone ring she had given her prince into her palm and departed.

She had lain beneath the tree for a day and a night, too stricken to rouse herself. How to live on, when the person who embodied her future ideal was dead in the service of a boy king?

Arthur. These fool knights and their love for a king! What was a knight's blind, idiot devotion, compared to her love? She hated him now, this boy king, as she would have hated a woman who had seduced Culwych from her bed.

When a shower of rain drove her at last to her feet, she had retired to her cottage and consulted pools and mirrors, falling even to the dark, forbidden ways Merlin had taught her. She had done everything but invoke the primer magic of prayer to God in order to find a path of revenge through the tangled hedgerow of her sorrow.

And then the spirits had revealed to her a terrible curse.

Now, Nimue stood in the cold dark hall of King Rience, the master of Snowdonia and Norgales, in Vortigern's old keep on rainy Mount Aravius, the instrument of her vengeance beneath her white fur cloak, stolen from the Isle of Avalon's own treasure house. Outside, thunder rumbled like a giant rolling across the roof of the keep. The rain pattered and lightning lit the high windows intermittently with splashes of blue-white fire.

A spindly page drew back the hide curtain and ushered her into Rience's presence.

Rience was a giant. The tallest man she had ever seen, with impressive even sprawled in repose on his stout throne of oak and horn. The chin of his prodigious curly black beard rested on one massive ringed fist. The other hand idly swirled a deep pewter goblet of wine. The dark eyes beneath his thick black brow regarded her frankly. He was a bit drunk. He wore a wine-red chiton and over his shoulders a long heavy cloak trimmed with fur patches of various textures and hues, as though culled from a bevy of different beasts. On his head was a tall, spiny crown of red metal, and around his neck hung a golden portrait of his late wife, suspended on a broad gold chain.

On one side of his throne leaned a great single edged sword in a furred scabbard. On the other, stood a wiry-haired young shield maiden in a coat of gold chased mail and a jeweled circlet. Rience's daughter, the mannish Britomart, almost as tall and solid as her father, yet somehow still alluring, like a stately elk cow.

"I was told," boomed Rience, his deep voice thunderous in the cave-like hall, "that an enchantress had come to see me with a gift. But I see only Nimue, that slip of a girl who once doted on the Merlin."

Britomart smirked at that, making Nimue want to slash the rough beauty from her face.

She drew herself up, unflinching beneath Rience's heavy gaze.

"As I am a pupil of the Merlin and a daughter of Avalon, you would be wise not to tempt my displeasure, Rience King."

"I'm sure Merlin taught you much before he cast you aside, my little nymph," said the giant, rubbing the end of his beard between two fingers, as though to keep it warm.

"I didn't come here to bear your insults, king," Nimue said.

"Yes, yes," he said, sipping from his cup. Wine dribbled through his beard like rainwater finding a path through a tangled shrub. "What's your gift, Nimue? Some lucky charm? Rabbit's foot?"

"I bring you nothing less than the destruction of your enemy, King Arthur."

"Of course you do," he said tiredly, rubbing his eyes. "See here, girl. It will take more than a few chaws of mandrake or a dash of toadstool power to oust Uther's bastard from the throne."

Exasperated, Nimue threw open her robe, displaying the gilded sword in the woven baldric about her thin waist.

Father and daughter both leaned forward as the jewels in the intricately fashioned hilt caught the torchlight. After a moment, Rience leaned back in his seat, his lids slipping down his eyes again.

"A sword?" He shrugged and touched the hilt of the weapon propped against his throne, for the first time deathly serious. "My family has borne Marmyadose since Heracles used it to slay the Hydra at Amymone. It was forged by Hephaestus himself, and two years ago broke the sword of Macsen at Aneblayse before my army was driven off. That is a sure sign from the gods that the High Kingship is rightfully mine. I will not trade my family's heirloom for that pretty trinket." His eyes slid to his daughter, still regarding the sword hungrily. "But perhaps my daughter…"

"This sword is not for either of you," Nimue said, closing her robe over it and breaking the avaricious trance of Britomart, who had taken a step forward at the notion of claiming the sword.

Rience smirked. "What is your intent, woman? To lead my army against Arthur yourself? My daughter would cut my throat in my sleep if I let any woman command troops before her."

Britomart squared her shoulders and looked as if she might take her father's sword and cut Nimue down herself.

"This sword is for the one that will shed Arthur's blood," said Nimue.

"You will slay him?" Rience said, befuddled.

"No. Not I. By my enchantment, the king will die at the hands of the knight who loves him best."

King Rience set his drink down and stared hard at her.

"That is a black curse indeed. Why would you do this, Nimue? My ear to the business of Avalon deafened when my wife died. But my spies say that the Lady of The Lake has thrown her support behind the bastard, and that when next I cross Marmyadose with his steel it will be the blade of the Excalibur."

"What the Lady of The Lake professes is her own affair," Nimue said. "*I* am not blind to the priests that crowd the court at Camelot, nor to Arthur's pining for the daughter of King Leodegrance."

A pied raven swooped in through the open window of the throne room and perched on the high sill, shaking the rain from its back. Rience took no note of it, but Nimue did.

"Leodegrance," Rience murmured. "My old, old enemy."

"A Christian king, as you know," said Nimue, watching the raven strut back and forth.

"So his daughter has the bastard's favor."

"Her name is Guinevere," Nimue said. "You and your queen served Avalon in the past, my lord. Will you do so now?"

"I paid service to Avalon as the husband of one of its daughters. My gods are not your gods. Why should I skulk and win by magic and treachery what the might of the arms of Hephaestus," and here, he brandished the old sword Marmyadose, "have declared is mine by right? No, I will take no part in your witch's curse. But you have brought me a gift indeed, whether it was the one you intended or not. I will take Arthur's crown, but it will be on the battlefield in open contest, where none may call my kingship to question, and I will not be beholden to any witch's favor."

At his side, Britomart smiled and laid a hand on her father's arm, then regarded Nimue with contempt.

Nimue curled her lip.

The raven flapped once and flew back out into the storm.

"You will fail," she predicted and went out of his presence.

CHAPTER
TEN

OR TWO YEARS Balin languished forgotten in the dungeon of Castle Bedegraine.

But that just confinement was nothing compared to the shame at having failed his beloved king so utterly. He had wept like a boy as he walked into the clearing with the body of Culwych cradled in his arms, and laid him at the king's feet. Arthur's anger had been all the more terrible because in the face of Balin's mortified tears, the young monarch had said absolutely nothing. He had merely lifted his cousin's body and walked away, leaving the fool Dagonet and one-handed Bedivere to tie him without protest.

They had led him, a prisoner from the forest, at the back of the train, behind even the butchered boar bouncing on a pole between Kay and Brastias.

In all, four carcasses had been borne from the wood that day, for what was Balin without his king to serve? Little more than a dead man.

Balin had never been brought before any court, never heard any pronouncement. He had simply been stripped of his arms and horse, of all honor and position, and deposited in the belly of Bedegraine Castle. There he had remained, fed and watered by the jailer daily, like some caged pet.

No man had visited him, and he had no word of the world.

Despite his anger at his brother's sin, he pined for Brulen's company. Yet he knew they would likely never meet again. On the field of Bedegraine, he had sought him among the Orkney knights, but hadn't found him, not during nor after the battle, among the dead. Brulen was damned for killing a holy man, so they would not even meet in heaven. The knights of Northumberland who had trained him thought him a traitor for taking arms against Clarivaunce, though his oath had been to Detors. Yet how could he stand in judgment of Brulen now, when not even the High King, chosen by God Himself, looked on Balin with favor.

He was utterly alone.

In his first year of confinement, he took a penitential oath of silence and did nothing but grow his hair and beard like Samson. He ate and drank only enough to sustain himself and spent his days in quiet contemplation of the act that had landed him in durance vile.

For a long time, he could not quite decide if he had killed the Welsh prince on purpose or if it had been an accident. He had never protested his innocence, or made excuse, though in replaying the memory of the moment in his mind, he swore the man had fallen on the point.

Still, Culwych's harsh words pounded like war drums in his ears. When he thought of the insult to his dear mother, Balin supposed he must have thrust the spear into Culwych's chest and murdered him in a rage.

This made him feel sympathy for his brother, Brulen. Confronted with the man whom he had blamed for their mother's death, he must have felt a similar rage.

Murder of course, was against the Lord's commandments. As a knight, he was given the right to bear arms and kill in the name of justice and in the protection of the defenseless, but no man was blameless in killing out of mere provocation. He was not some street brawling boy. A knight must be more.

By the end of his first year, he had decided it did not matter whether he had murdered Culwych or not. He was imprisoned, and so God must have seen the anger in his heart, the flaw in his knighthood, and thrust him into this maddening furnace of burning stillness to temper him.

The lack of news was a torture in itself, though. When the door had swung shut on him, his king's rule was still in question. The eleven rebel kings had retreated to their lands, and there had been word that Saxons had been mustering there. In a year's time, the kings had either repelled the invasion or been defeated. Maybe, as old Vortigern had, they had even struck a bargain with the Saxons. Whatever the end result, the threat to Arthur was not gone, it had simply been delayed.

How long before the winds blew war to Arthur's doorstep again? And here he was, negligent on his oath to protect his king due to his own childish folly.

Into his second year, he had found resolve.

He would not die here. Of that he was sure. God would not allow it. Eventually he would be released, or lightning would strike this castle and shake it down, and like Peter liberated from Herod by the angel, he would be freed. He was sure of this.

Then Arthur would need him once more.

So, he trained as best he could in his confines. He rebuilt his wasted body, consuming all the jailer passed him, and regained his strength through hard, relentless labor. He also found his quickness once more, hunting the rats that he had passively allowed to scurry over his sleepless body on their way to his leftovers, until perhaps, news of his terribleness spread through the colonies of vermin that wormed their way through the castle, and they visited his lair no more.

He began to speak in a hoarse and humble voice to the man who brought him food, and from him he learned Arthur was still king and loved all the more by his people. He had taken up his court in Camelot, the ancient city of the Black Cross, where the pagan King Agrestes had once sacrificed Christians in the time when Joseph of Arimathea had first carried the word of God to Albion. Now, the man assured him, good King Arthur had brought Christ to that once dark place, and he had erected a church to St. Stephen The Protomartyr to honor the nameless souls who had met their deaths in sacrifice to Agrestes' evil gods.

This news had filled Balin with pride once more. Pride in the king to whom he had sworn his life. He redoubled his efforts to be sure he was a knight worthy of such a ruler when at last he was released.

He spoke daily with the jailer, whose name was Matthew, and asked of the rebel kings and the Saxons. Matthew knew only rumors, that many had fallen against the wild invaders, but that one, Rience, had either united all the survivors and driven off the Saxons, or parleyed with the enemy and was now amassing a combined force to enact revenge upon Arthur for his earlier defeat.

Balin also came to know the names of the many good and wondrous knights who flocked to Arthur from around the realm.

Some he knew from his own brief career, such as Griflet, who had been a chased squire to Bedivere and was now made knight. Bedivere's brother Lucan was Arthur's butler now. Sir Kay had been made seneschal, and a count of Anjou besides. Old Ulfius was chamberlain at Camelot, and he heard that Brastias had retired to a hermitage. Dagonet, whom he had thought a fool, was said to now serve the court in exactly that capacity.

Some came to Arthur with royal blood. Serving as knights were Prince Marhaus of Hibernia and; Prince Bors The Younger of Gannes, son of the Gaulish king whom Merlin had disguised as a woodcutter's son at Bedegraine; Lamorak, Aglovale, Dornar, and Tor, the sons of King Pellinore of Galis; and Owain, Arthur's nephew by his sister Morgan and his former enemy King Uriens. Also in his service who had once counted him an enemy were the sons of King Lot, Arthur's nephews from Orkney: Agravaine, Gaheris, and Gawaine. Gawaine's strength, Matthew said, due to some enchantment perpetrated by his enchantress aunt Morgan, ebbed at noon and waned at dusk.

This word of pagan knights so near Arthur filled Balin with dread. There were also three heathen Saracen brothers: Safir, Segwarides, and Palomedes, by name.

The Lady of Avalon still spun her strands into the king's court like a lurking spider trapping souls. Matthew said that she had even bestowed upon Arthur the magic sword Excalibur, to replace the sword of Macsen, broken in battle. The old jailer said this last with pride. For all his Christian propensity, he still saw the endorsement of Avalon as some kind of honor. But Balin saw the replacement of Macsen's sword with a pagan treasure as harrowing. How long would the insidious evils of the dark Lady infect the folk of Albion?

Balin grew frantic. He needed to be free of this jail. Arthur needed him sorely. Perhaps, as a boy of only nineteen, the young king was unaware of the danger he was in. Perhaps the rumored threat of this Rience and the Saxons distracted him from the enemy infesting his court, no doubt whispering seductive evils in his very ears under the guise of advice.

There was something else, too, of which he was keenly aware. He was missing this golden age.

Camelot and Arthur were precariously balanced, as though God and the Devil were vying for control. It would take only a slight nudge to plunge the land into darkness or light. There was no other place for Balin but in the center of this holy conflict. He had to win the soul of Arthur and Albion for the Lord.

And for every new name that Matthew whispered to him through the bars—Sagramore, Maleagrant, Colgrevance, Dinadan—he wondered which were good men and which were bad. Which lions and which serpents?

When at last word came that he was to be transferred to the dungeon at Camelot, he rejoiced, for he knew his captivity was ending.

When Matthew opened the old door, Sir Dagonet strode in, wearing a richly embroidered but surpassingly bright tunic with a somewhat ridiculous heraldic device: *Or, a cockerel's head erased, gules.* He was much as Balin remembered him, long haired and trim-bearded, with a smirking lilt to his mouth, and yet now there was a dullness in his eyes, as though a deeper, more bitter jest hid there. It diminished his previous resemblance to Christ somehow. He made a show of pinching his nose against Balin's stink.

"Well, Sir Balin, like a green apple forgotten at the bottom of a bushel, you have surely ripened during your incarceration," he quipped.

"Sir Dagonet," Balin said, rising. "Have you come to free me?"

"Only the king can do that," Dagonet said. "Every Pentecost since he drew the sword from the stone, my lord Arthur has held court at Camelot and invited people from around the realm to come and air out their grievances. You could use an airing out, I think."

"I don't have any grievance with the king. It's quite the opposite."

"Let me finish," said Dagonet, leaning in the doorway. "As part of the Pentecostal celebration, he also evaluates every prisoner and frees them if their offense is deemed not so severe."

Balin lowered his head.

"Mine is very severe."

"Oh, I don't know about that. Arthur's cousins have proven to be equal blessing and bane at Camelot thus far," said Dagonet. "And Culwych wasn't even his favorite. I suspect his anger has cooled in two years' time."

"You mock me, sir."

"I mock everything, Sir Balin," said Dagonet. "You should be grateful that at last someone has included you in their catalog of everything, for I think that your situation has been an unfortunate case of misplacement, rather than lasting grudge. You're a good knife lost too long in the back of the drawer."

———

HE BADE GOODBYE to old Matthew and was led to a waiting cage on a wagon, where two knights sat on horseback, one a black Moor in the singular garb of English armor and Saracen head wrap, with a thick curved sword at his side, the other a slight, handsome fellow with a head of long black hair and fearsome blue eyes, a mantle of green plaid flung about his shoulders in the manner of a Hibernian. The former looked at him with silent curiosity, whereas the latter curled his lip at the sight.

Dagonet walked beside Balin, bearing his clanking harness, sword, and shield, which he moved to strap to a bow backed pack horse.

"I apologize for the conveyance," said Dagonet. "It's more suited to nightingale than knight."

Balin moved to the back of the cage wagon, saying nothing. He didn't care if he were brought to Camelot in a chicken coop, so long as he was at Arthur's side again.

The Moor jumped down lightly and unfastened the bolted door to the cage.

"Sir Balin, may I present my companions Sir Safir and Sir Lanceor," said Dagonet, indicating the Moor and the Hibernian, respectively, as he ported Balin's goods to the boot of the wagon.

"Balin The Savage?" said the Hibernian, grinning. "Is this the one killed a priest at his own accolade?"

Balin gritted his teeth behind his lips as he pulled himself into the cart and settled in the straw, but made no reply.

"You're mistaken, O Prince," said Dagonet, climbing into the driver's seat and taking up the reins. "That was Sir Balin's brother, Sir Brulen The Sinister."

Sinister? Was that what Brulen was called now? Was it because of his deeds or merely his left handedness?

"Ah," said Lanceor, looking back over his shoulder through the bars at Balin. "Then this is the one mistook the king's cousin for a wild boar."

"Yes," said Dagonet, "Have a care, Sir Lanceor, for Sir Balin is a danger to all wild boors."

Sir Safir smiled as he locked the door.

"You are wicked, sir," he said, mounting once more.

Lanceor frowned, still staring at Balin.

"Why are we wasting our time fetching this ragamuffin back to Camelot?" Lanceor asked.

"Because I have no hope for promotion with so many of the king's relatives at court," said Dagonet, cracking the reins, "and I hope Sir Balin's wild ways will thin out their number."

Lanceor and Safir both laughed and gave spur to their mounts as the cart lurched forward and Balin gripped the iron bars to keep his balance.

It was August, a full ten months before Pentecost came around again. But at least he would be nearer to freedom.

He had prayed for a liberator such as the angel that had come to Peter.

God had sent him a fool.

CHAPTER
ELEVEN

THE WOODS WERE dark, and Sir Dagonet, Sir Lanceor, and Sir Safir gathered about the fire eating while Balin watched from the darkness of his cage, hungry not only for the savory stag the Moor had shot, but also for the companionship they enjoyed. He had been too long alone, with only scuttling vermin and the voice of an old man through a bolted door for company.

They passed a flagon between them, and when they were of a mood, they clamored for Dagonet to produce his harp and play a tune.

"One day hence you two will mark this night you shared meat and reddish with the king of all Hibernia," said Lanceor.

"Radish?" said Dagonet, feigning to look about as he set his harp in his lap. "Have we garnish for this meat?"

"Reddish," Lanceor repeated slowly, and looked at Dagonet as if he were addle-minded.

Safir shook his head and laughed.

"I have never understood the custom of inheriting such a great thing as a kingdom," said Dagonet. "A bow, or a cabinet, that I understand. But to leave something so important as a country and its people to one's child, whether that child be unworthy or no, is something that has long befuddled me."

"Should we elect rulers by popular opinion, as the ancient Romans did?" Safir asked.

Dagonet shrugged.

"I have no head for such matters," he said. "Only God the Father ever had a son worth the kingdom, and some say Uther Pendragon, though it remains to be seen. As to all else, it is a few short letters from nepotism to despotism."

Lanceor took the flagon from Safir.

"What is nepotism?" he asked, but by the time he had upended the flagon, he had ceased to care about the answer, and Dagonet had begun to play.

It was not the lively song they had requested, more a sad and solemn dirge. It was well suited to staring into a fire, and made Balin think of the one which had consumed his mother and of the happy times before.

When Dagonet had finished, Lanceor gave voice to his approaching drunkenness with a deep belch. "Well that was just fine," Lanceor grumbled, "for a funeral."

"It was in honor of the stag Sir Safir slew," Dagonet said after a moment.

"Play something…better," Lanceor urged.

"Your pardon. My fingers are greasy," Dagonet begged off, stowing the harp away.

From observing them, Balin gleaned that of the three, Lanceor was the dullest. He was one of these knaves who depended like a woman on his beauty than on any real wit or even skill at arms. Dagonet had called him prince, and Balin wondered if that were just a joke or true. Dagonet had always been difficult for him to read. He knew the man to be a coward and had never understood how he had come to be a knight. But the alacrity of his speech and the mirth it seemed to engender in others made Balin think he must house some craft. Safir, the Moor, appeared appreciative of his verbal gambols but did not possess the cutting tongue of the fool.

The Moor was a source of boundless fascination for Balin, who had never before seen a black skinned man or lady in person. He wondered if this Sir Safir were a Moslem, and his curiosity overcame his discretion.

"Sir Safir?" he called to them.

The three of them turned to look in his direction.

"What is it, Sir Balin?" the Moor answered.

Balin was at a loss as to what to say next.

"I thought I might beg some of your meat, if there is any to spare."

Dagonet smiled, and Lanceor, looking like a pup at Dagonet, smiled too, though he obviously knew not why.

"Go on, Sir Safir," said Dagonet. "Take our charge some hart. He has gone long without, I think."

Safir carved a shank of meat from the carcass over the fire and stepped from the light.

Balin marked his progress by the sound of his boots, for when he came around the cage with only the dark forest behind him, only the glint of the moon on his breastplate was visible.

"Here you are, sir," said Safir, pushing the meat through the bars. "I regret that I cannot leave you my dagger."

"I will not begrudge, sir," said Balin, taking the hot venison in his dancing fingers and setting it on his knee. "Sir Dagonet is right. I have eaten only such gruel and pork as the jailer prepared. I haven't tasted a fresh kill in two years."

"I will leave you to it, then," said the Moor, and Balin heard his heel scrape as he turned away.

"Oh? Will you not stay?" he blurted, then regained himself. "That is, will you not talk a bit?"

"If it please you, sir."

"My news has been spotty at best. How fares Arthur?"

"Well, well. I am afraid my own knowledge of the events in this area may prove as sparse as your own. I am only recently arrived from Hibernia with my brother."

"Oh? You…you are Hibernian?" Balin said.

By his voice, Balin could tell the man was grinning.

"You are angling, I think, sir. No, I am not Hibernian. My father is King Astlabor of Galilee."

"So you're a prince…like Lanceor?"

"I am, but unlike him, I shall never see a throne, God willing."

This surprised Balin. He had never spoken to a noble who didn't want his father's throne.

"You don't want to be a king?"

"I should settle into the throne if it were required of me of course, but with nine elder brothers, I would rather be a poor man-at-arms than for my family to suffer the calamity necessary to set a crown on my head."

Nine brothers seemed a staggering amount to Balin, but he supposed King Astlabor must be a polygamist. Certainly no Christian woman would deign to bring forth that many babies alone.

"You are from Galilee? Are you a Jew, then?"

"There are not many Jews left in Galilee. My father is a Muslim. Myself, I was born here in Albion, with two of my brothers, and a sister. My father, by long and storied roads, came to save the life of King Pellinore from a beast in the Gaste Forest. Pellinore's friendship was such that my father visited often along with various of his wives, and four of his children were born here. My brother Segwarides made his home in Cornwall. We are both Christian, as is our sister Florine. But my brother Palomedes cleaves to my father's faith."

Balin found the man pleasant and wished they had met as two knights of good standing, rather than with shameful bars between them.

"And Lanceor, he will be a king?"

Sir Safir lowered his voice considerably.

"He is the only son of one of the minor kings of Hibernia, Elidus by name, and he will likely marry the daughter of King Anguish. My brother Palomedes and I were, until recently, knights of Anguish."

King Anguish had been one of the eleven rebels.

"Did you fight at Bedegraine? At Aneblayse?"

Safir sighed.

"We did, to our shame," said the knight. "But God taught us our folly that day. Were you there?"

"Yes. I fought against the Orkneys."

"We were to Lot's left flank with King Nentres, against Bors the Elder. I heard of your prowess that day. Sir Balin, I wish that we had met in better circumstance," said Sir Safir, holding his hand through the bars.

Balin grasped it.

"Such was also my thought, sir. Thank you."

"But not on opposite ends of a battlefield," Safir chuckled.

"Are you chewing the food for him like a mother robin, Sir Safir?" Lanceor called from the fire. He was deep in his cups, by the slur of his words.

"Excuse his manner," whispered Safir, before returning to the fire.

It seemed to Balin that the coarseness of the noble born related somehow to the eminence of their inheritance, and he considered the things Dagonet had said.

He settled in the straw and ate the first good meal he had had in two years.

THEY STOPPED FOR a time in Astolat, then followed the river road down through a lush forest and into a verdant valley that rivalled even Balin's nostalgia for his boyhood home. It seemed as if life flourished the closer they came to Camelot. It was the height of summer, but the air was pleasant and breezy, and wildflowers of every hue painted the land.

They came to a bustling village of prosperous folk, and though the children abandoned their chores to run alongside the horses and wagon, shouting up greetings at the knights whom they knew by name, none were scolded, and the parents waved from their houses, calling out to Safir, and Lanceor, and even to Dagonet, who made faces and threw playful insults and crossed his eyes at the little ones to their squealing delight.

The children were naturally curious about Balin, and some of the boys leapt up on the cage and shouted questions through the bars at him, but in so many shrill voices all at once, that he couldn't understand any of them.

The livestock he saw were plump and healthy as the people. God had blessed Camelot.

A grand, columned chapel festooned with leering gargoyles and stately angels and bright eyes of blazing stained glass stood in the center of the village. In its grassy courtyard, the massive obsidian Black Cross, on which Agrestes had once nailed Christians twelve at a time gleamed. A beautiful, proportionate white marble Christ had been affixed to its center, sanctifying it, and lush green ivy crept up it where it was said no growing thing would approach before. God had reclaimed this area, and Arthur's church had grown from the blood-soaked stone just as the climbing vines had come from the earth.

They rolled through a vast green meadow then, and Balin ached to see a fine tiltyard nearby, decorated with bright, flapping pennants, and to hear the crash of lance upon armor and the appreciative cry of the crowd in their boxes. More than ever he felt the keen sting of the sight of his own armor and blazon tied to Dagonet's pack horse, and he hung his head.

The castle itself rose on a hill across a brackish moat. The thick walls were of Agrestes' time, venerable, blocky, and formidable, but the crenulated battlements were hung with bright silken dragon banners which rippled like lake water. The pennant of Arthur and Uther was before him. Guards in gleaming armor and helms saluted them from the top of the wall.

It was agony to be taken from the cage and led across the sunny courtyard to the dungeon steps after a glimpse at such beauty and goodness, and it was made all the more tortuous by the passing of a group of maidens shaded beneath a canopy borne by four richly dressed young pages. Some of them giggled behind their hands at his scruffy appearance, and Balin keenly felt the breadth and knottiness of his unkempt hair and beard, and the threadbare state of his drab prisoner's clothes. But as they came nearer, the chief among them, a stately woman finely freckled with night black hair and forest pool eyes shushed them and admonished them for their rudeness. She even bowed her chin to him as he shuffled past and greeted each of the knights in turn. A golden cross caught the light at her silk-covered bosom.

"Who was that Christian lady?" Balin asked, when they were gone.

"That was the Princess Guinevere, daughter of King Leodegrance of Cameliard," said Safir.

"Curb your baser thoughts, Sir Balin," Dagonet warned in an exaggerated tone. "She will likely be our Queen in a few months' time."

"No such thing entered my mind!" Balin hissed, his face flushing.

It was horrible to think so of such a fine and goodly lady. He wanted only to know her name so that he might ask God to bless her in his prayers.

Lanceor chuckled, and Balin felt like turning and cuffing the intemperate Hibernian braggart.

The dungeon cell was spacious compared to his accommodations at Bedegraine, and a high barred window afforded him a view of the courtyard and a beam of warm sunlight, though he suspected that view would come to be a torture.

"And here you will stay for the time being, Sir Balin," said Dagonet.

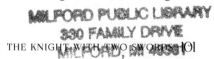

Safir grasped Balin's hand in parting. They had become friends on the journey, supping together often and speaking of their home countries.

"I will come and visit with you on Sundays after Mass while I am able," Safir said.

"You are my friend, sir," said Balin, his heart warming to the man. "And I am yours."

Lanceor picked his teeth with his little finger and went back up the steps without a word. Safir followed, and Dagonet watched the jailer shut and bar the door.

"Sir Dagonet," Balin called.

His eyes appeared in the little barred space in the door.

"Why did you bring me here, truly?"

"Truly?" Sir Dagonet repeated in the same tone. "The truth is, Sir Balin, that truth is the greatest virtue of a knight, and one that very few truly espouse. Many a knight who had slain the cousin of their king, without an eye to witness, it might have fled into the greenwood or fashioned some less damning version of the doing that would have cast them in a more favorable light. But you carried the body of Culwych from the killing ground and laid it at Arthur's feet. The truth is, he has need of men like you, whether he knows it or not. Truly, I am sorry I did not retrieve you sooner."

His face slid from the window, and Balin heard his boots on the stair.

Dagonet called down the passage in parting, "But now, farewell. Truly there are balls to be juggled and foolery to be done!"

CHAPTER
TWELVE

SIR SAFIR WAS true to his word, and visited Balin after every Sunday Mass when he was not out on some errand for the King. Safir kept him abreast of the news of the court and informed him of the official announcement of Arthur's engagement to the goodly Guinevere of Cameliard, a day which was marked by the ringing of St. Stephen's bells and the sounding of trumpets on the battlements.

"King Leodegrance is expected to give the Table Round that belonged to Uther as part of his daughter's dowry," Safir told him.

There was a hint of excitement in Safir's voice that mirrored Balin's own.

Balin had learned many of the legends of the Round Table while a squire. It was supposed to have been built for Uther by the Merlin, encasing the silver table at which blessed Joseph of Arimathea and his companions had once sat. In the days of Uther, it had seated a hundred and fifty of the greatest knights in Albion: Sir Caradoc The Thirteenth, Sir Abiron, Sir Brunor The Good Knight Without Fear, Sir Ulfius, and the greatest of them all, Sir Segurant The Brown.

"The knights of the Table of The Wandering Companions have been holding tournaments every month," Safir said, shaking his head, "hoping to determine which of them will be appointed to one of the sieges."

"I heard them jousting the first day I came here," said Balin. "But if the stories are to be believed…"

"Yes. No knight can claim a seat at the table unless first his name appears in golden letters on the back of the siege. Any unworthy knight who tries is driven mad." Safir shrugged. "In the meantime, it makes for good sport, anyway."

"Will you try, Safir?" Balin asked.

"If I am here. The king is not expected to marry until after the rebellion is put down once and for all. With the trouble stirring in the west, it could be years and many battles before they exchange the bands."

Balin said nothing but his heart hammered to be free of these prison walls. Though it was sinful, he prayed the trouble *would* continue, at least until he was free to face them among Arthur's companions, to clear his slate and earn the right to sit at that august table. He hoped Safir would be there too. In the absence of Brulen, he had come to love the Moor as a brother.

The sons of the traitorous Lot of Orkney had broken with their father and were now with Arthur. Did that mean Brulen too might find forgiveness in Camelot? Could he find his way back to the light?

"Do you think the Table would accept a pagan knight?" Balin asked.

"I have hopes my own brother Palomedes will find a place there when he's of age," Safir said.

"Palomedes is a Moslem. Although misguided, he is still a believer in the one true God," Balin said.

Safir chuckled. "You have a frank manner, Balin. It is expected that the Orkney brothers will sit at the Table. Gawaine in particular has made his name a great one. His aunt is a sorceress, and her gifts to him have helped him greatly. Do you disdain the notion of sitting across from an unbeliever?"

Balin did, in truth. He knew in his heart no godless knight could be trusted.

"Look you, Balin," said Safir, seeing the troubled look on Balin's face. "With all my father's wives and all the children begat by those unions, I have called Jew, Muslim, Christian and yea, even heathens, brother. I have fought beside knights Godly and pagan, and we have discoursed on our differences but also on our likenesses. Because of this, I have come to a certain understanding, which I believe our Roman forebears maintained also in their wisdom. Remember how the bloody temples of the Romans and the shrines of foreign gods once adjoined the same avenue as neighbors? God makes Himself known to every man in a way in which they may best understand. Mark how on the first Pentecost the Apostles were given the power to speak to men of every nation in a tongue each could fathom. I think that in every manner of worship there is a piece of the greater truth. One God with many names. That is why this talk of converting the peasants to one faith over the other baffles me. No man comes to God by the point of a sword. Even the Round Table is a miracle of heaven by the workings of a wizard."

Balin could not say he agreed. Safir had not witnessed the darkness which yawned and consumed those set upon the heathen path. He had not seen a brother give himself over to ultimate blasphemy, stain the altar cloth with unconsecrated blood, nor seen a mother burn unrepentant for her false faith.

"But now the hour's late, Balin," said Safir, rising from the stool on the other side of the prison door.

"Will I see you next Sunday, then?" Balin asked.

"I fear not, my friend," said Safir. "I have word from my brother Segwarides. He has need of me, and so I'm going to Cornwall."

He must have seen the grieved look on Balin's face, because he reached his fingers through the bars and entwined them with Balin's own.

"Don't despair, Sir Balin. In a few months' time, you'll be free of this place. When next we meet, it will be as two knights in good standing."

"As Knights of the Round Table, I say," said Balin. "Thank you, my friend."

Balin's only other visitor was a pied raven which sometimes lit in the high window of his prison cell and peered in on him.

He took the appearance of the strange bird as an ill omen. He cursed it and shooed it away at first, but on its second visitation he managed his foolish superstition better. He knew it was only a dumb animal seeking shelter and was ashamed of his earlier reaction.

He called it Brych, which meant "mottled."

He cooed kindly to it and tossed breadcrumbs up to it, watching it peck.

He took to leaving a dish of water there for the thing when it came. "Can tenderness turn black fortune white?" he asked the bird.

It squawked in reply, but whether it was an affirmation or a negative he couldn't guess.

These were the dark and lonesome days at the end of his sentence.

He feared that, except for Brych, he would be forgotten again, but after St. Stephen's bells sounded the end of Mass on Pentecost, the jailer unlocked his door and light spilled into his cell. Sir Dagonet stood limned by the sun in his bright courtly fineries.

"Make ready to stand before the king, Sir Balin."

Balin rose, looked about his squalid home of the past year. He left without remorse. He did worry briefly that Brych would return seeking food and water again and be left wanting. But his sentence ended, they both must find their own way now, he reasoned.

He was in an awful state. Unwashed, his hair long and knotted, his beard overgrown.

"May I bathe?" he asked.

"I'm sorry, Sir Balin," said Dagonet. "You must appear as you are. If Arthur decides to return you here, there's little point in making a fuss, is there?"

His heart dropped at the thought of returning to prison. He prayed Arthur's heart was not so hard. If it were, he thought perhaps it was better to request death than be caged again.

"I feared I'd been forgotten again."

"I never forgot you," said Dagonet, leading him up the stairs to the courtyard.

"You never visited," he murmured.

"I was questing. Sir Helior of the Thorn stole my wife from the box at the tournament of the Wandering Companions and rode off with her to Cornwall."

Balin caught his breath. He hadn't even known Dagonet *had* a wife.

"I didn't know. Was your quest…successful?"

"In a manner of speaking," said Dagonet, cryptically. "They were both of them slain; one when I drew my sword, the other when I kept it in its scabbard."

CHAPTER
THIRTEEN

THE GILDED, HIGH ceilinged throne room was festooned with blood red banners bearing descending white doves. Blazing arrangements of red roses and ramblers sprawled on every step of the dais leading to Arthur's high backed throne, atop which a rampant golden dragon perched like the soul of Uther, his father. Eleven tall red tapers adorned the chamber to commemorate the descent of the holy spirit upon the eleven disciples.

The crowded room milled with knights and their ladies, bedecked in their finest. Some, like Dagonet, wore richly colored clothes, but most of the men bore their arms and armor, polished to such a high sheen by diligent squires that the light of the tapers danced in them as though in a thousand mirrors. The knights of Arthur's hall appeared as archangels assembled for battle.

The attendant ladies shone beside them, flitting in rustling gowns of colored silk and velvet, trimmed with gold and silver. Their flowing hair encircled in glittering nets of gold thread, or their stately heads capped with bejeweled circlets.

But none, in all their rich adornments, could match the majesty of Arthur crowned and enthroned. He had begun a wispy growth of beard, but unlike the face of many an aspiring adult desperate for some outer sign of the manhood hidden within the boy, this was no source of mocking amusement. The king's bearing was ever dignified and inspiring. His blue eyes looked fondly on his subjects, smiling with pleasure even as his countenance remained ceremonious. Of the nobles and advisors gathered, any half dozen was finer garbed than Arthur's subdued red tunic and cloak, but none outshone him.

And there at his side in its golden woven, jeweled sheath, was Excalibur itself. Balin knew it from the dreams his mother's tales had woven into his sleeping mind. It outshone even the gilded sword of Macsen, which he had dared to touch. He knew his bravery would falter to lay a finger on that blade. That was Pendragon's alone.

The outer hall was crowded with petitioners from across Albion, come to make request of the High King. Dagonet led Balin past these to the back of the throne room. The knights were filing toward the throne one at a time, and Balin saw each man kneel at the foot of the dais and offer his sword, renewing his vows.

He balked and turned away, but Dagonet took him by the arm.

"What's wrong?"

"I am not fit for this honor," Balin whispered. "Look at the state of me."

"As the least in rank, I am the last to swear," Dagonet said. "If you follow me, there will be no offense. You will be taken as the first of the petitions, but offer your vow. Either Arthur will hear it, or he will return you to the dungeon."

Balin shook his head.

Dagonet gripped his shoulder. "Courage, man."

"I don't even have my sword."

"Here," Dagonet said, drawing his own and pushing it into Balin's hands. "Take mine."

Balin bit his lip and slowly advanced to the throne with Dagonet as each of the knights swore their oath and adjourned to either side of the hall with their ladies. Balin, envied them their dignity. He saw Sir Bedivere, grim as a statue, standing alone, perhaps as uncomfortable in the midst of all this pomp and ceremony as he was. He saw Sir Ector and Sir Kay, closest to Arthur, and Sir Lucan, in velvet robes of state. None of them looked on him, their one-time companion. His eyes lingered on a beautiful girl in a green and gold dress, a thin, willowy damsel with skin like crushed strawberries in a pail of milk and hair like curling corn silk. She met his gaze and whispered something to the knight at her side. Chagrined, Balin saw it was Lanceor, and he caught his mocking grin before he looked away. He squeezed the hilt of Dagonet's sword in his sweating fists.

He strained to hear the knights' oaths. Though the tenets were the same, in the end, each man swore by God or by Avalon, or by whichever pagan deity seemed to strike his fancy. Of these latter, he knew their promises were not binding, and even if he did not hear their names, he marked well their faces and blazons.

The time came for Dagonet to take his knee, and Balin was left alone, feeling naked. He kept his head bowed as Dagonet sauntered up to the throne and did a short turn, smiling broadly, to the appreciative chuckles of the men and women of the court.

"How now," said Arthur. "Which knight has come last? Is it my worst, or my greatest?"

"That remains to be seen, sire," Dagonet called back. "What quality of a knight do you treasure most? If it be truth, then your highness, I am your greatest man. If it be strength at arms..." he scratched his head, rolling his eyes comically. "Well..."

The hall rippled with laughter.

"So I see." Arthur smiled, leaning forward. "Have you come to swear your fealty upon an empty scabbard?"

Dagonet stiffened and grabbed the scabbard hanging from his belt.

He shook it, squeezed it in increments, and held it open with his two fingers, peering into it, then turned in circles looking left and right in an exaggerated pantomime that made the room resound with laughter.

Then, he opened his eyes and mouth wide and held up one finger as though he'd remembered, and turned to Balin, snatching the sword from his hands in mock anger and shaking his fist. If any had wondered at the dirty, wild figure accompanying Dagonet before, they now dismissed him as some beggar Dagonet had taken along as a component of his joking.

Dagonet turned back to Arthur, twirled the sword in his hand, and dropped it with a resounding crash on the marble. "Sorry, sorry!" he said, addressing the smiling men and women in turn. He snatched up the sword, then went to his knee and bowed his head.

Even the King laughed. Balin did not. It was shameful to profane such a solemn ceremony with base humor.

When the crowd's hilarity showed no signs of dying down, Dagonet raised his head and glared at them. He raised his hand for silence, and the laughter gradually ceased. Then, he lowered his head once more.

"Are you…?" Arthur began.

Dagonet cut him off with a prolonged crack of flatulent wind that sounded like a ship's canvas sail tearing slowly down the middle. He leaned sideways as it went on.

The windows of the hall rattled with the boom of laughter, and several of the gathered knights doubled over. Even the prim ladies could not hide their unrestrained braying behind their hands. The line of petitioners waiting in the doorway guffawed also…all but two, who remained conspicuously prim.

Balin's face reddened.

King Arthur held his face in his hands in an attempt to maintain dignity, then finally regained his composure and raised his hands for silence.

"Now then, Sir Dagonet, are you quite ready?"

"I am, my lord," Dagonet said, head still bowed, as if nothing had happened, and he raised the hilt of his sword and swore, "I, Sir Dagonet of Caerleon, swear never to do murder, and always to flee…" he pretended to remember, the effect eliciting more laughter, "…treason and falsehood, by no means to be cruel, but to give mercy unto him that asketh mercy, and always to do ladies, damsels, and gentlewomen… succor. This I do swear by the living God, upon pain of forfeiture of my worship and lordship of the High King Arthur for evermore. *Et cetera, et alii, et alibi.*"

King Arthur sighed almost in relief that the lengthy oath was concluded.

"Rise, Sir Dagonet of Caerleon," he intoned. "And now…"

Dagonet held up his hand. "A moment, King Arthur," Dagonet said. "I have a gift for you on this holy occasion."

"A gift?" Arthur smirked, putting his chin on his fist. "That is not our custom."

"Then may I institute the custom?" Dagonet announced.

"Very well. What is your gift?"

"I bring you a treasure I discovered buried beneath Castle Bedegraine."

"Such a treasure would rightfully belong to Leodegrance, as Bedegraine is within his lands."

"Ah, but this treasure you placed in Bedegraine yourself for safekeeping."

Arthur looked confused.

Balin wished the floor would crack open beneath his feet. It seemed as though he was to be the butt of one of Dagonet's jokes, nothing more. Yet he stood. What else could he do? He had faced death, a tide of bloodied steel, leveled lances and hurtling armored horses. That had been easier. He felt like a sinner naked at the foot of the cross.

"If this is a riddle you have me puzzled, Sir Dagonet. Speak plain."

"I will let the treasure speak for itself," said Dagonet. He turned to Balin and gestured for him to step forward.

It was as though Balin's feet were nailed to the floor, it took such an effort to approach those steps. Yet to find his voice, that was too much. He could not even look at Arthur.

"Sir Dagonet, who is this man?"

That cut him deeper than any reproach. He raised his eyes to Arthur.

"It is I, my lord. Balin of Northumberland."

Arthur blinked, as if the name meant nothing to him, but as realization dawned across his face, he rose from his seat and towered over him.

"Sir Balin," Arthur said, murmuring his name as if it were not a fit word to be spoken aloud in the court.

There was muttering among the gathered. Many had no idea who he was, and those who did, swiftly spread the account of his offense.

"I pride myself on the sense of humor my fool has engendered in me," said Arthur grimly, looking to Dagonet now. "But I must admit this jest has missed its mark."

"As well it should. It is no jest, your highness," said Dagonet. "You asked if the worst or greatest of your knights had come last. Here he stands. At force of arms, at your side at the battle of Bedegraine, he was the greatest. No knight here who values truth as a true knight should, can say otherwise."

There were heated whispers again at that, and Balin glanced at the angry faces who didn't know him. Lanceor's scowled.

Looking for any sympathetic face, Balin at last met the eyes of Sir Bedivere, whom he had bled at Aneblayse. Bedivere nodded to him in acknowledgement.

It was enough. Tears brimmed hotly in his eyes.

"And as to truth, he came to you red-handed with his offense, when there was no one to keep him from fleeing unseen into the woods he knows so well," said Dagonet. "No sire, the jest is your own. You have kept your greatest knight in a dungeon for a joke." He laughed, but no one laughed with him. "But a good fool knows when his jest has run its course."

Arthur glared at Dagonet, and Balin was aghast at the implication, but the king's face softened and he smiled.

"Do you call your king a fool, Sir Dagonet?"

"A good fool calls out the folly in every man, sire. The High King should expect nothing less from his own fool," said Dagonet, bowing low.

"Well said."

Arthur looked on Balin again.

Balin wiped his eyes with his filthy sleeves. "Sire, may I speak?"

"You may."

"In a moment of anger, I offended your Highness, who is more dear to me than my life. If I cannot serve you now as a knight, only grant me whatever duty is fit me. I beg you not to cast aside my loyalty entirely."

Arthur's eyes shined. Whether he had been moved by Balin's entreaty or by the memory of his murdered cousin, Balin didn't know. He only knew that Arthur's next words would save him or damn him.

"Take Sir Dagonet's sword and make your oath, Sir Balin."

His heart swelled to bursting as Dagonet stepped toward him, and the tears coursed down his cheeks, but Balin hesitated.

It didn't seem correct to him to swear fealty on another knight's sword, yet he didn't know where his had gotten to. Perhaps this was a sign that his penance was not yet finished. The face of Culwych dead on his spear flashed in his mind, and he held up his hand. "No, sire. I will swear on my own sword or not at all."

"Don't begrudge a fool's sword, Sir Balin," Dagonet whispered.

He fell to both knees, like a supplicant, and touched his head to the floor. "Nor will I spend any more of your precious time while I find where mine has been laid. I ask again, grant me some lesser duty. Let me earn the right to swear by a sword to you."

Arthur looked deep in thought as he sat back down. "Very well, Sir Balin. This day, as penance, serve the knights of my hall. Give them food and drink and whatever they ask. In that way, you serve me."

It was a humble task, humiliating even, but Balin welcomed it.

"Thank you, sire," he murmured into the cool floor.

Sir Dagonet helped him to his feet and led him aside.

"I owe you thanks, too, sir," said Balin, grasping his hand. "I mistook you greatly. I do not know how I can ever repay your kindness."

"No, Sir Balin, you have seen me for what I am from the start," he said, smiling thinly. "Now be off to the kitchen and bring me a goblet of wine, and we shall be settled."

CHAPTER
FOURTEEN

S
IR LUCAN DIRECTED Balin to the chief steward, a balding old man named Granger, who led him on a whirlwind tour of the bustling great kitchen. This cacophonous chamber of clinking crocks and hissing gravies went unheard in the serene chamber of the throne. Its sweaty denizens were as unaware of the weighty pronouncements outside as the king himself was of its many petty dramas, its spills and burns and undercookings, all of which secured the red-faced, trembling wrath of the screaming head chef, a man so gaunt that it seemed impossible to Balin that he had any practical experience with food himself. The place was a maelstrom, as loud and confusing as any battle, and Balin felt anxious passing through the bustling servants. They moved with such alacrity through such chaos that he worried he had volunteered himself for a duty which he lacked the coordination to perform.

Granger took Balin to a station where a harried looking dwarf called Barnock thrust a platter of wine goblets at him, not even looking up at him.

"Take these to Sir Lanceor and Princess Colombe, then come back for more."

He waddled off to a barrel tap to fill more empty cups.

Balin rankled at this first duty, serving a cad like Lanceor, but said nothing. It was a fitting penance. He carried the tray carefully through the kitchen back into the throne room, excusing himself to the milling people and guarding his charge from a spilling.

The petitions had begun. An elder knight with a rich marten fur cloak draped over his dented, spiked armor stood before the king. He had a cruel, hard countenance, and the brushy white eyebrow over his right eye was cleft by a scar that ran like a river from his snowy scalp. His close-trimmed white beard was partially obscured by the sweep of his bevor. Mud covered his greaves and spurs, as though he had just ridden here.

"King Arthur, I am a messenger from the court of King Rience of Snowdonia and Norgales," he rumbled.

Balin stopped still and looked. Rience. The strongest of the rebel kings.

Arthur knew him, too, and straightened in his high seat.

"King Rience. We've not heard from him in two years. What message do you bring?"

"Only this," said the ambassador with an orgulous air, putting one muddy foot on the bottom step of the dais with a heavy clank. "My Master attests that of King Arthur's enemies, Aguysans, including the captain of his Hundred Knights, Sir Morganore, are no more, and that King Cradelment of North Wales and Idres of Cornwall also have fallen to his sword."

That was good news. Was it possible Rience had at last recognized the authority of the High King, and had sent this knight to tell of his accomplishments, to treat for reconcilement?

"Brandegoris of Stranggore," the knight went on, "Clarivaunce of Northumberland, Nentres, Carados, Pinel, Eustace of Cambenet, and Lot of Orkney have all yielded their crowns and their beards."

So Clarivaunce had surrendered Northumberland to Rience. He wondered how many knights he had known had perished, or if Clarivaunce had even put up a fight.

"Their beards?" Arthur repeated.

"Aye," said the knight, without a hint of deference. "It is King Rience's pleasure to trim his mantle with the beards of his defeated foes."

Three knights rose at the mention of Lot. Balin had seen one of them give his oath earlier to Avalon and knew him to be Gawaine, the eldest of the king of Orkney's sons, a black-eyed brute whose flesh was marred by the blue woads of the pagans. The other two then were his younger brothers, Agravaine and Gaheris.

The old knight went on, unconcerned. "As to your servant kings, Pellinore and Pellam are little more than soft-bellied monks, and Uriens and Leodegrance are bare-faced weaklings. Your own beard is but half grown but will likely complete the trim when my lord comes marching across your kingdom to collect it."

Many stepped forward with strangled oaths at the affront to Arthur. Even the hall guards leveled their halberds and glowered.

Rience's knight appeared unconcerned, however, and kept his eyes affixed to the king's.

"King Rience sends word that if one of your servants will provide a mirror and razor, you might avoid the fire to come by sending your whiskers home with me."

Balin nearly flung his tray at the head of the old knight and charged him. He looked to Arthur and was grieved to see the young king's fingers clench at the arms of his throne. His right hand crept toward the pommel of Excalibur, and Balin inwardly urged him to answer the insult with that sharpest of blades.

Gawaine could not be silent. "Sire, let me send this old villain's head back to Rience in answer!"

Arthur's hands relaxed, and he sat back. "No, Sir Gawaine. Be still." To the knight, he said, "It is well for you that you come speaking another man's words."

The old knight gave no reply.

"You have delivered your message," Arthur continued evenly. "Now you will take back my reply. If ever King Rience comes into this hall, it shall be on his knees, else his own beard and the head it dangles from shall be forfeit."

The knight raised his eyebrows.

"If you hold that sword as well as you hold your temper," he said, "perhaps there will be a contest after all."

He turned to leave.

"What is your name, sir knight?" Arthur called after him.

"Segurant The Brown," said the knight, pausing to look back.

"The Knight of the Dragon!" someone exclaimed.

The dragonslayer. Greatest of Uther's Table. Had he been a squire again, seeing Segurant The Brown in the flesh would have sent Balin's mind wheeling. The scar over his eye must be his mark of courage. In the barbaric days of Uther, the king had permitted no knight to sit at his table who did not bear some mark or battle wound on his face. But why did this renowned champion who had served Arthur's own father treat him with such disrespect?

"You served my father," Arthur echoed.

"I served the High King Uther Pendragon," Segurant affirmed.

"Why do you dishonor his memory by fighting for a barbarian like Rience?" Arthur asked.

"Mark you, King Arthur," said Segurant. "Uther served the Lady of The Lake, and we rode beneath his dragon banner, not the cross. No true son of his would kneel before the crucified god."

"I am of a mind that every god is God," Arthur answered.

"That is why you will remain forever beardless," Segurant said and walked out of the hall.

The guards crossed their polearms to prevent his exit and he stopped. Arthur shook his head. "Let him go."

They put up their halberds and Segurant departed. The court listened to the rattle and clank of his harness and sword until it diminished.

CHAPTER
FIFTEEN

A HAND GRIPPED BALIN'S elbow and he turned to see the scowling, clean shaven face of Sir Lanceor inches from his nose.

"*Well?*" He hissed. "Do you begin your penance by leaving a prince and his lady thirsting, you ungracious ragamuffin?"

Balin blinked and looking past Lanceor saw Princess Colombe waiting. She averted her eyes, and her cheeks colored, but he could not tell if she was embarrassed by his staring or by her lover's boorish behavior.

Balin could find no words. He was still too furious at the insult to Arthur and yet confused by his admiration for Segurant's reputation to formulate any sincere apology. He feared if he spoke he might say something untoward. He carried the tray over and mutely offered it first to Princess Colombe, who curtsied as she took it, and next to Lanceor, who glared at him over the rim of the cup as he promptly tipped it back.

Balin turned to return to the kitchens, and Lanceor slapped his shoulder with the back of his hand. He had drained his cup in a single swallow and held it out now to Balin.

Balin set the tray under it. Lanceor released it with a clank.

"Bring more. And don't dally," Lanceor snapped with a sloppy grin.

This had not been his first cup.

"My prince, do you still thirst truly?" Colombe said lowly.

Lanceor wheeled on her, and Balin saw with narrowed eyes that she shrank from him, but Lanceor said, "I thirst always, my pretty, and when I am done with wine I shall thirst for something sweeter." He brushed her soft white cheek with his knuckles and when the corners of her lips turned upward slightly, Balin had his fill and went back to the kitchens.

Barnock was waiting with a line of cups and trays.

"What took you so long?" The little man barked. "This for Sir Dinadan and his lady. This for Sir Griflet, and this for Sir Bedivere. And this…"

"Sir Lanceor asks for another cup," Balin said, setting down Lanceor's tray and lifting up two others.

"That comes as no surprise," quipped the dwarf, waddling off to refill the empty goblet.

Balin went to the hall and served Sir Dinadan and his lady, then made his way across the hall to Sir Bedivere and Griflet. It was strange to see the mud-caked boy he had last seen polishing Bedivere's helm wearing a skin of steel himself now. Bedivere's missing hand had been replaced by a wrought one of iron.

Griflet took no notice of Balin as he took his cup, but Bedivere paused.

"It is good to see you again, Balin," the one-handed knight said.

Griflet blinked, realizing who Balin was, and lowered his cup.

"And you, Bedivere," Balin murmured.

"Do not lower your glass, Griflet," Bedivere said, lifting his own. "Pray raise it instead, to the man who shed blood beside me at Aneblayse."

Balin shook his head, embarrassed. It warmed him to know Bedivere had not forgotten him after all.

"No, no, no, sirs."

But Bedivere would not be dissuaded. "To one who was dead and has returned."

Bedivere looked expectantly at Griflet, but the younger man's gaze was at the edge of the hall and thousands of miles away. Bedivere looked, and so Balin turned and looked too.

The woman making her way down the scarlet carpet was lovely.

She wore a red robe trimmed in lustrous ermine, and a silver circlet about her black hair, which was bound and plaited with silver chord. Her skin was alabaster white, and the eyes that shone in her face bright as clean steel.

All eyes in the court watched her advance on the throne, as the previous petitioner bowed and took his leave.

NIMUE'S BROKEN HEART fluttered in the vicinity of her hated enemy, like the illusory contraction of a limb lost and forgotten.

King Arthur was young. Barely more than a boy. Too young and unassuming to have wiled Culwych from her side. Yet here stood this palatial hall, so bright and open compared to Rience's dreary fire-lit keep. The sun shone through the windows and illuminated the fine ladies and their bright knights, the flowing gowns and brimming silver cups. And this boy-king sat, the lord of it all, as though he were its keystone, as if it were all there solely because of him, and would crumble with his removal.

There at his side was Excalibur in its magic sheath. The Lady Lile had given it to him, the ultimate endorsement of Avalon. Could the weapon she carried match it? Pilfered from Avalon's armory with the aid of the Gwenn Mantle, it was a dark sister sword of Excalibur, forged by the god-smith Gofannon under the direction of the Lady Sebile during Alexander the Great's time, to bring about his fall.

She said nothing to the page's enquiry as to her business.

Her only answer was to unfasten her cloak and let it fall to the floor, revealing the ancient blade girded about her slim waist, just as she had to Rience and his daughter. She heard the gasps and exclamations of the men and women all about her, but her eyes remained on Arthur.

He leaned forward, screwing up his face.

"What does this mean? A lady with a blade?"

"It is unseemly!" some overwrought woman in the court exclaimed.

"It is indeed," Nimue said. "More so because it is my curse, your Majesty."

It was true. Part of the sword's curse was that if it were girded by one not worthy to wield it, it would not come unfastened. She had known this when she'd buckled it on after having spirited it from the Isle. For weeks, it had been a true burden to her. But she felt sure in this hall of great knights, it would be the least of her burdens to be lifted.

Especially the weighty thirst for atonement that weighed on her so heavily in the presence of this boy-king.

"Explain what you mean. What's this curse you speak of?" Arthur demanded.

"This sword may not be drawn, nor removed by me. Only a knight brave and loyal and pure of deed with truth can draw it from the scabbard. I've come from the west and visited the court of many a king. Lately, I have come from the court of the King of Snowdonia, where I was told there were to be many knights good and bold. As you see, I am yet burdened. Not even Rience could remove it."

Arthur's lips parted, his eyes shining so that she could almost see the glittering sword reflected in them.

"This is passing strange," he said at last, then struck the arm of his throne a blow. "Who among you will try?"

Arthur looked around the hall. Many of the knights looked from the woman to him and then at the floor or in the bottom of their cups.

"Well?" Arthur repeated.

A colorfully dressed knight with a head of curly hair cleared his throat. "Milord..." he said.

"Dagonet? Will you be the first this time?"

"No, milord," said Dagonet, holding up his hands. "You were right to say this affair is passing strange. By her own admission, the lady claims to have come from the court of your enemy, and with a cursed sword. I should recommend..."

Arthur fidgeted, then waved him off and stood.

"Come come. Recommend? You're not my counselor, Dagonet."

"I am, my brother," said another well-dressed knight with close cropped yellow hair and beard. "And I agree with Sir Dagonet. Who is this lady? Where does she come from truly? Who hung this sword from her?"

Nimue bowed her head to hide any expression of frustration.

"Perhaps you're right, Kay," said Arthur. "Will you tell of how you came to bear this sword, milady?"

"My lords, I know not. I am a maid of the Long Isles. My father gave me over to a nunnery, and it was there on my first night that I awoke to find this strange weapon about me as though by miracle. The old priest told me he had dreamed that the greatest knight in Christendom would be the one to draw it forth."

Arthur descended the steps as she spoke, and she had to catch her breath when she straightened and saw him standing before her. So close. He was so close. Why this elaborate plot? Why could she not now drive her thumbs into this boy-beast's eyes, who had taken her life and love from her?

He leaned forward and inspected the round, jeweled pommel.

"Do you know what it says here?" he asked.

"I cannot read the letters, milord," Nimue lied.

Arthur stooped and touched the pommel, tracing the golden inscription she knew so well with his fingers.

He read aloud, *"None shall take me hence but he at whose side I am to hang. And he shall be the best knight in the world."*

She looked down at the top of his kingly head. If she could but draw a hair pin from her plaits and drive it into the base of his thin neck! She could have done with curses and magic and heartbreak. But no! He deserved more than a quick, clean death. She was here to grind the pieces of her heart into a meal to salt the fields of Arthur's kingdom with sorrow and betrayal, in her Culwych's name.

He straightened. "Lady, will you let me try?" Arthur asked.

It was a disarmingly boyish thing to say. Or would have been, if she did not wish his death with all her soul. "Please, your Majesty."

She had heard Rience's insult to him. Now the sword was doing its work—calling to the pride all slighted boys had. If he could but draw the sword where Rience had failed, he could prove himself the greater man, the greater king.

Her heart seized up the instant he closed his hand around the hilt.

What if he *did* free it? What if he was everything Lady Lile and Merlin believed him to be? This true knight of knights, who was the only ruler intended for Albion?

But he struggled, and righteous hatred replaced her trepidation. He grasped the woven scabbard and tried to pull it, too, but it would not come.

"You need not strive so, dread king," Nimue said, fighting to keep the air of triumph from her voice. "The knight who is destined to draw it will do so without effort."

Arthur relinquished his hold on the sword and straightened. She expected to see a mask of frustration, but he just smiled.

"I know something of what you speak," he said, and turned to ascend his throne again, calling as he went. "Come now, my men! Which of you will succeed where your king has not? Remember your oaths and fear no ill magic. Here is a maiden in distress and perhaps a test from

God above. Shall Arthur's knights leave her dragging this sword down the lane? Step forth and try."

Nimue smiled thinly and turned her sad eyes on the court. The knights began to set aside their drinks and shuffle forward.

Which of them would be the edge that cut Arthur down?

BALIN STOOD STRICKEN, holding his breath as each successive knight approached the lady with the sword. He hated the secret joy he felt as each one, having tried and failed to free the miraculous weapon, returned to his place.

He rested his bunched fist on his chest and prayed silently for his prideful thoughts to die.

As each failed, Arthur called forth a new contestant. Balin watched them all, and put faces to names.

Maleagrant, Tor, Aglovale, Colgrevance, Owain, Agravaine, Gaheris. None of them could budge the sword.

When Lanceor made his try, he jerked and wrestled the blade, jostling the maiden almost to the point of putting his boot up on her hip for leverage.

Sir Kay stepped forward laughing.

"God's blood, Hibernian! Would you tear the poor lady in two?"

He took hold of the back of Lanceor's coat and pulled him lightly aside.

"Leave off and let men try."

Lanceor stared daggers at Kay, but the king's foster brother paid him no more heed and turned to the business of freeing the sword.

Sir Kay, too, turned away, shrugged, and offered his place to Gawaine.

Lanceor backed away, still glaring at Kay the Seneschal, and bumped into Balin. Seeing it was Balin, a knight far below his station, he spluttered, "Be off, you lout!"

Colombe took him lightly by the elbow and drew Lanceor aside, cooing in his ear.

In truth, Balin barely paid him any heed. He looked over the Hibernian prince's shoulder until he was pulled away, and watched, heart pounding under his fist, as Gawaine, Griflet, Bedivere, even Lucan and Dagonet tried their hand in quick succession.

Dagonet excused himself from the lady with a bow, a shrug, and a roll of the eyes. Though this raised a laugh from the court, it made Balin ease. No pagan had claimed the sword. No butler, no fool.

There was only one knight left in the hall who had not filed past the maiden now.

Arthur had stood atop his dais throughout the strange contest, so as to better view his hall and call on each of the knights by name. Now, obviously disappointed, he sank into his seat.

"I am heartily sorry, milady," he said. "It appears that your liberation is not in my power to grant."

The woman looked equally disappointed. Desperately so. She turned, looking frantically among the faces.

"Has every knight stepped forward?" she called plaintively.

Her bright eyes passed over his fellows and came at last to Balin. He could not deny them, even though his face flushed red to answer.

"Not every knight, milady," he found himself saying.

A murmuring rippled through the crowd, and Balin detected Lanceor's harsh but unintelligible whisper foremost among the questioning voices.

He left the crowd and came to slowly stand before the maiden, anyway.

He had remained silent, even as something in his soul had screamed in his ear, some hateful, misplaced pride that told him the sword was his; that this woman had come for him and him alone. How could that be? How could he, in the midst of humble penance, even think to claim such a reward as that intended for the greatest knight of all? And yet a small voice deep within him answered, how could it not be? Was he not truly the better in arms of every knight here standing? Was he not a man of great faith? His father's son? Why not think then, that God would deign to reward his humility now at his lowest hour? In truth, wasn't imprisonment penance enough for his crime?

"What is this?" the maiden smirked. "I've seen many a knight this day, in fine clothes and armor, bearing sword and cup and fine lady in hand. But this man comes in rags with a serving tray. Surely he is no knight."

"He is, madam," King Arthur answered for Balin, as he lowered his head in shame.

"Milady," Balin said, so quietly that all had to strain to hear, "I am grievously aware that I do not fit the ideal of a knight, but those virtues you spoke of…truth and loyalty and bravery, they are not woven into the fabric of a garment, but into the heart of a man."

He looked into her eyes then.

"Will you permit me?"

The lady stared and nodded slowly.

"You are well spoken, sir. Please."

There was real entreaty in the last.

He closed his eyes and said a silent prayer. On the surface, it was a simple prayer to free the maiden of her burden. Beneath that, it was a prayer to claim the sword and serve God's king. He set his mind to these pure aspirations and hoped to bury the base ambition that roiled like a serpent beneath. He hoped that if he filled his mind with just prayers, he might stifle the nagging demon that sought to claim, not the sword, but what it represented—greatness. Inarguable, undeniable greatness, such as he had always strived for. More than the greatness of his father, a true, everlasting, all-surpassing glory. Above Sir Ballantyne. Above Sir Segurant. Above even…no, even in his secret mind he forced that thought down. How could he hope to claim the prize with such a despicable, arrogant notion in his heart?

No mere knight could compare himself to God's chosen king.

He cursed his own black heart for bringing forth such a contemptible notion. His hubris had surely sealed his fate, and it could not now be bound to that which he so sorely wanted.

But when he opened his eyes, the sword was in his hand, and a sliver of the bright blade shone between hilt and scabbard. He knew he could draw it easily, and thrilled, catching his own breath.

The maiden laid her soft, cool hand over his and stopped him. She drew close, as intimate as a lover. She whispered close, and her sweet breath was hot and reddened the very porch of his ear.

"God save you, Sir…?"

"Balin," he whispered.

"Sir Balin. You hold in your hand the sword of destiny. The Adventurous Sword. It is yours to claim. Draw it. But then, I pray you, return it to me."

Balin stiffened.

"Return it?"

"Or keep it. But if you keep it, know this. For every glory you gain you will pay a price, just as for every crest there must be a trough. For every triumph, equal failure. Return it to me and avoid its many fortunes and its misfortunes. Live your life as you will, a good knight. Strive. Die. And never know to what heights you might have ascended. Keep it and you shall be the greatest knight in Albion. But in the end, you will fight to the death with the man you hold most dear."

Balin blinked. He stared down at the sword, quarter drawn at her waist, at the gilded, red-jeweled hilt and the golden cording which encircled the handle in his palm, but more so at the hint of the flawless blade tragically obscured by the sheath. There were etchings there on the mirror surface, and he drew it half an inch further, offering a more tantalizing glimpse at the wondrous craftsmanship. There was a fanciful image etched into the steel, of what appeared to be the dainty feet of a maiden in an embroidered gown. There was yet more to the design. It seemed to continue on down the length of the blade, and he sought to peek further, but the lady's hand arrested him, surprisingly strong.

"Make your choice!" She hissed.

"The sword...is cursed?" Balin whispered. "It is not...of the Lord?"

"Was Christ cursed to die on his cross? Or did he perish to attain a greater triumph?"

This reminded Balin of something Brother Gallet had told him once. Brother Gallet had said that the greatest of Satan's temptations did not end in the wilderness but remained with Christ all his days. Jesus Christ could have refused his cross at any time and lived and died the life of an ordinary mortal man. Even in the garden of Gethsemane, mere hours before his doom, he had wrestled with this. But in the end, he had chosen the cross.

The sword called to him, very like a cross itself.

"Choose," the woman urged.

Balin nodded.

"Choose it knowingly. Say it," she said, breathless.

"By my body, I will keep this sword. Nothing will part me from it."

She withdrew from him and smiled strangely.

"Then be you bound of your own will."

She released his hand.

He slid the sword reverently from its sheath, the sunlight gleaming off the perfect blade, more beautiful even than he had imagined it. Though the sheath was woven, it rang out in steel song as it cleared, and the gasps uttered by the court were like an answering chorus.

The belt about the lady's waist unfastened of its own accord and dropped to the floor.

Balin held the sword aloft to the ceiling, letting it catch the window light.

He could not help but smile beneath his prodigious beard at this great acknowledgement from God above. His spirit rose, filling his heart to the brimming.

He lowered it slowly, admiring its every angle and facet. The blade was not without flaw, apparently. There was an obscuring scuff over the flat where the head of the maiden whose feet he had seen etched into it should have been. The subsequent effect was of a headless maiden bearing a bushel of apples. He turned it over in his hands and held it out to Arthur, genuflecting at the base of the dais.

"My lord and king," Balin said. "Here is a sword I may swear upon, if you'll have me.

CHAPTER
SIXTEEN

UNSEEN TRUMPETS SOUNDED as the gates of the castle at the center of the apple orchard of Avalon groaned open and the Lady Lile rode forth on her white mare, a wild, shining flutter of pale hair, gown, and waving horsehair.

Through the evergreen meadow she raced, the hooves of her mount kicking up white petals of fallen apple blossoms.

She bent low over the horse's neck and gripped its braided mane as it made straight for the misty bank that ringed the island.

It should have plunged straight into the half-glimpsed water, but she was the Lady of The Lake, and all waters were hers to command. The horse bounded across the unbroken, clouded mirror of the water, cutting only the swirling mists, and crossed to the distant shore in no time.

No map could chart the lay of Avalon. All still waters were its entryway, and so the Lady emerged from the boiling fog onto the bank of a nameless green pond south of Astolat.

She slowed her panting mount to a trot and led it through the underbrush till its hooves clattered on the beaten road that led to Camelot.

Then she dug in her heels and headed once more into the rushing wind.

———

MUCH WAS MADE of the winning of the Adventurous Sword by Sir Balin. He was cheered by those who knew him, by Bedivere and Dagonet, Lucan, Kay, and Griflet, while many of those who did not know him locked their teeth behind their smiles and envied him in their hearts, none more than Lanceor, who loudly demanded more drink and went thirsty because Balin was not there to run for it.

King Arthur heard Balin's oath renewed on the Adventurous Sword and embraced him, and Lucan had his armor and his old sword found and returned to him. Arthur bade Sir Lucan lead him to the stables to choose a horse and saddle for his own. There was talk of giving him a squire, and many of the court boys looked earnest to serve the best knight in the world, but Balin begged off. He did not wish anyone to serve him in any capacity.

While Balin was off in the stables, King Leodegrance's daughter, Guinevere, came to court with her maidens, and Arthur took her hand in his and announced to the joy (but not to the surprise) of the gathering that once the Snowdonian rebellion was put down and the Saxons dealt with, he and the Princess of Cameliard would be wedded.

In this joyous din, only Dagonet noticed that the mysterious lady who had borne Sir Balin's sword was gone, and none would hear his concerns when Barnock hobbled out of the kitchens and announced in a strident voice the commencement of dinner in the hall.

NIMUE STOLE FROM the gates of Camelot unperceived. It had been small magic, barely worthy of the term, to remove herself from the attention of the court and pass between the guards and down the outer hall.

The sun had begun its slow descent, and she found her horse where she had left it tied in the shadow of the Black Cross. She would have been long gone but for the figure that stepped from the depths of that shade and grabbed her bridle, startling her and her mount.

"*Nimue,*" intoned the wild looking face, as if her name were a particularly improper oath. "You virago! What have you done?"

She overcame her initial surprise and let her lip curl.

"Tell me what I've done, Merlin, you all-seeing owl. Yes, tell me what you see. Do you see your precious boy king with the Adventurous Sword through his heart? Slain by one of his adoring knights?"

The horse shuddered between her thighs, but Merlin laid a hand on its forehead and it whinnied and calmed.

"Who put you up to this? Rience? The Queen of Norgales?" he asked, shaking his head in disapproval.

"I am not your dear Morgan." She hissed mockingly, insulted that he should think she would allow herself to be a pawn of King Rience or of the dreadful witch queen, a pernicious sensualist opposed to Avalon and in league with dark and bloody powers. Arthur's half-sister, Morgan La Fey, a formidable sorceress in her own right, had been tempted away from Merlin's special tutelage by the Queen of Norgales. "Do you think so little of me?"

"Then why?" he asked, and in his face there was…what? Disappointment? Sorrow? The Merlin she had known could not possibly feel such things.

"Revenge," she said, savoring the word. "Revenge for my Culwych."

"Against Balin?"

"Against Arthur!"

Merlin frowned, apparently confused.

"Arthur did not slay your prince of Celyddon."

"He coaxed him to his death. Away from me, where we might have both lived. When he left me to seek his fortune with Arthur, it rent my very soul! It…" She gasped, exasperated. It was no use trying to explain love to Merlin. "You can never understand me, Merlin."

"Then truly, it's revenge against Culwych for leaving you that you seek," Merlin said.

She wanted to strike him.

"But shooting arrows at ghosts, you always miss your target. Arthur will not die by your petty magic," he said.

She opened her mouth to argue, but by his puckish grin, and by the sinking feeling in her stomach, she knew it was true. Merlin would know. By the Sight he knew everything.

But how? How could she fail?

"*Petty* magic?" she exclaimed. "That knight Sir Balin bears the Adventurous Sword! I took it from Avalon's own armory!"

"Yes, if only you were as apt an enchantress as you are a burglar you'd have done your pilfering more selectively. That sword's just an antique," said Merlin, blowing out his lips dismissively and putting his chin on his staff. "Nothing more."

Just an antique? The Adventurous Sword?

"If it was such a trifle, why was it kept at Avalon?"

Merlin walked around the horse, stroking its flank.

"Oh, the Lady Lile intended it for a champion she has been raising, a Gaulish boy given over to Avalon to be raised. Just one final gift for Arthur's court. It is no matter. Your thievery has done nothing but usurp a boy's destiny and accelerated a man's meeting with his."

The words meant nothing to her. Was this a show he was putting on for her, to blunt her ambition and disarm her while he worked some crafty magic to undo her plot?

"You're a liar," she ventured.

"Not at all. You would've done better to have turned Arthur into a toad, you silly witch," Merlin said, coming around to scratch under her horse's chin.

Just then, a galloping sounded on the road and a blast of cool air tinged with the conflicting smells of rosemary, apples, and horse sweat blew past them in a flash of spectral, snow white.

Nimue watched in shock as the Lady Lile sped past them like a phantom rider. She raised her hand, and the gates of Camelot flew open to the utter terror of the sentries, who threw down their weapons and held up their hands against her terrible light.

Nimue turned to Merlin and saw that his mouth was agape, his face an expression of naked concern, more unguarded than ever she'd seen him before.

Just an antique. But enough of a worry to bring the Lady Lile from Avalon.

"You're not as certain as you were a moment ago, Lailoken," Nimue chuckled and struck down his hand with her fist.

Her horse reared, and she turned and thundered away from Camelot, fading from sight as she went.

Likely the Lady had come all in a rage seeking her. Best to be gone. Even if Merlin were right about the sword, it wasn't the only treasure she'd lifted from Avalon.

BALIN WAS BATHED and groomed.

Though he had retained his beard and long hair, it was clean and braided now. Sir Lucan returned to him his suit of armor, which had been lovingly polished and now shone like quicksilver. He selected a fine young gray destrier from the stables named Ironprow.

Lucan returned his lance and escutcheon, and Balin asked for his old sword.

"Your sword, Sir Balin?" Lucan repeated, evidently surprised. "You mean to say you want it?"

Balin still held the Adventurous Sword in its sheath. He had not yet girded it around his waist.

"If you please," Balin said quietly.

"As you wish," Lucan sighed. He departed, leaving Balin standing outside Ironprow's stall.

Balin eased the sword from its scabbard again and looked hard at his own reflection in the clear finish. He had not seen his own face in two years. But for his beard he had changed very little. He turned the blade and watched the hidden serpent in the pattern weld slither faintly across his features. He ran his thumb along the etching of the maiden where the steel met the golden crossguard. He could not detect the mar that obscured the figure's head. The steel was smooth and regular. It was as if the unknown artisan had deliberately omitted it or left it incomplete.

He had been well caught up in the miraculous moment of claiming the sword, but now, in a soberer mind, he thought hard about what the maiden had said, that should he choose to keep the weapon, he would slay the man he loved best.

By the time Sir Lucan returned with the trusty old sword he had nicked again and again on blade and shield at Bedegraine, Balin had made up his mind.

"AH. SIR BALIN!" Arthur called, when he had spied Balin entering the dinner hall.

A great stained glass window depicting St. George lancing the throat of the snarling dragon beneath his feet cast the dining hall in magic hues of gold, red, green, and purple.

The long tables were arranged in the usual manner, four forming an open square in which musicians played and tumblers cavorted as the dogs played tug of war with scraps and the nimble serving boys dodged and crisscrossed with precariously balanced serving trays. The tables were piled high with food and lined with knights and ladies, and Balin's eyes shone when he saw that a plaque had been affixed to a chair at Arthur's table with his name on it, between Sir Kay and Sir Bedivere.

The lady Guinevere was there, too, and he thought of Sir Safir's story that the Round Table of Uther was part of her dowry. One day it would stand in this hall in place of these long tables. Would there be a place for Balin there then?

Not if he was destined to slay the man he loved best.

˙ℂOME, JOIN US!˙ Arthur called, waving him over. "Eat! Drink!"

Balin crossed the square, but stood before Arthur's table, his head bowed, both hands resting on the pommels of the swords he had strapped to either side. His own proven blade hung on the right, the Adventurous Sword on his left.

Arthur frowned and signaled the musicians to cease their playing, and the knights and ladies to quit their chatter.

"My lord," Balin said, without preamble. "I must now take my leave of you."

Arthur looked at Guinevere, at Kay, and then back at Balin, consternated.

"But why? Please, say you do not wish to depart because I have treated you unfairly."

"Look at me, my King," Balin half-chuckled. He wanted sorely to stay, to be counted. But the sword which hung at his side and the promised doom it carried, could not be denied. "This morning I awoke on a bed of straw, less than nothing. Now I am offered a place at your table. Where is this unfairness?"

"Claim your place, then. Stay at Camelot."

"I cannot, sire," Balin insisted. But he could not tell the true reason why. How could he explain that the prophesy of the sword had been made known to him, and pride had driven him to claim it anyway? It would be a treasonous admission. There had to be a way around it, and until he found it, he had to keep well away from Arthur. "I cannot help but feel that I have yet to earn the honors I have been given this day. Here," he said, striking his breast with his gauntlet and eliciting a hollow ring. "I must quest down roads I cannot tell, until I've won the right to return."

"You feel the burden of prophesy," Arthur said shrewdly.

Balin's eyes widened and he nodded.

"Yes, sire, more than I can say."

"Go then, with my blessing," Arthur said. "But return, if not sooner, than in a year's time."

Balin bowed.

"By God, I swear," Balin said.

Arthur raised his cup and stood.

"Let us all drink to Sir Balin's return!" he called.

Balin smiled as all around him, goblets rose in toast.

"May God go with you, Sir Balin," said Arthur.

All drank, and Balin's heart trembled.

The door to the hall banged open then, and Balin turned to see a towering nightmare enter, so vivid and clear that despite two swords and a harness of good steel about him he nearly collapsed blubbering like the boy he had been when last he'd beheld it.

A woman atop a white palfrey trotted insolently into the dining hall, gleaming white and cast in red by the light through the red dragon of the window, like the blinding center of the furnace fire that had awaited Shadrach, Meshach, and Abednego.

The slender rider, enfolded in white, was almost unchanged from the day Balin had watched through the smoke of his burning mother. Still regal, otherworldly, and untouchable.

The servants shrank from her, and the dogs whined and cowered beneath the tables, so that the square in the center of the room was hers, but for Balin himself, who stood awestruck and agape as she swung down from her riding horse and addressed Arthur. The candles seemed to dim, relinquishing their meager light in deference to her own ineffable glory.

"Do you know me, King Arthur Pendragon?" she demanded, in a voice like the dawn burning away the night.

Guinevere clutched Arthur's hand and the cross on the chain around her neck. All at the table averted or shaded their eyes, all but Arthur, who nevertheless gazed at her askance, as if facing the sun.

"Are you…? The Lady of The Lake?"

"I am."

Guinevere made the sign of the cross. Balin hated to see the future queen so distressed, and his initial fear gave way.

Arthur set his jaw and touched the pommel of Excalibur.

"If you are the Lady, then what is the name of this sword you gave me?"

"It is Excalibur."

"And what do the old words upon the blade read?"

"They read '*take me*,'" the Lady answered immediately. "And on the reverse, '*cast me away*.'"

Arthur swallowed and nodded.

"Then you *are* the Lady."

Balin moved toward the table and put his hand to it, leaning on it heavily. Here was the Lady Lile, who had led his mother down the Devil's path and watched her burn. The chill of his departed shock began to warm into something else, a mounting heat that gnawed at the edges of his heart.

"When you were given that sword, King Arthur, you swore an oath to grant the mistress of Avalon a boon of her choosing when she came asking."

"You speak the truth," Arthur said. "Name your price, dread lady."

The Lady Lile lifted her hand and pointed one white finger directly at Balin, without ever taking her eyes from Arthur.

"I ask for the head of this knight, who lately claimed a sword which was taken unearned from my keep, or else the head of the maiden who brought it here, if she yet remains."

The knights and ladies of the hall gasped.

Balin's hand on the table became a shaking fist.

What was this now? The Mother of All Lies come claiming what God had granted him? Not only this sword, but his soul too? What did she want with his head? Had his mother's death not been enough to slake her blood thirst? Now she had come for him? The white serpent entwined about Camelot, about Arthur. She had shown herself, brazen, sure that her influence over Arthur would serve her. So, his claiming of the sword had been some sort of blow to her plotting. Of course, she had come to claim his life. As Arthur's greatest knight, he now stood between his king and her deviltry. Perhaps he was the only hamper to her returning the Black Cross of Camelot to its original purpose.

"Lady," Arthur said, lifting his hands, placating. "There was a maiden who brought that sword to my hall, and none could free it from her but the one who bears it now. If some misdeed against you has been done, it was by her hand, not Sir Balin's."

"And yet more misdeeds will be perpetrated if he keeps it," said the Lady Lile, looking at Balin now for the first time, her eyes like polar ice melting in a sea of rage. "This knight is cursed. His every act, despite his intent, will bring evil. He will not give up the sword. He cannot. There is but one way for him to relinquish my property. I demand his death, to avert what doom may yet come."

Balin glared at her, seeing the old fires framing her, smelling again the old memory scent of his mother's roasting flesh.

"My Lady, this is my hall, and Sir Balin is my servant," said Arthur. "Please, you must ask something else. Anything else."

"I will ask nothing else," the Lady Lile snapped, staring at Arthur again now. "Will you deny my right as your benefactress? Will you break your oath?"

Balin touched the Adventurous Sword. It seemed to hum in his fist. He released his grip on the table, like a man hanging from a precipice letting go his hold. He lurched toward the Lady, unsteady. What came next seemed inevitable. He verily hurtled toward it.

Blood drizzled down his chin from where he had bitten deep into his lip, and he spluttered now, flicking her pure gown with specks of red as he came:

"To speak of evil...and falsehood! The Devil take you, Lady!"

He relished the momentary glimpse behind her supernatural mask. Those pale eyes, in the last, knew fear, as the sword rasped free of its sheath.

In the corner of his eye, he saw Arthur throw out both hands and heard an unintelligible entreaty blast like an accidental trumpet from his lips.

Then he whipped the sword across. It passed under the Lady of The Lake's chin as though through a cloud of mist.

Her head tumbled from the stump of her swan-like neck, lips parted, eyes wide, hair flying in every direction, undone of all her damnable majesty in the ultimate moment.

Blood spewed into the air and the white-gowned corpse took two uncertain steps and fell across Arthur's table, pouring blood over the plates of the king and his betrothed.

Guinevere pushed away from the table and shrieked, and the sound was indiscernible from the scream of the white palfrey, which rose on its hind legs, its flank painted in its mistresses' blood.

It spun and galloped out of the hall, shaking its white mane and kicking as if to shake the stench of fresh death from its body.

But for the weeping of the ladies, the room was deathly silent.

Knights stood over their toppled chairs, some of them with their swords drawn.

Arthur stared down at the headless corpse of the Lady of The Lake lying across his table.

Balin turned in a slow circle, looking for a sympathetic face amid the assemblage as blood dripped down the length of the Adventurous

Sword, spotting the floor.

Not Griflet. Not Bedivere. Not even Dagonet. All were grave and condemning. The Orkney knights looked like slavering attack hounds only a hair's breadth from setting upon him.

"God," Arthur whispered, clenching his eyes as if to squeeze out the sight, leaning on his fists on the bloody table and lowering his head.

Balin struggled to find the words to explain himself. How could he encapsulate all that had expressed itself in that one bloody instant? How could he explain seeing this woman, knowing her to be the cause of all his sorrows? How could he make them see a helpless boy, only capable of watching the flesh blacken and drop from his mother's bones? How could he make known the secret anger that had dwelt at the center of his being his whole life and was now departed? He felt free, for the first time.

"Gentle lords," he said. "Dear...ladies..."

Arthur was staring at his hands. The Lady's blood had flowed around them and was now drizzling off the table edge. His hands were stained with it, and he rubbed them on his robe.

Guinevere retreated from the table, whimpering, flanked by other ladies of the court. They were all of them fleeing from his presence.

The knights drew closer.

There was strident ring of steel.

Arthur had drawn forth Excalibur, and that peerless blade shone with a light that was whiter than even the Lady's had been. It was terrifying to behold in the hand of Arthur, for his serene and youthful face was now struck through with stark veins and wrathful creases, a guise of unfettered rage.

He brought the sword up and struck the table with the pommel, causing the bloodstained dishes to shatter and the fragments to jump.

"You mad, pernicious villain!" He roared, and in the next, his voice was a tortured, disbelieving wail. "The Lady Lile was our *benefactress*!

Your shame is upon this whole fellowship!"

He heaved his breath, shoulders rising and falling, teeth bared like a wolf anticipating violence.

Balin's bloody lips trembled. He had thought the silent resentment of the king a hard thing when he had laid the body of his cousin at his feet. But this was an anger unreasoning and terrible as a storm at sea. This was the wrath of King Arthur's outraged heart.

Was this the moment the maiden had warned of? So soon? Would he die fighting Arthur here in his hall? No. By God in heaven if it came to that, he swore he would not defend. Better to fall upon his own sword than that.

"Go from my sight!" Arthur screamed. "If you were not truly cursed as the Lady said, then by heaven, I lay my own curse upon you! You will never live past this day if you linger here a moment longer!"

Balin trembled at that pronouncement.

The ring of knights wavered. He fancied he could feel their displeasure like the onset of inclement weather pressing in on him. They were never closer to disobeying their monarch than now.

His mouth worked, but there was nothing he could say. How could he explain himself in the face of this ire? The Lady of The Lake had turned all his peers against him, her last blow against him. He swore it. Her last. But he knew in his heart he was vindicated. He had saved them all from her wiles.

He half stumbled backward, almost tripping over the head of the Lady lying obscured in blood and tangled hair.

Without knowing why, he stooped over and snatched the head up by the hair and went quickly from the hall, ignoring their oaths against him, his trophy dripping blood.

He passed numbly into the outer hall. The guards shifted, unsure of what to do. Their captain touched his sword, but at a look from Balin, he lifted his hand, giving him passage.

He thought he saw a familiar, wild looking figure in black for a moment, but the figure passed behind a column, and when it emerged, he saw it was just a lanky squire with a black muffler.

The boy stared with wide, fearful dark eyes at Balin and what he carried.

Balin pointed to him with his bloody sword.

"Boy! Fetch my horse!"

The boy's eyes flashed anger for a moment, but then he bowed and scurried out of the chamber without a word.

By the time Balin had reached the outer gate, he found the boy waiting, holding Ironprow by the bridle, his shield and lance hung on the saddle with a bag of provisions.

Balin took the reins and climbed into the saddle. He propped the head of the Lady Lile on his lap, then reached down and snatched up the boy's muffler, pulling it from his thin neck. There was a flash of silver. The boy wore some sort of necklace. A torc that was oddly familiar.

Balin wound the muffler around the head and tied it off into a sack.

"You must find Sir Brulen of Northumberland. He serves Orkney. Give him this," he said, holding out the head in the makeshift bag. "He will reward you well."

He expected the dark boy to run from him, but the boy reached up and accepted the head quietly.

"What shall I tell him, Sir Balin?"

He paused. What to tell him?

At their knighting, when Brulen had slain Gallet, he had not understood. His brother had seemed like a stranger. But now…

"Tell him I forgive him," said Balin.

And he eased his spurs into Ironprow's flanks and rode, wherefore, he knew not.

CHAPTER
SEVENTEEN

K ING ARTHUR SAT troubled upon his throne, and Merlin leaned
on his staff beside him, gazing down at the floor.

Merlin had urged the shaken Guinevere and her entou-
rage to ride for Carhaix so that she could be with her father. Bedivere
and Arthur's nephews from Orkney had accompanied her.

In the door to the empty throne room, Princess Colombe gripped
the arm of Sir Lanceor.

"I beg you, my love," she whispered. "Do not."

Lanceor freed his arm and strode across the room to the foot of
the dais. He was bedecked in his full armor, helmet in hand. He raised
his gauntlet impressively.

"All Camelot seethes for want of justice, sire. In another day, word
of Sir Balin's deed will have spread to Cameliard and from there across
Albion. Only say the word and let me drive this false knight down for
you."

"Do you truly seek justice or simply to drive Sir Balin down, Sir
Lanceor?" Merlin asked, not looking up from the floor. "Have I not
heard you denounce the Lady of The Lake in your cups? Why would a
devout Christian such as you be her champion now?"

Lanceor reddened.

"The murder of a lady in the king's hall should not go unpunished, Merlin," the Hibernian answered. "Pagan or Christian. Only in Sir Balin's death can there be justice. Let me be its instrument, my king," Lanceor insisted.

Arthur looked to Merlin.

"Merlin," he murmured. "What should I do?"

Merlin shook his head.

"You are king. The decision is yours."

Arthur set his hands on the throne, looked at Lanceor, and grimly nodded.

Lanceor smiled, bowed, and went purposefully to the outer hall.

"Captain Albanact! Make ready my horse and lance!" he boomed.

Arthur and Merlin watched him go, and from the side door, Colombe flitted after him, sparing them both one rueful glance before disappearing into the hall in her lover's wake.

"He's right," Arthur said, with a hint of sadness. "I do not like to set my knights upon each other, but Sir Balin's crime is unforgivable. I should never have let him leave. Merlin, I don't understand. Was the maiden false? How could Sir Balin draw the sword when no one else could? How could the magic mark him true when by his action he has proven a villain?"

Merlin sighed.

"A man may be a hero in his own tale and yet a villain in some other's," said Merlin. "A woman too. Even the Lady of The Lake was benefactress to you and bane to him. As to the sword, a sword for all its magic is but a sword, and may no more lie than a brick may weep. There is truly no better knight than Balin in this land. He shall yet achieve great things for you, but in the end, as the Lady said…failure. And death."

Arthur pressed Merlin for more, and would have spoken long into the night, but the enchanter begged off, saying he had secret business and long journeys to attend to.

Merlin retired to his chambers, where a door at the back which was locked but had no key, opened to his crystal cave. There he dwelt, fortified by weighty tomes in languages both forgotten and yet to be spoken, many written in his own hand.

Nimue, and any other who observed him, would not have known him to be in mourning. His face seemed no more troubled than usual. In repose, he seemed always troubled. He mourned the loss of the Lady in his own way, by recording it in the pages of his books, as he recorded everything. Record was precious to one without a past. He mourned the loss yet to come.

Next, he set the black muffler sack with its dreadful burden on his workbench and positioned before it the ancient Cup of Jamshid. He stirred the liquid in the cup with the point of a polished dagger and recited incantations learned by long rote. By means scyphomantic and macharomantic, he looked into the seven levels and confirmed much of what he already knew, and learned far more than he wanted. In this knowledge unfiltered came the myriad dangers of his profession, the fardels of maddening secrets and unavoidable destinies which were wont to drive him running naked at times, howling through the wild rains of secret forests, hounded by visions wondrous and horrific, until he cowered in his crystal cave, huddled like a thing unborn fearing the noise and light of life impending.

He had seen men hurtling through black space in ships of steel on plumes of fire, heard songs gentle and cacophonous from ages hence. He had seen and lived the triumphs and calamities of men and women who would not be born until long after Arthur was dust. And he had seen Albion's fall and his own demise a thousand times. It came in many ways, from many avenues, from hidden archers and rolling fires, from men's violence and from the guile of women. The ultimate destiny was inexorable, but the tributaries by which they arrived, he had found, could be altered and diverted, to take less treacherous courses.

For as long as Arthur sat brooding alone on his throne, so sat Merlin, ruminating on how to avoid the worst possible doom and how best to bring about the lesser. That was Merlin the Cambion. Not the plotter and director men thought him, merely a fretting intermediary. Like a cosmic advocate, he pleaded on behalf of men with an uncaring fate.

When Sir Kay came in the morning and led his dozing foster brother and liege at last to bed, Merlin rose from his workbench and by forms fleet and strange, bore his grisly burden to the one Sir Balin had directed him to.

He wondered if Nimue had learned what had happened.

SHE HAD.

Through the Sight, Nimue had seen the death of the Lady Lile.

Merlin had not been bluffing. He'd been right about Balin. How had she not foreseen this turn? She fell from her horse, distraught, and lay in the forest weeping for the Lady of The Lake and the damage she had unintentionally done.

Lile had been the only Lady of Avalon she had ever known. She had been kind, like a beloved aunt, during her career on the Isle.

By dawn Nimue regained her wits and settled in the hollow of a tree, drawing the Gwenn Mantle about her to hide herself from all sight.

Avalon would swiftly elect a new queen. Nineve was a contender, but Viviane was more likely. If Viviane assumed the title, the maidens of Avalon would hunt Nimue down. Of course, Merlin might catch her first. The forests were no longer safe, nor any still body of water.

She flew far north as a sparrow, from dusk till dawn, to the Christian kingdom of Lystenoyse, where she had hid from the eye of Avalon after stealing the Adventurous Sword and the Gwenn Mantle.

She remembered the dewy fields where she had slept one night and the beauteous Castle Carbonek where the Christian King Pellam, custodian of the Sangreal, ruled inside the enchanted Palace Adventurous. Then, she had been unable to pass the walls of Carbonek with the Adventurous Sword, as no weapon could cross its threshold.

Now, free of the sword, she transformed into a bird and soared over the high walls and lit on the dark window sill of one of the tower chambers. She pecked furiously at the casement until a light lit inside and a pale hand pushed it open to admit her.

"Hello," said a sleepy woman's voice. "What is it that's so important, little bird?"

Nimue hopped past her into the dim room and became herself once more.

The lady at the window, Lady Heleyne, nearly dropped her candle in surprise.

"Oh my God! Nimue!"

She was older than Nimue but quite beautiful still. Her long golden tresses hung unfettered, and her nightgown was the color of Avalon mist. The cross around her neck marked her as follower of the crucified god, but Nimue trusted her now more than any other.

"I'm sorry to visit you like this unannounced," said Nimue. "I had nowhere else to turn."

Heleyne regained her composure and closed the window, coming across the room to embrace Nimue.

"You're shaking!" she whispered. "What's happened?"

She broke the embrace and stared at Nimue.

"Have you done it?" She gasped. "Is Arthur slain?"

"No," said Nimue, parting from her and dropping herself tiredly into a chair beside the door. She was exhausted. She opened her mouth to explain and fought back a wail. She put her hands to her face and squeezed her eyes against the guilt and sorrow.

Heleyne set the candle on the dressing table. She knelt and put her hands on her knees.

"But the sword! You don't have it," Heleyne said.

Heleyne had found her in the field outside the castle and pitied her. She had attempted to bring her to Carbonek, and when the Adventurous Sword had prevented her, Nimue had explained its curse and how she could be freed of it. She had hoped Heleyne would recommend some great Christian knight loyal to Arthur, but to her surprise, the kind lady of Carbonek had had no good words for the High King, and confessed that she hated Arthur, for he had personally slain her beloved brother at Aneblayse.

This mutual hatred had forged a sisterly bond between them, and Nimue had eventually confided her entire plan, relaying the tale of how she had used the Gwenn Mantle to infiltrate and steal, all to arrange the death of Arthur by the Adventurous Sword.

"Oh, Heleyne," Nimue said tiredly, rubbing her eyes. "I've been a fool. I should have taken your advice and just used the Gwenn Mantle to kill Arthur in his sleep."

"But a knight has claimed the sword?" Heleyne pressed. "A knight who loves Arthur best?"

"Yes, one Sir Balin. But he is a simple, raging brute, and he's used to…" She shook her head. As a Christian, Heleyne wouldn't understand the devastation of Lady Lile's murder. It was pointless to explain. "This was supposed to be a simple curse. But now the knight has misused the sword and been driven out of Camelot as an outlaw. I've failed. Spectacularly."

Heleyne laid her cheek on Nimue's knees.

"I'm sorry," she said. "But…will not the curse still do its work?"

"It should, but how much damage will it cause before it does?" Nimue said. "Every day the sword gets farther away from its target."

"Well then, you must simply steer your instrument back in the right direction," Heleyne said, lifting her chin to stare up into Nimue's eyes.

Her gaze flitted to the enchanted mantle about Nimue's shoulders, and she touched the hem lightly between her thumb and fingers.

"My movements are restricted," Nimue said. "The Merlin is hunting me, and soon, all of Avalon will join him."

"You can stay here, of course," said Heleyne. "As much as you need to. The women of Avalon cannot see into Carbonek. Not even Merlin can."

"I know. But after they've searched Albion and not found me, eventually they will think to come here," Nimue said. "And I won't bring them to your doorstep, not if I can help it."

Heleyne bit her lip and rose, pacing in front of the mirror for a few moments.

"Then what you need is something to distract attention from your movements," she said at last.

"Only a rampaging dragon would keep them from me now," she chuckled.

"I can provide something like that," she said, smiling. She left the candlelight and disappeared in the dark beside her large bed.

Nimue heard liquid splashing.

"What?"

Heleyne returned with a goblet of wine and held it out to her.

"Part of the reason Avalon hunts you is the Gwenn Mantle," she said. "You told me it's one of the Thirteen Pagan Treasures of Albion, like the Sangreal of us Christians. They seek to return it to Avalon."

"Yes…" Nimue said, taking the goblet.

"Drink," Heleyne urged. "You're cold. It'll warm you."

She tipped the goblet back, tasted the sweet flavor, and felt a pervading, heady warmth flood her body. She had intended to sip it, but it was good wine, and she was tired. She drained the cup as Heleyne went on.

"Give it to a knight opposed to Arthur," Heleyne said. "Let him use it to wreak havoc in Arthur's realms. Merlin and Avalon will recognize the work of the Gwenn Mantle and turn their attention to this knight. He can lead them on a merry chase while you herd your wayward Sir Balin back to Camelot. And should that prove impossible, then you have an invisible assassin at your beck and call. You can eliminate this Sir Balin or Arthur at your leisure."

Nimue thought about it. It was an audacious notion. She thrilled at the idea of it.

She stood up and rubbed her own shoulder. The dark bedchamber was cool. She could see her breath.

"You *are* cold," said Heleyne, coming behind and encircling her with her arms, drawing her in. She spoke close in her ear. "Come to bed. You can decide on your course of action in the morning, or the next day."

Heleyne's body was warm and soft. Nimue's flesh prickled at the heat of her breath.

"Do you have a candidate in mind?" Nimue said, as Heleyne reached for the candle on the dressing stand.

"As a matter of fact, I do," she said, and took her by the hand, leading her closer to the large bed.

The candlelight shone on it, and Nimue ached to burrow beneath its heavy bear fur covers and lose herself in the soft mattress.

Lying in the bed, his head propped against the headboard, regarding them both silently, was a broad, thick browed man with a head of unkempt dark hair and a beard streaked with white.

Nimue stiffened at the sight of him.

He lounged naked, one thick, hairy leg dangling out from under the black bear fur, idly pulling at the tuft of silver and black hair curling on his chest.

He smiled and reached toward the nightstand, where a pitcher of wine sat on a tray with another goblet. He closed his brutish fist around one and brought it to his lips, watching Nimue over the rim of the cup.

"This is Sir Garlon," said Heleyne, taking the empty goblet from

Nimue's hand. She set the candle on the nightstand beside the tray and sat down on the edge of the bed. Garlon slid his muscled arm around her waist and she took up the pitcher and poured wine in the goblet. "He's the brother of King Pellam, but he's secretly a pagan like you."

Nimue arched an eyebrow at Garlon as he replaced the goblet.

"You've heard a great deal," she said, "lying there on your back in the dark."

"I like what I heard," Garlon rumbled. "Don't fret. I've no regard whatsoever for that pup in Camelot. Life's more interesting without a High King pulling everyone in line. I can be a dragon for you ladies."

He pinched Heleyne's thigh and she giggled and held the wine goblet out to Nimue, smiling.

"Is that the cloak there?" Garlon said. "The one you've got on? The one that makes you invisible?"

Nimue tightened her fists beneath it. She didn't care for how Heleyne had let her go on knowing this man was in the room. She considered flying out the window again. But the thought of going back out into the cold dark did not appeal either.

"Take it off and let me try it on," Garlon said, wiping his mouth with the back of his hand.

She regarded Garlon. He was strong as a bull ape, and there was a copious amount of deviltry in his eyes. He was a villain through and through. Not like her Lanceor, but not entirely unappealing just now either.

She took the wine from Heleyne and dumped it down her throat, the strong spirits making her spine shiver.

She reached up with one hand and undid the clasp on the Gwenn Mantle.

"Perhaps later," she said.

Heleyne smiled and blew out the candle.

CHAPTER
EIGHTEEN

I T HAD BEEN many years since Balin had slept in armor, and now when he first awoke, and saw the green canopy of the trees above him crisscrossed by beams of morning light, he thought at first he was back in the woods of Bedegraine on campaign. For a moment he panicked, fearing that the ambush had left him sleeping. He jumped awake with a clatter, but there was no column to follow, no enemy to fight. Squirrels skittered off at the rattle of his steel, and flitting things swiftly departed for more peaceful vantages.

Then he remembered how preferable awakening to that bloody battle would have been to his current situation.

Outlaw. Hated. Feared.

He knew how his poor brother Brulen felt, understood at last the blind rage which had driven him to slay Gallet in the holy chapel. The sight of the Lady had overcome him. Yet he had cut away a great evil in the land and was so content in his deed, if not in his banishment.

Banished as he was, he had not been stripped of his title. Perhaps it was an oversight on the part of Arthur, or perhaps God had barred his tongue from speaking that final excommunication that should have left Balin bereft of all hope.

But hope he still had.

He was still a knight, and by quest and deed, perhaps he could still find some way to redeem himself in Arthur's eyes, some way to avoid the presentment of treason against the king the maiden had warned him about. It was a faint hope, but it was all he had. Only a heroic accomplishment equal to the crime he had committed could ever hope to expunge his record.

But what?

He groaned as he stood. He had ridden all night until even the stars had been blotted from his view, and only then had lain down where he dismounted, not caring where he woke up.

But of course, that had been in the dark night of his soul. The daylight and the utter strangeness of his surroundings renewed his concern, and he cursed himself for having ridden so far ignorant.

He had kept upon the road at least, but what wood he had spent the night in, he didn't know.

The trees were stately and gnarled with age, clothed in raiment of emerald moss and trimmed with lace of white flowering ivy. Spangles of toadstools adorned them like jewelry. It was quite a beautiful, ancient forest, the sort he would have run through with old Killhart as a boy, imagining hummingbirds as fairies and seeing gnomes in woodchucks crashing unseen through the brush.

He came to a great pine tree which straddled a clean spring bubbling up from underground, and when he drank the cool water, he felt greatly renewed. Looking up, he laughed, for he saw a pied raven very like the one he had fed in the Camelot dungeon.

"Are you the same bird? Are you Brych?" he asked the raven, which cocked its head at the sound of his voice. "So long as I can feed you, you will not lose faith in me, is that it?"

Chuckling, he went to his pack and brought out some bread crust, which he ground between his fingers and dusted on a stone.

The mottled raven watched him. When he returned to the spring, it squawked and swooped down to the rock, danced around it a bit, and then finally began to hungrily peck at the little pile of crumbs.

Balin took out the Adventurous Sword and knelt at the bank to wash the blood from the blade. After he had cleaned it and rubbed it with oil, he saw that above the engraving of the headless maiden, there was a new image. He was positive it had not been there the day before, and he hadn't detected any buildup of grime or tarnish that could have obscured it.

It depicted a skirmish between men at arms, maybe a dozen or more, all cluttered together on horseback. All but three figures were unarmored. One was a tall, bearded figure in richly ornamented harness and fur mantle who appeared in much distress. The other two were helmeted and visored knights who seemed to be opposing the majority, riding side by side.

He rubbed the etching with his thumb. His hackles rose at the sound of ghostly singing. It was a woman's voice, melodious and sorrowful, in a tongue he did not understand. He glanced back at the raven, which was still busily consuming the bread.

Then he rose and walked, following the sound of the voice.

He followed the little trickling spring as it disappeared under a dense old march dyke of hawthorn bushes. He pushed aside the thick brush as best he could and peered through.

A figure in green was moving deliberately among the beech trees beyond, stooping to gather sprigs of fennel adjoining the bubbling water, which on the other side of the hedge had matured rapidly into a healthy stream and widened far beyond that into a substantial brook which bisected a field.

The woman sang on, oblivious to his observation. She was not so fine as the maiden who had bestowed on him the sword, nor so clean and sweet featured as the Princess Guinevere, but there was an appeal to her strong frame and the prim, unpainted face that nestled among the bush of her hair, which was the color of a sandy beach and as fine and feral as a downy blowball.

She worked tirelessly, dipping into the tall grasses and pulling handfuls of herbs and plants such as used to grow in his mother's garden behind the cottage in Northumberland.

The pastoral simplicity of her dress and features combined with the elfin quality of her strange song tugged at Balin, and he wondered who she was.

"Like what you see?" came a startling voice from behind him.

He spun and saw, sitting on the stone where the raven had been eating, Merlin the Enchanter, his staff across his knees.

"Merlin?" he stammered, raising his sword warily and looking all about, expecting Arthur's knights to come charging at him.

"I am alone," said Merlin.

Balin was aware that the woman's song had stopped behind him. No doubt Merlin's voice had frightened her away.

"What do you want, you devil?"

"Of the both of us, which has comported himself more like a devil most recently?"

Balin glared at him.

"Have you come to avenge your evil mistress on me? If so, I am not afraid of you."

"Revenge." Merlin scowled. "Revenge is a man who slakes his thirst with salt water. You have taken *your* petty revenge and where has it left you? The same place revenge has ever led. Nowhere. You cannot ease your mother's spirit with blood any more than you can put an end to the Lady of The Lake with a stroke of a sword. Aye, even that sword."

Balin swallowed, and the Adventurous Sword dipped in his hand as a cold sweat broke out on his lower back.

"You mean...she still lives?"

Had Merlin come to aid her resurrected form in punishing him?

He looked all around, suddenly seeing her specter in every hollow and behind every leaf. Perhaps he had only bereft her of flesh, and now she could assault him as some harrowing spirit.

Merlin rolled his eyes. "You're not listening, Balin."

"Well, what do you want then, confound you, you godless fiend? Speak your peace and be off or I'll have your head as well."

"That's a fine way to address one who has come to help you."

"I don't want your help!"

"You asked for it last night."

"I never said aught to you."

Merlin pursed his lips and said, in the high voice of the page in whose black muffler he had wrapped the Lady Lile's head, "*What shall I tell him, Sir Balin?*"

Balin peered at the gleaming torc around Merlin's neck. The same as the one he had uncovered under the boy's muffler when he'd drawn it from around his neck.

"*You?*"

"Me. And I have delivered your unfortunate trophy and the accompanying message to your brother, as you requested," he said, with a mocking little bow of his head.

Balin's jaw fell slack.

"You...you found him? You saw Brulen? How is he?"

"He is well. He rides to meet you."

Balin approached Merlin, uncertainty hardening his heart again.

"To meet me? No. I don't even know where I am."

"You are at the Barenton spring in the Garden of Joy," Merlin said.

Balin frowned. He had never heard of this place.

"You wouldn't know it," said Merlin. "It is a place I come to untangle my thoughts. I grew all this from a handful of seeds I was given by Queen Gloriana of the fairies. We are quite alone."

Balin looked over his shoulder involuntarily.

"The Garden of Joy looks out from every forest," Merlin explained. "Just as all still waters may lead to Avalon. By that way," he said, gesturing to a section of the hedgerow that was thin enough to pass through, "a man might emerge in the wood of Broceliande, by that way, Sherwood, or rather, Bedegraine as it is called now," he said, frowning absent mindedly. "Take an unknown path and you could wind up on the other side of the world, in a wood whose name is known only to red-skinned men."

Balin shivered.

"This place is unholy. Why have you brought me here, Merlin?"

"You promised me a reward, remember? Now I will collect it."

"What do you want? My head, like the Lady? My soul?"

"Your thick headedness would try the patience of a stone, Balin. Listen to me now. That sword you love so well is cursed, and I fear you are under its spell."

Balin gripped the sword tighter. Of course Merlin would say that. He was an emissary of the Lady of The Lake, wasn't he? Why did they want this sword so badly? Had the maiden really stolen it from Avalon? If that were true, she must have had some purpose. Maybe it had been to turn it against them. In that way, it surely served the Lord's purpose. Hadn't it already dealt Satan's host a palpable blow by cutting down his mistress?

"It has served me well thus far."

"By earning you the enmity of the king you love so dear?" Merlin said.

Balin gritted his teeth. Gallet had told him the Devil's tongue was insidious, his plots innumerable. The knights of his youth had told him Merlin was a good man, consecrated. Was this a lie? How could he tell the falsehoods of the Devil from the truth?

"Now, let me tell you," said Merlin, sighing. "There is but one way to regain Arthur's favor, Balin, and if it is done, it will serve to bring even your brother, Brulen, out from under the curse of his own nefariousness. While I traveled to find your brother, I saw the Princess Guinevere depart for Carhaix with Sir Bedivere, Sir Gawaine, and his brothers. I also espied Sir Segurant The Brown, watching them unseen. I followed the latter. He reported his findings to his master, King Rience of Snowdonia, who is encamped with sixty knights near the border. In two days hence, he will pass the Northern Crossroads at midnight on his way to seize Guinevere at Carhaix."

Balin lurched toward Merlin, his blood boiling.

"He would use the Princess against Arthur? To make him yield? Merlin, is this true?"

"I heard it all," said Merlin. "And Sir Segurant rides west to gather Rience's Saxon ally, Osla Big Knife. King Lot is also bringing his men down from Orkney. Should Arthur attack Carhaix to rescue Guinevere, he will be set upon by Rience, Lot, and the Saxons."

Balin stalked back and forth impatiently, furious.

"This is monstrous! Merlin, have you told Arthur this?"

"Arthur cannot prevent King Rience from reaching Carhaix. Camelot is two days from Carhaix by fleet horse, and King Leodegrance is too troubled by the Saxons of Colgrin and Baldulf at Daneblaise to respond in time. But you can be at the Northern Crossroads at the appointed hour if you take that road," he said, pointing to a path through the wood Balin could have sworn wasn't there before.

"Sixty knights," Balin murmured, pacing still. Once he had been eager to throw his life away against three times that number on the Bedegraine Road. But now? "Merlin, I cannot possibly defeat sixty knights alone."

He turned to Merlin, but the black robed wild man was gone, and the pied raven stood hopping in his place. It beat its wings and rose into the air, circled once, and cawed.

And in that caw, Merlin's voice came down to him. "The road to redemption is hard, Balin! Christ taught that! But unlike him, you will not be alone!"

The bird went dipping and diving through the trees.

Balin watched it go. Had Merlin taken the shape of Brych, or had the raven always been Merlin? And if so, why had Merlin visited him daily in prison? To mock him?

"Blaspheming puck!" Balin called after it, crossing himself against the enchanter's evil wizardry.

Then he rushed to his horse.

CHAPTER
NINETEEN

S IR BALIN WAITED for an hour in the empty crossroads in full armor, no sound but the night insects and the swish of Ironprow's tail. It had taken him the entire day to reach this spot at the hour Merlin appointed and like his horse, he was winded, but tense and alert.

The moon was high and full, and the stars rendered the night a moth-eaten black mantle. Every sound from the narrow forest road to the north, every rustle of night creature and bowing of insects came to him as though through a trumpet, and every light and shadow was heightened.

He reckoned it was very near to midnight when, from the western road, he heard the approach of a lone horseman and saw a knight in armor appear, silent and faceless in his closed helm, bearing a long lance.

A shudder of supernatural fear went through Balin as he considered that it was Merlin the Cambion who had advised him to this undertaking. He was expecting a force of sixty knights, and here stood one lone, ghostly cavalier. He wondered what sort of face looked out at him from the dark slit of the visor, or if indeed, the armor contained any physical form at all.

The two of them faced each other before the newcomer slowly advanced.

Balin steeled himself, and called out, "Who goes? Name yourself!"

"Sir Brulen of Northumberland," came the muffled reply.

Balin's heart rose from the icy cold depth of fear. "Show me your charge!"

"It is customary that you name yourself first, if honorable knight you be."

"I am Sir Balin, also of Northumberland."

The figure turned its horse about, peering at him, and then lowered his lance and held up his shield in the moonlight. *Per pale indented argent and gules, two boars combatant, argent and gules.*

Balin raised his shield too.

"Is it…is it really you, Balin?" the knight asked, and Balin recognized his brother's voice at last.

Brulen lifted the visor of his helmet. As always, it was as though Balin were looking into a mirror.

"By the poor soul of our mother Eglante and the bones of our father Sir Ballantyne, it is," Balin said lifting his own visor, unable to keep from grinning.

Brulen rode up alongside his brother, and the two leaned from their saddles and clasped gauntlets awkwardly.

"Beyond all reason, my brother!" Balin exclaimed in awe.

He looked over Brulen. That armor was dented and tarnished though and did not gleam in the light as his own did. The shield at his side was equally battered, the paint of the charge chipped and flaking, attesting to its use. What roads had Brulen traveled in these intervening years? "Balin!" Brulen chuckled. "I confess I didn't believe the Merlin when he said I'd find you here."

"The Merlin said you were coming, but in my anxiousness, I'd forgotten," Balin said.

"He said you would have need of me," said Brulen warily.

Then Balin heard the rumble of approaching horses, and the clatter and creak of arms and saddles.

"He was right in that," said Balin. "Look."

Down the narrow northern road rumbled a long column of men, lance points bobbing in the sky, the torches of the vanguard blazing, lighting the five who rode abreast in hellish fire, like warriors culled from Satan's host. They rode in orderly rows of five, stretching twelve deep.

"What is this?" Brulen hissed.

"King Rience and sixty knights," Balin said. He leveled his lance. "Make ready!"

"Sixty!" Brulen whispered. "Balin, are you mad? There are too many. Let's withdraw till they pass."

Balin stayed firm.

"Go if you must, brother. I stay here. Tonight, I take Rience to Arthur a prisoner or die in these crossroads."

Beside him, Brulen drew back on his reins. His horse turned uncertainly in the road, snorting.

IN A LITTLE more than a week, King Rience anticipated he would be High King of Albion, and the bare patch on his kingsbeard mantle would be filled. The Queen of Norgales' vast spy network had led him to a steady series of victories against the other rebel kings, but the final move he was proud to claim himself.

Carhaix was a rich city, but secure in the south of Cameliard with allies at its back. Rience had directed Colgrin and Baldulf to take their seven thousand men and harry Leodegrance from the north through Northumberland, which the cowed and clean shaven King Clarivaunce had graciously allowed them free passage through. The threat of the Saxons had forced Leodegrance to pull the greater portion of his men from the south to reinforce Daneblaise in the north. Carhaix was barely defended, and the southern roads were empty, allowing sixty knights riding silently with their armor carefully bundled on their pack horses an uncontested ride under cover of darkness.

By morning they would take the town unawares and likely bloodless. The gate would be lowered for them by a paid turncoat on the wall. They need not even stop to don their armor. Then, once word reached Arthur in Camelot that they had Carhaix and his dear fiancé, he would come with his knights. King Pellinore would be no help, as he was busy dealing with the Saxon chief Cheldric raiding his lands. Even the greatest of Arthur's knights, Sir Gawaine and his two brothers, would not likely draw sword against their own father. Lot, Sir Segurant, and Osla Big Knife would pour in from the west with five thousand men and crush the boy king at the gates of Carhaix. Perhaps Leodegrance, fearing for his daughter, would even pull back from the northern skirmish and in his passion be brought down too.

Rience had Nimue to thank for the plan. Her casual mention of Leodegrance's daughter as Arthur's betrothed had sparked the notion in him.

The gods were with him, he knew. They wanted him to be High King. The breaking of Macsen's sword was only the first sign. Hadn't three of the most ambitious kings fallen to his sword by a combination of guile and luck? He had fortuitously caught King Aguysans without his famed Hundred Knights. He had slain King Cradelment when he had learned the disguised monarch had slipped from his fortress for a tryst with a sheriff's daughter and met him there instead. He had happily given King Idres to the Saxons at Wandesborow to appease their blood feud with Cornwall and provide a warning to the survivors.

Rience was wiling the time in the saddle alternately anticipating his meeting with Arthur and dreading negotiating the marriage of his fiery daughter Britomart with one of Lot's sons to solidify the union of

Albion beneath him, when the vanguard halted in its tracks, bringing the whole retinue to a stop.

"What's this?" Rience growled. "Why are we stopped?"

"Riders in the road, my king," called a man from the front.

"How many?" Rience called back, breaking into a sweat and gripping Marmyadose at his belt. These roads were supposed to be clear. Had he misread Leodegrance's mind or been misinformed as to the strength of his forces? They were caught in a narrow stretch of road which cut through the dense forest. His men were closely packed together.

"Two," was the reply.

Two?

"They must be an advance scout," muttered one of the knights at Rience's side, Sir Colivre.

Rience spurred his horse and moved up behind the point riders.

There in the moonlight, standing in the center of the crossroads, were two armored lancers, one mounted upon a gray destrier and the other upon a dark courser. He could not make out the blazons on their shields.

"Kill them," Rience ordered.

BALIN AND BRULEN spurred their horses and charged, bellowing a savage cry in unison.

They lowered their lances and cleared the distance in no time.

The five torch-bearing riders of the vanguard crumpled as Balin and Brulen hurtled headlong into them, spitting the lead horsemen fully on their lances, lifting them bodily from their saddles, and swinging them mightily into the surprised men to their immediate right and left, unhorsing the whole line.

Their lances were so entrapped, they dropped them and ripped their swords free of their scabbards. Balin discarded his shield and drew the

Adventurous Sword. He cleaved furiously about him, without any regard for his own defense. It was all or nothing. Glory or death.

THE WHISTLING OF Balin and Brulen's blades were like the constant whisk of hunters beating quail from the brush. Men fell screaming three at a time, nothing but their night cloaks between them and the swift, keen edges that bit into them to the bone. Even their shields were fastened to their saddles, and the first two lines of men tumbled bleeding into the road before this pitiless onslaught like harvest wheat before the reapers.

The torches fell into the road, flared hellishly, and were extinguished by the fear maddened hooves of the stamping horse train. The skirmish became a mad shadow play.

The third line of King Rience's men overcame their shock and managed to pull their swords, but the hasty blows they landed rang bootlessly on the brothers' mail. Balin felt nothing but the distant impacts. His answering ripostes parted flesh and muscle, sheared through limbs, sent hands spinning into the air like spiders fallen from their webs. Heads rolled in the road, still mouthing interrupted screams of terror and pain. Ropes of black blood snaked across the moon.

It was like slaughtering sheep.

The fourth row of five broke and tried to close around them, but the fifth hadn't expected the maneuver and faltered in confusion. Reins tangled, horses screamed as their flanks were cut by other riders' spurs and deflected swords. Some reared and shed their masters into the road or threw them end over end to crash upside down against the penning trees.

Balin and Brulen spun their mounts expertly, and the worthy animals partook themselves of the combat, horses and riders fighting together, crushing breastbones with terrible kicks of their muscled back legs and cutting enemies from their saddles.

"Their horses!" someone yelled from the back of the column. "Cut down their horses!"

Balin looked for the speaker and saw a gigantic man in a multicolored fur cloak hemmed in by a pair of burly men at arms who had managed to free their shields and swords and were fumbling with helms.

"Balin!" Brulen called at his side and pointed with his bloodied sword. "That's him! That's Rience!"

Balin knew it. He remembered him from the bridge at Aneblayse. This was the man who had cut off Bedivere's hand. Balin kicked his horse and pushed into the center of the column like a dagger point. He raised the Adventurous Sword and brought it down on the first of the bodyguards, shattering his helmet and washing the man's grimacing face with dark blood that splashed over his horse's shoulders as he grunted and slumped over its neck.

Brulen surged in behind and unhorsed the second.

Rience slipped from his saddle, drawing a bright broadsword and standing ready.

"King Rience!" Brulen yelled down.

"Here!" The king roared, and he passed its enchanted edge entirely through the neck of Brulen's dark courser. As the horse's head tumbled away, it crumpled to its forelegs and catapulted him over Rience's head.

Balin's heart leapt into his throat as Rience pivoted and chopped down at Brulen. Brulen managed to twist and bring up his shield in the last instant, and Rience's sword split his charge between the two rampant boars and wedged in the lower cannon of his right vambrace just beneath the gauntlet.

"Brulen!" Balin cried and swung down from his saddle, leaping for Rience like a panther.

Rience grinned and met the rush with his sword. Balin fully expected to break the king's sword and cleave that bearded, leering face. To his astonishment, the king's broadsword checked his magic blade and held. The meeting of the two swords, for a brief instant, lit the blood soaked road, glutted with mangled men and horses in an outward rolling flash of incandescent white light that made Balin flinch and shield his eyes till it passed into the dark forest and dissipated, leaving red spots pulsating across his vision.

Rience, too, looked shocked. Then he pressed in. He feinted, but Balin would not be fooled, and he sliced the king's right thigh with his other sword, bringing Rience suddenly down on one knee.

Rience cursed and slipped Balin's enchanted sword, intending to gut him swiftly at the waist. Balin saw his death in that instant, but from behind, Brulen flung out his bleeding arm and hooked his elbow, stymying the swing.

Brulen pinioned Rience's arms. The king snarled and flung all his great weight backward, forcing Brulen to the ground beneath him with a crash.

Then a slew of Rience's shattered retinue regrouped and leapt to his side rushing Balin.

Balin whirled his blades, dealing death to each man in turn, ducking or stepping out from their attacks and countering alternately with his left and right swords, not giving ground against the superior force, but slowly, inexorably, advancing against it, fighting to get to Brulen.

BODIES THAT HAD passed over Rience, roaring their intent to defend him, now sailed back the way they'd come, collapsing atop him, so quickly that he soon found himself buried beneath an increasing pile, unable to free himself even with his own great strength. The screams of his men were muffled by the corpses of their predecessors. Blood ran in his face, so that he, too, screamed at the horror of it. Rience did not know how long he lay pinned in the close dark beneath the corpse pile, but suddenly the moon looked down on him again, and the press was off his heaving chest. That awful knight with two swords towered over him, silhouetted by the milky brightness, blood dripping as regular as cave water from his two swords.

Rience had never before in his life feared any opponent.

But now he stammered like a chastised child, eager to spare himself the lash of the rod.

"Dread knight!" He gasped. "I yield to you. My sword, Marmyadose." He tried to free it, but his arm was still weighed down by corpses, "is yours."

The knight jammed one of his swords into the ground, or perhaps into a body that lay on it, for Rience could scarcely believe there was an inch of road not covered by corpses, and reached down, his blood slick gauntleted fingers closing around his tunic.

BALIN PULLED RIENCE free of the sliding corpse pile and flung him to the road, ignoring the proffered sword, ignoring the surrender and his own triumph. Suddenly none of that mattered.

He stooped and felt in the road for Brulen, found his blood stained harness, and pulled him up gasping.

Then all the night's labors fell upon him at once, and he fell to his knees and sagged against Brulen, who sucked in the night air gratefully.

"Are you alright?" Balin asked after he had caught his breath.

"Yes, I think so."

BALIN PULLED HIS brother close until they touched brows, grateful they had both survived. He mumbled his thanks to God, then turned to regard Rience, lying in the road, staring at the islands of dead in the pooling blood in the moonlight.

Balin got slowly to his feet and retrieved his sword. He went and stood over Rience, who held up a warding hand, real fear on his face.

"Rience, king of Snowdonia?" Balin said.

"And Norgales," said Rience, lamely. "Who are you?"

"Sir Balin of Northumberland. And my brother, Sir Brulen," he said, gesturing to Brulen as he struggled to stand.

Rience hastily held out the hilt of his sword again. Balin stared at it for a moment. Never in his life had he dreamed he would be offered a second enchanted sword.

He made no move to take it.

"I will not take your sword," he said. "That is for King Arthur to accept."

"King...*Arthur*?" Rience exclaimed, his whole expression sinking.

A chilly night breeze whipped briefly down the road, and he drew his kingsbeard mantle closer with a shiver.

CHAPTER
TWENTY

BALIN AND BRULEN rode in the predawn light to Carhaix with Rience before them, tied to the saddle of a bowbacked sumpter. Brulen had claimed the king's own destrier to replace the courser he'd lost.

"The last I heard of you, you were in the service of King Lot of Orkney," Balin said.

"I was. That was where I saw King Rience. You left Clarivaunce then?"

Balin nodded.

"I don't blame you, brother," said Brulen. "He wasn't fit to wear Detors' crown. You went for Arthur then?"

"I saw him draw the sword of God from the stone at Londres," Balin said. "A sword I could not myself free."

Brulen snickered.

"What?" Balin demanded.

"It's funny. You went to Arthur when he took up a Christian relic," said Brulen. "When I learned The Lady of The Lake had given him Excalibur, I knew King Lot's cause was lost."

"Did you fight at Bedegraine?" Balin asked.

"Lot gave me another task," Brulen said quietly. "I missed the battle."

"I thank God you did," said Balin. "Every man I faced, I feared it would be you."

Brulen smiled thinly, and they rode in silence for a while.

All was well. Despite his misguided reasoning, Brulen was on the side of the Lord now. Providence had directed them together again. He had so much to tell him. So much to ask. They were comrades at arms now. Surely the blood of Rience's men had washed away their enmity.

"You will join Arthur, too, then?" Balin asked, then.

But Brulen said nothing to this, only pointed ahead with his good arm.

"Here is Carhaix."

When they arrived at Carhaix, Cleodalis, the seneschal of the city, ordered the gate opened.

"Sir Balin and Sir Brulen of Northumberland," Cleodalis said with a bow when they entered, "Merlin the magician told me last night to expect you."

"How many men do you have here?" Balin asked.

"Four score and two hundred," said Cleodalis. "But Merlin said that Arthur and his knights will be here by nightfall to reinforce us."

Balin looked about the busy streets, at the children staring wide eyed at him from behind their mother's skirts. It was not enough. Even if Arthur took all his knights and soldiers and left Camelot entirely undefended, it wouldn't be enough.

A gray-haired knight with a great reddish falcon which clung to his black glove with sun yellow talons tipped in curved sable came forward with two guards and took custody of Rience and led him away to the dungeon.

"An epic victory, sirs," said Cleodalis, watching the king's mottled fur cloak receded with the clanking guards. But then he looked at Brulen and his expression fell. "Why, you're bleeding! Let me call for the surgeon."

Brulen swooned and had to be carried from his saddle by three stout squires. Though Balin begged to accompany the surgeon, an old cleric took him by the elbow and drew him aside.

"Please, sir knight. Tell me where you and your brother captured King Rience, that I and my acolytes might administer extreme unction to the men you slew."

Balin could not, in good conscience, argue against that. When he had given their number and location, Brulen was gone away to the house of the healer, and he was left alone in the courtyard with Cleodalis, who took his arm and led him up the stone steps to the keep.

"I pray you, do not fret for your brother. Our physicians are the best in the land. There is one here who owes you special thanks and has asked that I fetch you as soon as you arrived."

By various turns and ascents, Balin was led at last to a rich, guarded chamber, where he found himself standing before Princess Guinevere herself.

She was garbed in a long woolen dress that flowed over the floor, intricately embroidered and clasped with golden brooches at the shoulders and a purple silken tunic beneath with laced sleeves. She wore the cross he had first seen about her neck at Camelot.

"Here, Princess," said Cleodalis with jovial aplomb, "is one of the knights who by the bidding of Merlin has saved us all from the villain Rience this day."

When Guinevere saw who it was, recognition passed across her features and for a moment, revilement. To her credit though, she retained her noble poise.

"You are Sir Balin of Northumberland," she attested quietly.

He nodded and genuflected before her, lowering his head, self-conscious of his own bloody and grimy appearance in the face of her clean beauty.

"How is it that you are banished from Arthur's sight one minute and save his bride to be in the next?"

"My lady, all I do I do for King Arthur."

She said nothing, and Cleodalis fidgeted at his side.

"Princess," he said, "I must attend to the preparations for our defense."

"You may go, Cleodalis. I will be fine."

Balin heard the seneschal grind his heel on the flagstones as he left.

"Rise, Sir Balin," she said.

He did, but continued to avert his eyes from hers, which regarded him nakedly and somehow made him feel the same.

"You frighten me, Sir Balin," she said at last.

That surprised him, and he cleared his throat.

"My Lady has nothing to fear from me. I apologize for my appearance…"

"You appear at last as you are. When I first saw you, in the courtyard at Camelot, in chains, I pitied you. When next I saw you, clean and girded like a saint, and you murdered that enchantress, I was terrified. Now, bloody as you are, I am merely frightened, as I am frightened by the descriptions of the last plague on Egypt or by the angel that destroyed Sodom and Gomorrah. You are a bloody man, Sir Balin. But a Queen must not shrink like a blushing maiden from certain truths. My Arthur has need of bloody men like you. So do I."

Balin was conflicted as to how to respond, so he said nothing.

"I am a woman, and Cleodalis thinks I see and know nothing. He is a good man, but as he is blind to craft in women, so too is he blind to dishonor in men. In his daughter, I see my father's face, as plain as I see it in my own mirror." She looked away for a moment, sad.

Balin rankled. He had thought Leodegrance a pious, Christian king and an honorable man. He was ashamed to know such a base secret about him, if his own daughter could be believed.

"There is a traitor here in Carhaix," said Guinevere. "I have known it for a long time."

"A traitor?" Balin said, bristling. "Who, my Lady?"

"My father's best knight, Sir Bertholai The Red. He keeps a twice armed lanner falcon for hunting bustards."

"I saw such a knight down in the courtyard," Balin said, remembering the huge falcon and the black gloved knight who bore him. "What proof do you have of his treachery?"

"I have seen him fix messages to his falcon's arm and send it over the wall. When it returns, the messages are gone."

Balin gave pause, chewing over his next words carefully.

"Might he not be communicating with your father in the north?" Balin asked.

"What do you know of falconry, Sir Balin?" she retorted impatiently.

"Nothing, I admit."

"Bertholai taught my cousin, Sir Geraint. A falcon is not a pigeon. It will not carry messages as far as Daneblaise."

"As you say, my Lady," said Balin quietly.

Guinevere regarded him stoically and raised her eyebrows.

"I was terrified when I saw you behead the Lady of The Lake," she said. "But later, I thought that perhaps you were a Christian man who found the influence of Avalon on Arthur's rule abhorrent as I did. I heard you called 'savage' and denounced as a madman. But the angels of the Lord are not mad when they do His bidding, no matter how terrible. You called her false, and there were tears in your eyes. As Arthur raged against you, in my heart, I rejoiced at what you had done, and I suspected that you had some reason dear to your heart. I do not say this to engender your loyalty but to demonstrate my trust. Now I ask you, Sir Balin. Will you reciprocate my trust?"

Balin was so moved by the nobility of the Princess' entreaty, by her faith in him, that he felt his lip tremble, and he lowered his head once more. "I will see about this Bertholai, my Lady."

"In turn, I will soothe Arthur's anger against you when he comes."

"My Lady, I ask that you do not trouble yourself in that regard, nor even say that I am here. If the King is to forgive me, let it be of his own accord, by reason of my own actions."

Guinevere nodded.

"You are an honorable knight, sir. I will abide."

He went from her chamber and back down the tower steps into the courtyard once more.

He wanted only to head to the healer to check on Brulen, but the princess' words gnawed at him and he called for a man-at-arms.

"Where is the dungeon?"

The soldier pointed out the stair that led beneath the central keep, and Balin went over, seeing no guard at hand.

He descended the torch lit steps and found the bank of dim cells. Again, there appeared to be no man on duty.

He stalked down the short hall, seizing a torch from the wall and holding it up to the barred windows set into the thick cell doors. He saw only straw and a few scurrying rats until he reached the last.

There he saw a portly man lying face down in the bloody straw, a ring of jailer's keys on his broad belt.

He wheeled and raced back down the hall, taking the steps back up to the courtyard two at a time.

Balin drew frightened stares as he raced in his bloodstained armor to the gate, the dungeon torch still in his hand.

The two halberdiers at the gate crossed their pikes at his approach.

"Where is Sir Bertholai?" Balin demanded.

"He is gone with Father Amustant and the priests to the Northern Crossroads," said one of the guards. "He will be back within the hour."

"No, he won't." Balin growled, then shouted for Cleodalis, quenching the torch in the guards' water bucket in frustration.

The seneschal came running, holding his stately robes.

"Your Sir Bertholai is a traitor," Balin informed him.

Cleodalis met this accusation with a prim and indulgent smile.

"You have been speaking to the Princess, Sir Balin. Sir Bertholai has been King Leodegrance's best man since we were all of us boys. I would trust him with my own daughter's life."

Balin smirked, considering the revelation the Princess had shared with him about Cleodalis' daughter, but it was not his place to cut the man so completely. In truth, he pitied this man, cuckolded by his own master.

"As you trusted him to take King Rience to your dungeon? And yet your jailer lies dead and Rience is escaped, probably dressed as a hermit. Where is my brother?"

Cleodalis looked flabbergasted. He was already gesturing for a guard to confirm Balin's words about the jailer.

"He is there on the wall," Cleodalis said, pointing.

Balin found Brulen leaning on one of the battlements, staring off to the west. He was stripped to tunic and hose, and his wounded arm was bound with poultice and splint. His face and hands were clean.

A breeze stirred the vast field of green grass, which was level but for a diminutive copse of perhaps a dozen trees in the center, the lonesome remainder of the vast unnamed forest which had furnished the bones of Carhaix.

"Brulen," Balin said, gasping from having run up the stairs to the top of the wall. "Rience has been smuggled out of the city."

"In the hermit train?" Brulen asked, with an air of unconcern.

"Yes. The knight who accompanied them is false."

"Find me a knight who is true and I will call it news," Brulen said sullenly.

Though few had ever been able to tell them apart, the two brothers knew the subtle differences in each other. Their faces were like identical patterned garments commissioned and worn by different men. At a glance they were indistinguishable, but upon closer consideration, they bore the barely perceptible marks of vastly different owners. There had always been a youthfulness, a facileness to Brulen that was not present in Balin's rough expression.

But now that naivety was gone. The brightness of his eyes had dimmed somewhat. Not enough for anyone to notice save Balin.

"We must go after them!" Balin exclaimed.

"Rest, brother. They are too far ahead. If Arthur is coming as you say, then Rience will not go far ere he returns. With Lot and the Saxons, he will still have the advantage in numbers. His ambition will not allow him to fully retreat."

Balin sighed.

"It will be a hard fight," he said and dashed the battlement stone with his mailed fist, casting sparks. "I should have slain Rience when I had the chance!"

Brulen shrugged.

"You may yet get your chance to amend your mercy."

Balin put his fists to the stone and leaned on the wall as Brulen was doing. He felt the breeze that rippled the tree tops and grasses course through his hair, and he realized that they had said very little on the dawn ride to the city with Rience.

There had been no formal reunion between them. No full embrace, no talk of forgiveness or understanding. Perhaps there didn't need to be. Brulen had come at his summons to aid him, hadn't he? They had won a great victory together. What might have been said surely had been said, not in words, but in deed.

"How is your arm?" he ventured lamely.

"The cut is not so deep. It will mend quickly, I think."

"Brulen," Balin said unable to contain his enthusiasm a moment more, "since we were boys taking turns racing our father's horse along the old Roman wall, I have dreamed of what we accomplished last night."

He opened his arms to embrace the breeze and smiled into the sun.

"What we did, they will sing of it, brother."

Brulen said nothing for what seemed a long time before turning to look at his brother.

"Do you think they will?" Brulen asked.

"Two faced sixty and won!" Balin exclaimed, fairly bubbling over with excitement. "We're heroes, you and I!"

"Heroes?" Brulen repeated. "To whom?"

"To King Arthur. To the people of this city."

"To the men we left lying in that road, we were rampaging beasts," Brulen said, turning back to regard the land. "And as to the adoration of Arthur? What is that?"

Balin frowned.

"Where is your fire, brother? Is it that you do not recognize the High King? Do you dread opposing your former master, King Lot?"

"Lot took me in, yes," said Brulen, "after I left the kingdom of Malehault. He was a fair master, and you're right. I would rather fight Rience and the Saxons than oppose him, but in truth, in my travels I have found no king worthy of my devotion, nor known any knight truly worthy of the name. I'm surprised you cast your lot with Arthur, brother."

"Arthur is the chosen of God. He drew the sword of Macsen from the stone when no man could."

"You believe that fairy tale?"

"I told you, I saw the miracle with my own eyes, brother," Balin said. "Not a hundred men could draw it out. I myself tried."

"What is a miracle but magic?" Brulen said. "The Merlin inclines Arthur's ear at every turn. For all your hatred of Avalon, why have you not turned your sword against that black rascal?"

"Is your heart hardened because of how I dealt with the Lady Lile?"

Brulen shook his head.

"I cannot in good conscience fault you for that. I set the rash example myself in my own killing of that pernicious Gallet. We are a death for a death now, and I would leave it at that. Yet O my brother, how much greater is your crime. In my folly, I ruined only myself. Yours has damned all Albion."

"It was on a path to damnation before, I would argue."

"Do you think you have killed the Lady of The Lake truly, Balin? Don't you know it's an office, and that another has already risen to the title? Our own mother was offered it in her day. No Balin, Avalon endures, even without our poor aunt."

Balin frowned deeply at that.

"Our aunt?"

Brulen turned to him.

"The Lady Lile was our mother's sister. Yes. It's true. I have learned a great deal in my travels, Balin. More than I would have you know. About Avalon, about the God you worship, about Merlin, and about your precious King Arthur too."

Balin thought hard. His chest pounded with the revelation that he had slain his own kin. But what of it, really? Did a previously un-known connection to the Lady Lile make her any less of a villainess? If anything, her kinship with their mother made her sins against her even more offensive. Where sisterly affection should have restrained her, there had been nothing. In his eyes, that a sister had stood by and watched her own blood kin burned for forbidden knowledge she had bestowed, made her all the more monstrous.

But it was a truth. He felt it somehow. And what Brulen had intimated about Arthur troubled him.

"What have you learned? About Arthur?"

"Ask me anything else, Balin," Brulen rasped, tears in his eyes. "I see the love you bear for him and I would spare you. Ask me about the plots of Merlin, or the great and terrible ladies who have broken with Avalon. Ask me about the Sangreal and the Templeise. Ask me about my own deceits and unworthy deeds. Ask me about the Copper Tower or Sir Breuse Sans Pitie, or The Questing Beast. But O my brother, do not ask me about King Arthur."

Balin swallowed hard. What truth did he know?

Brulen grasped Balin's arm tightly. "But if you do dare ask me, then you must ask about King Lot and Queen Morgause, and about *why* the kings are rebelling."

"I know why," Balin interjected. "Clarivaunce…"

"Aye, that fool Clarivaunce! And Uriens, all the rest who were greedy or uncertain and yielded. But what of King Aguysans? And what of King Cradelment and King Idres? And what of good King Lot? Mark you, if I am right, he will not live past tomorrow."

"What are you on about, brother?"

Brulen shook his head and drew him into the embrace he had pined for before, but now Balin stiffened.

"A true knight may serve only one master, Balin," Brulen whispered in his ear. "Truth or delusion. Every man must choose."

Balin was vexed. He didn't understand anything Brulen was saying. What treachery was there here?

"Brulen," he asked, and cursed himself inwardly to hear in his own voice the same boy who had begged him to race along the Roman wall one last time with their father's horse when Brulen had wanted only to go and read somewhere, "will you not stay with me?"

"I will fight beside you again, my brother," he said, parting from their firm embrace to look into his eyes. "But not for any king."

CHAPTER
TWENTY-ONE

WITHIN TWO HOURS, Father Amustant returned with his
acolytes, much shaken and bearing two corpse wagons of
dead Snowdonian knights for burial.

He said that once they had passed out of sight of Carhaix, Sir Bertholai had flung his hawk into the sky, and while the two guards he had
taken along looked up to admire its flight, he had drawn his sword and
treacherously slain them. Then he had pulled one of the robed monks
up onto the back of his horse and galloped off to the west.

"That monk was Rience," said Balin, when he heard. "He will join
King Lot and Osla. They know our numbers and that Arthur is coming."

"Our only advantage is this fortification," said Brulen.

In that at least, Rience's original plan had still been foiled.

Night fell, and the women, children, and elderly were ushered into
the city keep.

There was a shout on the wall that announced the arrival of an
armed host, but it was not the thousands of Rience, merely Arthur and
the Camelot knights with a thousand footmen and archers, as promised.

Balin took hold of Cleodalis as the order to open the gates
was given.

"I beg you, sir, say nothing of my presence here. My brother and I are but knights in service to Carhaix."

Cleodalis agreed, though his face registered his bemusement, and he and Brulen replaced their helms and harnesses and Balin hid his charge. He left the Adventurous Sword hanging on Ironprow's saddle, fearing he would be recognized by it. He feared also, that perhaps in the heat of battle or by some strange twist of unlikely circumstance, he might use it to fulfill the maiden's prophecy and slay Arthur by accident.

Arthur rode in fully armored, with a steel company of cavalry at his back, all the heroes he had seen last at the dining hall. Arthur's squire Timias held his fluttering dragon pennant at the head of all.

Arthur greeted Cleodalis as Timias took hold of his stallion, and he swung down from the stirrups.

"Merlin told us that Carhaix was threatened by Rience, and that we must ride here at once. Is he here now?"

"I have not seen him since two nights ago, sire," said Cleodalis. "Rience rides at the head of five thousand men from the west, knights and Saxons under Lot of Orkney and the Saxon chieftain Osla Big Knife. He will be here by dawn, and we have but four score and two hundred defenders and those you have brought."

Arthur paced, thinking.

"Where is Leodegrance?" he asked.

"He fights the Saxons in the north at Daneblaise with the bulk of his army," said Cleodalis, wringing his hands. "If only Merlin were here. I wish he would return and weave some magic spell to open the earth and swallow Rience and his horde."

Balin pursed his lips disapprovingly behind his helm.

"Christian men should not put their faith in a wizard for victory, but in the Lord," came a strident voice from above.

The men craned their necks and saw Guinevere standing at the top of the stair in breeches and a leather jerkin, a spear in her hand and a seax at her belt like some Saxon battle maiden.

A cheer went up among the knights, though those among Arthur's company who were pagan took no comfort and looked grim. Arthur grinned widely to see his woman speak bravely to him.

"And in the king the Lord has chosen!" Balin called out, unable to contain himself.

Another round of cheers went up.

Arthur drew Excalibur, and the light of the torches shined red on its clean blade. He turned it over and held it up, cruciform.

"God may fight with us tomorrow, but he will not fight for us. Therefore, pray for the will to face the foe. Steel your hearts. If tomorrow they are to be broken, let their shards cut our enemies deep."

Every mailed fist raised in answer, and with a roar of unified assent, they broke to the walls, and Arthur, sparing a fond glance at Guinevere, turned to review the plans of the city.

Balin and Brulen insinuated themselves near Arthur's immediate retinue, which was Kay and Bedivere, Bors and Gawaine. Cleodalis pored over the city's defense plans, answering Arthur's pointed questions each in turn.

"It must be said also," said Cleodalis, "that one of our number has turned traitor. Sir Bertholai."

"Then Rience will know your numbers and every secret of this city," said Arthur. "Let every hidden postern and sewer be blockaded, and place a single runner at each to notify the defenders of incursion. We cannot spread ourselves thin. We must form a group of ten mounted men to remain in the city and defend these passageways as they are threatened."

"Let me, my lord," said Balin.

"And I," said Brulen.

Arthur looked to them and nodded.

"What are your names?"

"Sir Ballantyne," said Balin quickly.

"Sir Gernemant," said Brulen, taking the name of his old master at Sewingshields.

"As you know the city, take three of your fellow knights. I will assign you five of mine. Command them as you see fit. They are yours."

"Yes, my lord," said Balin.

They were given two of the Orkney brothers, Gaheris and Agravaine, as well as a Sir Marrok, and the sons of King Pellinore, Tor and Lamorak de Galis.

Though the two pairs of brothers brought horses and were armored, Sir Marrok came on foot unarmed and wore only a simple tabard emblazoned with an *argent wolf's head cabossed*. He was an older man, silver bearded, but hard looking, with rough hands and a weathered face with a crescent scar on his chin and sea blue eyes.

When Balin had explained the nature of their duty, he fixed his attention on Marrok.

"You are a knight, sir? Where is your horse and armor? Where is your sword?"

"Sir Marrok Le Bisclarvet needs none of those things, Sir Ballantyne," Gaheris volunteered for the older man, smiling wryly. Like all the Orkney brothers, he had a shock of red hair and pale skin that offset the dark pagan woads which intruded upon his face.

Marrok lowered his head at Gaheris' words.

"I move faster without harness, sir," he said quietly, in a voice as grizzled as his appearance.

"Do you move faster without a horse as well?" Balin quipped.

He nodded seriously.

"And do you strike harder without a sword?"

"Perhaps not harder, but swifter, yes I do."

Balin had about decided the fellow was mad when the Cameliard knights arrived, introducing themselves as Geraint, Guy, Landens, and Purades.

"King Arthur bade us report to you, Sir Ballantyne," said the eldest, Geraint, whom he remembered was Guinevere's cousin. "And Cleodalis has told us we are to obey your every command." He saluted and looked at Balin intently, his meaning plain. The Cameliard knights would not divulge his or Brulen's identity.

"Very well," said Balin. "For now, I charge you with showing Arthur's knights the ways we will be guarding. Sir Landens, recruit from the volunteer runners equal to the number of points of entry. The rest of us will begin building blockades."

In this way, Balin and Brulen were able to surreptitiously learn the city's weak points under the subtle direction of Guy and Purades.

All of them toiled till deep into the night breaking up furniture and hauling stone into the sewers and escape tunnels to block the passages. They also set bundles of spears and bows and arrows at every entrance on the city side. Runners were culled from the citizen volunteers, and it was decided that Sir Marrok and Sir Landens would act as the hub, relaying information from the runners to the armored knights as needed.

When all the passages had been blocked and assigned a lookout, there was nothing more for Balin's command to do but wait in the center of the city for dawn as the rest of the defenders busied themselves on the walls.

A servant brought them dinner, the roast carcass of a lamb, and all but Balin and Brulen ate and drank.

The odd Sir Marrok sat alone beyond the edge of the cooking fire and ate quietly.

"Why does Sir Marrok not sit with the rest of us?" Sir Geraint asked.

"Is he truly a knight?" Balin asked.

"Did you note his mark of courage? He was a knight at King Uther's table," said Gaheris. Then, a bit lower, conspiratorial, he whispered, "He is a werewolf."

"You jest with us," chuckled Sir Guy.

"It is sadly true," said Sir Tor. "How he came by his curse no man knows, but he must be chained on nights of the full moon for he becomes wild. Other nights, he may change at will."

Sir Guy laughed and shook his head, sure he was being led.

"He came to Camelot as a gray wolf," said Agravaine, completely serious. "Arthur brought him home from one of his boar hunts, because the wolf approached his horse and licked his boot in the stirrup like a friendly dog. As a tame wolf, it was an oddity, of course. It rested beside his throne and dinner table, and slept at the foot of his bed. It would suffer the most nervous of ladies to stroke its ears. Children could hang about its neck. Then one day a year ago, a certain knight and his lady came to court and presented themselves. At one look the wolf leapt down from the dais and tore the knight's throat out. It would have mauled the lady, too, had not Arthur ordered it dragged away, barking and slavering as it never had before.

"The tearful woman confessed all over the body of her dead paramour that the wolf was her true husband, Sir Marrok, whom she had observed stripping off his clothes in the forest one night and transforming. She was a faithless woman and had loved the other knight, so she stole her husband's clothes and went off with her lover, thinking she would never see Marrok again.

"Arthur ordered that clothes be laid out for the wolf to test the lady's story. At first the wolf would only sniff and stare at the clothes, but then Merlin suggested the wolf be given privacy, and so it was shut up in a certain chamber. After a few moments, Sir Marrok emerged wearing the clothes Arthur had laid there, and the wolf was seen no more. For seven years, he said he had lived as a wolf, and he swore fealty to Arthur then and there as his savior and the son of the king he had served."

The Cameliard knights looked at each other and smirked, but none from Camelot smiled, and Agravaine raised his hands.

"By all the gods, it is true," he said.

"Anyway," said Sir Landens, "he has a passing odd manner."

"His manner is not odd to him. He lived in the forest six years, so his etiquette needs some oiling," said Agravaine.

"Why do *you* keep your helmets on, sirs?" Sir Gaheris countered, directing the question at Balin and Brulen.

"You should eat and drink," Sir Tor agreed. "This meal may be your last."

"We are fasting," said Balin. "If victory comes, then we'll partake."

"Victory?" snorted Lamorak. "How can we hope for survival, let alone victory?"

"We stand a good chance, I think," countered Agravaine.

"Aye, *you* do," Lamorak muttered.

"What does that mean?" Agravaine demanded.

"It means if the siege turns against us, it will be no great matter for the sons of Orkney to go to their father's side."

Agravaine and Gaheris both jumped to their feet.

"We have sworn our oaths to Arthur," said Gaheris.

"So did your father, King Lot, after Bedegraine. But he seems to have had a change of heart," said Lamorak.

"We may share our father's blood, but not his heart," said Gaheris, putting a hand to Agravaine's breastplate to stop his brother from advancing on the still seated Lamorak.

"Let us hope so," said Lamorak.

"That's enough, brother," said Tor.

"I agree," said Balin, getting to his feet. "Reserve your ire for the enemy."

"What if it's Lot that comes up one of those tunnels tomorrow?" Lamorak said. "Can we trust these two to fight?"

"Lot would not enter a city but by the front gate," said Brulen. "We'll be killing skulking Saxons in the morning."

"What do you know about Lot?" Lamorak demanded.

"I know he's an honorable king," said Brulen, "as kings go."

"Do I know you, Sir Gernemant?" asked Gaheris. "Your name isn't familiar, but your voice…"

Brulen sat silent for a moment, then rattled at his helm straps.

"No," Balin said, laying his hand on one of Brulen's pauldrons.

"Leave off, brother," said Brulen, wrenching the helmet from his sweat soaked head. "This thing is stifling. Men should not die alongside strangers."

"Sir Brulen!" Gaheris exclaimed, smiling and coming across to clutch Brulen's hand, an act which perturbed Balin. Here was the knightly camaraderie he had always coveted from his brother.

"Hello, Gaheris," Brulen smiled thinly, and to Agravaine he nodded.

"What are you doing here in Cameliard? We thought you perished at Bedegraine."

"Perhaps I did," Brulen said stiffly.

"Aye, there's that old sunshine manner," chuckled Agravaine. "It is surely Brulen The Sinister."

Gaheris' smile fell then, and he turned to look at Balin. He drew his sword, and the other knights leapt to their feet.

"But if this is your brother," Gaheris said, "then he is Sir Balin The Savage, murderer of the Lady of The Lake."

Arthur's knights drew their swords.

"Traitor!" Agravaine spat.

"Villain!" cursed Lamorak.

Brulen stood in front of his brother, and the two Orkney knights wavered, but Tor and Lamorak circled. Marrok's nose wrinkled, and his lip twitched. Apparently despite his aloofness, he had heard everything, for he entered the firelight now. His anger was so deep he could only growl its expression.

"What foolishness is this?" Sir Geraint demanded, standing beside

Brulen. "Will we start the battle early here amongst ourselves?"

"A Christian knight, in a Christian city," said Agravaine. "Defending the crime of one of his own. Typical."

"*We* are Christian," said Lamorak on behalf of Tor. "And we do not condone the beheading of a woman in the presence of the High King."

"Is this so?" Sir Geraint said, looking aghast at Balin at the accusation.

"I did what I did," said Balin, taking off his helm.

Geraint's eyes lingered on Balin, then he turned back to the others.

"Yet I swore to my cousin, who will be your Queen, to serve this knight who saved Carhaix from destruction only this morning."

In answer to their quizzical expressions, Geraint explained how Balin and Brulen had slain Rience's bodyguard and ruined his plot to take the city and Guinevere unawares, and how but for the betrayal of Bertholai they would have the lord of Snowdonia in their dungeon even now.

"*You* did this?" Lamorak repeated in awe.

Balin nodded reluctantly.

"I and my brother. But grant me this boon, sirs. Do not inform Arthur of my presence here, either by my death or arrest. Let me defend him this last time by your side."

The two pairs of brothers and Sir Marrok looked at him strangely, then at each other. They lowered their swords.

"Very well," said Gaheris, speaking for them all. "Put your helmet back on, Sir *Ballantyne*."

"Yes," said Sir Tor. "But do go and fetch your wondrous sword. It may be we will have need of it in the morning."

CHAPTER
TWENTY-TWO

THE ENEMY HOSTS clattered over the horizon as if to welcome the dawn, and the shout of warning rippled the orbit of Carhaix's battlements down to the ten men waiting by their horses in the city's center.

From their vantage, they could not see the might of Rience's army, but a water woman up on the wall shrieked at their appearance and spilled her bucket. Sir Aglovale had to carry her away.

"We will die here! We will all die here!" she screamed, as he clamped a hand over her mouth and took her to the keep where Princess Guinevere commanded the maidens and old women.

Them that were Christian in their number—the Cameliard knights, and Balin, and the sons of Pellinore—knelt and prayed, while Sir Marrok, the Orkney brothers, and Brulen drew their swords.

They saw Arthur ascend the wall and call down words. He was answered from below by the ox-bellow voice of Rience, but what was said between them, Balin couldn't hear.

They all watched the inscrutable exchange with hearts hammering, when a boy came rushing up to Balin and shook the hilt of his sword in its scabbard.

It was a dirty faced child, yellow haired with wide, scared blue eyes. He wore a threadbare tunic and running hosiery.

"Men in the east postern." He gasped.

So, whatever parley Rience was engaging in with Arthur was a mere stall as his infiltrators attempted to gain the city.

He rose from his knee.

"How many?" he demanded.

"It was hard to see. More than two dozen," said the boy.

"The postern!" Balin roared to the others. And to the boy, he said, "Take word to the defenders on the wall."

The boy raced off.

Purades, Tor, Guy, and Agravaine swung up onto their horses and clattered off to defend the postern.

Almost before they had rounded the corner, the runner from the sewers ran up and screamed shrilly that he had seen men trudging down below. The south passage runner almost collided with him and said the same.

Rience had sent men into all three passages at once.

"Lamorak, Marrok, Landens, and Gaheris defend the south passage," he ordered.

He clapped a hand on the shoulders of Brulen and Geraint.

"The sewers for us," Balin said.

"How appropriate," Brulen snickered.

They mounted and swung their horses about. Balin noted that Marrok ran behind his fellows, stripping his clothes as he went.

He pursed his lips at the madman and the three of them galloped for the sewer entrance.

Geraint led the way, riding down narrow alleyways that cut quickly through the labyrinthine city. They passed through the eerily empty streets till they reached the central entryway down into the old Roman subterranean drainage tunnel and swung down from their mounts.

Brulen pulled open the heavy barred door which led down, and the three of them clattered into the dim tunnel, each grabbing a handful of spears from the bunch they had left there. They splashed up to their ankles in the foul-smelling water which passed over the floor.

The tunnel ahead they had crammed with detritus, but over the edge of the pile they saw the glint of steel helmets and swords and heard guttural Saxon words bouncing off the sloping stone walls.

Balin signed for his fellow to crouch down, and they silently laid their spears at hand on the sides of the tunnel and waited.

The Saxon captain or chief reached the blockade, and after some querulous back and forth with his lieutenants, gave the command to heave to and pull the debris down.

As soon as the first large obstruction was pulled down and the Saxons reached to pull away the next, Balin gave the order and his men thrust over the barrier in unison, driving their spear points through necks and hauberks and sending three men tumbling backward screaming, to splash in the filthy water.

Balin, Geraint, and Brulen, withdrew their weapons and sprang up then, jabbing again, and sending more confused Saxons howling.

The voice of the commander sounded again and a roar went up in the tunnel.

Answering spears were flung over at them, and they cast their own and reached for the spares, exchanging missiles blindly back and forth.

The Saxon infiltrators were lightly armored, and the defenders' spears naturally did more damage, whereas the Saxon spears, thrown from confused, close quarters, sailed over the barricade, and for the most part, glanced harmlessly off the knights' heavy armor.

Yet the Saxon commander hollered again, and the flight of Saxons' spears ceased. Balin, Geraint, and Brulen kept throwing, but they heard a great deal of diminishing splashing as the enemy retreated down the tunnel.

For a brief moment, they thought they had repelled the invaders, but an instant later they heard the cry of the commander again, a little further down the tunnel, and a deadly whistling was heard.

A volley of feathered arrows came flying over the barricade just as Brulen yelled, "Shields!" and brought his up in time to catch three.

Balin avoided the shafts, but Geraint grunted as one arrow cut his face and a second pierced his shoulder, knocking him on his backside in the water.

Balin helped Geraint to his feet under cover of his shield as a second flight blew like an ill wind over the barricade and pierced his shield.

Geraint brought his own shield to bear and a third flight riddled their shields.

The commander shouted the order to let loose, and his voice grew steadily louder.

"They're advancing!" Brulen said, and Balin saw blood dribbling from the wound beneath his vambrace where Rience had cut him.

The arrows outranged their spears. They couldn't hope to reach them without succumbing to the Saxon archers.

All three knights dove for cover behind the barricade and leaned against it as flight after flight whistled through the tunnel, splashing into the water, imbedding in the walls, clattering on the stone staircase lit by the sun shining down on the street above their heads.

Then they could hear the tramp and splash of the advancing Saxons and the yell of the commander. Soon they were close enough to hear the twang of bowstrings.

And then there came another command and a chilling demon scream of charging men.

Balin, Brulen, and Geraint braced themselves against the blockade and shuddered as the full strength of the Saxon force charged against it.

It groaned and pieces clattered off, but it held.

The Saxon captain called out in cadence, and the army on the other side of the blockade heaved. They were irresistible.

"We can't stop them!" Geraint shrieked.

"Spears, then swords!" Balin called. "Cut down as many as you can! Geraint! Go upstairs and lock the gate!"

And so here he would meet his end, in the putrid bowels of this city in a hopeless fight. But at least Brulen was here.

"I won't leave you!" Geraint yelled.

"Go and lock the gate! Then ride for reinforcements! Bring the Orkneys! Anyone you can find!"

No doubt the Orkneys and the other Cameliard knights and the sons of Pellinore had their own troubles. Rience had Saxons to spare after all, and if there was enough of a force arrayed out on the field before the city to mask the maneuvers of so many down here in this tunnel, no doubt each of the secret passages was equally threatened. They didn't need to besiege Carhaix or batter down her gates. The city would fall from within.

The barricade buckled with the latest push, and Geraint reluctantly withdrew and stumbled toward the stair. Brulen took up a spear and his sword and Balin did the same, the gleam of the Adventurous Sword in his hand almost lighting the passage.

Then a great shadow stymied the sun on the sewer stairs and he looked up and saw a great dark furred form as of a sharp-eared beast come padding down the steps on all fours.

Its eyes caught the shine of the sword and flashed like jet in its broad face. It was a silver wolf, yet larger than any such beast Balin had ever seen.

A great, evil dread seized his heart at the sight of the terrible creature, and he nearly cast his spear down its maw.

At that instant the Saxons burst through the barrier, sending its components tumbling in every direction. Balin spun and spitted a rushing warrior on his spear, then swung the Adventurous Sword and cleaved through the helm of a second, halving the grimacing face beneath in a burst of teeth and blood. A sharp ringing sound reverberated along the tunnel, and the sword shook in his grip. Its inherent shine flared into a lightning bright flash that illuminated the surprised visages of the tangled cluster of bearded soldiers, all of them in scale hauberks and wielding long swords or spears and round blue and white painted Saxon shields.

Time seemed to freeze in that moment.

Balin recognized the commander in that single strobe of incandescence, a broad shouldered man in a chain shirt and peaked aventail helm with accents of brass around the eyes and nose, and a broad axe in his fist. A signal horn hung from his belt, to be blown when Carhaix had fallen, no doubt. But the dead could sound no horn.

The supernatural white blaze of the sword penetrated the dark eyelets of the commander's helm and showed bright eyes, wide and dilated in awe.

The wolf on the stair let out a terrible howl that echoed down the tunnel like the plaintive wail of an arch demon lamenting the torture of hell. There was something unearthly in that animal call. It was like no wolf Balin had ever heard and contained much of the moan of a man in it.

That beastly din, combined with the light of the Adventurous Sword, caught every man in the Saxon charge up, and in their eyes and in their manner Balin saw for an instant a withering dread that surpassed his own, perhaps born in the long ago superstitions of their northern blood. This knowledge, that they were greater in number and yet more afraid, blew fire into his heart and limbs and quickened his pulse.

The blast of strange light faded, and so too did that howl dwindle. It was as if the illuminated Saxons plunged, drowning men sinking into a fearful night eternal. Balin's last sight of the Saxon commander was as the man reached out, as if to catch the dying light in his grasp.

Into that darkness Balin leapt, striking first two-handed with the sword, smashing shields and snapping swords. He cut the shaking hands that grasped the broken weapons. He split in twain the fear-filled hearts behind them. As if the bloodletting was not enough, he drew his second sword to better glut his hunger for the slaughter.

The wolf sprang from the stair, too, and Balin smelled its musk and heard its horrific snarling at his side. He was splashed by the blood of its victims, just as he was sure it was bathed in the same from his own.

Brulen was there, too, in the dark, expulsing the cry of a man seeking to beat death at his own game, to overwhelm death with more death.

These were the ancestral enemy their father had faced in the service of Detors, and Balin delighted in taking up his birthright. The half-hearted blows of the dying picked at him, making his armor chime. One heavy blow from an axe tore the helmet from his head, but he fought on, ears ringing.

He did not know how long they cut their way down the length of that tunnel, but when his forward momentum carried him to the end of his opponents, he nearly fell sprawling into the water, tripping over the dead. He turned to look back, and the light of the stair was a ways off, the view unobstructed.

The great wolf panted beside him, but he did not shrink from it. He heard Brulen's labored breathing, and Geraint's.

"My God," said Geraint. "Are we alive?"

Balin gasped and leaned against the tunnel wall. Many islands had formed in the water, still and barren. The stink of blood and piss and dung was heavy in the dank air.

"If we are not, this is surely hell."

CHAPTER
TWENTY-THREE

WHEN THEY HAD waded back down the stinking tunnel, now choked with floating bodies, and climbed the sunlit stair back up to the street, they were greeted by Sir Lamorak and Sir Gaheris who came riding up on their horses.

"Goddess!" Lamorak exclaimed at the sight of the three blood splashed men and the large wolf, whose maw and flanks were soaked in Saxon red.

Gaheris dismounted and took from off his saddle Sir Marrok's tabard. He moved to the sewer stair, and the wolf followed him closely, wagging its tail like an eager hound. Gaheris flung the bunched up garment down the stair and the wolf eagerly bounded down after it, like a dog at play.

Balin could only stare after it, fearing what form it would take.

"We repulsed the south tunnel assault handily," said Gaheris. "There were only a dozen or so, and we set the tunnel afire. They won't try that way again. How many fought you?"

Brulen shook his head.

"I could not count them in the dark. There were many. Too many."

"Where is Sir Landens?" Geraint asked.

"He took a wound from a Saxon axe beneath the knee, but he will neither die nor lose the limb," said Lamorak. "He is a game man. We carried him to Princess Guinevere."

Sir Marrok emerged from the stairwell, wearing his tunic and otherwise bare beneath. His arms and legs bore open cuts, and there was blood beneath his nails and splashed across his teeth and lips.

Sir Balin shuddered and crossed himself, doubting the werewolf's tale no more.

"Collocaulus was in command of our lot," said Marrok. "I remembered him from King Uther's day. One of Osla's lieutenants. Sir Balin slew him."

He looked at Balin with admiration, but Balin would not meet his gaze, afraid he would see a beast's eyes in Marrok's face. He pitied the man his curse. It was an evil fate to consider.

"We must ride and relieve them at the east passage," Balin said hastily.

They wasted no time in mounting and riding hard for the eastern postern, which was a secret way that opened up into a toolshed off the central keep and was intended for the nobility of the city to make their escape.

When they arrived, they found the shed sundered into splinters and the secret postern door exposed.

Sir Tor sat at the edge of it with Sir Guy in his arms, and Sir Agravaine pulled the broken helm from Sir Purades, revealing his bloody face.

Sir Tor looked up with tears in his eyes.

"Sir Guy de Cameliard is dead," he announced sadly.

Sir Guy lay as if sleeping. His armor was much dented and bloodstained, and there was a great rend in the steel from which a tide of blood still leaked.

"He slew that traitor, Sir Bertholai, down in the passage before he fell," said Sir Purades.

Geraint got down and fell to his knees beside the dead knight.

"He was my uncle's son," Geraint said, stroking his face with one gauntlet.

"There will be time for grief later if we live," said Balin. "How fares the east passage?"

"We fought men of Snowdonia," said Agravaine. "We accounted for half their number, then they retreated at a command and surrendered the passage."

They heard Saxon signal horns bellowing from the field then, and the whistle of a storm of arrows, followed by a tremendous crash.

"That sounds like the front gate," Sir Purades said.

Balin bit his lip and looked to Brulen.

Brulen read his thought and pointed out a nearby wagon yard.

Balin nodded.

"We have to reinforce the gate," he said. "Those wagons over there can be used to block off this entry entirely if we knock the wheels off."

"I will stay and do it," said Sir Purades, wiping the blood from his eyes.

"As will I," said Sir Tor, gently pushing the corpse of Sir Guy into Geraint's arms.

Marrok limped up, took quick stock of what was needed, and spoke, "I'd be no good in another fight. I'll stay."

"Sir Geraint?" Balin pressed.

The knight of Cameliard looked up absently, as if he didn't know where he was.

"Geraint!"

Geraint blinked and nodded, laying Guy down on the stones.

"I'll go with you."

"When the work is finished, guard the Princess Guinevere," Balin said to the others, wheeling his horse about.

Agravaine and Geraint mounted, and the six of them rode for the gates. Balin looked once over his shoulder and saw Sir Marrok raise his bloody hand in farewell.

DEAD DEFENDERS WERE draped over the wall of Cameliard as their dwindling fellows launched arrows down on the besieging army. As Balin and his coterie rode up, they saw a Saxon climbing over the edge of a battlement as he topped a besieging ladder. A badly wounded Cameliard man, bristling with arrows like a porcupine, rose slowly, ran straight at the Saxon assailant and tackled him. They heard the howls of every man on the ladder as it fell backward, even above the din and clash and the singing of feather shafts.

Balin was surprised to see Arthur's knights mounted and waiting in an orderly line before the gate, whose iron and thick oak were splitting apart. Squires ran up and down the column passing up lances and shields.

Arthur was astride his horse Hengroen, trotting magnificently up and down the line, shouting encouragements as he had at Bedegraine, his helm in his hand.

Sir Lamorak recognized his brother Aglovale at the back of the line and rode up to him, Balin and the rest falling in behind.

"What goes on here?" Lamorak asked.

"The gate is failing," Aglovale said. "We are lost!"

Balin looked to Brulen as Arthur rode up to them.

"Sir Balin!" he exclaimed at the sight of him. "What are you doing here?"

Balin had completely forgotten he had lost his helmet in the sewer.

"My lord, Sir Balin and his brother have faithfully defended Cameliard this day," Gaheris interjected.

"I will swear to that," said Sir Geraint.

Arthur looked from his nephew to the cousin of his future queen, if ever he would live to see the day of their wedding. Then his eyes settled on Balin. His face was strained, eyes bloodshot. A Saxon arrow had pierced his besagew and hung there unnoticed, like some bit of decoration.

"You were the Sir Ballantyne I ordered to guard the hidden ways," Arthur said, his voice hoarse. "How do they fare?"

"They attacked from all avenues, sire," said Balin. "We repulsed them all. The south passage is aflame and the sewer infiltrators were killed to a man."

"What of the east tunnel?" Arthur asked with some sense of urgency.

"The Snowdonians were driven back. Sir Guy de Cameliard fell in battle with the traitor Sir Bertholai The Red, who was also slain. I left three knights to block the way."

Arthur sighed in heavy relief and closed his eyes, muttering a prayer of thanks. Balin realized that Arthur was not defending only his ally, nor even his kingdom from Rience, but his love as well. The east passage was closest to the keep, where Princess Guinevere and the other ladies were secured.

"Sir Landens is wounded but guards the Princess Guinevere," Balin added, "and I instructed the others to join him when they finished their work."

Arthur's eyes opened.

"Yet her cousin Sir Guy is slain," Arthur said.

The gate shook and crackled again with another impact that sent rivets and splinters tinkling to the ground.

Arthur snapped out of his melancholy and gritted his teeth at the sight of the gate. "The gate fails," he said, donning his helm.

He stood in his stirrups and shouted over the heads of the knights. "The men of Cameliard on the wall are faltering! The city cannot hold! But I will not die shut up in a trap like a rat! When the last blow sunders the door, I will ride straight into the enemy host and cut my way to Rience himself, if God will grant me that!"

The knights raised their shields and hollered their approval.

He turned and looked at Balin, then reached forward and clapped his pauldron soundly with his gauntlet.

"You are supposed to be the best knight in the world," said Arthur. "Ride with me now, Sir Balin. I would have the Adventurous Sword at my side. Perhaps it and Excalibur can carve a clean path through the waves to our foe before they fall back upon us."

Balin's heart swelled so great he thought it would burst his cuirass. He clasped his king's hand and his only answer was a joyful sob that burst unbidden from his lips as he bowed his head in assent.

Arthur closed his helm, took his dragon shield from his squire, and fitted his lance into its rest.

Another did the same for Balin, and they took their places at the head of the knights with Bedivere, Kay, and Gawaine.

The door shivered. Bearded faces peered through the splits in the heavy wood. At the sight of the gathered knights, the eyes widened and they retreated fearfully, shouting a warning to their fellows.

Arthur raised his lance and bellowed, loud enough to be heard by all his men, "Now! By the powers that made you!" To the beleaguered guards manning the gates, he shouted, "Throw the bar!"

Balin was exhausted from the hard fight through the sewers. Every steel encased limb felt encumbered by lead even atop that. But he couched his lance and raised his bare charge, and prayed to God to cross swords with a king once more before he died.

The shattered timber need hardly be lifted from the gate. It fell to pieces when the guards laid hands on it and the horde beyond, throwing the weight of their makeshift ram upon it, tumbled in like eavesdroppers surprised at a chamber door.

Those that had tried to warn the others scrambled to get away, their alarms lost in the confusion and exultation.

Arthur, Kay, Balin, Gawaine, and Bedivere kicked their horses and charged, and all the fighting pride of Camelot and Pendragon thundered behind them.

CHAPTER
TWENTY-FOUR

L ANCES PIERCED STEEL and muscle, lifting men screaming into the air. Others exploded with lightning cracks, pounding metal and pulverizing the bone beneath it. Limbs flailed wildly and without reason as evicted souls departed their broken, bloody cases.

The great ram and the wet hide canopy above it collapsed as the besiegers suddenly found themselves besieged.

In the initial tangle of retreat from the hammer charge, men died, bones snapping beneath iron shod hooves or the heavy boots of their own fleeing warriors. In the wake of the great push, the squires swarmed over the groaning wounded, dealing death as quick as the flicking tongues of adders with dagger edge and spear point.

A hundred and forty knights smashed into the numerically superior Saxons, and for one storied, effervescent moment, successfully drove them back. But behind them waited the dream crushing armored cavalry of Orkney and Norgales, and the hard knights of Snowdonia, led by Sir Segurant The Brown, two thousand strong.

These spread into a steel shield and thundered across the plain to catch the rebounding Saxon footmen and check Arthur's spear point.

The forward knights of Camelot and Cameliard had lost their

lances, and so those in the rear that had kept theirs intact, doubled their speed to take the front. Arthur, Kay, Bedivere, Balin, and Gawaine fell back and drew their swords.

Balin saw Geraint, Agravaine, and Gaheris fly past, leveling their lances as they went. He looked for Brulen, but did not see his brother.

Lance point met shield and plackart and helm as it had in hundreds of bright tournaments on the sunlit tiltyard before Camelot. But this was no war play now for token or gamble, and knights crashed to the ground with a tremulous cacophony of sound, some never to rise again. Horses screamed, pierced or broken legged, and flopped about the bloody field, rolling over their masters.

The superior force of Segurant caught and crushed the charge, then enclosed them like a fist, riding in with chopping swords and swishing flails to rake and batter those that had fallen and struggled to rise.

Excalibur and the Adventurous Sword rang out and struck alongside each other as they had only once before in forgotten times, until the melee became a writhing knot of steel clad riders and unhorsed fighters. Balin and Arthur were separated like leaves in a storm swift eddy. Balin blessed this turn. Every moment he spent at Arthur's side, he feared the sword in his own hand.

There was no easy gauging the battle now. It took effort for Balin to remain in the saddle of Ironprow. At every turn the enemy came, faceless juggernauts of iron and steel, tarnished and bright, bloody and spotless, of every fashion, pauldrons heavy and winged, helms flowing bright plumes or flapping with silken ribbons, arms tied with soft remembrances of women who would grieve them before the sun set. Balin's sword and shield met axe and mace, morning star and greatsword, until finally the latter caved and broke apart.

Then, Balin let slip his ruined shield and drew his second sword, or rather his first, the trusty weapon with which he had trained and been dubbed so long ago. He lay about him as he had at the crossroads, no longer giving any though to defense, merely turning and cutting, stabbing and slashing, casting himself heedless into the unending fray. He locked his knees and let the reins fly wild. Ironprow understood somehow, and wheeled and jumped, switching its master's facing constantly, as if the worthy animal knew that the heavy, roaring thing on its back would meet and end every impending threat to its own sweaty hide.

A ring of armor began to form around Balin's pitching mount as more and more Snowdonians took note of the wild enemy fighter in their midst and rushed forth to seize his life for their glory, meeting instead their own inglorious endings. Men swore vengeance at their fallen fellows and then swiftly joined them. Others lay whimpering final prayers as fresh dead came slamming down atop them, the foundation and brick of a wall of dead, with blood and viscera the mortar.

For an instant, Balin found respite, like a summoner safe inside his warding circle of steel-clad corpses. His swords had built a makeshift berm which destriers and coursers, and even the most battle hardened chargers balked to leap, fearing either the heavy scent of death or rolling eyes at the sight of the devil horse and its demon rider waiting on the other side like a consuming fire. New attackers dismounted to clamber clumsily over the dead and get at him.

Balin saw beyond the clash of arms where the remainder of the spirit-broken Saxons, still thousands strong, milled anxiously, watching the fight, eager and yet fearing to join. They had not yet flowed through the broken gate of Carhaix, though. A group of Saxon chiefs and their mounted bodyguard hovered near the entrance, preventing their subordinates from looting.

No doubt as part of their pact with Rience, the city was being held for him to claim.

Balin looked across the field then and spied the King of Snowdonia and Norgales himself, tall in his saddle, freshly armed and in his beard-trimmed cape. He was behind a line of archers and footmen which seemed innumerable to a lone knight in the midst of his last stand. All his commanders were there with him too. There was the wraith-like King Lot beside him, and the bright blonde Osla Big Knife, all calmly watching their utter destruction from afar.

And behind them, empty grass, and that lone island of old trees.

Then above the ring of steel and the screams of men, a familiar voice called to him, "What is your name, knight?"

Balin looked down from Ironprow and saw a powerful, lone knight with a white beard and cruelly spiked pauldrons, bearing a bloody greatsword. He had cast off his bassinet and great helm. The knight stood insolently on the pile of corpses Balin had made. Though he was of their number, they were not his peers, and were but a footstool to his own purpose.

Sir Segurant The Brown. The greatest knight of King Uther's Round Table of old.

"Sir Balin of Northumberland," Balin called down.

No one else was coming in to fight him now. Segurant had claimed him.

"I am Sir Segurant The Brown. Step down into this arena you've made for us, Sir Balin," he said, descending nimbly down the bloody limbs like a stair until he stood underneath the snorting muzzle of Ironprow.

Balin breathed heavy. His arms were trembling, hanging at his sides. Having given them a brief rest to observe the enemy, they had failed him now, perhaps thinking the fight was over.

But he could not let the challenge go by. Segurant may have been a great man once, but he was a servant of the Devil now, and his haughty pride was loathsome to behold.

"God grant me strength," Balin muttered and leaned forward to kiss the mane of Ironprow before sliding out of his saddle to light upon the ground.

He had barely discharged his faithful mount with a light slap on the rump when Segurant was upon him, the huge sword falling toward his exposed head.

Perhaps the danger spurred his overtaxed muscles to one last effort. He raised his arms and crossed blades to catch that splitting blow.

Then he turned, the scrape of his swords sliding off Segurant's blade was a harsh whisper which became a whistle of wind as he swung for the older knight's neck.

But the heavy sword spun expertly and batted the double strike aside. The heavy pommel of the weapon lurched forward and struck Balin in the ear, and he reeled back, head ringing, barely dodging the stabbing point.

Both combatants had dealt much death this day, and perhaps had they met each other fresh, the duel would have been swifter, more impressive. As it was, technique hid its face from naked aggression as understanding dawned in the minds of both men.

Early into the fight, Balin knew Segurant's reputations was no idle boast, no minstrel's fabrication. He surely faced the greatest knight of yesterday. But would the maiden's prophecy bear out? Would the Adventurous Sword make him the greatest knight of this day?

Rience, Arthur, the Saxons, Carhaix, though a hundred and more such dramas as their own were even now playing out in the bloody show of war all around them, there was nothing in that circle of bodies but Balin versus Segurant.

SEGURANT HAD SLAIN real dragons and giants in his day, but this young knight's death eluded him with every last instant parry and preternatural duck and spin. The veritable boy before him knew. He instinctively *knew*, as only one natural born to the martial path knew. He knew which blows to allow through his defense, which would merely dent his harness, and which would kill or maim. He knew when to lunge for all he was worth and when to feint and hope for an opening to exploit.

He knew as Segurant himself knew, and so not a blow was landed that drew blood, for the one that did would be a killing blow.

He wept to know he would have to kill this fine knight.

BALIN HAD NEVER met a fiercer opponent.

The old knight had the strength of a bear and the swiftness of an arrow flying, which should have been impossible with so heavy a weapon. Segurant used the massive blade unconventionally, more like a quarterstaff at times, hand flying up from the long handle to brace the blade against Balin's attacks, then sliding back down to grip the pommel and put a bull's might behind his riposte.

This was the sword Wyrmspit, with which Segurant had laid dragons low in the old days. There was no magic to the ugly two-hander but what its wielder brought to it, and yet it was more than a match for Balin's Adventurous Sword. Perhaps the hot blood of dragons had tempered the steel somehow. Balin had broken steel, yet whenever Wyrmspit met the Adventurous Sword, there was a flash of hot sparks as from a smith's hammer.

His own knight's sword trembled to meet that elder weapon. Balin could almost feel the steel crying in pain deep in his fist with every savage kiss of Wyrmspit, threatening to shiver at the hilt.

He released his grip on the sword as a whim, and Segurant, suddenly meeting an utter lack of resistance, overstepped ever so slightly.

It was enough. Balin closed, his gauntlet beating down in quick succession Segurant's wrist, pushing Wyrmspit low, too low to ward against the point of the Adventurous Sword, which punched through his bevor with a screech of tearing steel.

Segurant's momentum carried him further down the shining blade, until the tip burst from the back of his thick neck and he fell against Balin, dropping his sword and embracing him in the last.

Balin groaned with his weight.

Segurant stared up at him, eyes bulging, pouring tears. He opened his mouth, perhaps to speak some valediction, but blood was all that came out, staining his snow white beard like the gory trail of some stricken winter prey.

Balin let Segurant fall, his weight pulling the Adventurous Sword free, and tearing most of his head from his neck.

He stared down at the body in amazement for a moment, as realization dawned on him that truly, he was now the best knight in the world.

Somewhere a Saxon horn sounded.

He plunged its point into the ground and looked around wearily for his next challenge.

CHAPTER
TWENTY-FIVE

BEYOND ALL HOPE, a hundred of the knights of Camelot and Arthur still stood or rode.

The field was littered with dead knights, the victors in some cases entwined with the defeated.

As Balin reclaimed his other sword and pushed the short wall of dead down to stumble through, he saw the Snowdonian and Norgales knights, still greater in number, had formed a perimeter around the survivors of Arthur's charge, watching alongside the Saxons with wary uncertainty.

Many of them had died. So many that the commanders had blown the signal to disengage.

Balin staggered forward, dragging his swords in the bloody earth.

Bedivere stood, and the Orkney knights, Kay still on his horse next to Arthur atop the blood spattered Hengroen as always, Griflet, Geraint, and others. All were battered, cut, and bloodied. All spent past their limits.

Balin looked about for Ironprow, but did not see him, and nearly tripped over the body of a knight whose face he had seen at the banquet in Camelot, but whose name he didn't know.

Someone caught him.

It was Brulen. His helmet was gone, and blood ran from a cut at his hairline, as well as from the wound in his arm, opened anew and now hanging limp at his side.

Balin smiled, but could summon no words.

Brulen smiled back and they touched foreheads, glad to have met each other on the field of slaughter one last time.

RIENCE HAD SEEN enough of his men die, or perhaps he had taken the fall of Segurant as an ill omen. He had ordered his men back, and now the Saxon archers were raising their bows and crouching in unison.

A chief rode back and forth behind them, urging their aim be true, preparing them to let fly.

Balin let his swords drop from his tired hands and threw his arms about his brother. He wished they could be free of their armor, to feel their hearts beat one against the other before steel pierced them.

"Forgive me, Brulen, forgive me," Balin bawled into his brother's ear.

"Forgive *me*, brother," was Brulen's sobbing answer.

Then there was a commotion from far off where the archers stood.

Balin glanced over and saw the captain of archers fall quietly from his saddle, their execution order dead with his last breath.

Panic and chaos erupted among the Saxon bowmen. Arrows. Arrows were falling into their midst from the sky. But how? There weren't that many archers left on the wall of Carhaix, and they were well out of range of the city at any rate.

These arrows came stinging from behind.

But there was nothing behind the archers but their own footmen and King Rience. And nothing behind them but bare field and that small copse of trees.

And then, something stirred that bunch of trees. Something that was not the wind.

A wild, black clad figure atop a piebald horse, bearing a staff. He paused, turned, and raised his arm as if gesturing for someone to follow.

A COLUMN OF charging cavalry, under a flapping black banner burst from the stand of trees.

On the banner: *Sable, a lion passant, Or.* The gold lion banner of King Leodegrance.

Balin watched open mouthed as the silver column of warriors grew like a snake emerging from its hole. It was impossible that those men had been hiding there. There were dozens of men. There was not enough area to hold them all.

"It's a miracle!" Balin remarked.

"Not quite," Brulen chuckled wearily. "Merlin."

And then, to compound the impossibility, two more lines of knights came flying from the left and right of the copse, both bearing glorious standards.

Azure, a lion rampant or, armed and langued, gules.

The golden lion, red clawed and red tongued, of King Uriens.

And on the other side: *Or, semy of plain crosslets, azure.*

The blue field of gold crosses. The emblem of King Pellinore.

It was as if the copse had dammed some silver river and suddenly burst, spilling three coursing streams out onto the land.

As Leodegrance's army bore straight for King Rience's back, and he and his immediate men turned to face them, the armies of King Uriens and King Pellinore flanked the terrified Saxons.

Merlin remained behind, the knights coursing around him. Finally, a line of archers marched out, raised their bows, and arced another volley into the air which rained down on the enemy, just before Leodegrance's knights smashed into their midst.

"Horses, if you have them!" Arthur roared from his saddle, wheeling the shimmering Excalibur above his head. "If you hear me, you are not dead men yet!"

Balin and Brulen both heaved a cry that was taken up by the other survivors of Camelot and Cameliard. They were not alone.

The surge of spirit made the enemy ringing them quiver. They gave ground, uncertain whether to turn and meet the new threat or dispatch the ones at their mercy.

Then Arthur's men charged in all directions, on foot, on horse, renewing the attack, their half-dead bodies invigorated by what some of them called magic, and others said was the Holy Spirit.

Balin and Brulen rushed into the thick of the enemy and pulled a pair of bewildered Snowdonian knights from their saddles, seizing their destriers for themselves.

They rode hard, splitting the host of Saxons and knights with unrelenting violence, their swords knocking heads spinning from their shoulders and leaving the dead sprawling in their wake.

THEY RODE DIRECTLY for King Rience and the commanders.

A wild arrow shot up and skinned Balin's chin, but then they crashed into the thick of the retreating bowmen, cutting their bowstrings, cleaving their sallets.

When they burst side by side through the contingent of archers to the bodyguard, they found the knights of Pellinore engaged, and The King of the Isles himself fighting the lanky King Lot horse to horse. Balin had not seen Lot since the courtyard of St. Paul's, when he had renounced Arthur. His face was shorn clean, the black beard gone to Rience, no doubt.

Balin grinned savagely to see Rience, Lot, and Osla Big Knife grimacing in awe at the sudden ill turn of their assured victory.

Balin spurred his horse for Rience, shouting the king's name, but a horse came up fast alongside him, and its rider cried out, "No, Sir Balin! He's mine!"

It was Arthur, bent low over Hengroen, snarling as he swiftly cut across the nose of Balin's horse and rode straight at the tall king.

Rience saw him and turned to meet him, readying Marmyadose.

Balin watched the two monarchs clash, saw the blinding flash of their enchanted blades, and then saw King Lot deal Pellinore a blow that knocked him clean from his horse.

Balin kicked his destrier and collided with Lot, sending them both crashing down in a tangle.

They rolled back and forth, wrestling for dominance, until Balin got hold of his sword again and struck his face with the crossguard, laying Lot out.

All of Lot's bodyguards were engaged or fleeing. Balin sat, panting, his sword point to the pagan king's throat. The battle was crumbling to a chaotic rout all around them.

"Yield," he demanded.

"*Yield*?" Lot gasped, laying spread-eagled and staring up at the blue sky. "Tell me your name, sir knight."

"Balin of Northumberland."

Lot chuckled tiredly.

"I was about to appeal to your sacred duty to your rightful king, but it *would* have to be a knight of that craven oaf Clarivaunce that conquered me at last. Perhaps even that murderer Arthur is a better lord than him. How very far the apple fell from the tree of Detors."

"Why do you call King Arthur murderer? He will grant you leniency if you but surrender. Anguish and Uriens swore fealty, and they still rule their lands, as do Leodegrance and Pellinore. And I am told you are a good king."

"Who told you that?" Lot asked sharply.

"My own brother, Brulen, who served you. And I have served alongside your sons, Agravaine and Gaheris."

"My sons." Lot spat.

"You think them traitors?"

"No," he sighed. "They follow their hearts, and know not the source of their father's enmity toward their uncle."

Balin leaned forward.

"What *is* its source?" he ventured.

Lot looked into his eyes, then over his shoulder as a shadow fell over them both.

"Good day to you, King Pellinore," said Lot in a flat and unwelcoming tone.

Balin looked up and saw the tall, faceless king in his glorious, cross-emblazoned great helm and gold-chaised armor, a scarlet, ermine-trimmed cape over his shoulders. Beside him stood his son Lamorak, his sword naked in his hands.

"Stand aside, sir knight," came Pellinore's muffled voice.

"Do as he says, Balin," said Lamorak. "It's proper that we take charge of the king of the Orkneys."

Balin stood slowly, nodding. He supposed a king must surrender to a king to save face.

Lot's gauntlet shot up and caught Balin's wrist, pulling him down with considerable strength until his ringing ear, bleeding from the blow Segurant had dealt him, was near to Lot's lips.

"Sir Balin," he said hastily, his voice strained and urgent. "In St. Stephen's, where they will bury me, there hangs a certain painting of a serpent. Number its clutch and count the rebel kings. Then you will learn the High King's secret shame."

Balin frowned at Lot, puzzled.

"Bury you? Are you badly hurt, sire?"

Balin could see no serious wound on him.

Lamorak pried Lot's hands from around Balin's wrist and parted them.

Balin straightened.

"Unhand me, Lamorak!" he snapped, not liking the rough way the son of Pellinore had forced him.

"Go your own way, Sir Balin, and peace to you," said Lamorak, holding up his hands. "Only let my father and I deal with King Lot."

"I never said I would not," Balin began, but then movement caught his eye, and he saw his brother Brulen only a few feet away, engaged in combat with a Saxon captain wielding a two-handed axe.

He spared a hard look at Lamorak, then hurried to aid Brulen.

By the time he reached his brother, however, the Saxon had been dispatched. Brulen leaned exhausted on the pommel of his sword, still sticking in the axeman's belly.

"The Knight with The Two Swords," Brulen chuckled. "You still live."

Balin sheathed one of his swords and put his hand on Brulen's shoulder, past exhaustion himself.

"I may yet collapse in this field and sleep."

"I will sleep beside you, brother," Brulen said. "Is this over yet?"

Balin turned and looked about.

The clash of arms was noticeably lessened. The combined force of Uriens, Pellinore, and Leodegrance were more than a match for Rience, Lot, and their Saxons. He saw hundreds of the latter throwing down their swords and shields, axes and bows, and being directed to sit like scolded children amid a guard of knights.

Then a long, unmistakable howl rang out over the field.

Balin's heart stopped as he saw a dozen Saxons stealing unnoticed through the broken gates.

He pointed them out to Brulen.

"Bent on murder-revenge, or stealing what they can before they sneak away," Brulen muttered.

"Princess Guinevere is still inside," Balin whispered.

Brulen looked about for a horse and spied Ironprow himself, grazing nearby.

"Isn't that your horse?"

THE TWO OF them tore at their armor, flinging down their gauntlets and kicking off their greaves, shedding steel and harness until they were stripped to their doublets.

Balin whistled as he approached the horse, for fear it would bolt, but it looked up at him and trotted over like a faithful hound.

"One more task, my friend," he whispered, then pulled himself up into the saddle and reached out to Brulen.

Brulen swung on behind and gripped his waist. They tore across the field at speed for the city.

IT SEEMED AN eternity before they reached the ruined gates, and still he spurred Ironprow cruelly on, the sight of the dead Carhaix watchmen lying within gnawing at his heart.

The brothers galloped through the empty city, not stopping the winded, heaving horse until they were at the keep.

The eastern postern was blocked by heavy carts.

They rushed to the stair and found the door to the keep broken off its hinges, the doorway glutted with bodies, but they breathed relief when they appeared to be uniformly Saxon.

Balin saw Purades and Tor then, and in front of them all, standing proud with her bloodied spear, Guinevere in her hauberk, her cross dangling outside. At her side, the gray wolf that was Sir Marrok panted, his muzzle dripping fresh blood.

Balin and Brulen both fell to their hands and knees in prostrate exhaustion.

"Bring water!" Guinevere called to the women behind her and exchanged her weapon for a bulging skin.

She genuflected between them and gave them cool drink, first Balin, then Brulen.

"How goes the battle?" she asked, when they'd drunk and thanked her.

"My lady!" called a familiar voice from down in the street.

Balin looked to see Arthur, leaning in Hengroen's saddle, smiling through grit and blood up at her.

"King Rience's own beard will complete the trim of his mantle now," said Arthur.

Guinevere went between Balin and Brulen and came down the keep steps, going gingerly over the dead Saxons, then running when the way was clear.

Arthur got down from his horse and the two embraced, even pressing lips hard to each other in a decidedly uncouth display that made Balin blush and Brulen smile thinly.

Balin looked away and saw a familiar pied raven preening itself on a barrelhead near the blocked entry to the escape tunnel.

Merlin!

Clattering up the street came King Leodegrance, King Pellinore, King Uriens, and several knights. Sir Gawaine, Balin noticed, had the great sword of Rience, Marmyadose, across his saddle.

"My daughter is safe?" Leodegrance demanded in his booming voice, before he saw the princess in Arthur's arms and broke into a winning grin.

"Leodegrance!" Arthur called, in high spirits. "By what miracle do you come? We thought you detained at Daneblaise in the north! And you, Pellinore. What of Chief Cheldric?"

"Cheldric's boats were swallowed in a sea storm," said Merlin, who was now sitting on the barrel where the raven had been.

"And Uriens rode out of the woods outside Daneblaise and trounced Baldulf. Then Merlin bid us ride back into the forest, saying you had need of us," said Leodegrance. "When we emerged, it was here."

"The same wizardry brought us," said Pellinore.

"I am glad I didn't listen to old Cleodalis and institute more civic improvements. That stand of old trees would have been felled at the beginning of the year." Leodegrance laughed heartily.

Arthur parted from Guinevere long enough to clasp Merlin's shoulder. The display made the wizard look uncomfortable.

"Thank you, Merlin," Arthur said.

"You are not entirely out of the woods, as it were," said Merlin, disengaging Arthur's hand. "Osla Big Knife is neither among the prisoners nor the dead."

"Yet all his lieutenants are accounted for," said Uriens, "and his army is gone."

"He will sail for home and return with another, be assured," Merlin said.

"That will wait for another day," said Arthur, returning to Guinevere's arms. "The rebellion at least is over."

"Peace!" Pellinore trumpeted, raising his fists, and the men cheered.

"Let the people know!" Leodegrance called to the serving women peering anxiously from the doorway of the keep. "Our city is safe. And when the dead are buried, and the blood scoured from the streets, when the last remnant of the war is cleansed, then I shall bring my daughter to Camelot, with the Round Table of Uther."

More cheering.

The children came streaming down the steps of the keep, waving kerchiefs and twigs and whatever they could lay their hands on to dance around Arthur and Guinevere. Balin's aching smile slipped as he saw Brulen inching away alone, his countenance dark and heavy.

Balin pushed his way through the crowd, past the kings, who were now passing a flagon of red wine between them and past the knights and soldiers who were raucously clashing each other's armor and singing conflicting songs.

He finally caught up with Brulen at the smashed gates, leaning against a pillar away from the noise and press.

"Where are you going, Brulen?" he called, when he reached him.

"Truly, I know not, my brother," said Brulen. Balin could see something in the lines of his brother's face, as though they had been scored deeper by some great troubling thing.

"Won't you stay? Return with me to Camelot and await the coming of the Table. Do you remember the tales of the wondrous sieges Claellus used to tell us?"

"I remember," Brulen said, smiling faintly, "and I'm sure your name will be there in gold."

"Maybe yours too," Balin said hopefully. And why not? What other knight approached him in skill, if he was the greatest?

"I will not sit at any table of Arthur's," Brulen said, looking off into the distance.

"*Why?*" Balin insisted, striking Brulen's chest with the back of his fist. "Will you not tell me the ill you perceive in him?"

Brulen's face hardened, and he pointed.

"Look for yourself, brother," he said through his teeth. "Look as I told you and *mark it.*"

Balin looked.

The prisoners were being escorted into Carhaix now, hemmed by guards.

Rience was driven first in clinking chains, stripped of his beard-trimmed mantle and armor, his empty scabbard at his side an inglorious reminder of his defeat. He hung his head and met no man's eye as he passed.

Behind him, his defeated warriors bore their dead leaders on makeshift biers of shields and crossed spear-hafts. The Saxons held aloft their slain chiefs, and Balin saw Sir Segurant's body carried on the shoulders of the Snowdonian knights, his own solemn head resting upon his breastplate, hands over his ears as though to shut out the cheers of the victorious.

Behind him came the soldiers of Orkney. Alone among all the other prisoners, they wept and wailed with unseemly abandon. There were not enough knights left to bear their burden, so common soldiers shared it alongside bleeding noblemen.

It was King Lot of Orkney, his face pale white, his arms crossed over his chest, like a martyred saint carried aloft by ecstatic adorants.

Balin crossed himself as the sorrowful procession passed. He was too stricken to say or do anything else.

When he turned to speak to Brulen, to demand some explanation, or perhaps to haltingly make one himself, his brother was gone.

His heart sank in his chest, but he pounded one mailed fist against the stone wall and resolved to find Pellinore and Lamorak and demand answers.

He had done no more than stomp around the corner, pushing through reveling commoners, when two armored men barred his way.

Gawaine and Gaheris stood before him, glowering, and their swords were drawn.

Balin took a step back, and a gauntlet reached from behind and clapped over his hand when he touched the pommel of his sword.

Agravaine leaned forward and hissed like a viper in his ear. "Draw, and die, you damned villain!"

"Why did you kill him, Balin?" Gawaine growled, as heedless of the celebrants capering around them as the peasants were of the barely controlled violence straining like chained hounds between the four knights. "Why did you kill our father?"

"I didn't," Balin said.

"Liar!" Gaheris yelled, trembling.

Gawaine angled his sword in front of his younger brother, to stay off bloodshed for the moment.

"Sir Lamorak said he saw our father offer up his sword to you, and you cut him down," said Gawaine.

Balin's fist clenched so hard at his side the steel of his gauntlet creaked.

"Lamorak is false." Balin growled. "He and King Pellinore came to me on the field when I bested Lot and demanded to take charge of him. I swear by all the saints and prophets…by my very soul…I left your father in good health."

Gawaine stared hard at him, and Gaheris looked to his elder brother as though awaiting the order to kill.

Balin eased his hand out from under Agravaine's and let it hang easy at his side.

"Take my swords," Balin said. "And let's go together to Pellinore and Lamorak. Let me prove my word."

Agravaine whisked Balin's sword free of its scabbard, but when he tried to jerk the Adventurous Sword loose, he found he could not draw it.

"You can't draw it. Permit me," said Balin.

He felt the prick of Agravaine's sword point at the side of his neck.

"Move wrong and I'll butcher you here," Agravaine promised.

Balin grasped the hilt in reverse and drew the magic sword easily. He dropped it in the street.

Gawaine lowered his sword and motioned for Agravaine to do the same.

Gaheris hesitated but let his own guard down.

"You don't believe him?" Agravaine exclaimed, aghast at his brother.

"Let us see what Pellinore says," said Gawaine. "And Lamorak."

He turned to go and Agravaine shoved Balin after.

Gaheris hesitated and stooped to retrieve the Adventurous Sword from the street.

"Leave it," said Balin. "It will be there when I return."

"*Return!*" Agravaine scoffed.

They stalked purposefully through the increasing crowd of revelers, until Geraint and Marrok came out of the press at them, tankards brimming and sloshing ale on the flags.

"Where are you going looking so serious?" Geraint slurred. "Come, let's find a barrel for you to lighten your expressions!"

"Where are Lamorak and Pellinore?" Gawaine demanded.

"Gone," said Marrok.

"Gone where?" Balin asked.

"Back to the Outer Isles," said Marrok.

"They're missing the party," Geraint said regretfully.

"When did they depart?" Gawaine asked.

"You can't catch them. Merlin's taken them through the woods by magic. Pellinore wanted to prepare his country's defenses in case Osla's ships should double back and think to take it undefended."

"Come and show us how pagans drink!" Geraint said, spilling some of his drink across Gawaine's feet.

Gawaine shoved him away into Marrok's arms, and Gaheris took his elder brother by the arms.

Marrok, sensing something wrong, drew the drunken Geraint away before he could regain his senses and escalate the situation to a brawl.

"Brothers," said Agravaine, from behind Balin. "Let us show these Christians how pagans fight."

"What purpose would that serve?" Gaheris snapped.

"Shut up, you little pup!" Agravaine barked back. "It's obvious they meant to kill father all along. Pellinore and Lamorak charged this assassin with slaying him, as he slew our Lady of The Lake."

"I didn't kill King Lot!" Balin insisted.

"You confess to killing the Lady!"

"I would not kill a man who surrendered to me," Balin argued.

"But you'd slay a defenseless woman? What sense does that make?" Agravaine chuckled ruefully.

Gawaine grasped his own head and turned in place, closing his eyes and thinking.

"Why would he charge Pellinore and Lamorak with the crime if he were under their orders?"

"To give himself an alibi, that we do not slay him for a villain!" Agravaine countered. "He knew they were returning to the Outer Isles and would not be here to defend themselves. This man is as much an enemy of Avalon as our dear father was its friend."

"I agree that Pellinore's departure was convenient, brother," said Gaheris. "But for Pellinore. That tyrant's dislike of Orkney is well known, and Lamorak has ever been the wolf in sheep's clothing their priests so rail against."

Gawaine opened his eyes and looked at Balin, coming to a decision.

"We should slay this murderer, Gawaine," Agravaine said.

"Let's take our case to Arthur," Gaheris pleaded.

Gawaine ignored them both.

"Take your swords, Balin," he said. "If ever it comes to light that you slew our father, you will have need of them."

"We're letting him go?" Agravaine exclaimed.

"We should at least take him before Arthur!" Gaheris said.

"So he may be locked away in a dungeon again?" Gawaine said. "If he is guilty, then I want him out in the world, where I can cross steel with him. Do as I say."

Balin nodded to Gawaine as Agravaine released him and held out his sword.

Gawaine only turned and pulled Gaheris along with him.

Balin took his sword, but Agravaine held it for a moment, glaring into his eyes, before he let it go.

"Even the best knight in the world falls eventually," said Agravaine.

He went off after his brothers.

Balin wondered again where Brulen had gone.

SECOND PART:

THE
DOLOROUS
STROKE

CHAPTER
ONE

THREE DAYS AFTER the siege of Carhaix, which became known as the Battle of The Copse, the long funeral procession of King Lot of Orkney arrived at Camelot, where his youngest sons, Gareth and Mordred, and his daughter, Soredamor, awaited with their mother, Queen Morgause. The old Queen of Norgales was there, too, and King Uriens' wife, Queen Morgan La Fey.

There was something in those three austere and aloof queens that made Balin shiver. Garbed in sable mourning clothes and faceless beneath night black veils, they stood arm in arm before the great Black Cross in front of St. Stephen The Protomartyr's, inscrutable in aspect and silent and still as ancient monoliths. Morgause was heavy with the last scion of Lot, and somehow the matronly swell of her belly made her all the more imposing and phantasmagorical, as though she were some dread progenitress of darkness, a malevolent and willful Pandora, or a mysterious Nyx, in whose womb God had somehow stuffed up the primordial denizens of antediluvian chaos. Why Balin had these ill feelings toward Lot's widow, he did not understand. She was one of King Arthur's half-sisters by the late Igraine of Tintagel. Family.

Of Arthur's other sister, Morgan La Fey, Balin knew very little, only rumors he had heard from Matthew and Safir during his imprisonment. He knew that she had been a student of the Merlin, and that she had left his tutelage for greater, deeper instruction from the Queen of Norgales.

The Queen of Norgales, it was said, had courted the Devil and King Rience for power and protection, respectively, after Sir Aglovale and the knights of Pellinore had slain her wicked husband, King Agrippe. Agrippe had been a vile persecutor of Christians, the worst since Agrestes. He had invaded the kingdom of Pellinore's brother, King Pellam of Lystenoyse, Matthew said, because the Devil himself had tasked him to do so for the promise of absolute rule over Albion. Safir had told Balin the Queen rivaled even the maidens of Avalon in knowledge of the magic arts, yet stood in opposition to them.

No one knew her given name. Matthew had said she'd hidden it from the world, so that no man, angel, or demon could have power over her.

But for all his dread of these three terrible queens, Balin felt only pity for Lot's orphaned daughter, Soredamor, a flush faced girl of thirteen, eyes red from crying, her red hair bound away in black barbette and black fillette like a young nun. Gareth, too, only fourteen, cried openly at the sight of his father's covered corpse, borne stoically by his elder brothers Gaheris, Gawaine, and Agravaine, as well as Arthur himself, and King Uriens. As for Mordred, he was no more than a pudgy babe clutching his mother's skirt and stuffing his own fist into his mouth. He would never know his own father.

All of Camelot turned out to mourn King Lot and see him entombed at St. Stephen's, even Archbishop Dubricius and all the clergyman of the countryside, for despite Lot's stolid paganism and rebelliousness, he was remembered unanimously as a goodly man.

Only King Pellinore and his sons were noticeably absent.

Balin knew well why.

He had trusted King Pellinore and Sir Lamorak as good standing Christians to do right by King Lot and had left the defeated man in their care as he would have left the Christ child in the arms of the immaculate Mary and gone in bliss.

Though Arthur's doubt in Balin had fled, no doubt in part due to Guinevere's soft words in his ear, the other knights were still hardened against him. The pagans could not forget his killing of the Lady Lile, and despite Gawaine's clemency, Agravaine perpetrated the story that he had treacherously slain Lot after securing his surrender. The Christians, too, seemed to believe this, likely at Lamorak's urging.

So, in the midst of the finest fellowship in the world, Balin, finally counted as one of their number, found himself alone. Not even Bedivere or Griflet had any words for him anymore.

Their armor had been repaired and polished to a bright gleam for the occasion of Lot's funeral, and they made a magnificent show. The Black Cross had been decked with white lilies by the clerics, and the white petals and emerald vines reflected in the mirrors of their harnesses so that each knight seemed to shine with supernatural light in the sun.

Arthur and the pallbearers stopped before the three black clad queens. Soredamor wailed and staggered toward her dead father with her arms outstretched, but her aunt Morgan caught her by the arm and drew her back.

Queen Morgause disengaged herself from her sister and the Queen of Norgales, and stepped forward quietly.

She lifted one hand and laid a white lily on her husband's breast, then, taking Gareth gently by the shoulder, turned and walked into the church. Morgan followed, consoling the distraught Soredamor. The toddler Mordred had sat down to play in the dust and began to wail as he was forgotten, but the Queen of Norgales hushed him and held out her hand. He got to his feet, snuffling, but in control of himself, and wrapped his hand around her middle finger.

The pallbearers turned the body and waited for the Queen of Norgales, but she took two steps back toward the cross behind her.

Her meaning was plain. She had come to pay her respects to Lot, but she would not, perhaps could not, set foot in the church.

Gareth released his hold on his father's body and crouched, opening his arms. Little Mordred smiled and scurried to him, giggling, his dark eyes wide and happy.

Arthur and Uriens bobbed their chins and they, Agravaine, and Gawaine bore the body of Lot in, Gareth setting his youngest brother on his shoulder and carrying him after.

The knights dismounted as a body and handed their reins to a line of squires. Then they shuffled into the church behind the corpse and its chief mourners.

As Balin passed the silent Queen of Norgales, he heard the squawking of crows and saw Merlin in his favorite form of the pied raven, Brych, disturb a murder of its black fellows into flapping exodus as he settled blasphemously on the left arm of the Black Cross above the Queen's head.

Something in the angle of the view of the pied raven struck Balin as familiar, and he went into the church troubled, trying to call to mind a long-forgotten picture in his memory. He suddenly wished Brulen were here beside him.

He was once again cross with his brother, resentful of the secrets he kept, and that he had not stayed by his side, nor even bid him farewell in the parting.

Brulen's assurance that Lot would not live through the battle had come back to him again and again since, as had Lot's own last words to him:

In St. Stephen's, where they will bury me...

How had they both been so sure?

But they both laid treachery at the feet of Arthur. Was not Pellinore to blame for Lot's cowardly execution? Or Lamorak?

He couldn't believe that Arthur had known anything about it. Surely there had been no secret edict calling for his demise.

What had Arthur to hide in Lot's death?

In St. Stephen's, where they will bury me, there hangs a certain painting of a serpent. Number its clutch and count the rebel kings. Then you will learn the High King's secret shame.

Balin steeled himself as he entered the archway of the church.

He passed into the marble atrium and followed the body of Lot as it was advanced down the center isle of the nave toward the crossing, where a bier adorned with blooming flowers waited.

From the chancel, the choir's voices rose like the praise of angels before the Throne and echoed high in the white dome above the transept intersection.

The Archbishop and his attending priests waited solemnly, majestic in his satin cape trimmed in ermine, tall in his miter.

As the pallbearers and family moved to the front, the knights began to split off into orderly rows. Balin found himself on the south end of the wide nave. He craned his neck to take in the opulent decorations of the altar. There was a richly finished rosewood cross with a carved Christ upon it. There were golden sconces and marble cherubs, and on the east wall behind the gleaming golden Tabernacle where the rising sun must blaze, a colossal depiction in stained glass of the radiantly haloed St. Stephen, all in white, holding aloft the bloody stones which had martyred him.

Yet wherever he looked, Balin saw no painting of a serpent.

The mass commenced, and Balin and the other congregants stood, and knelt, and responded. The pagans were easily marked. Like the grieving widow and children of Lot, they stood throughout the mass, unaware and uncaring of the observation of the ritual.

Arthur eulogized Lot, calling him a good king loyal to his own heart and cited his upstanding sons and daughter and the number of his mourners as proof against his damnation. Surely, Arthur argued, he was merely biding his justly allotted time in purgatory.

He then offered the congregation the opportunity to rise and speak of Lot if they were so acquainted.

Balin met Lot in the last moments of his life and had nothing to say about the man, though it seemed every other man and woman here did, and that the ceremony would go on for much longer than he had anticipated.

His bladder began to swell, and when even Sir Griflet deigned to rise and speak about the gallantry of the deceased he had observed from afar on the battlefield of Bedegraine two years ago, Balin took the opportunity to slip unnoticed from his place and go quietly out to the atrium, to gain the outside and perhaps the stand of trees behind the churchyard where he could relieve himself in private.

That was when he happened to glance up and see the vast fresco above the exit.

It was a strange thing to see decorating the house of God.

It was painted in a nightmarish style, inelegant and verging on blasphemy in its vivid and realistic depiction of a pale, naked male figure twisting, almost trussed like a sacrificial beast in his purple sheets, as an immense serpent coiled about his entire bed. The serpent's great and hideous green head reared over the waking sleeper, its jaws open, fangs dripping yellow tears of poison which appeared to burst into flame wherever they touched the coverlet. The sleeper had a sword poised like a phallus aright from his body, set to impale the serpent through its head when the deadly jaws closed and killed him. Alongside the bed, an empty scabbard draped across a table beside a tipped chalice, which spilled red wine across the floor like blood.

The body of the snake wound twice around the bed and then continued out the bedchamber window. At the window stood a black garbed servant, tipping what looked like a nest that had been constructed on the sill. A strangely familiar two-headed eagle was diving out of the sky, enraged, and on the wall outside the window, archers could be seen aiming for it. Where had he seen such a creature before? He couldn't place it. It had been an emblem on a banner. But whose?

From the nest four eggs were tumbling, down past the body of the serpent, to splash into the crashing, foaming ocean below. Some of the eggs were cracked, and from one, a small, pale arm reached out imploringly. The tail of the great serpent emerged from the fourth egg, which was greater than the rest.

Cavorting demons with grimacing, terrible faces bordered the bottom of the fresco, as though they lay beneath the moat and foundation, and across the top, sorrowful archangels with bright, multicolored wings looked down from the moon dappled clouds.

Balin breathed, his heart clenched in fear at the sight of that terrible work. Surely this was the painting Lot had described. And the figure in the bed, he resembled Arthur more than a little. But what did it mean?

He did not know how long he stood transfixed by the work, before a hand touched his shoulder, breaking its spell.

CHAPTER
TWO

AS THE BELLS tolled the commencement of Lot's funeral and the last of the mourners passed into the church, the Queen of Norgales spoke, seemingly to the empty air, "You can come out now, grandson, and speak to me, if you please."

"Don't call me that, harridan," said Merlin, stepping from behind the Black Cross. "We are not kin."

"What shall I call you then? Lailoken? Myrrdin Wilt?"

Merlin shook his head.

"You're fishing... *Optima*."

She laughed and turned to face him, the black of her gown swirling like ink in water, whispering across the stones as she approached.

"As are you. No, Merlin, you will have to do better than that. Your god may show you the future, but it's by the Devil that you knew the past. Your dear mentor, Blaise, estranged you from your true master in hell with his precious baptismal rite, and your rechristening cut you off from your true destiny. Now you are like an accursed horsefly, existing only in the moment, yet plagued by the knowledge of every future. Have you seen Camelot in ashes yet? Have you seen the skulls of those holy priests dashed once more against the Black Cross?"

"I have seen no future in which you win, *Joan Go-Too't*."

She wagged her finger as she passed him, walking casually into the churchyard.

"Try again."

Merlin frowned behind his tangled beard, and she paused and looked over her shoulder.

"No? Nothing more from your books?"

"*Mariana!*" Merlin blurted in frustration.

She shook her head and kept walking, forcing him to follow.

"I buried my true name deep well before I ever summoned the spirit that fathered you, Merlin."

It was true. Her true name and any power he might gain over her had thus far proved unattainable.

"Now tell me why you are here. Are you waiting for Morgan?" She giggled lightly. "She tells me a great deal about you."

"To hell with Morgan La Fey." Merlin spat. "I came to ask about Nimue."

"Who?"

"You know very well who she is."

"You mean the girl with the sword? Does she still have it?"

"You know she does not. Did you send her?"

The Queen of Norgales rested her hand on a weathered tombstone, the name rubbed away by years of rain and wind.

It was said that the spirits of the dead who lie in unmarked graves are restless, but what of one whose marker has been erased by time and the elements? Is their peace disturbed? Merlin wondered.

"Another of your little doves, Merlin? You do have something of your father in you after all."

Merlin stared at her, reading her, then sighed.

"You did not. I can tell when you're being enigmatic and when you don't really have your hand in something."

"Can you really? I *have* visited this Nimue. In dreams. I heard her crying in the night, and when she reached out for succor, when she turned in the witching hour to black arts to divine the cause of her sorrow, I followed the scent of her broken heart on the midnight wind and gave her the answer."

"*You* told her Arthur was responsible for her lover's death. You hid Balin from her."

She curtsied.

"But you did not send her," Merlin said thoughtfully.

"I gave her a nudge in the appropriate direction, the little starling," said the Queen.

"To have all this power..." Merlin mused.

"...except over one's only rival," the Queen finished. She leaned across the headstone and spoke in a hushed whisper, conspiratorial. "We could tell each other our names, Merlin. It's become wearisome, hasn't it? We could end this long, long game, tip the board, forgo the clumsy pawns for once."

She passed her wrinkled hand over the old grave.

In a few seconds, the dirt began to turn, and bony fingers strung with rotten sinew broke through the turf.

Merlin tapped the grave with the end of his staff. Immediately fresh green shoots sprang from the turned earth and grew over the weakly groping hand, the roots pulling it back down into the earth, until it was as though it had never been.

"What entertainment would our lives have then, your highness?"

She straightened and sighed.

"Until next time then, grandson," she said, and walked into the trees beyond the churchyard.

MERLIN WATCHED HER fade into the shade of the canopy, knew it was useless to follow her. She was his reason for being. She and King

Agrippe had called upon the darkest powers, forged the most damning pacts to beget on his mother, Adhan, a scion of hell to counterbalance the Christ. But blessed Blaise had taken a page from the Queen's own book and countered their plot, christened him by a new name at his birth, a name unknown even to Merlin, so that neither they nor any demon could have any power over the other. Blaise kept Merlin's name locked in his own heart. The holy man was ever his conscience.

Now Merlin and the Queen struck at each other through intermediaries. She, through rogue sorcerers and enchantresses like Morgan La Fey, he through his shaky alliance with Avalon, but more via myriad kings and their errant knights. She had foiled his plans for Uther with Igraine, but he had turned her victory into Arthur. She had very nearly defeated all his plans with Morgause.

And how he had foiled *that* plot. Had Blaise known, it would have broken his heart, maybe tempted the old man to bind and destroy him.

She would not best him through Nimue and Balin, though. He had taken steps already to insure she would not. As for Balin, the doom of the Siege Perilous awaited him. Now he must only find Nimue and turn her from her wrath with the truth, perhaps convince her to return to Avalon, for her dogged persistence made her almost unpredictable.

Merlin could not afford to allow Nimue's random, underhanded attacks at Arthur to go on. She was growing in power and could well fall to the wiles of the Queen, who would make her into more than a mere thorn in his side.

He turned and went to the church. Passing behind the Black Cross, when he gained the steps of St. Stephen's, he was no longer Merlin, but the image of Preudom, the old painter and bell ringer, who was even now dozing in the belltower. The old man had trained himself to awaken at the *Ite, missa est* and perform his duty, but would not awaken for some time yet.

Merlin passed into the shadows of the vestibule and waited. When

Balin stepped out of the church proper and examined the painting above the door, Merlin waited until he had taken it all in before putting his old, gnarled hand on the knight's shoulder.

THE OLD BELL ringer bid him outside and Balin walked into the churchyard.

He was a completely hairless fellow, a feature which made him somehow unseemly. He was old, but wiry, as the bulge of his shoulders through his mantle attested. There was a roll to one of his eyes.

"You like my painting, sir knight?"

"I do not think it belongs in a church," said Balin carefully, not wanting to offend.

The priest cackled.

"Nor do I! It was commissioned by the king himself, and he insisted on its placement in the vestibule. It is called *Somniamus Arturus*. The Dream of Arthur. He described it to me in great detail. Even pointed out the place he wanted it, right over the door where you saw it."

"But what does it mean?" Balin asked.

"I asked the very same of the King, and he said to me, 'Brother Preudom, let it stand as a reminder to all who leave this hallowed sanctuary, that the Devil coils like a serpent, even in a good man's shadow, ready to strike him when he is at his most vulnerable.'"

Balin chewed his lip.

"Is there any significance to the number of the eggs? Why does a child's hand reach out from one of them? And why is one egg a serpent's?"

Preudom grinned and held up his hands.

"I was only told what to paint, not the meaning behind every detail. It was a nightmare after all, and only a dreamer may truly understand the reason in his own dreams."

Balin thought of the black clad figure at the window, dumping the nest into the waters. It did remind him of someone in particular.

"Or a wizard," said Balin darkly. "Tell me, good Brother, where in Camelot can I find the enchanter, Merlin?"

"Ah," said Preudom. "The Cambion comes and goes, Sir Balin. When he comes, he comes there," said the bell ringer, pointing to the castle. "Where he goes, no man can say."

Balin went to find Ironprow.

MERLIN WATCHED HIM go through Preudom's eye, then flew ahead to the castle as the pied raven Balin had dubbed Brych.

Most of the servants were busy preparing Camelot for the wedding of Arthur and the Princess Guinevere, and the majority of the nobles were attending Lot's funeral. Merlin leapt down unnoticed from the open window and became a kitchen boy.

BALIN HAD TO lead Ironprow to the stables himself, and he wandered the deserted halls of Camelot for some time before he found a harried looking young serving boy whose collar he had to grab to stay him.

"Where are Merlin the wizard's chambers, boy?"

The boy looked flustered.

"Pardon, but I do not know, sir! I don't see much of the castle past the crocks and me own bed."

"Doesn't he take supper?"

The boy shook his head, eyes wide.

"Barnock says he sups on our swevens while we sleep," the boy whispered.

"He must frequent a certain part of the castle over others," Balin said.

"I have only ever seen him in the throne room and the dining hall. He never eats, but often counsels the king there." The boy sucked his lips thoughtfully. "Truly, come to think of it, I have never spied him anywhere else in the castle."

Balin released the boy and passed through the empty throne room to the dining hall, where he very nearly gasped at what he saw.

The long tables had been pulled from the center of the room and stacked against a wall, where they waited to be hauled out.

In their place, in the center of the room, was a vast oak table, round and surrounded by many baroque, high backed chairs, each with a gleaming golden plate set into the back.

Balin felt his knees tremble. All thought of the painting and Merlin washed from his mind as he approached the immense table. He could see the seams where it was disassembled for transport, and with one shaky hand, he reached out and stroked the grooves cut into it, old marks of utensils wielded by storied, mighty hands. In the pit of the deepest marks, he saw the gleam of the silver beneath the wood. The legends that this was the table of Joseph and his disciples were true.

Next, he turned his attention to the sieges with their red velvet cushions. There were more than a hundred. On the back of the one nearest him, the unblemished golden plate shimmered, and he was taken aback by the sight of his own name in a bold, regal script:

Sir Balin of Northumberland

"They change as warranted," said a familiar voice from across the room that made Balin start.

Sir Dagonet stepped out from an alcove, sloshing a goblet of wine. He went to one of the chairs and plopped down into it, lackadaisically throwing his boots up on the table.

"Try it. Look at that seat over there," he said, pointing with his goblet to a siege four places over.

Balin went to it and saw his name on the plate again. He squinted at the one next to it, saw it shimmer, and read his name. It was as though the plates bore no name at all until they were observed.

He laughed uncontrollably and ran like a boy around the table, watching his name appear on each chair as he passed it.

"They all change. Except that one," Dagonet said, pointing to another.

Balin stopped behind it. This one, the plate did not alter to show his name. It bore no inscription at all.

"What does it mean?" Balin whispered.

"Merlin brought the table with Leodegrance's knight, three days ago. He told me that was Joseph of Arimathea's chair and can only be filled by the holiest, most pure knight."

Balin's heart pulsed in his ears, and he touched the chair.

"Be careful, my friend." Dagonet hissed, standing. "He also told me that four knights in Uther's time tried to sit in it and were burned away by a column of heavenly fire."

Balin paused. But surely, he was the greatest knight. He had been told so at every turn. What had he to fear?

"I know what you're thinking," Dagonet said. "The sword said you were the greatest. But pay attention to the words. Are you the holiest? Are you the purest?"

Truly, Balin believed he had no guile that he was aware of, and the sins of other knights, the pettiness and the feuding, these were not in him. But was he correct?

He touched the hilt of the Adventurous Sword, and a flicker of doubt passed through him. Something held him back from claiming the seat.

What was it, this unmanly doubt?

Surely he felt no guilt at the beheading of the Lady of The Lake, which he had done the last time he'd set foot in this hall. He had murdered no innocent woman. He had destroyed a dangerous witch. A succubus. A servant of the Evil One.

No, it was not that.

The seat called for the purest knight, not the greatest.

Was he a pure man, indeed?

This sword.

Could he rightly say his claiming of this sword had been an act pure of intent?

He recalled again the words of the maiden who had borne it.

Keep it, and you shall be the greatest knight in Albion. But in the end, you will fight to the death with the man you hold most dear.

Arthur. There was still the promised doom of the king. He knew that if he did claim this seat, and sat here, eventually, it would mean the king's death at his hand.

Then why had he taken it?

For his own glory? To be the knight he had always wanted to be as a child? But what did that achievement have to do with serving the Lord's own king?

Now this very symbol of his merit was an impediment to his taking his rightful place at the Round Table.

He drew the sword, of a sudden impulse to fling it from him, and he caught sight of the beautiful blade once more, of the carvings on it.

There was the depiction of the Battle at The Crossroads. He realized it now. The two knights shown were himself and Brulen, attacking Rience.

Above it, there was a new engraving.

It was a double headed eagle, like the one he had seen in the painting in St. Stephen's vestibule, the one that had seemed so familiar to him at the time. A lion was devouring it.

The attitude of the lion was familiar too. It was the same lion on the pennant and shield of Pellinore and his sons, but he could not puzzle out what this meant.

And now, two more designs had appeared on the sword.

One, a circular wheel orbited by smaller circles, was undoubtedly the table before him. The Round Table.

The second made no sense. It was of two hearts, pierced by a single lance.

Dagonet stood beside him now.

"The sword tells your future, does it?" he asked. "Or is it your past?"

"What do you mean?" Balin stammered.

Dagonet pointed out the headless maiden.

"Here is the Lady of The Lake beheaded."

He pointed to the crossroads battle.

"And here is your battle with King Rience. Yes, I heard tell of it. Who hasn't? Good show."

"But what does this mean?" Balin asked, exasperated, pointing to the lion and the two-headed eagle.

"A lion devouring a two-headed eagle," Dagonet observed. "The lion is the symbol of King Pellinore or one of his sons."

It was customary for knights to bear on their own charges emblems inherited from their fathers. Pellinore and his sons all bore variations of the golden lion on their charges, just as he and Brulen had the red boars of their father on their own.

"And I've seen a double headed eagle on Sir Gawaine's shield," said Dagonet.

Gawaine. That was where he'd glimpsed it. On Gawaine's shield as he charged by him at Carhaix.

If Gawaine bore a double-headed eagle, then his father had too.

"Lot," said Balin quietly. "The double-headed eagle is The King of Orkney. I saw an eagle like this in a painting at St. Stephen's."

Dagonet looked sharply at him, his eyes, usually half-lidded and cynical, suddenly alight.

"Brother Preudom's painting," said Dagonet.

"Yes! What does it mean? The eagle…was attacking the king in his bedchamber? Attacking his castle?"

"No, he wasn't. Think harder, Balin."

"If you know…"

"It's not for me to know. It's for you to discover. Think."

Balin thought back to the painting.

"The eagle was…attacking the servant in black. Protecting its nest."

Dagonet nodded. "And?" he pressed.

"But the nest, had a serpent's egg in it."

"Yes!" said Dagonet.

"Lot told me, on the field at Carhaix, the last time I saw him. He told me to look at that painting. He told me to count the eggs. There were four."

"Yes, Balin," said Dagonet patiently, but still with a hint of excitement.

"He told me, if I counted the eggs and counted the number of rebel kings, I would know Arthur's secret shame. But there were eleven rebel kings. I don't understand. And why…?"

"There were eleven rebel kings, yes, Balin," said Dagonet. "How many were killed?"

He tried to think back to the day Segurant came to the court and proclaimed the defeat of the rebels at Rience's hand.

"There were three," he said at last. "The King With A Hundred Knights, the King of North Wales, and the King of Cornwall."

"And now the King of Orkney," Dagonet finished.

Four. Four eggs, four dead kings. But what did that mean? Were the eggs the kings? Which was the serpent? What did Merlin have to do with any of it? Why had Lot told him these things?

"Why is Arthur shamed?" Balin asked bluntly. "Tell me, if you know."

"I have sworn not to speak it, Balin," said Dagonet. "Even a fool keeps his word sometimes. Especially a fool knight."

"I didn't kill Lot," Balin said.

"I know," said Dagonet, with a look of sad empathy.

"It was Pellinore, or Lamorak."

"I expected that," said Dagonet. "Balin, my friend," he said, looking down at the Adventurous Sword and tapping it. "I wish you had taken your oath with my sword. Believe me, the sword of a fool is no great burden. But the sword of a hero…"

"What is happening, Dagonet? The painting. The serpent. This damned sword. What does this all mean?"

Somehow, it was all of it tied together. Somehow. He could feel it. He wanted to press his hands against his head, to squeeze the answer from his mind, if it was there.

Dagonet put his hands on Balin's shoulders.

"*May* the *day* never come when you understand, Sir Balin," he said strangely. "*May* the *day* never come. It will break your heart twice over."

Balin put the sword away, his eyes lingering on the perilous chair.

"I'm going to claim that seat one day, Dagonet. I swear it to you now. I'll claim it or I'll die trying."

"I know you will," said Dagonet.

Balin turned angrily away.

"I must find Merlin."

"Yes, perhaps you should. Goodbye, Sir Balin," said Dagonet.

DAGONET WATCHED BALIN pound across the hall like a frustrated child.

When he had departed, Dagonet saw a child standing in the shadows, glaring at him. A serving boy from the kitchens.

Dagonet smiled at him.

The boy stomped away in Balin's path, the very mirror of his frustration.

CHAPTER
THREE

BALIN PACKED IRONPROW with lance and shield, and donned his armor.

Merlin had all the answers, as he always did.

But where to find him?

In the forest, of course. He would ride for the forest, go calling for the damned Cambion if he had to, or cut his way through every brush and hedge until he found himself back in the Garden of Joy. Then he would put the point of the Adventurous Sword to the wizard's throat, along with every question, and by God, he would be answered.

He rode out from Camelot without a word to anyone, skirting the Black Cross and St. Stephen's, where Preudom was tolling the bell signifying the end of poor Lot's funeral. He wanted to stay awhile and see Lot interred, but he could not tarry in Camelot, not until this riddle was solved.

He had a dilemma with the Adventurous Sword. A part of him told him to get rid of it, to cast it at the foot of the Black Cross and put leagues between it and his person.

But many things nagged him. His faith in the weapon, for one. It had served him well and he was fond of it. Perhaps he had too much faith in it. Could he still be the greatest knight in the world without it?

It served another purpose, too, though. Dagonet was right. It told his future. Maybe it could help him find Merlin somehow.

Dagonet had told him something else. He had said that if he found the truth, it would break his heart twice over.

The latest design to appear on the sword was a pair of hearts, pierced by a lance.

But what did *that* mean? Was the sword telling him his future or his past?

He pondered these things for many miles and came at last to the edge of Camelot, where a stream emerged from the green wood and cut a meadow in two.

In that forest, he knew he would find Merlin. He was sure of it.

Ironprow was winded and tired. They had ridden a long time and it was well after noon, so he dismounted, stripped off his harness and the saddle from the war horse's back, and led him to water.

He fed and brushed the beast, and had just plucked a fat silver fish from the stream with a thought to dinner when he heard a splashing and saw a mailed knight atop a lathered rouncey.

Balin dropped his fish back in its abode and ran for his swords, but the mailed rider stopped in the center of the stream and twisted in his saddle to look back the way he'd come, and made no move to even acknowledge Balin. His armor was sorely used and dented. He had lost his shield, and his lance was shivered, his horse in poor shape.

As he watched, the horse began to dip its head toward the water around its ankles, but the knight cruelly pulled hard back on the reins, keeping it from drinking.

Balin stepped forward.

"Ho there, knight!"

The knight tensed and grabbed at the sword hanging on his saddle.

"Wait!" Balin urged. "If it's blood you want, allow me to get my armor, or at least, to mount."

The knight gripped the handle of his sword, but did not draw.

"It is not blood I want, sir. Only water and a moment's peace."

Balin jammed his sword in the earth and held out his hands.

"Take it, then."

The knight looked at him for a moment, and again over his shoulder, then swung down and dropped to his knees on the bank, setting aside his broken lance. He pulled off his helmet, revealing a red face and yellow growth of beard, before plunging into the water and thirstily lapping beside his mount.

"Your horse is nearly dead, sir," Balin said. "To what purpose are you pursued and by whom?"

The knight laughed.

"To what purpose?" he glanced furtively upstream yet again, and then got to his feet, as if remembering his peril. "Who are you, sir?"

"Sir Balin of Northumberland, knight of Camelot."

"Camelot." The knight looked around wonderingly. "My God, am I in Camelot?"

"The border. If you require sanctuary, I can take you to King Arthur."

The knight looked tempted, then shook his head vigorously and prepared to mount.

"No, no. It would only do me harm and Arthur not much good."

The knight tried to pull himself back into the saddle, but gasped with the effort and sank back.

"Your horse is near collapse, and you aren't much better," Balin observed.

The knight looked back at Balin.

"Sir Balin, will you promise me safe conduct?"

"I will, to Camelot," Balin said, "on my honor. Provided you are no outlaw."

"On the contrary. It's a base villain who pursues me. But you're right." He gasped. "I am past spent, and my horse…"

He stopped speaking and stood bolt aright, listening.

Balin heard it too.

It was nothing, deafening in comparison to the prior incessant, hushed discourse of bird and brush, bug and brook.

Beside the trickle of the stream around the stones and the horse's labored breathing, the ambient chatter of the meadow insects and the trilling of birds in the trees had ceased.

Then Balin heard a fast galloping from the road leading into the forest mouth, and an unexpected rush of violent wind kicked up, howling like the primordial death rattle of some beast from the very belly of the woods. It bent the grasses and kicked up dust from the road and blew the leaves from the trees. A mossy robin's nest crashed at his feet, spilling a clutch of twitching, half-blind, mottled juveniles across the ground.

"We're too late!" wailed the knight, pulling himself into his saddle with effort and grabbing his sword.

A terrible, cockle raising laugh insinuated itself through the howling wind. The galloping became deafeningly loud along with it, as if a gigantic horse were pounding across the meadow.

Balin whirled all around, both swords leaping into his hands now. Ironprow fought his hobbles and reared, but there was nothing but the bending boughs and grasses, and a shower of leaves stripped from the trees.

The knight spurred his horse, but the exhausted beast was sluggish, and stumbled rather than bolted.

There was a rapid series of splashes in the streambed, followed by a clang of steel on steel.

Balin squinted through the swirling maelstrom of blowing leaves and dust and saw the right side of the knight's harness rend and split outward with a burst of blood, as if something irresistible had torn through him.

Another row of splashes erupted downstream followed by the pounding of those thunderous hooves again. The devil wind and its accompanying laughter dwindled, and as the storm of leaves at last settled to the ground, so too fell the knight from his saddle, splashing facedown into the stream.

Balin rushed up and dragged the wounded knight clear. The great cut in his side was dumping blood without surcease.

The knight blinked as his eyes filled with blood and the stuff trickled darkly from his drawn lips. He looked as surprised as Balin by what had happened.

"What was that?" Balin stammered, horrified as blood poured over the hands that he clamped bootlessly over the terrible wound.

"A mad knight, with some foul enchantment that renders him invisible. His name is Garlon. He has slain many innocents. My quest was to find him, but…I suppose…he has murdered me." With effort, the knight reached out and gripped Balin's fingers. The metal of the gauntlet was ice cold from the stream. "I beg you, Sir Balin. Take my body to my lady, Lorna Maeve. She is at the Castle Meliot. Lay me in the churchyard there, as befits a Christian."

He let out a groan and shuddered.

Balin held him close.

"I promise," he said. "And I will find this evil knight and avenge you. I swear it."

But the knight heard nothing of that. He was dead.

Balin cleaned the nameless man and rolled his body in a blanket and tied him over the saddle of his horse.

He prayed that God would accept the knight's soul.

He knew the animal would not go much further today. Still, he did not wish to camp in the open meadow beside the stream now that he knew there was an invisible murderer about, so he led Ironprow and the tired horse and its dead master into the mouth of the forest, where he felt he had a better chance of avoiding an ambush such as he'd seen.

Yet what could he truly do, if this Garlon decided to come skulking in the night to push a dagger under his chin?

He made camp just within the forest, unsaddled and rubbed down the knight's horse, and laid his body gently in the ditch.

He spent the night in his armor, sitting with his back to a moss covered old oak, his swords in his hands, dozing, but never quite sleeping.

CHAPTER
FOUR

BALIN JOLTED AWAKE at the sound of horses approaching from deeper in the wood. It was well past dawn. He took up his swords and lurched into the road, joints aching from having slept in his harness.

Two riders came trotting around the bend in the woods. Their mounts were startled to rearing by his crazed appearance, brandishing his swords like a brigand in the road.

It was a knight and his lady.

More, it was the Hibernian, Sir Lanceor and his lady, Princess Colombe.

They looked to have been on the road for some time. The lady's hair and dress bore all the signs of having slept for some time beneath the stars, and their palfreys were shaggy and ungroomed. Lanceor's armor was mud splattered and bore a film of trail dust. His put upon young squire came up behind, plodding along with a bow-necked pack horse bearing his lance and all the accoutrements of a long journey.

Balin stammered a mostly unintelligible greeting, he was so astonished to meet them.

They blinked at the sight of him, as if waking from a long sleep, and Lanceor immediately grew animate.

"At long last!" he declared with a broad grin. "When I had given up hope of finding you, here you are. Praise God!"

"Have you sought me, Sir Lanceor?"

"For a week or more, aye, but no longer. Now is my quest fulfilled. Now do I bring you the overdue justice of the King."

He turned in his saddle to gesture hurriedly at his squire, who was already working to remove his helm and lance from the back of the packhorse.

"What are you talking about?" Balin asked, blinking in confusion.

"Don't play the fool. To think I rode all the way to your cursed Northumberland to find you and was given over to returning empty handed. But here I have caught you practicing the highwayman's trade at the very doorstep of Camelot."

"I'm no robber, you fool."

"No, not when facing your betters you're not," Lanceor scoffed, as his squire ran up and passed his helm to him.

He pointed to the body of the murdered knight bundled in the ditch.

"No robber, yet you lead an empty horse and hide a body in the ditch."

"I'm not hiding anything, you clod," Balin said, his old annoyance at the Hibernian prince rising in him, dispensing with all courtesy. "I saw this knight killed by an invisible rider, and I've sworn to bear his body to Meliot Castle and see him buried."

"An invisible rider!" Lanceor laughed, sliding his helm over his head. "And *I* have sworn to ride you down, you murderous villain, on the order of Arthur himself."

Balin's heart sank. Was it true? Had Arthur sent this fool to kill him?

"I don't believe it," Balin said resolutely.

"What you believe hardly matters," said Lanceor, grabbing his lance from the squire. "Arthur put me to your scent not an hour after you slew the Lady of The Lake. I lost your trail in the forest, but now I'll put an end to your mischief."

Balin shook his head.

"The King must have forgotten your quest."

Lanceor laughed again, as though such a thing were impossible.

Colombe, silent at her prince's side, now looked concerned.

"Hear me," said Balin anxiously. "You said you have been riding for a week. Then you cannot know all that has happened."

"*What* has happened?" Colombe asked.

Lanceor looked sharply at her.

"My lady," Balin said, bowing his head seeing in her a reasoning spirit, "Carhaix was attacked by Rience and Lot with their Saxon allies, but they have been defeated. The Saxons have been routed and the rebellion is over. Lot is dead. He is even now being entombed in Camelot, and King Arthur is to wed Princess Guinevere in a few days' time."

Colombe looked open mouthed at her prince.

He was locking his lance into its fittings, unconcerned.

"Even if all that were true, it does nothing to stay your sentence," said Lanceor.

"It does," Balin said. "I fought at Carhaix. I charged at Arthur's right. I slew Sir Segurant The Brown. I was pardoned."

Lanceor's only answer was to slam down the visor of his helmet.

"Lanceor!" Colombe protested. "What if what he says his true?"

"Stay your tongue, woman, you do not know the lies a villain will tell."

"They are *not* lies," Balin said angrily. "I *am* pardoned, I tell you. I have a place at the Round Table."

Lanceor scoffed.

"You see how his falsehoods grow, my sweet? Next he will tell me he is Arthur's chosen champion. From ragamuffin prisoner to glorious hero in less than a fortnight. Ready yourself, savage. One of us is going to lie down in this road in a little while."

The Hibernian turned his horse and rode a respectable distance up the road, turning once more to face Balin. His palfrey pawed at the ground and he fancied he saw it glower at him beneath its barding, a mirror of its rider's determined arrogance.

Balin bunched his fists.

Colombe looked from Lanceor to Balin, anxiously. There was pleading in her soft eyes, but Balin dismissed it with an angry, exasperated swipe of his hand.

"Alright, you Hibernian popinjay," said Balin through his teeth. "Let God judge the truth!"

"Don't blaspheme, you shameful damned blackguard," Lanceor called. "You will stand before Him in a little while, and you will have to answer for your tongue."

Balin stalked angrily off the road and unfastened Ironprow, hauling himself up into the saddle alone. He didn't bother with his helmet. In his outrage, he took only shield and lance and urged the destrier into the center of the road to face his opponent.

Lanceor's squire pulled at the bridle of Colombe's palfrey, trying to extricate her from harm's way.

"Get out of the way, Colombe!" Lanceor roared.

"Sirs!" Colombe called to them both as the squire struggled with her horse. "This is rash and will come to no good end! We should take this before Arthur or some other impartial…"

But Lanceor had kicked his horse and was charging, even before she was out of his path.

The squire got her clear with a final effort.

Balin roared and stabbed Ironprow's flanks with his spurs, perhaps too exuberantly. The horse launched itself up the road. He had less momentum than Lanceor now and was at a disadvantage.

But he would dive willingly into hell rather than let this ill-mannered, soft-bellied, wine-guzzling Hibernian fop unhorse him today.

He leaned forward and leveled his lance.

He saw Lanceor, a hurtling thing of steel and blazing plumage peering out from the depths of his helm over the lip of his shield, which bore: *Azure, three crowns in pale, or, bordure argent.*

A royal charge, the three white crowns of his father, King Elidus, borne by Hibernian royalty since before Vortigern's day.

Balin was a poor knight, the son and brother of poor knights. To his heart that royal crest was as haughty a thing as the scornful manner of its bearer. It enraged him that a wealthy man might be born into the title "nobility," when this prideful whelp who bullied his lady and drank to excess like a common tavern lout was as far from embodying the noble qualities of a man as a rat was from the High Crown of Albion.

How many wealthy knights had he known were worth the rich arms they bore? How many did not kick the peasantry from their path like chickens, or cuff tardy servants, or speak in whispered laughs about the shabby appearance of their own peers if they came up from the lesser ranks?

He had no doubt his own father had suffered such insults from so-called men even worse than Lanceor.

As the clash became imminent, he steeled himself, and in his wrathful heart demanded of God in heaven, *demanded*, not begged, swift and total victory over this unworthy princeling.

Lanceor's spear touched his shield and he angled it away, feeling it slide along, glancing, scraping, whereas Balin's own lance struck that blue field of white crowns dead center and somehow found a miniscule but fatal flaw in the shield's design. Steel pierced steel and rammed through almost to the hilt before the wood handle shook and shattered in Balin's fist, and he released it as he passed, his hand thrumming.

Balin pulled back hard on the reins and turned, ready for a second pass, grabbing his swords.

Lanceor still had his lance, but he had stopped and was not regrouping. His palfrey shook its head and slowly turned about.

Balin sat aghast at the sight of him, and murmured aloud, "*Heaven!*"

Balin's lance had pierced Lanceor's shield and pinned it to his chest. It was an impossible stroke. He had never seen, never even heard of such a thing ever happening. How had the lance survived punching through three layers of steel? Its dark tip protruded at a skyward angle from Lanceor's back as he slumped forward against the neck of his horse, which swiftly ran with bloody rivulets, causing it to rear, spilling Lanceor with a clatter into the road before trotting past the thunderstruck Balin, shaking the blood from its mane.

Balin turned to watch the horse disappear around the bend in the road. It was a surreal sight, slow and dreamlike, the blood stark against the palfrey's pale snowy hide.

Then he nearly leapt from his armor at the spine-raking shriek that sounded from Colombe.

Balin watched her, distraught, drop from her saddle.

The squire tried to restrain her but she shoved him to the ground, hiked up her dress, and ran to her fallen lover, skidding to her knees beside him.

Balin opened his mouth as the woman fell across the dead man.

Had he really done this? Had he really *prayed* for it?

Had God answered him? What other explanation could there be for such a colossal stroke?

He swallowed, heart hammering, face flushing at the sound of Colombe's heart breaking. She heaved uncontrollable shrieks into the corpse of her man, wrested out strangled entreaties, and was met only with the silence of the dead.

He urged Ironprow closer.

He passed the young squire, on his knees in the ditch, wild tears cutting through the mud on his face. The boy was scarping up clots of dirt and flinging them down again in feral grief.

Had Lanceor touched this boy's heart so? How? It seemed impossible that the loutish, boorish prince had been so well regarded.

But then he came to Colombe, and as he dismounted, she snapped upright at the sound of his greaves clinking. This was no playacted grief. She was *destroyed*. Her lovely face was drawn near to splitting, lips in a leering grimace, cheeks blotched fire red, her eyes running with tears to match the copious life that pooled scarlet around her knees.

He fully expected her to spring for him, tear him to shreds in her outrage.

But her grief was too great to leave room for wrath, even. She wailed like a ghost as she struggled to form words that came out in breathless bursts.

"Oh…Sir Balin…it is two bodies…you have slain here."

She lifted Lanceor's lifeless hand and gently took off his gauntlet to press it to her breast.

She kissed it, rocked with it as though it were a newborn babe, dried her tears with the pale back of it.

"Two bodies…in one….heart, and…one heart in…two bodies," she babbled into his dead knuckles.

She leaned over him again, like a penitent.

Balin reached out to her, unsure of what to do to comfort her. He had never seen such grief, not since he had seen Brulen while their mother burned. It embarrassed him, more so because he felt less than miniscule for having caused it. He was wretched. Lanceor had been right. He truly was a villain.

Colombe fumbled with Lanceor's helmet and slid it off at last, then planted loud kisses all over his still face.

She had loved this man, and Balin had slain him, even called on the Lord in his sinful rage to aid him.

Colombe straightened a second time, and rose shakily to her feet, the front of her dress stained with Lanceor's blood. As she rose, the dead prince's sword rasped from its sheath and dangled from her hand.

She looked at Balin, calmer now, her eyes placid and faraway.

He backed away warily. Now would she strike him?

"And one soul," she murmured.

Then she turned the sword over in her hands, let the pommel touch the road, and flung herself forward.

Balin lunged, but he couldn't stop the point of the blade from sprouting like a steel sapling from the middle of her back with a rip of skin and fabric. There was one horrid, dwindling shriek of agony.

She twitched across the body of Lanceor, then lay unmoving.

Balin wavered on his unsteady legs and then pitched backward. He fell on his rear in the road.

The squire wailed, an orphan's lament, and ran off, directionless as a frightened fawn into the trees.

It was just as the image on the sword had foretold.

CHAPTER
FIVE

I N THE WAKE of the death of Lile, a new priestess had ascended to the office of the Lady of The Lake, and Merlin came into her parqueted hall to dutifully present himself.

He knew her of course, as he knew most of the women of Avalon. As a natural or perhaps unnatural font of latent infernal power and occult knowledge, most all of the sisterhood had come to slake their individual thirsts at his spring at one time or another, and being of a puckish nature, he had exchanged many secrets to them for their attentions.

The Lady Viviane was no different. Being the daughter of the Baron of Briosque in sensuous Gallia, if the old adages were to be believed, she was perhaps most equal to him in terms of amorous prowess. Truly she understood most of all the women of Avalon the inherent power of her own womanhood, and her efforts to educate her sister priestesses in recognizing and harnessing that power in themselves had begun to frustrate Merlin's bartering, and to put a damper on his already sparse leisure.

She had learned much from Merlin and taught him a good deal. She was level-headed and calculating. She would make a formidable

Lady of The Lake, but would her rule be friendly to his purposes? She made very little of her opinions known. She had served Lile dutifully and without question, but would she uphold all that Lile and Merlin had planned together? Would she approve of a compromise between the Goddess and the crucified god?

He found her not in her rich audience chamber, but reclining on a marble bench in the sun in her back garden, glorious in her samite gown, observing a surpassingly handsome young man expertly maneuvering a horse through the apple orchard at a dangerous pace.

Merlin was amused at the swell of jealousy he felt observing Viviane's appreciative eye on the young rider. That was the sort of power she wielded. It could not be taught in any grimoire.

He cleared his throat, and after a moment, she took her eyes off the young man to acknowledge him.

She was slightly older than Merlin, but the enchanted air of Avalon, which was a province of Fluratrone, the land of the faeries, had served her. One would have thought her a blushing maiden of cream skin and thread of gold hair but for her frank and worldly eyes which were the same blue that called mariners past their prime back to sea to die.

In his youth, Merlin had visited her home country with his foster father Blaise to deliver the extreme unction to her father. The old man had told them he had once spared a wounded white hart while hunting in the forest, and Viviane had been given the blessing of the moon goddess, Diane, herself.

Merlin didn't doubt it. She was damnably alluring.

"Merlin, so you have come at last."

"As always, to vouchsafe my service, Lady," Merlin said, bowing slightly.

She smiled and returned her gaze to the young rider, who was urging his horse to vault over moss covered boulders now, using only his strong knees as he spread his lean arms like a bird in flight, fearless and trusting wholly in the animal not to throw him.

The horse was frothing with sweat, as was its rider, who opened his tunic and let the wind fill it.

Merlin rolled his eyes at the gaudy display, and Viviane's barely perceptible but undeniable appreciation of the well-muscled form of the rider.

This was the boy Viviane herself had taken from Benwick in Gaul at the behest of Lile all those years ago. The loyal champion that she had insisted on raising to insinuate among Arthur's company, to insure a true knight of Avalon sat at The Round Table. Besides Merlin and the Red Knight who guarded the entrance to the castle, he was the only male allowed on the enchanted shore.

"Have you reclaimed the Adventurous Sword for young Lancelot?" Viviane asked, smiling as the youth in question executed a particularly bold leap and urged his horse on, laughing gamely.

"Are you certain he could claim it if I had?"

"Do I hear jealousy in your voice, Merlin?" Viviane laughed, and her voice was a melodious trill.

Surely there was some, and he hated that she could detect it. But there was more. Merlin did not care for this Lancelot overly. He had never been a part of Merlin's vision for Arthur, and until he left the Isle of Avalon, its magic kept the boy from appearing in his prognostications. He was an unknown factor. Merlin had no notion of the qualities of this man. He had heard he was a very accomplished knight, but what of his heart? He was brave, but was he humble? He was fair, but was he true?

Merlin had looked into his parentage. He was of good stock, the son of the late King Ban of Benwick, descended from Bron, the first keeper of Joseph of Arimathea's Holy Grail. That was how he had discovered the purpose of Lile's choosing this boy. She had hoped not only to introduce a knight loyal to Avalon to Arthur, but also to marry the traditions of the crucified god and the Goddess in the person of

Lancelot. That was why Merlin had not done more than raise questions and not objections. It was a worthy notion, complementary to his own plan for Arthur, and not dependent on the already notoriously volatile knights of Orkney.

But Viviane's influence made him question the Lancelot scheme all over again. She was certainly no mother figure to the boy, and he wondered by her candid looks what else she might have taught him.

"Your silence answers both my questions," Viviane said. "Is it still in the hands of Sir Balin The Savage then? Was he not immolated by the Siege Perilous as you planned?"

"It will be returned in time," Merlin assured her.

"Why you do not simply destroy this knight personally is beyond my ken."

"It's the location of the Gwenn Mantle which concerns me more," said Merlin, changing the subject.

"Yes, I agree. Nimue shall answer for her crimes against the sisterhood," Viviane said coldly.

"You will not deal with her too harshly, I trust?"

"How should thieves of her stature be treated, Merlin?"

"She was distraught. She acted out of a broken heart. And," Merlin said, hesitating to add, but finally deciding, "her dreams were influenced by the Queen of Norgales."

Viviane looked at him sharply.

"Influenced? To what extent?"

"I do not believe she is aware. I think if she were made aware, she would repent her actions and work to rectify them."

"If she has befuddled you, Merlin…"

"I assure you she has not," Merlin chuckled.

"Don't be *too* sure of yourself, Cambion," Viviane said. "You are half man, and some might argue, not the better half, either. Find her and find the Gwenn Mantle."

Merlin bowed slightly and turned away, taking an apple from the golden dish beside her seat.

"What if she returns the Gwenn Mantle to the treasure room herself?" he asked, biting into the golden fruit.

Viviane thought for a moment.

"I will take it as a gesture of repentance and consider it when I pass judgment, but it must be soon. Goddess knows what mayhem she will enact with it. Already the sword is doing its work to unravel its bearer. We shall be fortunate if Sir Balin doesn't take half of Albion with him."

"What do you mean? What work has the sword done?"

Viviane looked up at him, frowning.

"Have you not been keeping your weather eye on Sir Balin, Merlin?"

"I left him in Camelot. I went seeking Nimue, and when I heard of your elevation, I came straight here. Why? The last I knew, he used the sword to best King Rience and win the day for Arthur at Carhaix."

"Fly to Carteloise Forest at the edge of Lystenoyse and see for yourself," said Viviane.

Merlin wheeled and stormed from her presence, intent on doing just that.

CHAPTER
SIX

S IR LANCEOR'S BLOW had marred Balin's shield, leaving a jagged slash that joined the two boars upon the charge, cutting them through the middle. He had decided he would not seek its repair. It was a mark of his shame, and he further debased his crest by using the point of the shield as a spade to dig the graves of Lanceor and Colombe.

Long hours he worked gouging their beds beside the road, stripped to his braies, toiling and scraping in the earth like a goblin.

He lay Lanceor to his rest first, and then Colombe beside him, and when he had finished covering them, knelt between the two grave mounds and prayed fervently and quietly for forgiveness, from them both, from God.

By midday, clouds had gathered and halved the dim forest light, so that all was bathed in appropriate gloom and flecks of cold rain spat upon his bare back like the derision of the angels.

He set about lashing sticks together to make crosses and hung Lanceor's shield from his so that all would know him. He puzzled over how to mark the grave of Colombe, and it was in this attitude that the column of nobles, knights, and attendants riding south discovered him, filthy and stripped to the waist with his ratty beard like a wild man's.

Above them flapped a banner bearing *Azure, a lion passant, or, on a chief argent three Cornish choughs.*

"Is this the man?" demanded a barrel-chested, thick bearded noble in a blue and white cape with a gold circlet upon his head.

Balin stood slowly, as from the crowd of knights, Lanceor's squire pushed forward. He had been cleaned, probably fed, and now he nodded deliberately.

"Sir Balin The Savage," said the king.

Balin bowed his head, rankling under that nom de plume.

"I am, sire. Who is it addresses me?"

"Wretch, do you not know the golden lion and beckets of the King of Cornwall?"

This was Mark, then, the newly crowned son of Idres. Balin knew something of his reputation. He had heard in his squire days that he was a cruel poltroon who had murdered his brother out of petty jealousy of the latter's glory at arms.

"I did not know your charge, sire. Forgive my ignorance and the state of my appearance."

"This boy tells me you are a murderer. That you slew a prince of Hibernia and his lady both. And here I find you burying the evidence, rash, and blood-soaked villain that you are."

"The boy's grief and rage have made his tongue false," Balin said evenly. He looked up into the glaring eyes of the squire and the boy looked away. "Sir Lanceor challenged me in fair contest and by ill fortune I dealt him a mortal blow. Colombe, distraught, fell upon his sword. I was only giving them their due Christian burial."

Mark sneered and kicked his horse, riding over to tower above Balin.

"Yet they would have no need of such arrangements but for you."

He pointed to the body of the murdered knight lying nearby, swaddled in tabard and blanket.

"And who is this? Another victim of your ill fortune?"

"His own, rather. I do not know this knight's name. He was slain while under my protection, by an invisible rider. I am bearing his body at his request to Castle Meliot."

Mark's booming laughter drowned out the last of Balin's words, as he looked back at his company.

"An invisible rider?" he repeated. "Tell me, Sir Balin, does this invisible attacker manifest only when the moon is full? Is his appearance preceded by the onset of headaches? Did he slay these young lovers also?" He roared the last, down at Balin.

"By God's blood, I told you, sire, what transpired here," Balin said through his teeth, feeling his anger rise to match his shame. "Of this knight's death, I am blameless. Yet of this young pair I have admitted freely my culpability. In an unknightly rage I faced Sir Lanceor, and my wrath guided my hand to bloodshed. Colombe's words cut me worse than had she taken her lover's sword to my unworthy hide. 'Two hearts in one body,' she said. 'And one heart. And one soul,' she said, ere she ended herself."

He stammered the last and put his face in his hands to hide his overwhelming emotion.

There was a ruckus from the train, and two knights separated from the company. They were both of them black skinned, one in the armor of a knight of Albion, the other in a familiar eastern hauberk, bearing a curved sword and a white turban upon his head.

The latter was Sir Safir, and part of Balin's downtrodden heart swelled to see his comrade. Yet his face was rigid and cold as stone, only the pathways of tears on his dark cheeks marking any emotion.

"Your majesty, I do beseech you to temper your judgment of this knight," said Safir, his voice strained. He did not look directly at Balin.

Mark turned, very nearly rearing like an enraged lion.

"On what grounds?" he demanded.

"He is a good man," said Safir, though by his flat affect he seemed to be struggling to say so. "There is no lying in him. I will vouch for his veracity, as will the knights of Camelot and their king."

"And I will vouch for my brother's judge of character," said the knight beside him, older, and bearded, and yet bearing no small resemblance to Safir.

"Do you stake your honor on this man, Sir Segwarides?" Mark asked the elder of the two.

"It is the word of a distraught boy over a knight's," said Segwarides, riding over. "As to this man," he said, indicating the dead knight. "Sir Balin, will you permit me to view the body? It may be that I know him, as I have been a guest of Castle Meliot."

Balin nodded wordlessly, brushing at his own leaky eyes. He had not only never been to Meliot, he had never heard of it before.

"Please, sir."

Segwarides handed his reins to his brother and dismounted. He knelt over the body and parted the wrappings about the face, then crossed himself, said a short, quiet prayer, and stood again.

"He is Sir Herlews le Berbeus," Segwarides announced. "One of the knights of Count Oduin, the lord of Castle Meliot."

"Are you certain?" said Mark.

"I am, sire," said Segwarides. "I saw your nephew Allisander unhorse him once during a contest at La Beale Regard."

Mark frowned and regarded Balin once more.

"A knight who would bear a man all the way to Castle Meliot to fulfil his dying wish would hardly murder another knight and his lady and take the time to inter them and mark their graves." He looked back at the squire, who had hung his head. "Truthfulness is the first step to knighthood, boy."

Mark dismounted and genuflected between the graves. He prayed for a few moments in silence, and Sir Balin wondered if perhaps the stories he had heard of Mark of Cornwall were untrue.

When the King rose, his eyes were red and he brushed at them with the back of his hand.

"The truth you tell touches me deeply, Sir Balin," he murmured. "The devotion of this Colombe to her prince is much to be admired. We are on the way to Camelot to see Arthur wedded. I will report this unfortunate affair, and when I return, I will build a tomb befitting these lovers."

Balin's lip trembled and he bowed to Mark. On a whim, he took the King's hand and kissed it.

"True love and fidelity are rare treasures," said Mark absently. "They should be guarded, and housed accordingly."

Then he raised a benevolent hand and turning his horse south rode on alone without another word.

The train galloped behind to catch up.

Segwarides hung back and pulled his horse alongside his younger brother. The two spoke whispered words and touched foreheads, and Balin pined once more for Brulen. Then Segwarides said to Balin, "Follow the Itchen River for five days and you will come to Meliot, Sir Balin."

"I am indebted to you, sir," Balin said.

"God go with you," said Segwarides and fell in with Mark's train.

Safir, still shedding silent tears, waited in the road.

"It's good to see you, Safir," said Balin.

"With all my heart, Balin," Safir said, trembling, fresh tears spilling down his chin. "I do wish I could say the same."

"Faith, my friend," Balin murmured. "Have I hurt you also in some way?"

"To the quick, Balin," Safir groaned. "To the marrow of my bones. Remember, I was raised in the court of Colombe's father. We were playmates. She was as dear to me as my own sister."

Balin remembered. The court of King Anguish.

Balin stared up at Safir, miserably. He opened his hands. He had no words.

"You bear two swords now," Safir said, observing the weapons hung on Ironprow's saddle.

Balin looked back at them, dropping his arms to his side. He felt as if something deep in the earth pulled him, and it was a struggle just to stand. He wanted to lie down and rest with Lanceor and Colombe.

"A knight bears his shield to defend love and virtue," said Safir sadly. "A knight with two swords can hold no shield. He can only attack and slay."

Safir gave him no chance to reply, but spurred his horse and raced after the clatter and rumble of King Mark's company.

Which was well and good, as Balin had none to give.

He watched his one-time friend disappear, and stood alone in the forest road for some time, until the light rain which had been flecking the ground grew into a deluge that made the leaves patter and dance on their boughs and that lashed his skin with an icy sting.

He stood a long while, until his trousers were plastered to his shivering legs, his hair hung from his bowed skull, and the chill of his skin equaled the cold that had settled in his heart.

The rain hid his grief.

CHAPTER
SEVEN

ALIN RODE WELL into the night through the rainy forest, trusting his course to Ironprow. The horse seemed to sense its master's melancholy and share it. Its head hung low. The horse of Sir Herlews plopped behind in the muddy road with its sorrowful burden.

He did not hurry. There was no eagerness in him to be quit of the dark forest road. Let it go on forever.

The whisper of the rain in the brush and trees was like the gossip of the departed. The ghosts of Colombe and Lanceor walked with him, and Lot, too, and Segurant. A legion of disapproving spirits and saints shook their heads at him in passing, and the rain was the murmur of their condemnation.

He deserved it. He had never felt so low. He wished almost that God would put that invisible knight in his path. Let death come unseen and snatch this joyless existence from his tired bones.

But this was the curse he had taken upon himself. His career was a wave, just as the maiden had warned him it would be, and he was buffeted upon it like a castaway in an oarless boat. Crests and troughs. Crests and troughs. Slave to the wind, like a weathervane cock. He felt as though he scrambled for new purpose, yet his overall life had none.

The rain did not stop for five days.

He followed the course of the clear Itchen, a wide chalk stream bordered with lush wild watercress, its surface diamond clear down to the flint gravel bottom, where brook lamprey wriggled like the serpent in Preudom's painting, heedless of the raindrops rippling the shimmering surface.

Families of otters cavorted playfully. Silver mailed graylings swam with spotted brown trout, and he saw a shaggy hart raise its black muzzle dripping from the water at the sound of Ironprow's snorting, and watch him pass before returning to its refreshment.

The countryside was verdant and lush, the earth black and rich-smelling, no doubt teeming with nightcrawlers.

Yet alongside this busy watery thoroughfare across this populous animal kingdom, Balin had never felt so alone.

He felt as apart from the company of men as he did from animals. The loss of Safir's friendship had gutted him. No comrade would welcome him in Arthur's hall, no aged father waited to embrace him in a warm cottage, and there was no elderly mother's lap to lay his head in. No maiden's either. No children to clutch his legs and beg him to stay awhile longer. No brother to ask after his health and prospects.

The myriad rain drops, each one somehow heavier on his drooping shoulders than the last, two weary horses, and a corpse were his only constant companions.

He shivered in his intermittent sleep, jolted awake again and again by dreams of the dead, cut, bleeding, burning, screaming his name.

On the fifth day, Balin came alone in sight of Castle Meliot, which was a small, modest keep of dark stone with a high wall and swollen moat.

The rain renewed its vigor, a slashing downpour punctuated by deep thunder over which he had to bellow several times before a figure wrapped in a heavy cloak appeared on the battlements and called down, "Who are you?"

"Sir Balin of the Round Table! I bring word of the fate of Sir Herlews le Berbeus!"

The faceless figure on the battlement peered down at him from the depths of its hood, then disappeared.

After a few moments, there was a rumbling and the heavy oak drawbridge lowered on clanking chains and settled into the mud at his feet.

A portcullis raised jerkily, and Balin dismounted and led the horses across and beneath the arch of the sallyport. The oasis of dryness was a shock to his waterlogged body. He had been so long exposed to the rain that he had lost a sense of self, become indistinguishable from the torrent. Exiting the incessant storm, he was like a shapeless thing forced to assume form, a fetal being divorced of its amnion, born anew into an arid, material world.

He looked into the small, gray courtyard, and the same figure who had spoken to him on the wall stepped forward with a raised lantern. Her hood had fallen back, and he saw that she was a portly, rough-handed woman, likely a chambermaid.

There was a flash of lightning and accompanying roar of thunder, and above it all, from a high window of the keep, a tortuous scream echoed down to Balin's ear, raising his hairs so that he gripped his sword.

"What was that?" Balin demanded. "What goes on here?"

The maid bowed her head in excuse.

"It is for the Count to say, sir."

Across the gray courtyard, the door to the keep opened and a man stormed across the distance, clutching an otter fur robe to his shoulders.

He was an older man, with a full gray beard, sparse hair on his head, and vigorous black, angry eyebrows.

"What is this? Who calls at this hour?"

"Sir Balin of the court of Camelot," Balin answered, as another plaintive shriek came from the tower. "What is that?" he demanded again.

"Sir," said the older man, putting up his palms. "Please…"

Balin pushed past the man and drew his sword.

He crossed the courtyard to the door of the keep, ignoring the protestations that followed him. Someone was imperiled, by the sound of that agonized wailing.

The keep was modestly decorated, mainly with old arms and hunting trophies. He found the winding stair and followed the painful screams to their origin, a closed door at the highest point, which coincided with where he expected the lit window to be.

A hand restrained his arm from behind. It was the bearded man, his soaked fur mantle flecking rainwater, his bald head shining from the wetting.

"Please, Sir Balin. I beg you to temper yourself for what you will see."

Balin shrugged the man off and opened the door, ready to attack any half dozen villains within.

He was not prepared for what he saw.

The room was lit by a series of stubby candles in some predetermined, meaningful arrangement. In the center was a bed, where a young man lay naked to the waist, his skin crisscrossed by a series of bleeding, open slashes.

A figure in white bent over him with a dagger.

Balin rushed into the room, but the man behind him threw his arms about his shoulders and arms and checked his advance.

"No, sir knight. No! I beg you! My boy will die if you interfere!"

The figure turned at the interruption and Balin caught his breath, for he knew the face that looked at him like an alabaster sculpture framed in unruly, straw yellow autumn brush. All fight fled from him, and the point of his sword struck the floor as it sagged in his grip.

He had seen this woman before, peering through the hedge of Merlin's mystic garden. She had been hunched in a meadow, picking herbs. He hadn't remembered, or perhaps hadn't seen, the startling quality of her green, bird-like eyes, which were strange in that plain but fine featured face. They fixed directly upon his own, made him shrink inwardly, and blush, as if they knew every rash and amorous fancy that flashed through his glamored mind.

Standing there, the keen dagger held at the ready, the candlelight glowing orange on her pale skin, she was as fearsome as the Lady of The Lake had been, and yet, somehow, more real, immediate, and desirous.

She stared at him, then her green eyes flitted back to her strange work, and it was like the light of divine favor had passed from Balin. He felt lesser and desperate to regain her attention.

She drew up one of her sleeves, revealing dark woad snaking up her arms, like the cursed marks his mother had borne when working her spells. She traced one of the serpentine symbols with the point of the dagger, and let her blood dribble into an iron pan on the bed.

"What evil is this?" Balin whispered.

The man, his lips near Balin's ear now, replied in a matching hush.

"No evil, sir knight. But the fruit of evil."

The woman took a clean white linen bandage from the bed and wound it tightly around her wound, then took a second bandage and dipped it in the pan of her own blood.

The boy on the bed screamed again and trembled as the window lit with lightning and thunder shook the room.

The woman took the blood soaked bandage and pressed it to the greatest of the wounds. Before Balin's eyes, the scarlet drained from the linen until it was snow white again, as though the boy's wound had sucked the blood from it. She removed the bandage when it was clean, and Balin saw the grievous slash beneath it had closed and was now only an angry scab. She dipped the bandage again and reapplied it to another of the boy's cuts.

"This is my son," said the man in Balin's ear. "He was attacked in the forest by something invisible. After we found him, he could only scream and could neither eat nor drink, and lightning exacerbated his condition. Thank the Lord that the Lady Lorna Maeve was at hand and saved his life. He may only sustain himself on the consecrated host and blest wine. The blood of a noble born maiden is all that can alleviate his suffering. I am beholden to this lady. For many weeks, she has stayed here nursing his terrible malady. The blood of his assailant will cure him entirely, but we do not know who or what did this."

"It was a knight," Balin said, appalled and fascinated to see the lady's blood drain from the bandage again. "An invisible knight, named Sir Garlon."

The man released him, open mouthed.

"Who told you this?"

"His last victim," said Balin.

Balin looked again at the woman. She was binding her cuts and straightening from her task. The boy had fallen into an exhausted slumber.

"He will sleep for a while, Count," said the woman.

"Thank you, my lady," said the man, whom Balin realized must be Count Oduin. "Please, may I present Sir Balin of the court of Camelot."

"My lady," said Balin. "I came here to Meliot for you."

Lorna frowned, still gathering her bandages, dagger, and pan.

"For me? Do I know you, sir?"

"No," he said regretfully, "but you knew the one who sent me, I think. It was Sir Herlews le Berbeus."

She stopped.

"Where is he now?"

"My lady," said Balin, trying to decide how to best choose his words. "In the forest at the border of Camelot, I saw the invisible knight strike him…"

The pan, dagger, and bandages slammed down on the floor. The boy jerked on the bed, but did not awaken.

She rushed past both of them and took the stairs three at a time.

Balin went to the open window and Count Oduin went with him.

They looked down into the courtyard, where the maid had been left with the horses.

Balin saw her race across the courtyard, go to the second horse, and attack the bindings about the head of the corpse. When the gray face was revealed, Lorna let out a wail that matched the Count's son in its ragged pain.

CHAPTER
EIGHT

THE RAIN FELL without mercy the next morning, soaking the churchyard behind Meliot Castle's chapel and bedeviling the gravediggers who toiled in mud to lay Sir Herlews to rest.

The priest and mourners stood beneath a white canopy held aloft by four servants, and the patter of the drops above Balin's head was like incessant, mocking applause.

The priest recited Latin as they lowered the good knight into the ground, and Lorna Maeve, in garb of black, watched without expression as the diggers covered her love in clumps of mud.

Balin's heart ached for her. He longed to comfort her, to thaw the mourning frost that had settled on her spirit. He knew he was stricken by her, knew it unseemly to so pine for a woman grieving, yet he could not help himself. All his previous worries, his dark thoughts of Arthur and Merlin, Safir and Brulen, had departed from his mind. He had lain awake in the guest chamber of Meliot, wondering solely about her. He was convinced that his meeting her again after that long-ago glance was not happenstance, but a sign of Providence.

He had knelt before the High Queen of Albion and encountered princesses and enchantresses and miraculous maidens, women whose bearing and beauty were as undeniable as they were renowned. But this Lady Lorna Maeve alone had taken root in his heart. He knew she was a pagan, knew it a hopeless sin to love her, and yet here he was, with a hollow space in her outline carved into his heart.

He re-dedicated his quest to find this Garlon. He would do it to avenge Herlews, yes, and to bring a godless villain to God's justice. But he would also achieve this to mend and so perhaps to win the heart of Lorna Maeve.

Sir Herlews had been well regarded, and the servants of Meliot wept for him, as their master eulogized his life.

"He was the best knight I have ever known," said Count Oduin. "A strong man-at-arms, and yet never hesitant to lay down those arms in emulation of our Lord, Jesus Christ. He knew the secret of knighthood that eludes many a proven warrior; that the soul is the sword and armor, not the meager steel that encloses the transient flesh, not the keen yard that may fall from the mailed fist. It is the soul that must be polished and tempered to shine and cut. The heart of Sir Herlews shone so very brightly, that this dark earth we lay over him cannot douse it. It bursts forth like a shoot and illuminates the hearts of all who knew and loved him."

When the last spade had disgorged its load of mud, the Count motioned for Balin to accompany him back to the keep.

They left the servants and the awning behind with Lorna Maeve, who did not stir from the melancholy graveside.

As Balin left the churchyard behind Count Oduin, a young tonsured acolyte in a hermit's habit stepped from behind a moss covered tomb and called him.

"Sir Balin!"

Balin stopped and looked at the boy. He did not know him. How could he?

"Why do you stray so far from Camelot?" said the boy. He had bright, steely eyes, strangely familiar.

"Who are you?" he asked sharply.

"A loyal knight should not stray so far from his king," said the boy, backing away.

Balin advanced on him. Something in the boy's manner of speech raised his hackles. The eyes that looked out at him, it was as if they did not belong in that face.

"We do not take leave of those we love," said the boy, retreating further back behind the tomb. His voice was familiar too. High and yet husky. Not a boy's at all. "Do you not love your king?"

Balin lunged to grab him, and the boy slipped behind the tomb.

Balin turned the corner and saw nothing but the tail end of a small white mouse disappearing through a hole under the churchyard wall.

He shivered, looked all around, skin prickling. He crossed himself and fled the haunted place.

IN THE DRY warmth of the dining hall, Count Oduin broke bread and the maid poured wine, which Balin gratefully drank to calm himself. What had he encountered in the graveyard? A ghost? A fey spirit? Some damned enchanter or enchantress he knew nothing of? The words about Arthur filled him with dread. It knew of the curse of his sword, whatever it was, and wanted him back at Arthur's side.

"Do you fancy a game of gwydbwyll?" the nobleman asked, producing a richly stained teakwood box.

Balin agreed readily, eager to have his mind off the thing in the graveyard. The Count laid out a polished marble board with playing pieces of mahogany and holly wood, much like the one Sir Claellus had taught him and Brulen to play on at Sewingshields.

"You're a fine speaker, my lord," said Balin, as they began. "Any man would be honored to be so well eulogized."

"You embarrass me, Sir Balin," the Count replied graciously. Then the nobleman cleared his throat and eyed him as though he were about to deliver an executioner's blow. "You will pardon me…but I fear you are preparing to embarrass yourself as well."

"My lord?" Balin asked.

"With the Lady Lorna Maeve," Count Oduin whispered, raising his eyebrows. "She is a lovely woman, and attraction comes naturally to a man, but in the very wake of her lover's death…you must tread carefully, sir."

Balin stiffened and blushed. Was he so obvious? He shook his head as if ridding himself of the accusation.

"You're mistaken, Count," he said hurriedly.

"As you say," Count Oduin said, though there was a smile behind his eyes Balin didn't like.

"Tell me of this Sir Garlon," Balin said, making the first move on the board hastily, to change the subject.

"The only Garlon I know is brother to King Pellam of Lystenoyse," said the nobleman, going immediately on the attack with his draughts.

"What do you know of him?"

"He is of legendarily foul temperament. Though Pellam and his brother Pellinore are devout Christians and Pellam is the last of the holy Fisher Kings and master of the Templeise, Garlon is the worst sort of bloodthirsty pagan. He is a backstabber and a ruiner of women. It's said he was once the paramour of the Queen of Norgales, and though it was never proven, some say he betrayed his brother to King Agrippe and aided in the invasion of Lystenoyse, only joining with his brothers when Pellinore arrived to turn the battle."

Balin shuddered at his memory of the Queen of Norgales.

"He is certainly the one," Balin whispered, mounting a bold counterattack. "How can I find him?"

"In spite of his brother's villainy, King Pellam is goodhearted to a fault and keeps his brother close by at Castle Carbonek."

"Direct me to this castle, then," said Balin.

Count Oduin smiled, halting Balin's advance with a deft maneuver of his mahogany men.

"You do not know Carbonek, Sir Balin?"

"Should I?"

"You have heard of the Sangreal surely?"

He frowned, staring at the board and its arrangement, which had become ill favored to his victory.

"I don't know that word."

"But you know of Joseph of Arimathea."

"Of course." Brother Gallet had told him all about Joseph of Arimathea. "Joseph lent his tomb to Christ after the crucifixion. He was chosen by the Messiah to bring the word of God to Albion. He and his followers spread the Gospel through all the kingdoms."

"The Gospel wasn't the only treasure Joseph and his followers brought to Albion," said Count Oduin, settling in. "These are sacred matters, Sir Balin. A sacred, hidden history. Pellam is the latest of a blessed lineage, The Fisher Kings, entrusted with an immensely important duty. The pagans in the days of Agrestes were sinful, base creatures, firmly entrenched in this material, perceptible world. They would never have accepted the word of God had Joseph not provided them with proof of the miracle of Christ."

"I knew that he was a miracle worker…"

"More than that. Joseph housed the body of our Lord in his own tomb, yes. He was also the owner of the Cenacle, the upper room where Christ and his disciples observed The Last Supper. A wealthy man, he was a secret supporter of Jesus. He bore to Albion two sacred relics from Palestine. The spear of the centurion Longinus, which pierced the side of Jesus while He hung on the cross, and the cup of the Last Supper, the Holy Grail, with which Joseph caught His blood."

Count Oduin called for more wine and smiled indulgently. He knew he had won their game and now was toying with Balin.

"Please forgive me if I go on. The lore of the Fisher Kings is something of a hobby for me. Where was I?"

"Two treasures," Balin murmured, leaning on his fists and wishing he could take back his last three turns.

"Two treasures, yes! The Holy Grail. The tales of Joseph and the Grail are myriad. At Rock Castle, for instance, he found the Saracen lord, Argon, had been mauled to death by a lion. He used the Grail to raise him from the dead in Jesus' name. When Argon's brother Matagran learned of this, he thought Joseph a necromancer and attacked him. His sword pierced the thigh of Joseph, but Joseph broke the blade and removed it. The Grail healed Joseph's wound. Both brothers converted to Christianity.

"The Grail is not only miraculous, it can be a terrible curse upon the evil hearted. The pagan King Agrestes invited Joseph and his people to bring it to Camelot, where he professed to accept Christ. Once Joseph and his wife and son departed, Agrestes treacherously slew several of his followers and fixed them to the Black Cross. He filled the Grail with mead and drank from it at a feast. It drove him horrifically mad. He murdered his queen and sons in their beds before consuming the flesh from his own hands and leaping into the hearth fire."

Balin narrowed his eyes, the game forgotten in the face of that sobering tale.

"Do you know the stories of Joseph's miraculous table?" Count Oduin asked, sipping his wine.

"I know that it became the Round Table," said Balin. "I have seen it in King Arthur's hall."

"There is one seat which cannot be filled. The Siege Perilous."

Balin leaned forward, eager to hear of this.

"I was told that a knight who sat in it and was deemed unworthy was burned with holy fire."

"That is the seat of Bron. He married Enygeus, the sister of Joseph of Arimathea. Once, when preaching the Gospel to the pagans of the Outer Isles, Bron caused a great fish to beach and so fed thousands. Ever after, he was called The Fisher. Bron's son, Alan, used the Grail to cure King Kalafes of Lystenoyse of leprosy, and so Kalafes built Carbonek for him. Alan and his brother Joshua built the Palace Adventurous within Carbonek to house the Sangreal. Joshua married the daughter of Kalafes and thus established the line of Fisher Kings, giving over stewardship to his own son, Amandap, who established the Templeise Order, elite knights sworn to give their lives in the guarding of the Sangreal. That is why King Agrippe invaded Pellam in his time. Agrippe and his vile queen were charged by Satan with destroying the Sangreal."

Balin was impressed, but part of this holy pedigree irked him as much as losing this game. King Pellam may well be descended from Joseph of Arimathea and be the keeper of the treasures of God, but what of his brothers? Pellinore or his son Lamorak had murdered King Lot, and Sir Garlon was a traitorous madman who used the dark arts.

"You see," Count Oduin went on, "getting into Carbonek is no small matter. It is a miraculous place and cannot be simply visited. It is impossible to find by all who would seek it."

"How can that be?"

"The miracle of the Palace Adventurous," Count Oduin said. "In King Amandap's time, the wizard Tanabos enchanted the place at the King's request. No man may come to it who seeks it out but by the permission of the Fisher King, and no weapon may pass across its threshold."

"Then Garlon is unassailable," said Balin. "He rides out invisible, and then hides under his brother's protection. Yet, there must be some way."

"There is a way into the castle. A way I have no doubt was provided by God as it coincides with your coming and the revelation of this villain's identity."

"What way?"

"The Queen of Lystenoyse has recently given birth to a daughter, Helizabel. King Pellam has declared fifteen days of celebration at Carbonek and invited the titled nobles to attend the feasting. The invitation has also been extended to knights, should they attend with their ladies."

"Then we will go to Carbonek," came a flat voice from the doorway.

Both men turned to see the Lady Lorna Maeve, as terrible as the Queen of Norgales in her midnight gown, her usually wild hair plastered to her head by the rain. Evidently, she had left the servants behind.

"I will go as Sir Balin's paramour."

Balin felt himself blush and looked away.

"My lady," said Count Oduin, pausing, perhaps to gather his thoughts into tactful speech, "do not burden this knight unduly. His task ahead is hard enough."

"No," Balin said hastily, half-rising from his seat. "My lady, you could never be a burden. That is... I would be honored if you would accompany me."

He sat down just as hurriedly, feeling foolish.

"How shall we induce Sir Garlon to accept Balin's challenge and leave Carbonek?" Count Oduin said. "By all accounts, he's a rascal without honor."

"We will appeal to King Pellam," said Balin. "If he is a righteous king as you say, and we accuse his brother publicly before all his guests, he can't refuse us justice."

Count Oduin scratched the side of his face, musing.

"Can you beat him, Sir Balin?"

"A skulker who attacks unseen and from behind? If I keep a weather eye for him, I can't fail."

"Don't dig his grave yet," said Count Oduin. "Lystenoyse is ringed by evil country, and you have nothing to look forward to at the journey's end but combat with a treacherous foe."

"No knight who is false can stand against one who is true, even with all the power of hell at his back."

"Amen!" said Count Oduin, slapping the table. "Very well. I will outfit for the journey, and send word ahead that I am attending. I shall have to find some present for the baby…"

"Don't name us," said Lorna Maeve.

"Or if you must, give the name Sir Ballantyne," said Balin.

Count Oduin rose.

"And his blood. We must carry away some of his blood to cure my son."

Lorna Maeve held up something, a conical piece of steel. The pointed tip of Herlews' lance.

"When he falls, I have sworn to sink my Herlews' lance in Garlon's body. Your son shall have his cure, Count Oduin."

Count Oduin looked nervously to Balin, then nodded to her.

"It is three days to Lystenoyse, and no easy journey. We'll depart in the morning."

Count Oduin touched Balin's shoulder and departed.

Balin rose, too, and found Lorna Maeve still standing in the door-way.

"My lady," he said, lips trembling even to address her. "I will avenge your Herlews."

"Honorable challenge or no," she said impassively. It was an edict, not a question, and he shivered inwardly, love-struck even by her mercilessness. "Swear." It was almost a command.

He touched his closed fist to his own breast and bowed his head.

"I swear it."

When he looked again, she had gone without even a rustle of her skirts.

CHAPTER
NINE

HE RAIN CEASED at last, as if God approved of Balin's latest undertaking.

Count Oduin procured a chest of gold for the baby Helizabel, and they set out from Castle Meliot, the nobleman with four of his servants, Balin, and Lorna Maeve on a black palfrey. She had insisted upon the dour mount, as she had cast aside her mourning clothes to pose as Balin's lady.

They rode throughout the day, and it was a surpassingly sunny and pleasant country. The fauna and beasts they saw along the way seemed to rejoice on the first clear, bright day after such a long rain. Sparrows circled them, wending even through their horses' legs as they rode, and squirrels chased each other up and down the trees.

Though Lorna Maeve's expression was morose and listless, Balin could not help but see her as a human culmination of the natural beauty all around. Though her heart had passed into darkness with the death of Herlews, her arrival in Balin's life had dispersed the clouds that had gathered around his own mood. Oduin was right. He was desperate to win her.

"You put your heart in a broken container, my friend," the Count advised candidly as they rode behind. "The Lady Lorna Maeve loved Sir Herlews with all that she was. His death has emptied her."

Balin wouldn't be dissuaded. "Tell me about her, sir. Tell me about how she was. I can see the remnants of her. They're like the tracks of a deer in new snow."

Count Oduin shook his head.

"She was a lively lass, when she and her knight first came to my keep. Her blood is of the Summer Country. Avalon. It's where she learned her healing arts. The ladies of that land are always full of life, and they fill their lives with love."

"You do not decry them, as a Christian?" Balin asked.

"Jesus did not shun the tax collector or the harlot. Who am I?" Oduin said with a shrug.

Balin did not wholly agree with this, and yet his feeling for Lorna Maeve denied him any argument.

Oduin went on, "When she was with Herlews, it was as if…as if the sun and moon had come together. They would sing old songs, and in their hearts, in their eyes, they were like the couples in them. It's the happiest thing, when two such lovers meet, and it is the saddest tragedy when they are parted so."

"Do you think?" Balin ventured, watching her. "Do you think she could be healed? Could she be made to love again?"

"Love comes, Balin. It grows, but gradually," Oduin said sadly. "It can't be made or hurried, any more than you or I can force a tree to grow."

But it could be coaxed. It could be nurtured. Balin resolved then to plant a seed.

He urged his horse beside hers. She was not watching the road, allowing the black horse to carry her. Her attention was on the lance-tip of Herlews, resting in the nest of her cupped hands before her like a baby bird of iron.

"How fare you, my lady?" Balin asked.

She glanced up at him, as though she had been dreaming.

"That is, do you have need of anything?" he pressed.

She smirked and looked at him with a disbelief that cut him. He felt a fool.

"Water?" he said hurriedly. "Are you thirsty?"

"No," she said.

"This is beautiful country to go riding in," Balin said. "There were woods like these around my mother's cabin. The trees were so green in the summer…" His words failed him and he struggled to bring to mind something that should bring her back from the dark, to his side. "My brother and I used to climb the apple tree on the hill just to sit and look over it all. The breeze moved the meadow grass like waves,"

The analogy pleased him.

She turned to him.

"Apple tree?"

"My mother planted it."

"She was of Avalon?"

He wondered how she had guessed that. He found himself in a strange place, wanting her to speak, but not wanting her to ask more.

"She was, in her youth, before she married my father."

"He was Christian?"

"And a knight, yes."

"Like my Herlews," she said. "The sisters told me he would prove false, but he never broke an oath to me, except when he died," she murmured.

She was back in her sorrow.

Balin fell back, hunching in his saddle a little, feeling as far from her as Lucifer from heaven.

A FEW HOURS from dusk they sighted a great growth of forest stretching out like a thick drab green fog and run through with wisps of murky white mist. The winding road disappeared into it, and a few miles to the west, Balin saw a bare hill pushing up through the dense canopy, the black spire of an old keep fighting to escape its growing confines.

"That is Carteloise Forest," said Count Oduin. "On the other side lies Lystenoyse. I told you Pellam's kingdom was bordered by an evil land. There is an old curse upon Carteloise. At its heart is Aspetta Ventura, the Castle of the Leprous Lady. We must spend the night here, well away, and traverse the forest tomorrow."

"Who is this Leprous Lady?" Balin asked, as they dismounted.

"I know no specifics," Count Oduin admitted. "I don't even know if such a lady resides there. I know only that the forest should not be traveled by night, and the keep is to be avoided."

As the servants unpacked the camp gear, Lorna Maeve stood watching the sun descend over the forest and stared long at the lonesome stone tower.

The pavilions raised, the servants cooked supper, and still she sat atop her horse. The moon had risen, casting silver light on the edge of the tower.

Balin brought her food to her. As he approached, he heard her murmur:

"White as the face of the moon,
You traverse the wasted land
bringing pestilence to all you meet."

"My lady?" he asked tentatively. "It's getting cold."

She did not stir, but for the night breeze passing through her wild hair. He cleared his throat.

"Why do you stare so at that place?"

"I do not know," she said absently, as if waking from a dream. She looked about, as if surprised to see darkness. He offered his hand, but she let herself down, and he took the bridle instead and offered her a dish of stew.

"I'm not very hungry," she said.

"May I walk you to your pavilion?"

She gathered her skirts and placed two fingers on his offered elbow.

As they walked to the silken tent, she spoke softly, "You saw Herlews die."

"Yes, my lady."

"Did he…did he speak? I know that he named his assassin."

Balin swallowed. She sought some comfort about her lover's demise. Some final word, maybe. There had been nothing, but she didn't know that.

"He named his assassin," Balin affirmed, "and he asked that I continue his quest. And that I bring him to you. He told me how I would know you."

She said nothing.

They skirted the firelight and headed for her tent. The light within made the blue silk glow like a paper lantern.

"He described me your face. The aspect of your eyes and your hair," said Balin carefully. He could not stop himself, though something urged restraint. "He said that of the earthly things which he would yearn for, he would miss your embrace the most. Above the excitement of the hunt, and the glories of the quest, there rose your sweet face before his fading gaze. Your name was the last thing to issue from his lips. 'Lorna Maeve,' he said. 'Sweet summer spirit. I love you.' And so he passed."

He praised the darkness that hid his coloring face. He could never have dared to speak without it.

At his side, he sensed her stiffen, and her fingers, two points of unbearable warmth and closeness on his arm, retracted as if burnt.

"Those aren't his words," she said.

She turned on him, and he saw the furious flash of her eyes in the light from her tent.

"If he'd had more life," Balin said lamely, "he would have said them."

"Have you no honor, sir, to assail me so? My love lies fresh in his grave. The dust hasn't yet settled on his face."

Balin thought to deny. But how could he? He had bumbled into stupid deceit, like some sweaty lothario, and now he curled like a snail under her outrage.

"Forgive me!" he stammered.

She would have none of it. "Would you have me as your *lover*?"

Now the blood pulsed behind his eyes, and he felt as if his head would burst. This was nothing he could cut his way out of.

"Please, my lady. I know that…I have no tongue…"

"You don't? Your tongue was quite evident but a moment ago."

Her voice was shrill, and some of the servants at the fire looked over.

"Please, I sought only to comfort you."

"I know well what comfort you offer." She spat, pulling open the tent flap. She started to go in, then spun on him. "Is that why you took on Herlews' quest? Did you hope to bed me? Do you love me? Speak!"

That angered him. He didn't like being belittled or having his intentions called into question. He was hurt and struck back, flinging down the iron dish of stew with a crash that made Count Oduin jump up from the fire.

"No! I am a knight of the Round Table. My heart is for my king and quest. There is little room in my heart for else."

Her blazing eyes grew half-lidded. "My Herlews had room for the whole world in his heart."

Balin's teeth jammed together, and he drove his fingers into his palms. He wanted to hit something. *Herlews again. He was like a saint to her.*

He turned away with an inarticulate snarl and stomped out into the darkness. There was a thick copse of trees a few hundred yards distant, and he made for it. He stumbled over something in the dark, cursed, and let his momentum hurl him into a ragged run.

He heard Count Oduin call his name, but he didn't stop.

He drew his swords and when he reached the trees, he attacked them with fury, hacking down saplings and dulling his blades in a mute and frenzied tantrum. His assault took him through the stand of trees to the other side, where, panting, he drove both weapons into the ground, sank to his knees, and sobbed his frustration.

The world was an abominable disappointment. He had been reared on fairytales, weaned on the belief that God was in His heaven insuring the deliverance of the just and the punishment of the wicked; that battle lines were clearly drawn between good and evil, and he could be a shining champion of the former, assured victory by the law of the universe.

Yet here was this woman who, like his mother, should represent to him all that Gallet had warned him against, and she had unmanned him as easily as a low branch checking him from a horse. There was Arthur, the personification of his highest ideals, guided by the machinations of lurking sorcerers and harboring some darkness he did not have the intelligence to decipher or even the veracity to believe. His brother, who by the stories, should have been his merry companion throughout every grand adventure, was a brooding murderer given over to black moods and bitter pessimism What was he himself, when he looked beneath the veneer of knighthood he sought so hard to build and maintain?

Wasn't he just a brute? Wasn't he the savage they all said he was? What ideal dwelled in his heart? It was no abode of honor and truth and faith. Wasn't his heart a ramshackle home for envy and lust and violent, frustrated rage?

All this pounded in his angry brain, until the chirping of the night insects was lost in the rush of blood in his ears.

He glanced up through the tangle of his fingers and hair. On the blade of the Adventurous Sword, above the two hearts of Lanceor and Colombe, there was now an etching of tall tower against the full moon, or perhaps the noon sun. A knight was falling end over end from its highest window.

Good, he thought. *Let that be my fate. And let it come quickly.*

He almost didn't hear her scream.

It was Lorna Maeve.

And there was more: the shriek of Oduin's maid, the angry yells of men, and the exclamations of horses.

He ran back through the trees. It was an easy, clear path, he had cut, but he still managed to catch his foot on a limb he had himself severed, and bowled over into the grass.

Picking himself up, he saw the far off light of the campfire and the black shapes of men on horseback circling it like demons.

He saw Lorna Maeve's tent pulled down, saw thrashing figures pulled over the saddles of the riders. There were five or six strangers.

They galloped away in the direction of the forest, the screams of their prisoners diminishing with the thunder of their hooves.

One remained behind, sawing the hobbles from the horses with a dagger.

Balin ran across the meadow for the fire.

The last of the assailants wore armor and a long head of black hair. He turned and straightened as Balin came out of the dark, but he did no more than get both feet under him before the Adventurous Sword sent his head spinning into the campfire.

His body crashed down with a clatter.

Balin stood in the shambles of the camp. The three male servants had been killed, but the maid, Lorna Maeve, and Count Oduin had been taken. For ransom, or for some other sinister purpose? He checked Count Oduin's tent. The small chest of gold for Pellam's daughter was still there. They were not robbers, then.

Whoever they were, there was no doubt they were bound for the keep at the middle of the forest.

He had to pursue, though it was black night.

He saddled Ironprow, freed his armor, and hastily began to don it.

He was halfway through the laborious process when he heard hoof beats on the road.

The raiders returning for their missing comrade? He shook off his unfastened greaves and leapt into Ironprow's saddle.

There were three armored riders, and they came not from the direction the others had gone, but from the southern road.

One stopped short at the sight of Balin, and the other two slowed, but drew their swords.

"Sir Peryn! Sir Garnysh!" called the one who had stopped. "Do not draw!"

"He is one of them!" yelled one of the others.

"He's not," the unarmed knight insisted, reaching for the shield hanging on his saddle.

Balin tensed, ready to fight should one of them charge.

"How do you know?" demanded the other.

"I think I know my own brother," said the third, and he held up his shield for Balin to see the charge of the two boars.

CHAPTER
TEN

BRULEN," BALIN SAID in disbelief, peering at the shield. Then, because the last time they'd seen each other, the sword of Rience had cleaved Brulen's shield in two, he asked warily, "Is it really you?"

In a few moments, his helmet was off. It was indeed Brulen, unless some goblin of this evil land had taken his form. Though his shield had been replaced, there was still the rent in his right-hand vambrace, where Rience's sword had lodged.

"This is my brother, Sir Balin," said Brulen to his two armored companions.

One lifted his visor, revealing a clean-shaven face and guileless eyes.

"I have heard of the Knight of The Two Swords. I should have known you by your arms," said the knight. "I'm Sir Peryn of Montebeliard."

The other knight raised his charge, that Balin might know him. *Gules, two barbel addorsed, or.*

"Sir Garnysh of The Mount," he said, and then, hurriedly, "Sir Balin, did you see the six riders who attacked this camp?"

Balin nodded.

"Five of them took Count Oduin and two ladies, and slew his manservants. I killed the sixth man as he tried to steal our horses."

"Killed him?" Brulen repeated, his face drawn in concern. "How, Balin?"

"I beheaded him," Balin said, pointing with his still drawn sword to the head burning in the fire.

Brulen looked relieved, and Sir Peryn said, "Thank God for that."

Sir Garnysh threw up his visor, revealing impressively cultivated upper lip hair underlining a long nose and furtive looking eyes.

"Was there a woman with them?" Sir Garnysh pressed.

"I saw no woman," Balin said. "But I was off by that stand of trees when they struck."

"Why were you not on watch with your people?" Peryn asked.

Balin felt his face color again and stammered to answer.

"Never mind that! Where did they go?" Garnysh interrupted.

"I saw them ride for the forest," Balin said, thankful for a way to avoid Peryn's inquiry. "There is a castle there, a keep."

They all looked across the darkness, and in that instant, a single yellow light shone like a beacon over the tops of the silver-chased trees.

Somehow, the appearance of that light sent a shiver through Balin's bones.

"What is that castle? Do either of you know it?" Brulen asked.

"Its name is Aspetta Ventura," said Balin. "It's called The Castle of the Leprous Lady. But I know nothing more. Brulen, what is going on? Why are you here?"

"I might ask you the same, brother."

"We were on our way to Lystenoyse, to celebrate the birth of the princess of that kingdom," said Balin, seeing no need to elucidate further.

"We are on a quest to retrieve Sir Garnysh's lady, the daughter of the Duke of Harniel, who was stolen from her bedchamber by some band of villains on the eve of their wedding. We have been a day behind them for two days and finally tracked them here."

"We are losing time!" Garnysh barked. "Let's ride!"

Garnysh spurred his horse and went galloping down the road.

Peryn spared them each a look and followed.

"These are not ordinary men, Balin," Brulen warned.

"What do you mean?"

"One of their party fell back and ambushed us on the road last night. I've never faced so terrible a foe. He fought on despite wounds that would have slain you or me outright. He was strong enough to throw Sir Peryn and his horse bodily. His eyes…"

"Your companions will leave us behind if we don't follow. Go. I will gather my armor and be along."

"I'm glad to see you again, Balin," Brulen said.

Balin bit back a thousand questions. Where and why had Brulen gone from Cameliard? What did he know of the painting at St. Stephen's which Lot had spoken of?

Balin only nodded and slapped the rump of his brother's horse and watched him go, before returning to his armor.

Two hours into the night they rode through Carteloise Forest. Balin discovered an overgrown ascending lane, little more than an animal run, branching off in the direction of the hillside keep.

The forest was dense, dark, and unnaturally silent, lit only by slivers of moonlight and their own torches. The trees were so close together that the path was like a dark cave tunnel.

"I do not like the look of that way," said Sir Peryn warily, "but I see no other avenue. We know they have gone this way. They cannot but pass us to come back. If a keep waits at the end of this, we should wait and attack at sunrise."

"And give those villains a night to fortify themselves, a night unopposed with my lady in their power, in their own haven?" Sir Garnysh veritably shrieked. "We go now!"

"Peryn may be right," Brulen said thoughtfully. "They could lay in wait for us like last night, and this time we are outnumbered."

"Our horses could stumble in that pitch black."

"They can see by the torches well enough," Garnysh argued.

"Then they will see us coming," said Peryn.

"They already know we pursue them, you fool!" Garnysh snapped.

"Balin?" Brulen asked. "What say you? What course?"

"Count Oduin said the keep was to be avoided at night, but the ladies these fiends took…" Like Garnysh, the thought of Lorna Maeve subjected to some unworthy dishonor by these strange knights brought his blood to a boil. "Garnysh is right. We shouldn't tarry."

Garnysh lit a torch and led the way, not waiting to hear Brulen's course.

Balin fell in behind, and then Brulen and Peryn, the last with a final mutter of protestation.

The path was treacherous in the dark, and though, as Brulen predicted, the horses stumbled, none fell.

It was another hour's ride up a steep incline before the tangled roof of the forest gave way to a night field of blooming stars, and they came to the foot of the grassless hill atop which the Aspetta Ventura sat like a forgotten pagan idol. Its battlements were crumbling, and some broken blocks lay on the ground where they'd fallen. Its walls were covered in climbing vegetation. Its single leaning tower bisected the bright moon.

The light that shined around it disclosed a stone walled graveyard with one old crypt and nine tombstones, the latter incongruously new and well-tended among the ruinous surroundings. The grass on one grave was short, and they saw that a tenth had been dug recently. The laborer's spade still stood upright in the disinterred earth like a bare sapling.

The yellow light in the high window flickered, the upper reaches of the keep exposed to the wind that howled mournfully above Carteloise Forest.

They approached the great, solid door. They heard an abrupt groan. It swung outward and a gust of strong, cold wind blew out, upsetting the horses.

Two black armored, bare headed pale figures stood in the doorway, their long white hair whipping about them. One bore an axe.

"Knights! Steer clear of this keep! You are not welcome here and may come no further!" boomed one of them impressively.

"You hold my bride-to-be against her will!" Garnysh yelled back.

"And two ladies and a nobleman unjustly taken on the road!" Balin added.

"The two ladies and the man you speak of are guests of the Lady Verdoana, chatelaine of this keep," said one of the pale knights. "As for the one who was to be wed, she came of her own volition and is even now with our captain, Sir Guthkeled."

"Liar!" Sir Garnysh thundered and slammed down his visor.

"Depart!" the second of the pale knights ordered. "Or it will go badly for you!"

"Say you so?" Sir Garnysh said arrogantly and spurred his horse.

The chill wind from the keep kicked up once more, howling, so that they had to lean into it. The two black armored knights bellowed in answer to Sir Garnysh's rash charge, and leapt into the air as no men possibly could, so laden down in plate. It was as if they were astride the ill wind itself and flew spinning through the very air at them.

Garnysh's horse balked at this unnatural sight and threw him to the ground, turned, and bolted back into the forest for all it was worth.

The two devilish knights passed over him and instead bore Sir Peryn down from his horse. Brulen fought to keep his mount steady, while Balin atop Ironprow galloped to his aid.

Yet though it was a short distance, by the time Balin reached Peryn, the two figures atop him had bodily torn his harness from him like paper, and were gleefully rending and tearing at him with axe and bare hands as he shrieked in agony, great gouts of blood and flesh flying over their shoulders like the clots of earth flung back by two digging dogs.

Balin fought his urge to flee in the face of such horror and hewed down, sending the upraised arm of one of the pale knights tumbling into the churchyard still grasping its axe.

The inhuman warrior wailed in pain and surprise and leapt desperately at Balin before he could draw his second sword.

Brulen was there though and swung a spiked flail into the thing's face.

To Balin's chagrin, the metal ball smashed like a glass egg and the weapon broke apart in a burst of steel and chain links. The knight was distracted but entirely unharmed.

The leaping knight swept its surviving hand inches past Balin's face, and he saw long clawed fingernails yellow in the moonlight, heard them scrape against his helm.

The tremendous jump took the knight entirely over Ironprow's back, and Balin twisted in his saddle to jab at the thing with the Adventurous Sword, suspecting his second weapon would be no avail and remembering that the enchanted blade had passed through its arm easy enough.

The pale knight jumped back, right into the path of Brulen, whose horse reared and struck with its hooves, then came down with its full weight.

The knight thrust out its arm though and gripped the horse's thick neck, actually holding it aloft for a terrifying moment, long enough for Brulen to tumble off its back in an awkward heap.

Balin swept across the fiend's chest with the Adventurous Sword, and the keen, supernatural edge sliced it from pauldron to cuisse. It stumbled, and when the terrified horse at last came down, it was because the creature holding it had slid apart in two halves.

There was no time to reflect on the victory or the nature of the enemy though, as Balin felt himself jerked from the saddle by an irresistible hand and flung down on his back.

The second knight straddled him, and the face that loomed in his was the very essence of nightmare. Its bulging eyes were unnaturally black, yet flecked throughout with scarlet like resolute cinders in a bed of ash. Its marble white flesh was spattered in Sir Peryn's shining blood, and its dripping red lips pulled back from a hellish maw that included a pair of long, wolf-like fangs.

Balin recoiled from a hot blast of rotten breath, tinged with the sharp scent of steel and blood. Its foot pinned his wrist to the ground. Balin could not lift his sword. He struck out with his free, mailed hand, but it was like punching a solid trunk of oak.

Brulen rose over the thing's shoulder and leapt upon its back, wrapping both arms about its neck, trying to twist its head off, but evidently its bones were as resilient as its flesh.

The thing hooked its fingers in Brulen's rerebrace and pitched him lightly head over heels to the ground, so that now he lay helmet to helmet with his brother on his back.

Then it leaned in closer, grinning that feral grin of a devil frolicking in hellfire. Its hair was putrid bone-yellow, a color born of diseased follicles.

"Cease!" came a strident woman's cry from somewhere high above, yet with such vigor that it seemed to make the trees quake.

The pale fiend straightened and looked up, and Balin could not but follow its gaze.

High atop the keep stood a figure even more terrible and harrowing than the diabolic creature that had brought Balin down.

It was female, and the very image of the Queen of Norgales, covered head to toe so that not a glimpse of humanity showed through. Yet where the Queen's garb had been black, this woman was all in purest white. Her face was shrouded beneath a long white veil and barbette, and even her hands were covered in white fabric.

She was not alone.

Beside her on the roof was Count Oduin, his hands bound behind him, his eyes blindfolded. The woman in white gripped him by the shoulder and called down, "Cease your contest! Each side has forfeited a man. Lay down your arms and enter peaceably, else I will cast this nobleman down to a hard death."

Balin's beastly opponent looked down at him, one white eyebrow cocked.

"Do you yield?" it queried.

"I will abide," said Balin through his teeth, for he had never surrendered to any knight before.

"I agree," said Brulen beside him.

"Never!" Garnysh bellowed.

Balin strained to look, and saw Garnysh standing where he had fallen, his sword and shield raised.

"Garnysh, you fool!" Brulen hollered. "Your rashness has already cost Sir Peryn's life! You will not be responsible for another! Accept the offer! If your lady is within, we will treat for her!"

Garnysh lowered his arms with hesitation, but let them clatter, as three more of the black knights marched from the dark keep bearing spears.

The one that pinned Balin stooped down and tried to pluck the Adventurous Sword from his grasp but grunted in surprise.

Balin smiled as it straightened again and called up to his mistress, "This one's blade is enchanted! I cannot lift it!"

"Leave it in the road!" The woman in white replied, ushering Count Oduin back into her keep.

The evil knight instead grabbed Balin's sword hand in a Herculean grip and taking Brulen's arm with the other, hauled them both to their feet. In spite of the gravity of their predicament, Balin's memory cast back to the misadventures of his childhood with Brulen, when their mother would hoist them up from some disaster and carry them away to be scrubbed or paddled.

Balin looked across at his brother, dangling from the knight's other arm.

Brulen caught his look and evidently read the memory in his brother's eyes. The fear slid from his face.

They very nearly smirked at each other.

"Come along, sir knights," the fiend said with more than a hint of gloating. "Avail yourselves of the hospitality of the Aspetta Ventura."

As they were pulled rudely along, Balin whispered to Brulen, "What does the name mean? Aspetta Ventura?"

"Expected Fortune," Brulen answered. "In this case, I expect, not the welcome kind."

CHAPTER
ELEVEN

I F THE PALE knight's jest about hospitality had been misconstrued as anything but a jest, the three knights swiftly found their expectations righted. The black knight flung them unceremoniously down the stone steps of a dim dungeon beneath the keep. The heavy door slammed shut behind them, a lock clanked into place, and the thud of a thick timber bolt fell resoundingly, sealing them within. Balin and Brulen picked themselves up in the dark. Garnysh had dashed his head on a step and was unconscious and bleeding.

Balin tore a scrap of cloth from his padding and bound up the knight's head.

But for a dim glow that shone through the small barred window in the prison door, cast by the torch sconce in the outer hall, they were in total blackness.

"Have you ever seen anything like those creatures?"

"Never," Brulen answered. "Not in all my travels."

"They were *devouring* Sir Peryn," Balin said, shuddering uncontrollably.

"No, not devouring. Not exactly. I saw clearly. They lapped his blood like a dog."

"Well," said Balin, chuckling nervously. "Then instead of cannibals, they are...what?"

"*Baobhan sith*," said a small voice from the darkness that made both of them jump nearly from skin and armor.

They gripped each other's arms, not full grown men anymore, not proven knights, but brothers trembling beneath their sheets at some imagined goblin at the window, some lurking bodack that reverted to a harmless kindling pile at dawn.

They waited tensely, their own laborious breathing and the steady breath of Garnysh the only sound, so that for a moment, they thought they had imagined the voice.

Then it spoke again, high and small, a child's voice.

"Are you still there?"

"Who speaks?" Brulen whispered.

"A prisoner, like yourselves. But I've heard of the *baobhan sith*. The bloodsuckers of the Caledonian highlands. That is what I think they are, though I had thought they were always women. Maybe they are the *droch-fhola* of The Black Stacks in Hibernia. And maybe they are all the same thing. Who can say?"

"That is no child," said Brulen. "It speaks in the voice of a child, but in this castle, who knows?"

"I didn't say I was a child, Sir Brulen," said the voice. "Just a prisoner like you. Bound in cold iron to a dank wall, caught like some clumsy poacher in these accursed woods."

Balin heard a clink as of chains shifting from somewhere across the chamber.

"How do you know my name?" Brulen demanded, his voice quavering at having been personally addressed by the dungeon's unseen occupant.

"Who that knows of knights has not heard of Sir Brulen The Sinister? Who is that with you?" the voice countered.

"Sir Balin of the Court of Camelot," Balin answered, a bit more curious than afraid now.

"Don't answer, you fool!" Brulen hissed.

"Of the Court of Camelot," the voice repeated. "No longer of Northumberland, no longer The Savage? And what of the Knight of The Two Swords? Have you cast aside that appellation as well, finally?"

"Who are *you*?" Balin asked.

"And who is the third knight I hear breathing?"

"Sir Garnysh of The Mount," said Balin.

Brulen struck Balin's shoulder with his gauntlet. The sound was like a gong in the dungeon.

The unseen prisoner sucked its teeth.

"Alas that *he* has come. He shall not like what he finds here."

"What will she do to us, this Leprous Lady? This Verdoana?" Balin asked.

"Even I don't know that," said the child-voice, "but if these chains were unlocked, we could find out together."

"You mean to say you could free us from here?"

"Almost certainly," said the child-voice.

"Don't be tricked, Balin," Brulen urged. "This thing screams of faerie. Remember our mother's stories."

"Yes yes, Sir Balin," the voice said, annoyed. "Remember faerie rings and hollow hills and mad dances and maypoles, thousand-year slumbers and pixie dust. I'm no sprite! Unchain me and let's be off from this place!"

"You haven't yet said who or what you are," said Brulen.

"Who are you speaking to?" Sir Garnysh muttered drowsily.

The third voice nearly made Balin shout his surprise. "Curse this damned darkness!" he blurted out.

Garnysh clanked and shifted between them, sitting up. "There is flint and firesteel here in my belt," said Garnysh. Then after a moment,

"Yes, I still have it."

Brulen tore a piece of fabric and in a few moments, Garnysh was striking primordial sparks that lit the three knights in brief flashes like lightning.

"Steel yourselves, knights," said the boy-voice as the charcloth flamed and the fabric lit in Garnysh's hand, "for I was apprehended in the midst of making my escape."

Garnysh raised the makeshift light. It only burned away a few feet of darkness, and the three of them, huddled together, rose and moved across the black room toward the sound of the voice.

Vermin scurried across the straw-strewn floor, retreating from them.

"I may be a sight," said the voice, just as the light reached the far end of the chamber, and suddenly the wall and the figure chained to it emerged from the pitch black like something surfacing from a pool of oil.

Garnysh dropped the firecloth with a start, nearly setting the sparse straw on the floor ablaze. Balin caught it, and fixed his horrified eyes on the thing that had spoken.

It was chained to the wall by its manacled wrists and fitted with a collar around its thin, bent neck. It was the size of a man, but thin in the extreme, its frame skeletal and the muscles underdeveloped. It was naked and mottle-skinned, yet not fully flesh. It's head and shoulders were covered in a strange, wet-looking mane, consisting of something between hair and feathers. Its face was set with two huge, gleaming black eyes situated on opposite sides of its head and darting independently of each other, like a lizard's. Its mouth tapered into a long, curved point with a pair of pursed human lips and small, nubby teeth at the end, and a shaggy black beard shot through with feathers hung beneath, almost to its swollen belly. Its ears were mere holes recessed in the sides of its head, but long wiry hairs sprung from their depths like cat whiskers. The hands that protruded from the manacles were long, fingerless points, where the stubs of rudimentary thumbs twitched uselessly at the base of each. Its legs below the quite human knees were beaded and leathery, and ended in splayed, spindly claws that could grasp a man's head. In the axis of its legs was a mass of tendril hair and shaggy feathers, wreathing a disconcerting mélange of pitch black cloaca and giblets.

Garnysh stumbled backward.

"God's bones, douse the light, Sir Balin!" he wailed. "Return that demon to the darkness."

Balin was revolted by the sight of the thing and wished for a blade to slay it with as he could not even stomach striking it with his armored hand. What kind of a horror was this? Surely Garnysh was right and it was a demon of some kind. He began to mutter prayers against it.

Brulen was curious. "What are you?"

"Remove this iron from me and you will know," it pleaded, and the child voice was more horrendous coming from that strange maw.

"Why don't you tell us what you are first?" Brulen pressed.

"The iron forbids me."

"We should kill this thing in its chains," Balin muttered. "It's a demon of hell."

"I second that!" Garnysh said.

"Who chained you? The Lady Verdoana?"

"Her servants," said the thing. "They trapped me in the forest."

Brulen stared for a long time at the thing shifting in the fluttering firelight.

"If Verdoana's servants trapped it, it may not mean us ill after all," he ventured.

"Or maybe she harnessed it to bolster her fell powers," Garnysh said.

"When it was a child you were afraid of it, and now that it's a demon you think it means us no harm?" Balin said, exasperated.

"I don't think it's a demon," said Brulen. "Faerie, maybe, but no demon."

It looked from one to the other of them, but its inhuman face betrayed no emotion, and it said nothing.

"Gallet told me that faeries are angels caught outside of heaven after the Fall of Lucifer. With no home in hell and barred from heaven, they grew mad," said Balin.

"Not a demon, though," said Brulen, shrugging.

"But not harmless," Garnysh added.

"I was taught the Fey always repay a kindness," Brulen said.

"A faerie's notion of kindness is to invite you to a dance that lasts a thousand years, or to take your human burdens from you by turning you into a fox or a snail," Garnysh muttered.

"I think it can free us from here," said Brulen. "Will you eschew its help it if means your lady's life?"

Balin had been set to leave the thing languishing and find some other method of escape when his brother had said that. And for his part, he knew his answer.

"I am not willing to wait. If the thing can help us, free it," he said. "Our time may be as short as our need is long."

"I don't like this," said Garnysh, backing out of the light, a wide, scared expression on his face. "I'll have no part in it."

"Then you hold the light," Brulen said, handing the burning cloth to Garnysh, who reluctantly held it high. Then to, Balin, he said: "Help me, brother."

Balin curled his lip to approach the thing. It smelled of wood smoke and sweat, and his skin crawled when he laid fingers on the pin of the manacle enfolding its malformed wrist. He had to take off his gauntlets to pry it with his fingers, and grimaced to feel its clammy skin brushing his knuckles.

He was forced to lean close as he worked the pin loose. Brulen struggled with the other. He turned his face from the thing and saw, with a shudder, a small white mouse very like the one he had seen in the cemetery at Castle Meliot. It was sitting upright on its haunches and staring up at them with pink, knowing eyes, nose twitching.

He spat at it, and it retreated into the darkness. He could feel it there in the black, watching still. It made him rethink this plan of action, but even as he did so, the pin popped loose and the spindly arm fell from the iron fetter.

"Get to work on the collar, Balin," said Brulen, still painstakingly working the left-hand manacle pin.

Balin put his hands about the collar seeking out its weak point. The fleshy throat of the thing undulated against the backs of his fingers, and the fine feather-hairs tickled his flesh, which seemed to scream in disgusted protest at the unwanted interaction.

Brulen freed the creature's other arm. It made no move, but stood there patiently with its bent arms before it in the attitude of a mantis.

The light of the small tinder fire was dying by then, and as his fingers tore and bled from the hard exertion, it died altogether, and they were again in total darkness, the hissing breath of the thing close in their ears.

Balin didn't like to free this thing blindly and urged Garnysh to make another light, but by the time he had fished out his steel again and begun striking sparks, Balin felt the pin pop free and the collar clanked open.

Balin stepped back as though from a hot stove.

There was no sound from the creature at first, but then he heard it give a sigh of contentment.

Bare feet slapped across the floor, and they heard Garnysh give an exclamation, heard his armor scrape and clatter.

"What is it?" Balin asked urgently.

"Nothing! It just moved past me, to the door," Garnysh whispered.

They marked its progression. It seemed to move with purpose. No stumbling or cursing. Evidently it navigated the darkness with no ill effect. They heard it ascend the stair and cautiously crept after it, clattering against each other in the black.

The door clanked, and on the other side, the bolt hit the ground with a thud.

The heavy door lurched open, spilling a cone of light into the dungeon, against which, their liberator stood limned.

But it was not a hellish monstrosity any longer.

It was Merlin, and he was naked as a hatchling jay.

"Well come on," he said, waving them up, impatiently. He stepped out of the dungeon into the torch-lit hall beyond.

"Merlin," said Brulen, in as cold and bitter a tone as ever Balin had heard his brother speak. "Better to have left him chained."

CHAPTER
TWELVE

THE NAKED ENCHANTER led the three knights through the corridor and cast one disparaging look over his bare shoulder.

"The three of you make a racket like a gang of kitchen boys dropping crocks down the stairs," Merlin grumbled.

"How did you end up in this dungeon, Merlin?" Balin asked.

"I came looking for you, Balin," Merlin said. "I was told you would be in the Carteloise Forest, but I suppose I was too early. More likely you were late. As I said, I was set upon by the same knights who captured you. I tried to escape, but they were surprisingly fast. They clapped me in cold iron mid-transformation. I did not expect to see you again, Brulen."

"I would not have freed you had I known it was you," Brulen said. "I should've listened to Sir Garnysh. He was right. We have unleashed a demon."

"Only half, on my father's side," said Merlin, peering around a corner.

He waved them closer then, and strode in.

"Your weapons."

They found themselves in an old, long unused guardroom, and

sure enough, their swords and shields were neatly arrayed on wall pegs intended to keep the arms of the castle guard.

"These won't do anything against those things," Balin said. "I need my sword."

"For once I agree," said Merlin. "Where would they have put it?" he wondered aloud.

"It's still in the road in front of the castle," said Balin. "They couldn't lift it."

"Of course."

"The Lady Verdoana," said Garnysh, strapping on his sword, "she must be like her servants."

"I know next to nothing about her," Merlin admitted. "There were stories of the Leprous Lady in my boyhood. That she preyed upon passing maidens, I knew, but nothing else. We must assume she is of the same dreadful race as her knights, yes."

"Then they will want the ladies' blood!" Garnysh despaired. "Oh, my sweet Ettard!"

"But if that is so," Merlin went on, ignoring Garnysh's outburst, "there may be another way to dispatch her. Of the *baobhan sith* I have heard it said that a shaft of yew through the heart will destroy them and that they cannot abide the light of day."

"We have no yew, Merlin." Balin hissed. "And we're pretty far from dawn. Think of something else."

Merlin twisted his beard with his finger.

"No holy water among you? Crucifix? Eucharistic host?"

"We're knights, not deacons!" Brulen scoffed.

Merlin thought for a moment. "Bulb of garlic?"

"We're not cooks either."

Merlin threw up his hands. "Then, Balin, I think we shall have to get your sword."

"How can we hope to pass through this abominable keep undetected?" Balin said.

"That's easy enough," said Merlin. "I'll weave a spell to mask our presence."

"Can't you conjure some clothes?" Garnysh burst out. "God's blood!"

"My clothes and staff are still in the forest where I left them," Merlin said.

"Merlin, do not turn us into beetles or rodents, or something," said Balin.

Merlin spared Balin a look and then set one hand on his shoulder and another on Garnysh's. He looked at Brulen. "Touch shoulders. Gather close."

Brulen hesitated but put his hands on the shoulders of Garnysh and Balin, and they did the same to him.

Merlin lowered his shoulder for a moment and closed his eyes, muttering secret words they could not decipher nor hope to repeat. An instant later he opened his eyes and released them. "It's done. Let's go."

Balin didn't feel any different, but they fell in behind Merlin as he strode up the corridor to the bottom of a cracked stone stair.

Merlin ascended, and they climbed behind. At the top of the stairs they halted, sighting one of the terrible knights standing guard with a halberd, but Merlin kept going. He ducked easily enough beneath the guard's arm and moved on, so they did the same, each being careful not to jostle the sentry.

Balin passed right in front of the knight, watching its impassive face. Sweat leaked down his sides. He expected the unearthly knight to seize him any moment and tear out his throat with its fangs, but the creature took no notice of them, and they slipped from its presence.

Every flat surface in the dark keep lay beneath a thick frost of dust. Every table, every chair, every step, was covered. Faded tapestries hung moldering on the walls, and the dry, dead leaves of many an autumn passed lay scattered across the floor. It was as though the castle had not served as a proper abode in centuries. Perhaps, in a way, it hadn't. Verdoana and her servants put no effort into its upkeep. It was merely their citadel against the light of day, a place to drag their screaming victims.

There was no illumination. They followed Merlin's pale backside, for he alone seemed unhampered by the darkness. He stepped surely, pausing only to peer left and right down intersecting passages before decisively choosing a direction, as if he knew the layout well.

He led them at last to the main foyer, where a single light burned in a sconce on the upper landing. They could see the main gate down a hall to their left.

Merlin led them to the gate, and as he approached, he spoke, "Thus far our little adventure has been easy, but I cannot mask the noise opening that gate will make. You must be ready, Balin, for whatever comes."

"I'll be ready."

"Ettard is being kept upstairs, I'd wager," said Garnysh.

"And Lorna Maeve and Count Oduin as well," Balin agreed.

They expected Merlin to blow the heavy gate from its housing with a wave of his hands, but he went to the heavy timber bar and motioned for Garnysh to help him.

"Ready?"

Balin nodded, and at his side, Brulen prepared to bolt, looking warily behind them for any sign of pursuit. Merlin and Garnysh grunted at the bar and threw it up, then pushed open the heavy doors. Balin rushed out into the night down the mist covered road, Brulen clanking along at his side.

He saw the Adventurous Sword, gleaming through the fog where he'd dropped it.

"Balin, look!" Brulen hissed.

In the cemetery, one of the knights held a shrouded white body in its arms. It was lowering it into the open grave they'd seen earlier.

Its head turned at the sound of the keep door, and it dumped the body unceremoniously into the fog shrouded hole and began running across the graveyard to intercept them.

It was unbelievably fast. Balin feared it would beat them to the sword. Praying, he slid in the dirt for the weapon.

In the same instant, the knight leapt up over the fence of the graveyard and soared at them, sharp teeth bared, hair flying, clawed fingers groping in anticipation of their flesh.

Balin rolled and grabbed the hilt of the Adventurous Sword. He brought it up and swung in one motion, swiping through the knight's head just above the eyebrows. Its face slackened and it crashed dead on top of him, the crown of its skull rolling off down the road like the discarded lid off a jar.

Brulen pulled the corpse off him and yanked him to its feet. Garnysh was waving frantically for them to come. Balin didn't see Merlin. They ran back to the entrance, breathless.

"Where's Merlin?" Brulen asked.

"As soon as you two left he became a raven and flew off over the trees!" Garnysh growled.

"Bastard!" Brulen cursed.

"You mean he abandoned us?" Balin said in disbelief.

"Now you know never to trust that lying devil, Balin," Brulen said, scouring the dark forest with his eyes as though if he could locate Merlin, he could destroy him with a baleful look.

"We don't need him anymore," said Garnysh. "We have your sword, Balin. Come on!"

Garnysh turned back to the foyer, but Brulen took hold of his wrist.

"No, Garnysh. We can't just storm in here without a plan again."

"The plan is to rescue my bride and your people and slay any of those foul things we meet. *And* put that Leprous Lady to your sword."

"No, Balin!" Brulen said. "Merlin said these things avoid daylight. We should wait till dawn and then find them."

"Did you see that body lain in its grave? We don't have time!" Garnysh said.

Balin stiffened. In the rush of things, he had forgotten all about the body the thing had dropped.

Without a word, he left the castle at a run for the cemetery, Brulen and Garnysh first calling out, then running behind him.

MERLIN HAD TENSELY watched Balin run for the Adventurous Sword, ready to offer what aid he could.

That was when he'd seen the white mouse dart from between Garnysh's feet and go scurrying off for the edge of the forest.

He knew it was Nimue. It was her favorite form to take.

What was she doing here? Trying to steer Balin back to Arthur, no doubt.

For a half a moment he stood looking between her pale little form and Balin clashing with one of the Leprous Lady's knights. In that half a moment, Balin handily dispatched the fiend and rolled out from under his corpse with the sword.

Without a word, he assumed the shape of the pied raven and beat his wings after Nimue, ignoring the frightful exclamation of Sir Garnysh.

The wind rushing in his ears, he banked and dove at her, seeking to snatch her up by the nape of the neck or perhaps catch her tail in his beak.

She saw him though over her shoulder and shifted into the form of a mole which hastily burrowed a tunnel under the tree line.

Merlin did not check his dive, but became a viper and slithered down after her, blinking back the clots of flying earth and ducking under tangled roots in her wake.

He nearly jammed his fangs into her hind end when she shrunk into a nightcrawler and slipped between his jaws, breaking once more for the surface.

Merlin became a stout brown rat and scrabbled after her.

This time Nimue changed into a raccoon, too big for his maw but small enough to scuttle under the bushes of Carteloise.

Weary of this play, Merlin grew into a yowling panther and crashes heedlessly after her. He pounced to trap her beneath his claws, but she sprang for a birch tree and mid-leap became a gray squirrel that skittered up the pale trunk. Merlin crashed into the tree as a young black bear, jaw popping, sable claws raking the bark and shimmying up just beneath her.

She grasped a bough and jumped into open space, turning into a quick little sparrow. Merlin followed as his namesake. Hunting hawk and prey plunged through the canopy like shark and sea lion navigating the grasping, scraping treachery of a dense coral reef.

Merlin had not had such fun in years. Nimue had grown strong indeed. He watched her fleeting tail feathers with his yellow hawk's eyes, mind racing to guess her next move as he gained, talons curling in anticipation.

Would she become a fly and zip through his grasp or drop spinning from the sky into a body of water as a turtle?

She made for a particularly thick tangle of oak branches and a few seconds before she crashed into it, folded her wings and plunged downward.

She was exhausted. It was a pity to end so lively a chase in fatigue, but Merlin closed the distance.

Suddenly she let the wind fill her wings, but they were no longer a sparrow's. They had become the leathern skin of a small bat.

She climbed, and miniscule, slipped deftly through the dense knots of oak wood and Merlin, taken by surprise, smashed fully into them like a moth that had fluttered thoughtlessly into a spider's web.

Dazed, he hung there for a second and strained his eyes.

Nimue was gone.

Merlin hung in the branches for a few seconds, catching his breath and stifling the urge to screech giddily before he became a man again and dropped down to the forest floor.

"Damn it." He hissed and turned to go and find his robes.

BALIN CROSSED THE threshold of the graveyard and stumbled through the tangled weeds and tombstones to the fresh open pit. What if Lorna Maeve were the body in the shroud? Then his quest was already at an end and the hunt for Garlon meant nothing.

He did not hesitate, but leapt down into the foggy grave. Straddling the bent corpse in the bottom, he tore open the head wrappings.

He laid bare the face of Count Oduin's maid, stark white, an expression of petrified terror forever on her face. He felt a pang of guilt at the rush of relief that flooded his heart at the sight of the dead woman. He had never even learned her name. He looked up to see Garnysh and Brulen looking down at him. He raised his hands, and they hoisted him out of the grave.

"Look, Balin," said Brulen, waving his hand across the sky, which was now purpling like a healing bruise. "The sky is lightening. Dawn is very near."

"We go now," Balin said and left the cemetery without waiting for protestation or encouragement.

Moments later they were back in the foyer.

Balin sprang for the stair and gained the landing, Garnysh and Brulen right behind. Their swords were drawn, though they knew it was bootless. If any threat appeared, Balin would have to deal with it alone. He peered down the passageway, found the first of four doors, and kicked it open savagely.

An empty bedroom, the grand bed strung with a canopy of old webs.

Onto the next. Brulen urged caution. Garnysh urged him on.

This one a grand master bedchamber, well-tended, and Balin noticed the windows were shuttered and locked, the cracks filled with pitch against any possibility of intrusion of light.

Nothing in the next room, and the fourth was a door leading to a staircase.

The tower rooms.

A cold sweat passed over Balin's body and he felt the chill of the grave. The sword had shone him falling to his death from the window of a high tower.

Was it this tower? Was his own death upon him?

They ascended unopposed, and that made their progression all the more sinister. There were fresh footprints on the dusty stair, and the way was torch-lit.

They came to a landing where two staircases continued on in opposite directions.

Balin chose the right-hand side, and they came at last to a locked chamber door. Balin struck off the lock with his sword in a shower of sparks and glowing iron.

He pushed the door open and strode inside. If death waited for him, let it come now.

The room was well kept. Another bedchamber, and in the bed two figures lay entwined and apparently naked beneath the red coverlet, a man and a woman.

A strangled exclamation escaped Garnysh's lips, and he shoved past Balin.

The man was one of the pale knights, and the auburn-haired woman resting her face against its bare chest opened her blue eyes at the intrusion and furrowed her brow at the sight of them. There was alarm, but she did not throw off the creature's arms and flee the bed for Garnysh.

"Ettard?" Garnysh stammered, leaning on the edge of the bed, as if stopping himself from collapsing upon it.

"You came? All this way?" Ettard exclaimed. Then threw her head back into the pillow and began to softly giggle.

The sound caused her paramour to stir and open its red-black eyes. Garnysh already had his sword out.

He raised it and brought it whistling down. It cut Ettard's laughter short in her severed throat. He swung down twice more before Brulen took a hold of him and pulled him away.

The knight, surely the Sir Guthkeled one of his subordinates had mentioned, sat up in alarm, covered in his mistress' blood.

"Whore!" Garnysh shrieked, throwing Brulen off him. "Whore!"

Balin looked aghast at the bloody mess on the bed. Sir Guthkeled was meticulously picking the matted hair from Ettard's ruined face. Dark red tears were leaking from its unholy eyes. Balin looked over and met Garnysh's eyes.

"*Why?*" Garnysh yelled, his voice rising into an ever-sharper pitch. "*Why, Balin?*"

Garnysh saw the window at the far end of the room. Like the others they had seen, it was shuttered and filled. He charged it without another word and dove at the casement. The bulk of his steel-clad body shattered the flimsy wooden shutter.

The first light of dawn had risen beyond, and once Garnysh's body had cleared the window and gone noiselessly into the void outside the tower window, those newborn rays coursed like floodwaters through a broken levy and fell full upon the gruesome bed.

Sir Guthkeled raised one pale arm to its face against the light, and then its skin flared with golden fire, blackened instantly to cinder, and blew apart with a rustle like a pile of leaves. The thing never had time to scream.

Balin stumbled and Brulen caught him.

"Garnysh, you damned fool," Brulen muttered.

"I didn't…" Balin whispered. He was stunned at what Garnysh had perpetrated. Yet, had he, Balin, listened to Brulen, perhaps Garnysh would not have found them. Was he culpable?

Brulen gripped his harness and dragged him stunned from the room. "Come away, Balin!" he choked.

They stumbled down the stair to the connecting landing and Brulen gasped.

Balin was still looking back toward the charnel room. Down in the dimness, looking up into the sunlit doorway, he could just make out the blood staining the bed skirt. The thought in his mind was, had he appeared as monstrous as Sir Garnysh when he'd slashed the head from the Lady Lile in Arthur's dining room?

That was when a female voice rasped, "*What have you done?*"

Balin looked and saw standing at the top of the opposite stair in the doorway of the room above, the Leprous Lady, ghostly and luminous in her trailing white veil and barbette, face and arms wrapped in swaddles of altar white linen, but for her dark eyes, obscured behind the fog of the veil like shadows. One protruding crooked, yellow-nailed finger emerged from the bandages, bubbling with angry red and white sores, pointing down at them accusingly, seeming to carry in its cracked tip all the pestilential rot that crept beneath the foundation of this dilapidated fortress.

Balin gripped his sword. His heart felt as if it would implode, retreating in horror into itself. His skin prickled. He wanted to shrink within his armor.

The Leprous Lady advanced.

CHAPTER
THIRTEEN

ALIN STEELED HIMSELF. and his armor rang lightly as he moved unconsciously shoulder to shoulder with Brulen against the satanic apparition looming above them, the Leprous Lady Verdoana, blood drinking mistress of the Aspetta Ventura in the black heart of dread Carteloise.

To Balin, the gentle clink of their armor touching sounded like the ring of the altar chimes, signifying the transubstantiation of the Eucharist. Somehow, it gave him hope.

Let me die here, he thought, with my brother, against this unspeakable evil. This is how life should go.

He readied his sword, but could not find any voice to defy her. He merely waited for her to unmask, show some terrible true form and unleash all her hellish powers upon them.

"Where is the Lady Ettard and Sir Guthkeled? Why do I smell blood from their chamber and see the sun?" she asked, raising one arm to bar her already shaded eyes from the indirect light spilling into the hall from the bedchamber behind them.

Balin knew he need only get her into the light. She would perish as had the seducer, Guthkeled. He took a step forward.

"Wait, Balin," Brulen whispered. "Look. Is that not your lady?"

He blushed, even in the anticipation of battle to hear her called so, but his heart thrilled to see Lorna Maeve appear behind Verdoana in the doorway, gripping her own bandaged forearm.

"Sir Balin!" called Lorna Maeve.

The Leprous Lady turned to regard her. "Do you know these knights, who have shed blood in my sanctuary?"

"This is the Sir Balin we told you of," said Lorna Maeve, looking down with confusion from him to his brother. "The other is his mirror image."

"Brulen, my lady," said Brulen. "The blood you smell is that of a lady named Ettard, spilled by our companion, Sir Garnysh, who has thrown himself from the tower."

The diseased fingers of Verdoana clenched into fists and slipped once more beneath her veil. "Twisted, foul murderer!" she rasped. "She was the guest of my captain, Guthkeled. Why was she slain?"

"My lady, Garnysh told us Guthkeled had stolen her, that she was his bride."

"Falsehood," said Verdoana. "Her father was Duke Hamel. He promised her to that unworthy knight to seal a political alliance. She loved Guthkeled."

"That *thing*?" Balin burst out.

"That thing, Sir Guthkeled, was a great hero in his home country," said Lorna Maeve reproachfully. "He contracted his curse from another and fled many years ago, driven off by his people for his affliction. The denizens of this castle are to be pitied, Sir Balin. This is not a fortress of monsters but a haven for the accursed."

"My lady, this creature has ensnared your mind," said Balin.

"No, Sir Balin," came another voice, that of Count Oduin, who stepped out of the room, unharmed. "The Lady Verdoana has granted us her hospitality, in exchange for a service."

"Last night she was set to cast you from her tower to your death!" Balin challenged.

"A regrettable action," said Verdoana.

"But not of Lady Verdoana's volition," said Count Oduin, stepping forward. "I volunteered to play hostage in the hopes of stopping more bloodshed, but I fear I am responsible for a terrible misunderstanding, We warned the Lady you would come looking for us, Sir Balin, but alone. The Lady mistook you for the three knights who had been hounding Sir Guthkeled and his men. Had I not insisted on being blindfolded, I should have recognized you. I'm ashamed to admit, I'm terribly frightened by tall heights."

"But your servants on the road! And your maid lies dead in the cemetery!"

Oduin sighed heavily. "The cursed knights defended themselves from my servants, who would not see the Lady Lorna Maeve and I delivered into their hands. As for Irena, she grew hysterical last night when the custom of the castle was explained to her."

"She resisted to her detriment," Verdoana croaked, "and like your Garnysh, brought about her own end. She thought submitting to the custom would damn her soul."

"She killed herself?" Brulen asked.

"You don't believe this!" Balin exclaimed, wheeling on his brother.

"Sometimes a sword is not the tool a knight needs, Balin," Brulen whispered.

"What is the custom you speak of?" Balin demanded.

"Pity me, knights," Verdoana rasped. "For I would submit no one to such evil were I not compelled. In my youth I was as lovely as this lady," she said, indicating Lorna Maeve at her side, "and I drew the unwelcomed attentions of a wizard named Klingsor. When I spurned him, he cursed me to this undeath and incarcerated me within these walls, from which I cannot pass."

She lowered her masked head, as if relating her doom physically pained her. Lorna Maeve laid a hand upon her bent back and drew her into a comforting embrace.

"Only the blood of a pure maiden of a certain bloodline can free her," Lorna Maeve continued, "and so for years her servants, all who have been similarly afflicted though by various means, have set out and waylaid women on the road through Carteloise Forest, to try and break their mistress' curse."

"Bless the Lady Lorna Maeve," said Count Oduin, "she kept her wits and opened her heart, where others, as Irena and Garnysh, acted from fear and hate. We are not prisoners here."

Verdoana sobbed softly, and two bloody stains had appeared on her veil, near her hidden eyes.

"You let that…that…*witch* drink your blood?" Balin exclaimed.

Brulen touched his arm but said nothing.

"I *am* a witch of sorts, remember. It is only blood," said Lorna Maeve, with a shrug, "and haven't I given plenty of the same already to Count Oduin's stricken son? I pitied this lady and wanted to help her. In exchange, she offered us her hospitality for the night."

"Yet I fear now that hospitality will be rescinded thanks to Sir Garnysh's lamentable actions," said Oduin. "Perhaps we should spend the daylight distancing ourselves from Carteloise."

"Never by me," cried the Leprous Lady, drawing herself aright. "But Guthkeled was beloved by my knights, and I am their mistress only in name. His destruction may overwhelm their pity, and I have no true power over them. They can leave this castle. I cannot. Alas, that I cannot vouchsafe your safety."

"We will depart, Lady," Oduin said.

"We just leave her?" Balin exclaimed, trembling so that his sword shook. This woman and her knights were evil abominations. Driven to evil, perhaps, but evil nonetheless. How could he turn from this stair, knowing she or her knights would be in that slaughter room above as soon as they departed, lapping the blood of Ettard from the walls like plague dogs?

"We will go below and find our horses," said Brulen, drawing him away.

"But they're abominations!" Balin hissed.

"Not by choice, brother," Brulen counseled.

"Is there so great a difference?" He growled, looking over his shoulder at the lady in white.

"Yes, very great a difference," said Brulen, "between deliberate evil and evil by necessity."

"What is the necessity? They kill that they might live! How many maidens will fall victim to her or her knights? We should burn this castle in our wake. Were I so afflicted, I should stand in the sun and be done with it."

"Then, by your own beliefs, you would be damned as a suicide," said Brulen. "The Lady Verdoana does not kill. She seeks her own salvation, as do we all, in our own ways."

As they descended the stairs, he heard Lorna Maeve recite quietly:

"Turn aside, White Lady,
And do not come whilst we slumber
Lest you come arm in arm with easy Death.
White as desert bones,
White as ash sifted from the pyre,
White as the Lady who walks alone."

The horses proved to have been well tended in the stables behind the keep. Balin and Brulen gathered up their saddles and gear and made them ready to ride out, while Oduin and Lorna Maeve took a pair of palfreys and saddled them.

Balin's heart burned in the shadow of the evil keep. He wanted only to be gone from it. After their night of horror, he once more felt the wedge between himself and his brother, who worked lightly, untroubled.

Count Oduin and Lorna Maeve's acceptance of the Leprous Lady and her knights vexed him too. He felt as though he were out of step with the whole world. He felt alone.

"Your traveling companions are unique," Brulen remarked when Count Oduin and Lorna Maeve had ridden across the courtyard to wait by the gate. "I never expected you to keep such level-headed company."

Balin said nothing. *Level-headed?* The world was mad. He sought for some anchor to grip and found that he did feel some relief now that the Count and especially Lorna Maeve were safe. It figured his brother found their strangeness praiseworthy.

"The lady is especially interesting," Brulen went on, smiling wryly, teasingly at his brother.

"Keep quiet," Balin said lowly, reddening, not wanting to think of the humiliation of the previous night. "She is in mourning."

Brulen looked her over as she rode away.

"She will not be in mourning forever." He looked closely at Balin, until Balin's face split and he smiled and shook his head. "Where are you bound now?"

"To Lystenoyse," Balin said. Despite everything, he wanted to invite Brulen to join them. Nothing would make him happier.

"Some quest for Arthur?"

"No," said Balin. "There is an evil knight there, whose blood will cure Count Oduin's afflicted son." He didn't think the vengeance of Sir Herlews worth mentioning just then.

"A blood quest?" Brulen said with a hint of surprise. "Not the usual fare for a Christian knight, is it?"

"I see nothing wrong in bringing God's justice to a pagan villain," Balin said, eyeing his brother sideways, repaying his mockery a bit.

"Every man thinks himself justified and no man a villain."

"Sage words from Brulen The Sinister," Balin quipped.

"If our nom de plumes are any indication of our character and judgment, what does yours say about you, Balin The Savage?"

They stared at each other a moment, and Balin wondered if they were still joking.

Then Brulen chuckled, and Balin felt easy again and laughed too.

Yet something had been gnawing at him, and as they worked on in silence, he couldn't hold it to himself any longer.

"Brulen, before he died, Lot told me to seek out a painting at St. Stephen's in Camelot. I saw it. It was of a serpent attacking Arthur in his bedchamber, and a servant in black was dumping a nest of eggs into the sea. I saw Lot represented by the double headed eagle, attacking. A priest told me the whole composition sprang from a dream of Arthur's."

"Gernemant used to tell me that the dreams of the guilty are the whispers of conscience they ignore by day," Brulen said grimly.

"Then Dagonet told me..."

"Dagonet," Brulen scoffed. "Does that clown still serve his master?"

"He told me that the number of eggs was the same as the number of the rebel kings who had died."

Brulen clenched his jaw. "What else did Sir Dagonet say?"

"He told me my heart would be broken twice over if ever I learned the meaning of the painting. But I don't see how I ever shall. You know I don't have a mind for puzzles. Yet I think you know the answer."

Brulen turned on him, eyes fiery, his previous mirth burned away. "I had asked you not to pursue this line with me. Twice now, by myself and by Dagonet, you have been urged not to dwell on this. You have a good heart, brother. A hero's heart. If you would keep it, stop."

Did he, though? Balin wondered.

"You know Dagonet. That is why you share the secret, isn't it? What do the eggs mean, Brulen? What do they have to do with why the kings rebelled? What does it all mean?"

"It *means*, brother," Brulen snapped, "that once, on a May Day, I did your beloved king a service. The last I will ever do for him, or any other king, so help me mercy."

Balin stared at his brother's back. He was trembling as he worked to cinch the saddle of his horse. He wanted to reach out, to touch him, to give him some assurance. Yet, how could he? He did not know what troubled him and was baffled by this revelation. For surely there had been a revelation, one which it pained Brulen to speak of. Yet, what had been revealed, Balin cursed his dimwitted mind, he couldn't guess.

May Day. What had Brulen done for Arthur once upon a May Day?

"I am going to pack feed for the journey," Brulen announced and stormed away to the stable shed to fetch grain, empty feed sacks over his shoulder.

Balin watched him go, frustrated.

"Will your brother be riding with us to Lystenoyse, Sir Balin?" Count Oduin called from across the courtyard.

Balin opened his mouth to answer that he didn't know, when Merlin strode over from some unobserved spot in the courtyard, fully clothed now, and once again bearing his staff.

"Lystenoyse?" he said, frowning. "Why are you going to Lystenoyse?"

"Merlin!" Balin spat angrily. "You abandoned us last night and now you have the gall to show your face?"

"I was momentarily distracted by the appearance of someone I had been keeping an eye out for. It was urgent and couldn't be helped. Besides, you all seem fine."

"Sir Garnysh is dead!"

"Yes, I know," said Merlin, "but Sir Garnysh's pride had dug him a grave some time ago," he went on, touching the side of his nose impishly, "and his course was quite unalterable. As is yours, if you do not at last heed my advice and be rid of that wicked sword of yours. I suppose it is the reason you are going to Lystenoyse."

"I'm on a quest," Balin said. "To avenge the Lady Lorna Maeve's knight and bring her killer to justice."

Merlin glanced across the courtyard to where Count Oduin and Lorna Maeve sat atop their horses waiting. He looked disinterested at Balin, then narrowed his eyes, looked back again, and came away with a broad grin.

"You are in love!" he exclaimed.

Balin's eyes widened involuntarily and he shushed the impious wizard. First Count Oduin, then Lorna Maeve herself, and Brulen, and now Merlin. Was he that transparent?

"Oh, but it's true! It's all about you!" Merlin continued. "Well, the beginnings of it, anyway, for you do not yet know what love is. But what of that?"

"Keep your voice down!" Balin snarled.

"Hah! Not a hint of denial, though. Well, this is something. This is a start," he mumbled to himself. "Isn't she the same one you saw through my hedge? How interesting. Yes, maybe there's hope yet. Nimue's hate put the sword in your hand, maybe love can take it from you."

"Who's Nimue?" Balin asked, even more confused than ever.

"Never mind, never mind," said Merlin. "Let me worry about her. Tell me of this woman now. Does she reciprocate your affection?"

"She loves a dead man," Balin murmured sadly.

Merlin rolled his eyes. "Too much love of death these days and not enough vested in the living. This business with Lanceor and Colombe…"

Balin felt his heart seized by a fist. The shame brimmed in him again. "How did you know about that?"

"What matters is this," said Merlin, taking him by the shoulders. "It is not yet out of your hands. Abandon your quest. Abandon all questing. Choose the life of the one you love or take that life yourself. In your right hand, the sword of a poor knight, unsung, but true. In your left, the curse of a storied hero, born from the death of your mother. Choose!"

"My mother?" Balin hissed.

What did his mother's death have to do with any of this?

"Balin…" said Brulen, coming out of the stable behind him.

He turned and saw his brother. Merlin released him. Brulen looked past Balin, and seeing the enchanter, he scowled, but in that same moment, his face grew slack and he dropped the four full sacks of feed, so they burst open on the cobblestones.

Balin looked back and saw Brych the pied raven, flapping off over the trees.

When he looked again at Brulen, his brother was reeling, and leaned hard against a support post, apparently to stop himself from falling. Balin went to him and gripped his arms. "Are you alright? What's the matter?"

"Balin…" Brulen mumbled. "Merlin."

Balin began to relay the wizard's explanation as to why he had left them the night before, but Brulen shook his head furiously.

"No, no. That mottled raven. That was Merlin."

Well, that was obvious, wasn't it? Hadn't Brulen seen him change?

Brulen seemed to gather himself, breath coming out in wrathful huffs that flared his nostrils, until he expelled an anguished cry, "MER-LIN, YOU BASTARD!"

It startled even the horses of Count Oduin and Lorna Maeve across the courtyard.

"My God, what is it?" Balin said, shaking his brother. "What is it?"

"That damned *villain!*" Brulen hissed, and tears of rage spilled from his red eyes.

Balin could only embrace him, and it was a clumsy embrace of steel against steel, like feeling for the flow of a river through shoes.

"Brother, speak to me," Balin urged. "What is the matter?"

Brulen hissed in his ear. "How could you not know? Have you ever seen a raven like that? Ever?"

"I don't know what you're talking about."

"Think, you *imbecile*! Have you ever seen a raven mottled in color like that one?"

Brulen had never spoken to him so harshly, in such a passion.

"Yes," he mumbled in confusion.

"Where?"

"I don't know, all over."

"No, you haven't! There are no such birds. Think, Balin. Where have you seen it?"

"In my prison window at Camelot…in the forest of Bedegraine…"

"All those times," Brulen interrupted. "It was Merlin, wasn't it? Now think back. Have you ever seen a bird like that when it was *not* Merlin? What about *that day*?"

There was no question of what day Brulen meant. Throughout their lives, in the history of days, *that day* had always been the day they had seen their mother burn. There was no other day, really worth remembering. How could there ever be? What day could ever hope to measure up to *that day*?

"In the tree, Balin! Don't you remember?"

He did remember, the pied raven cawing in the boughs of the apple tree on the hill overlooking their cottage.

The raven that had flown in the face of Gallet.

The pied raven, which was Merlin.

Merlin had been there the day their mother died.

"He's been there! Even on *that day*. He's been there *our whole lives*, the fiend!" Brulen babbled. He shoved away from Balin, who was too dumbstruck to react. He went straight to his horse and practically vaulted up into the saddle, for all his weight. The horse reared, but Brulen fought him down, savagely drawing the reins.

"Where are you going?" Balin whispered.

"Do you know what I did for him and his damned boy king, Balin?

Do you know what I *became?*" he screamed.

He didn't. He still didn't understand.

"Where are you going?" Balin asked again, louder this time, finding his voice.

Brulen shouted to his horse and spurred it, and went galloping down the forest road away from Aspetta Ventura.

Balin could only watch him go.

CHAPTER
FOURTEEN

SIR BALIN PUZZLED mightily over what had transpired. He did so on the back of Ironprow through Carteloise Forest, as he and Count Oduin and Lorna Maeve left the shadow of the castle of the Leprous Lady.

He could not answer his companions' questions about Merlin and the unexpected flight of his brother. He had no answers. None at all.

He rode in quiet at the head of their trio, turned inward, thinking not even of Lorna Maeve, only of serpents and wizards, eggs and kings, and May Day.

Once upon a May Day, Brulen had done Merlin's king a service, he'd said.

One upon a May Day.

And something about May Day stuck in the mire of his hopelessly whirling thoughts.

May Day.

Dagonet had told him: "May *the* day *never come when you understand.* May *the* day *never come.*"

Dagonet had been trying to tell him, hadn't he?

May the Day.

But he was no closer to understanding the mystery.

The revelation about Merlin distracted him further.

Merlin had seen their mother die when they were boys. He had been there. Balin had always known about Merlin's ties to Avalon, but Brulen had told him the Lady Lile of The Lake had been their aunt. Merlin dealt so closely with the ladies of Avalon. Maybe it was understandable that he had been there. He had flown at Gallet, tried to stop the burning in a small way.

Yet Merlin could have stopped the entire affair. He was certainly powerful enough. Why hadn't he?

The curse of a hero, born from the death of your mother, Merlin had said.

It was too much for him to think about.

Mulling over this riddle made the time pass quickly. The sun sank, and they were well away from Carteloise and in a deep green valley when Count Oduin suggested they stop and sleep, near a small lake. On the shore of the lake there was a twisted old oak half leaning on a tall, rounded, moss covered sarsen menhir.

Distracted, Balin tended to the horses while Lorna Maeve built the fire and Count Oduin brewed a broth that was bubbling by the time he joined them at the fire.

Count Oduin said grace and then ladled out the warm broth, first to Lorna Maeve, and then to Balin. Then he settled in himself. They ate as they had ridden, in silence, until Lorna Maeve spoke, "Are you alright, Sir Balin?"

He was pleasantly shocked by her concern but knew better than to take it as anything but concern that the only man-at-arms among their party had lost himself.

"I'm fine," he said quietly.

"Is everything alright with you and your brother?" Count Oduin said. "I was sorry to see him ride off."

But Lorna Maeve was not content with this civility. "He seemed beside himself. Did it have to do with Merlin's departure?"

"More to do with his appearance, I think," said Balin. Then he shook his head. "It's old family business," he said apologetically. "I am sorry you saw it."

"We are already in the borders of Lystenoyse. Tomorrow we will come to Carbonek," said Count Oduin. There was a hint of worry in his voice. They were very close now to their purpose, and it would not do to have him lose his wits here.

Balin nodded, looking into the fire. He did not want to involve these people in his personal tragedy, but he couldn't help but think he might not have another chance for help in solving this perennial riddle he struggled with.

"What is the significance, please, of May Day?" Balin blurted out. "Maybe I have lapsed as a Christian. I remember the crowning of Mary the Blessed Virgin from my boyhood, but what else?"

"It goes back further than that, Sir Balin," said Lorna Maeve, smiling somewhat indulgently. "To the Goddess, whom the Romans called Flora. My mother called it Bealltainn. When I was a girl, two bonfires would be lit, and the cattle would be driven between them to their summer pastures. The people marked the beginning of summer with songs, and drink, and dance."

"My people kept some of the old Roman customs when I was a boy," Count Oduin said. "The maidens would bind wild vetches and lupins, and throw them at each other, and in April, the men would trap and keep wild hares and set them loose by the hundreds for the boys to chase across the field."

These stories reminded him of some of the queer customs of his mother. They called to mind a long forgotten memory, of he and Brulen shrilly screaming, of Killhart barking excitedly, as their mother chased them round and round the outside of the cottage, each of them letting fly with fistfuls of hard, dried beans and laughing till their bellies hurt when they scored hits on each other. She had gone with purple garlands in her hair, and they had all visited the village, to see the children dance around a birch pole strung with colorful ribbons.

None of this was helpful, of course, and they saw that he was vexed.

"Why do you ask, Sir Balin?" Lorna Maeve said.

He shook his head, grimacing.

"I don't know," he groaned. "Is there nothing else either of you can think of? Something that might concern the rebel kings?"

Lorna Maeve and Count Oduin looked at each other, and in Lorna Maeve there was no spark of insight.

Count Oduin stroked his beard thoughtfully. "Much of the rebellion has taken place far from my country," said Count Oduin. "But news from Malehault necessarily came my way now and again, as King Aguysans was my neighbor for many years. I lost more than a few of my own household knights trying to go off and join his famous Hundred. But I recollect that it was on a May Day two or three years ago that some of the Hundred came to Meliot searching for a pair of boys."

"Boys?"

"Yes. Just infants. One of them was the son of the captain of the Hundred. The other was Aguysans' own. What was his name? Margon or…Malaguin or something," said Count Oduin. "Yes, it was ghastly business. They found their cradles empty that May Day morning. They were never found. The common folk all attributed the disappearance to faeries. Who can say what truly happened? And the strangest thing, they shared the same May Day birthday. It would have been their first."

Balin narrowed his eyes, thinking hard. There was something here. But what? What?

"Are you certain you're alright?" Lorna Maeve asked, laying a light hand on his elbow which burned him like a glowing brand.

And then the thought was gone, leaving only a vague sense of trouble.

"I'm fine," he said, standing up abruptly, so that her hand fell away. "Both of you should sleep. I will keep watch."

"Wake me at midnight," said Count Oduin, gathering up the crocks. "I will relieve you."

Balin did not. He stayed up through the night, thinking. Thinking, and watching the gentle rise and fall of Lorna Maeve's shoulders.

CHAPTER
FIFTEEN

CLOUDS OF BLUE-BLACK rolled in agony as white lightning scourged them and they bled rain. The vast dark sea beneath raged and rose to terrifying heights, then fell in impotent tantrums of white foam.

A lone knight in blood red armor stood alone on a slick stone jutting from the angry waters, slashed by silver rain and spray. The knight stomped furiously upon a robin's nest like a spoiled child, and three of the bright blue eggs within broke apart and spattered his strange, tapering sabatons with dark blood.

The knight stooped down and lifted a single unbroken egg from the ruined nest, then lifted the beak of his pointed visor, revealing the horrendous face of a black billed crow, shining bead eyes rolling madly in its mottle-feathered head. It stuffed the egg hungrily into its mouth, then fell to its knees, cawing horribly, and vomited a long, curling black serpent onto the rock, which had the face of a mewling child.

And when the infant drew its primal, gasping breath, it expelled not a babe's wail or a monster's roar, but Brulen's own voice.

"MERLIN, YOU BASTARD!"

———

BALIN NEARLY FELL sidelong from his saddle.

Count Oduin reached out and caught him.

"Sir Balin?"

All the world was bright and sunlit, and every resplendent hue of the rainbow seemed represented in the costumes of children who giggled at Balin's near mishap.

They were in procession down the center of a prosperous village of smiling, waving peasants.

THEY HAD SIGHTED it not long after breaking camp, and Count Oduin had said the beautiful white walled castle beyond was Carbonek.

He must have dozed in the saddle as they rode through the hazy, warm green country. He blinked rapidly and patted Count Oduin's hand in thanks for saving him from a spill.

To his right, Lorna Maeve rode in her finest dress, and the sun and goodness of the country seemed to fill her.

A brook bisected the village, and they saw a buxom old washerwoman with brown hands and a face like a raisin beating wet clothes against a stone as a naked child splashed along the bank.

At the sight of them, the child inched bashfully closer to the woman, until he grew too close and caught a pair of sopping wet britches full in the face, hard enough to knock him on his bottom bawling.

Lorna Maeve exclaimed sympathetically at the boy's plight. He could be seen huffing through the pants, and when the washerwoman peeled them from his face and began assailing him with kisses, he forgot his distress and tried to push her off.

The three of them laughed.

Lorna Maeve and Balin looked to each other, it being the first time either had heard the other laugh, and it was as though they had seen each other anew. Balin did not look away in shame, and Lorna Maeve smiled and turned to watch her path.

Count Oduin nodded to himself, looking pleased.

Balin thought that maybe there was hope.

Maybe what Merlin had said…but he didn't want to think about Merlin anymore. There was still bloody business to be done. He was reminded by the glint of the steel that encircled the tail of Lorna Maeve's meticulously styled hair. It was the lance point of Sir Herlews, waiting for its measure of blood.

As they passed out of the village and came to the gates of Castle Carbonek, they saw a short line of country nobles before them, inching slowly under the portcullis, where the richly armed guards checked the weapons of the attending knights and ushered their animals, handing them off to a bustling relay of squires and pages moving between the gate and the nearby stables. Tall royal blue banners hung from either side of the entrance. *Azure, a cup, or.* The Holy Grail emblem of the Fisher Kings and the Templeise, the sign of the lord of the Palace Adventurous.

Balin had strapped the Adventurous Sword to Ironprow's saddle, knowing no page would be able to take it from him. They dismounted as they neared the entrance.

A well dressed and prim looking herald stood before the guards with a squinting young tonsured scribe at a podium beside him. On the herald's left stood a broad shouldered, somewhat unkempt and brutish looking knight with a head of salted black hair encircled by an ostentatious gold circlet and sporting a silver streaked beard. Dark eyes looked over the line of entrants in half-lidded interest from beneath a pair of unruly eyebrows. He was in fine, black armor filigreed with little gold crosses and cups, and a rich evergreen cloak was about his shoulders, trimmed in silver thread with old runic symbols. He was loudly crunching a green apple, the juices and detritus running down his beard, when Count Oduin stepped forward.

"The names and titles of your party, please?" the herald asked.

"Count Oduin of Castle Meliot," said the Count.

"Sir Balin of Camelot," said Balin, helping Lorna Maeve dismount. "And this is the Lady Lorna Maeve."

As the scribe scribbled away on his parchment, the herald eyed Count Oduin. "Pardon me, Count. But have you brought no lady with you?"

"I hope King Pellam will pardon me. The Countess, my wife, died last year," said Oduin. "I still thought it rude not to honor his daughter's birth."

The knight in the cloak was eyeing Lorna Maeve brazenly over the top of his apple, as if he were devouring her and not the fruit. Balin looked hard at him, but the knight didn't even notice.

"Please leave your mounts with our pages. They will be tended. And sir knight, your sword," said the herald.

"In my country," said Balin, still staring at the ill-mannered knight, "it's not customary for a man to relinquish his weapon."

The knight looked at Balin for the first time and slung aside his apple core as the two guards stepped closer. "Well this isn't your country, is it?" he said, bubbling over with challenge.

The herald intervened deftly. "Your pardon, Sir Balin. Weapons are not allowed to pass the threshold of the Palace Adventurous. Ancient magic forbids it."

Balin looked hard into the eyes of the knight in the green cloak. He wanted to cuff him for his disrespect, but instead he unbuckled his sword and held it out to the page who held the bridle of Ironprow and stood waiting. The page took hold of it, but Balin did not release, and the slight boy looked from him to the herald.

"If it is stolen," Balin said directly to the knight. "*You* will be responsible."

The knight shifted, showing the flash of his teeth, but the herald spoke first. "It will be safe, I assure you."

———

NIMUE, IN THE guise of the young page, watched Sir Balin and his two companions pass under the archway of Carbonek, casting one hard glance back at Sir Garlon.

Garlon looked angry enough to stab Balin in the back, as was his wont, but then his eyes fell on the glittering hilt of the Adventurous Sword on Balin's horse.

Nimue led the horse off to the stables and noticed Garlon was following her.

Good. She needed to have words with him alone.

The past few days had seen the continued unraveling of her plan. Balin had ventured further and further away from Camelot, delaying her vengeance against Arthur even more. Garlon had so far proven to be as undependable and unpredictable as Balin. Now, her two pawns were on an inexplicable course toward conflict with one another. One of them would not survive. Merlin made all this scheming and manipulating seem so damnably easy!

When she had learned Balin was in the vicinity of Meliot, she had disguised herself as a young acolyte in the churchyard and tried to urge him back to Camelot, but her approach had been borne of frustration and, she admitted, clumsy. She had followed him to Carteloise as a flea on his horse, and then as a white mouse into the dungeon of the Leprous Lady's castle, where she'd been amazed as he to find Merlin imprisoned. She hadn't known he was susceptible to cold iron. That at least was a valuable bit of information.

Merlin had nearly caught her outside the Aspetta Ventura that night. After eluding him, she had gone to ground for a day, curled up in a soft, dark rabbit warren, indistinguishable from the rest of its denizens, till she had been sure she'd lost him, then she had flown ahead to Lystenoyse.

When she'd learned at Meliot that Balin was heading here to Carbonek and that King Pellam had declared a feast, she had hoped

Arthur would attend, but his wedding to the princess from Cameliard had skewered that plan.

Merlin would be watching Balin from afar, looking for her. It wasn't safe to try and speak to him again, but she still had Garlon, brute though he was. She dutifully led Balin's gray horse into an empty stall and set his other sword nearby.

Garlon entered the stall behind her, ignoring her, and pawed like a hungry urchin in a bakeshop at the pommel of the Adventurous Sword hanging on the saddle.

She watched Garlon's fingers close on the handle and stood back, amused as he struggled to pull it from its scabbard, upsetting the horse so that it turned in place, forcing him to follow it stupidly.

"You can't take it," she said.

Garlon shot her a look. To him, she was just an impudent stable boy.

"Be off, boy, or I'll fetch you a clout," he grunted, returning to his comical labors.

She revealed herself and folded her arms. "You would add petty thievery to your long list of crimes, Sir Garlon?"

He started at the change in her voice and marveled for a moment before settling into his easy, roguish smile; perhaps charming in a man half his age and handsome, but in his thick face, more akin to the leer of a mangy old jackal. She wondered how she had ever thought him anything other than an ugly animal.

"So. Nimue," he purred.

She stepped forward and touched the hem of the ancient cloak draped about him.

"I gave you your power for a reason, Garlon. You have misused it."

Garlon pulled the cloak from her hand and scoffed. "Don't play the righteous benefactress with me, girl. This is the cloak of an assassin, not the robes of the Pope."

"Yet you ride around slaughtering innocent knights, thieving, and likely attacking women."

"Just testing out the goods, dear. Think of it as a rehearsal for the last act. You wanted me to be a dragon, remember?"

"I wanted you to strike against Arthur."

"Don't fret," he said, running his eyes down her figure like a hungry tomcat. "Incidentally, I haven't found your Sir Balin yet."

"You fool! You saw him only moments ago! This is his horse and these are his arms! Your bloody deeds have earned his enmity and now he's here for you."

Garlon looked momentarily confused, then shrugged and began pacing idly about the stable, hooking his thumbs on his belt.

"All the better. Once he sets foot in the Palace Adventurous, he'll be unarmed and no threat. I can poke a hole in his throat with a dinner fork at my leisure."

"You were never supposed to kill *Arthur*," Nimue said, exasperated.

"Yes, yes, I know," said Garlon, "but Arthur is surrounded by knights, and attended by that foxy Merlin." He fingered a bit of straw in the manger. "That game's not in season yet, love. I'll see to him soon enough, don't you worry. In the meantime, I've another throat to cut."

Nimue looked hard at him. There was something behind that deliberate nonchalance. "You're not talking about Balin," she said slowly. She reached out to him, using the old way, the Sight she had been taught. Garlon's mind was shrouded but easy enough to see into. Her heart quickened. "You mean to kill your own brother! King Pellam."

Garlon turned on her, raising his ridiculous eyebrows, and set the bit of straw between his yellow teeth. "You're a clever one after all, girl. I haven't been in my brother's good graces since Agrippe's invasion. Oh, they accepted me back ready enough, but they've never quite trusted me. You know how insufferable two older brothers can be when each of them's got a throne and you don't? Been lording it over me their whole lives. With all these strange knights in the palace, if Pellam springs a leak and trusty old Garlon finds and kills the invisible culprit, maybe your Sir Balin, for instance…he's a testy sort… I can take him aside and bandy him into a challenge, slip a blade into the back of his neck somewhere quiet, stow him away for later. I unveil him after the deed's done, say I caught him with the blade that struck my brother low. Then Garlon's a hero and above reproach. And since Pellinore has his Outer Isles and Pellam's weans are all yet nursery-bound, it's King Garlon at last. Arthur be damned. I'll be swilling wine from the Grail by this time tomorrow."

As he spoke the last, he raised the hood of the mantle and before Nimue could utter a hex, he vanished.

"Damn!" she cursed. She leaned against the stable wall and put the heels of her palms tiredly to her eyes. How had she deigned to trust her revenge with this base thug? In hindsight, it seemed like the most foolish step she had taken. "Merlin, what have I done?"

"I don't know, Nimue. Illuminate me."

Merlin stood in the stable doorway, dark and terrible, blocking her escape.

CHAPTER
SIXTEEN

ORNA MAEVE TOOK Balin's offered elbow and they passed through the sallyport into the courtyard and joined the procession of exquisitely dressed ladies and gentlemen filing into the palace.

The majesty of the Palace Adventurous had been partly obscured by the tall white walls of the castle around. It surpassed Camelot in the sweep and majesty of its architecture, which was cathedral-like in its complexity. Prophets and saints in relief traversed among the many arches bordering the brilliant stained-glass windows, which in turn, depicted momentous scenes from Scripture in ascending order, with the seven days of Creation in the ground floor windows, and the Ascension of Christ in the top. The seven white spires that assailed the heavens were guarded by masterwork statuary which mimicked the rank and file of heavenly spirits in their arrangement. Each tower tip was capped by a golden, seven-winged archangel, the central and tallest being capped with a tall golden cross encircled by four six-winged seraphim. Four solemn, angelic watchmen guarded the corners of the towers at each of the three floors of the Palace. Ringing the entire structure were an innumerable host of cavorting granite cherubs, beaming down at the guests who one and all craned their necks to take in all the celestial glory before passing within.

It was unquestionably the greatest, most beautiful structure Balin had ever seen. For a moment, he actually dabbed at his eyes, wondering at the intensity of love and artisanship and the incalculable human effort that must have gone into erecting this singular monument to the Almighty. What was his own offering of the sword, pledged to profanely disassemble God's creations, next to this divine assemblage of stone and gold, marble and silver? He thought of Guinevere's observation that he was a bloody man. As Arthur had need of bloody men, did God? Was there a place for the angel that had slain the first-born Egyptians on this edifice? He felt like fallen Lucifer, or an envious Cain watching Abel's more heartfelt offering, yet unlike his wretched ancestor, Balin's envy moved him to humility. As God had taken the stuff of the earth and molded man, here man, in his own way, had taken of the earth and aspired to the Father, rendering it into an artifice to honor the Divine. Surely, it was the closest mere man could ever hope to come to reciprocating the immeasurable affection of the Creator.

Lorna Maeve noticed the wetness of his cheeks as they entered the great foyer and touched his hand with hers.

He looked into her querulous eyes with shame at his naked emotion, but in her he saw something. Something new that had not been there among the deadness, something blooming like the first shoot through the winter frost. She understood his emotion and appreciated what he felt.

Could she though, a woman who knew nothing of God?

Whether she knew Him or not, she was His creation. As Balin looked on her beauty, his emotion was renewed, and he marveled on her as he had on the architecture, for while the building was of man, Lorna Maeve was of God, and she was not dead stone and metal. She lived, and breathed, and his pulse fluttered at the warmth of the blood flowing beneath her soft fingertips, precious blood she had selflessly given again and again, just as Christ had given His own, for others.

Yes, she was of God.

Was Arthur right? Was every god, God? Did she honor God as she saw Him?

Did he imagine the moment of connection between them? The passing of understanding between their eyes? What did it signify? If he could love her, could she love him? Did she require the offering of Cain? Could they but turn from this bloody quest as Merlin had urged? Would she come with him if he suggested it or curse him for a coward? She did not move her hand away, and a slight smile curled in the corners of her mouth.

He was overwhelmed with the desire to lean in and touch his lips to her own, for a brief moment only. Would it be misconstrued as lust? He could not bear to have her think that. What he wanted was to thank her in that instant for her empathy, in the most chaste and heartfelt way he had immediately at his disposal.

But he thought of how she had cut him outside her tent, and he cowered. Better Sir Garlon kill him unawares in this instant than that. Oh God, he could not bear to be unmanned by her withering words a second time.

He returned the briefest of smiles, and looked away, pretending to admire the décor, seeing nothing, and aching to his soul.

Though she remained poised at his elbow, her other hand returned to her side, and a tear slid from him, hot as first blood. He caught it with the back of his hand, and they moved on.

The procession through the Palace was a blur. He was aware of ancient portraits, of Count Oduin naming the Fisher Kings of the past. He did register that while the spell on the Palace forbade the passage of weapons across its threshold, apparently those that had been kept within prior to the casting of the enchantment were here still.

The guards of Pellam, the elite Templeise, with their illustrious armor, gilded with golden grail motifs as the black harness of the rude knight at the gate had been, bore old style, but perfectly kept swords. Polearms, flails, maces, and axes of antique designs adorned the walls too. If he had to fight Garlon within these hallowed walls, there was no shortage of weapons.

They came at last to the throne room of Pellam, where the wizened Fisher King sat upon a throne of burnished gold, its high back suggesting the shape of a great chalice. King Pellam was quite old. His white beard tapered to a point midway down his chest, and soft white hair cascaded from beneath his bejeweled diadem over his narrow shoulders. His wrinkled, unadorned hands were spotted, and yet there was a vigor in his old face, a light in his kindly blue eyes, when they looked upon the tiny pink babe slumbering peacefully in the golden, silk shaded cradle set before him, around which lay piled all the fine gifts of the visiting gentry, laid like a magnificent pyre of riches arranged by the magi of old.

Pellam's queen was yet a young woman, though her rust colored hair was shot through with fine silver, and she rested her elbow on her throne, and held the hand of her husband.

On a small golden stool beside his mother sat the king's young son. Count Oduin had said his name was Eliazar. He was a handsome boy in fine silks. He leaned his head sleepily on his mother's leg.

There was love between this family.

Balin was also glad to see red robed priests among the courtly advisors. Perhaps even more than Arthur, this king ruled under God.

Count Oduin spoke blessings upon the baby Helizabel, though in the hushed tone of a knowing father, so as not to awaken her, and when he had introduced Balin and Lorna Maeve as his guests, he laid the chest of gold among the other gifts, bowed low, and they departed for the banquet hall.

"He's so old to have a young child," Lorna Maeve observed.

"The Fisher King and his family and the Templeise and priests here celebrate Holy Mass with and take communion from the Grail itself," said Count Oduin. "It grants them all miraculous strength and vigor well beyond their years."

They were seated at one of the four long tables that bordered the concourse. The tables all bore cloths that could have adorned the altar at St. Stephen's, and the plates and utensils were not of iron, but gold and silver.

Count Oduin took his place beside a portly noble with an immense red mustache and deep set eyes who called for more wine at regular intervals and whose equally large wife sounded as if she were being eviscerated whenever she laughed.

The thin young woman on Balin's left was deeply infatuated with her table partner, a mop haired nobleman with a long nose and sleepy eyes, as transfixed apparently by her presence as she was by his. They spoke in passionate tones so low Balin was amazed they could hear each other.

Balin cast his eyes about the hall, taking in the opulence of generations, such as he had never known in Northumberland or Camelot. Everything was so clean and fine, he hated to touch any of it.

Lorna Maeve sipped wine, and Count Oduin engaged the fat noble beside him, asking the names of the various seated dignitaries, cleverly trying to discern which was Sir Garlon, if he was here.

Balin looked down at his own reflection in the golden plate and beside him, Lorna Maeve remarked, "These could be melted down and the gold used to feed a family for a year outside these walls. Why do your Christian kings festoon themselves with such gaudery?"

He had thought Prince Clarivaunce extravagant, but he was a pauper compared to Pellam.

"I don't know if that is confined to Christian kings, or if it is the province of kings altogether. When my brother and I came to Sewingshields as boys, to be trained as knights, that was the first time I realized I had been poor. It was a thing I learned from other men, men who never let me forget the lesson."

"I had thought you came from Camelot. Aren't all the knights there wealthy?"

"Not at all, my lady. Dagonet was a common man, a lowly minstrel, knighted by Arthur at Cameliard. Sir Marrok came to Arthur without even a stitch of clothing on his back," he smiled at this, for he was perhaps being a bit misleading, though it was true that Marrok had lost his lands long ago.

"Wasn't your father a knight?"

"That doesn't always mean wealth, my lady. Fortunes come and go. As I said, we were poor, but with our mother's cottage, and the clearing, and the apple tree on the hill, we thought ourselves well enough. We lived, and breathed, and we ate and drank. We wanted for nothing."

"You say your mother's cottage. She built it?"

"She would not raise us in the castle of King Detors. She wanted us to dwell among green things."

Lorna Maeve smiled and rested her chin on her interlaced fingers. "Don't your priests warn you knights about godless women like your mother and I?"

He reddened and chuckled.

"I'm being quite serious!" She laughed. "How did your father, a Christian, cope with his pagan wife?"

Balin thought for a moment. "I couldn't say, but he did die when we were very young."

She looked at him for a moment, and then he smiled and she playfully slapped his elbow and laughed.

Then Count Oduin leaned across. "There, at the door!" He hissed. "Sir Garlon!"

They looked to the entrance, their merriment forgotten, and sure enough, the herald called out Garlon's name. It was the very same ill-mannered knight they had encountered at the gate.

He was in a foul mood and looked over the whole hall, at each of the guests, scowling. Then his eyes fell on Balin, and he found a grin to match the leers of the Leprous Lady's knights and made his way toward where they sat.

A servant happened to cross his path. Garlon reached out and took him by the front of the tabard, pulling him in close, and upsetting his tray of golden goblets noisily.

"Where is the Lady Heleyne?" he demanded, ignoring the mess he'd caused and the heads swiveling to observe him.

"I do not know, Sir Garlon!" the serving boy stuttered.

"Well find her," he said simply, and pushed him out of the way roughly, before continuing his advance on their table.

Balin pushed himself back from the table. Another serving boy was just finishing laying out their wine when Garlon arrived and without a word, plucked Balin's goblet up and guzzled it down.

When he had finished, he set it back on the table and grinned past Balin at Lorna Maeve.

"Hello, pretty," he said, leering awfully, and then to Balin, "Much too pretty for the likes of you, muckrake."

"Garlon!" Balin snarled and to his surprise, Garlon planted a strong, gauntleted hand over his mouth.

"I'll see you after supper, boy. Enjoy the free meal. It will be your last." He released Balin and crossed the open area to his own seat at the king's table.

Balin was beside himself at the insult. He stood so abruptly his chair tipped over.

"Challenge him!" Count Oduin hissed. "Challenge him!"

"No!" Lorna Maeve said. "No, something's not right. Don't!"

"Sir Garlon!" Balin shouted.

The knight didn't even turn around but called over his shoulder airily. "After supper. Then you can do what you've come to do."

He sat down as if nothing at all had happened, though every conversation in the hall had ceased, and every servant stood frozen. Every eye passed between Balin and Garlon expectantly.

"Wine," Garlon said to a dumbstruck waiter, his voice echoing in the silent hall.

Balin's teeth clenched together so hard he thought he would crack them. His blood rushed and pounded in his ears. Lorna Maeve grabbed his hand and he shook her off.

In doing that, he turned and saw, on the wall behind him, an old sword set on hooks.

He grabbed the handle and tore it from the wall, the hooks pinging as they bounced along the floor. He stalked across the open concourse toward Garlon's table. The people rose in their seats, their voices rising in an unintelligible crescendo, warning, exclaiming, pleading.

Garlon had a goblet tipped back, so Balin was halfway to him when his eyes spotted him over the rim of the cup and widened in surprise.

He jumped up and grabbing the edges of the hood of his green cloak, threw it up over his head. He vanished completely, eliciting a new volley of screams from the onlookers.

Balin lunged across the table, swinging down. The blade struck something that sucked at it like a ripe squash, and its cutting edge disappeared for a fraction of a second, before Garlon's head reappeared about it. The green hood of the cloak parted and slipped from his head.

Garlon stared at Balin, mouth open, blood dribbling down his nose from the cleft in his skull.

Balin viciously drew the sword out with a whisk of blood and brain, and Garlon fell back into his chair.

Balin thrust the point into Garlon's neck and ripped it free again, sending gouts of blood shooting across the table. It spattered Balin's chest and the side of his face.

The feel of the blood doused his rage. He looked back across the screaming, scurrying guests, and saw Lorna Maeve standing and Count Oduin beside her, both of them agape.

He held out his blood drenched hand.

Lorna Maeve recovered admirably fast and came around the table to him. She reached behind her head and pulled the tip of Herlews' lance point free of her hair, sending it springing out again, wild and unfettered.

She was beautiful as she strode, heedless of the pandemonium erupting around her, like a terrible goddess herself, uncaring of the blood running down the table, pooling on the floor, covering him, until she knelt and held the small lance tip cup to the blood, patiently letting it run and fill it, dipping the point in, as she had sworn to Sir Herlews.

She looked up at him. She was terrifying. A witch, yes, in the midst of some blood drenched spell.

But she did not shrink from him. He loved her. Completely.

She smiled and took his hand. He lifted her gently to her feet. Hand in hand, they walked back to where Oduin stood wringing his hands.

Blood enough. Enough to heal Oduin's son. Enough to quench the angry fire in her heart, perhaps? Enough for Balin.

But not the end of blood.

For at that moment King Pellam and his retinue of Templeise burst into the hall. They had no doubt responded to the noise of the shrieking guests, and Pellam opened his mouth to demand explanation, but then spied his brother face down in his place, the place beside Pellam's own.

He rushed to the table, grand, purple robes rustling, the Templeise clattering to keep up.

King Pellam touched his brother's open wound, ignoring the blood that soaked his ermine-trimmed robes or the matter that tumbled wetly down his trembling hands when he lifted his brother's head and looked into his dead and gaping face.

He pressed his own face to his brother's and mourned.

All around, the guests pointed to Balin.

"Balin!" Oduin whispered when they reached him. "My God, hurry. You must state your case…you must…"

But then there was an unexpected roar, a wail frightful and vital, and it came from the black mouth in the bloodstained beard of the frail looking Fisher King, who glared across the hall at Balin still holding the bloody sword.

The command was unintelligible but unmistakable. A half dozen Templeise rushed at them.

Pellam went to the opposite wall of the chamber and wrenched an axe from its hangings.

CHAPTER
SEVENTEEN

N IMUE AND MERLIN strode side by side from the stables. She had told him everything. She had had to. It had gotten too far out of her control. Too much was at stake.

"We must be quick," Merlin said. "Garlon and Balin will be like two bears brawling in a potter's shop. Everything hangs in the balance now."

"I know!" Nimue said. How could she have allowed them both to come so close to the Sangreal? She knew well its power, the hold it had on this country. Christian or no, many lives were endangered, maybe all of Albion.

"Well done, Merlin," came an imperious voice from the courtyard, "I see you have caught our wayward little magpie at last."

They both stopped.

It was Viviane, the Lady of The Lake, in her scintillating samite gown of office, her platinum hair plaited and bound by a circlet of silver. What was she doing here?

"Viviane!" Merlin exclaimed.

"Now, Nimue," said Viviane, advancing. "We will take you back to Avalon, to face the consequences of your crimes."

"You followed me?" Merlin asked, evidently perplexed. "No, you could not have. Else you would have intervened in Carteloise. What are you doing here?"

"The Sight showed me you both. Do you think you're the only vaticinator in Albion?"

"Of course, of course," Merlin said, furrowing his brow, as if trying desperately to understand something. "But why did you send me to Carteloise prematurely to begin with?"

"I don't know what you're talking about," she snapped impatiently. "Come, we must to Avalon."

He pulled his beard, thinking, then shook his head vigorously and waved his hand. The matter at hand was more pressing than whatever it was that was troubling him. "There will be time to decide Nimue's penance later. We must first intervene here."

"I will have nothing to do with anything in this Christian fortress," Viviane announced.

"Viviane, you must know where you are," Merlin spluttered, exasperated. "This is the stronghold of the Sangreal. The very heart of Christendom in Albion. Two men are about to fight."

"Yes I know," said Viviane, with a light smile.

"You know, of course," Merlin said, "but there is a very great chance they could disturb the Sangreal within."

"Oh, more than a chance, Merlin," said Viviane. "It is practically an absolute. The only thing that could possibly keep it from happening is *you*."

She extended her index finger toward Merlin, and the cobbles beneath his feet suddenly exploded outward. Thick black roots burst into the light, shedding crumbling earth, and spiraled like tentacles up his legs, twisted around him, and pinned his arms to his sides.

Merlin glanced at Nimue, expecting it was her doing. She saw in his eyes the confusion that came when he espied the shock in hers.

Above their heads, the sky darkened as clouds rolled in like an avalanche of black snow over the sun.

"What are you doing?" Nimue exclaimed.

Thunder rumbled, and a chill wind picked up the loose straw and dust, stinging Nimue's eyes.

"For four hundred years, more, the seeds of the Way of the crucified god which Joseph of Arimathea planted in this land have been allowed to sprout and take root," said Viviane. "Today they will be weeded out."

"Viviane, this isn't the way," Merlin said, struggling against the thick roots constricting him. "The roots are too deep. We must…"

She twisted her extended hand a bit, and the roots lashed themselves across Merlin's mouth. Then they began to draw him down.

"Yes, Merlin, you dirty fingered old gardener," said Viviane. "I know well what you and the Lady Lile proposed: that the Way of Avalon and the Way of Christ be allowed to grow beside each other in harmony. You are operating on the assumption that I am a servant of either."

Merlin's eyes bugged as he was pulled up to his knees into the ground.

"Don't you recognize me yet, grandson?"

Merlin fought furiously against the roots dragging him low.

Nimue still didn't understand. "Who are you?" Nimue asked. "You aren't Viviane…"

"Oh, but I am. I have always been. And I am the Lady Heleyne." She said, in the Lady Heleyne's voice, with a wink at Nimue, exactly as she had that hazy night she had flown here to Lystenoyse, "*Drink. You're cold. It'll warm you.*"

Nimue blinked rapidly. The drink. The remarkably strong wine Heleyne had given her that night, potent enough to coax her into bed with her and Garlon, but more, to give him the Gwenn Mantle!

"And of course," Viviane went on in her own voice, "I am also…"

The vines stopping up Merlin's mouth suddenly burned away in a flash.

"She's the Queen of Norgales!" He gasped. "Kill her, Nimue!"

Nimue raised her hands, describing a mystic pass. She had never killed with her magic before. She struggled to call to mind a curse or hex.

Viviane raised her hand aloft and pointed at Nimue with the other. A crack of brilliant lightning streaked earthward, streaming down her upraised arm. It traveled the length of her body in an instant and then lashed straight at Nimue from her guiding hand.

Nimue raised her palms and managed to deflect the bolt, but she was blown backward and crashed against the wall of the stable ten feet away, her palms scorched red.

The roots around Merlin burned to ash and fell away, and he corkscrewed up out of the ground to stand before her once more. He thrust his staff at Viviane, and a crackling bubble of white flame emerged from the end and roared toward her.

Viviane shielded her eyes as the sphere of furnace fire burst across her, blackening her gown and singeing her hair.

"You've known all along you can't win like this, your Majesty," Merlin said, as she flung the fire from her in all directions, setting the straw on the ground, a nearby blacksmith's hut, and a hay cart aflame.

"I don't need to defeat you, Merlin," said Viviane, with a fearsome, mad grin on her burned face. "I only need to delay you for a little while."

With that, she rose into the air, not as a bird or a bat, but undisguised, in a vulgar display of power, the scraps of her tattered gown flapping about her. The lightning played about her white flesh and flashed blue-yellow in her terrible eyes.

Nimue got painfully to her feet, every bone in her body vibrating.

Merlin ascended in the sky to meet her. As he did, he looked back at her.

"Don't just sit there!" he yelled.

But what could she do? She was an enchantress, yes, but this was a battle of gods.

IN THE DINING hall of the Palace Adventurous, the chamber doors were flung open and more Templeise knights stormed in. Somewhere a bell was tolling, calling the castle to arms.

Oduin was seized and pulled away protesting his cause to ears that had been deafened by the blood of Sir Garlon and the donning of war helms.

A knight reached in to take hold of Lorna Maeve, and Balin kicked him in the chest and sent him flailing back into his fellows. He turned constantly, meeting armored foes on every side, and Lorna Maeve clung to his back, screeching warnings.

"I seek parley!" Balin roared. "Parley!"

Across the hall, bloodstained old King Pellam came bounding with the speed of a very young man, the heavy axe over his shoulder.

"Do not attack!" he yelled. "Leave him to me!"

Lorna Maeve leaned in close, her lips brushing his ear, her sweet, warm breath flooding it as she whispered, "He will not listen. You cannot fight and fret for me. Make your escape. I will be fine. Thank you, Sir Balin. Thank you."

Did her lips touch his ear in a kiss?

He opened his mouth to protest, but she had already released him and stepped backward into the throng of knights, who snatched her up and carried her off.

He caught a glance of her wild hair as she was borne away, and in the midst of it, her sweet face, her glorious eyes, glistening and seeking one last sight of him. In the deepest core of that gaze, was there something else? Was it mere concern or longing?

He moved to pursue her, but the old king burst through the ranks and swung the mighty axe. Balin brought up his sword to stop it and came away with only the broken hilt in his hands.

He dropped it with a clatter as Pellam swept the axe back at him. He caught the haft in his hands and grappled with it, but the strength of the Fisher King was astounding. It took all his effort to keep Pellam from breaking free and splitting his head.

"Slay him!" Pellam yelled through his teeth, and the Templeise moved in with their swords.

Balin released Pellam and jumped back, narrowly avoiding the jabs of a half dozen swords. A pike still managed to cut his cheek as he ducked under a spear and dove underneath one of the tables.

He did not stop to recover, but rolled out on the far end and ran for the only unguarded exit in the chamber, colliding with such momentum that he took the left-hand door off the hinges with a great crack.

Beyond was a bare and empty corridor. As the clash of arms and shouts increased behind him and King Pellam rode forth on a tide of knights, he ran pell-mell down the passage, praying it did not come to a dead end.

THE BLACK SKY was lit up with lightning as Merlin and the Queen of Norgales traversed mysterious drafts of frigid air up the tall towers of the Palace Adventurous. The faces of the graven angels took on malevolent airs as they were illuminated by sorcerous flashes, while the two archmages unleashed every hellborn arcane assault and divine counterspell either knew.

They were figures out of nightmare, man and woman, each bearing the burns and scars of their terrible combat, each one's costume reduced to streaming rags as they wheeled and turned, dove, fell, and regained.

And through it all, orbiting the outer edge of the colossal battle, was a madly flapping starling, a tiny and furtive witness to this titanic contest.

This was Nimue.

She was astounded by the ferocity of the battle, more so because for all that Merlin had taught her, for all she had learned in the tutelage of Avalon, of Viviane herself, she could not begin to understand the magic the two combatants employed against each other. They drew on resources totally unknown to her, plunging their arms to the elbows in untold mystic reserves and coming up with fistfuls of crackling power she could scarcely comprehend.

Viviane drew the surrounding air into a white, frigid cloud and flung it at Merlin, and his staff froze solid and fell, shattering into pieces on the ground below. The enchanter countered with a complex gesture that produced a thick swarm of black hornets from the sleeves of his garment, to coat every inch of Viviane. With a shrug of her shoulders, they fell dead from her body and plummeted down, rattling like some accursed hail out of the Bible.

They spoke no words but their unrepeatable incantations, the forgotten spells gleaned from thousands of rare and long lost grimoires, the sum total of both their considerable occult libraries. The power on display shook the windowpanes of the Palace Adventurous and sent the villagers down in Lystenoyse scrambling for cover, terrified by the thunderous storm of colors that played out across the mad sky.

Nimue sensed that, despite the violence of the struggle, it was doomed to a stalemate, as unwinnable as it had been inevitable. The crash of the waves on the stones.

So she did not seek to intervene, not there.

No, she was needed elsewhere. Inside the Palace. To that end, she hurtled herself down at a great glass window depicting the giving to Moses of the Ten Commandments and became an immense white-tailed erne. She hated to destroy the ancient masterwork, but her need was great, and so she tucked in and smashed through, tumbling to the floor of the chamber beyond as a spry little calico cat.

She was in the dining hall, and it was deserted to the tune of spilled goblets still dribbling purple wine, broken carafes, and tipped chairs. She leapt lightly up onto the table and hurriedly padded along its length, stopping and laying her ears back when she saw a single figure still seated in the room.

It was Sir Garlon, and he was very dead.

She sat down and licked her paw in relief. Balin must have killed him at dinner. It was something of a habit for him, apparently. Yet another rash act in a long line of impulsive violence. No doubt he had been apprehended on the spot and taken to the dungeon or dragged before Pellam for justice. Then they were safe, and she and Merlin could concentrate on defeating Viviane, or rather, the Queen of Norgales, if such a thing were even possible.

But then she started, nearly leaping from her whiskers, as a group of six armed knights ran in from an ulterior corridor and raced purposefully out another door.

She heard them as they departed:

"He's on the second floor, the villain!"

"The King pursues!"

Balin had not been taken prisoner. He was being chased through the Palace Adventurous like a wild boar. The danger had not passed at all. She turned and leapt back out the window, regaining an eagle's wings, beating the air to gain the turgid, sorcery-lit sky.

CHAPTER
EIGHTEEN

MERLIN LIT UPON the roof of the Palace to catch his breath, as Viviane streaked earthward, encased in a whirling globe of pecking ethereal ravens formed out of the very shadow of night.

How had she escaped his detection all these long years? How had he not known her nature? Avalon, was of course the answer. The nature of that Fey place wreaked havoc on his vision and senses. All this time he had thought his nemesis had erected some occult citadel with magic enough to hide her from his sight, when in fact they had shared the very same bed in Avalon on occasion. He cursed himself to think that some of the magic she now used against him he had personally taught her.

She had manipulated Nimue from the start. She had already admitted to feeding her Arthur's name to give Nimue a focal point for her rage and grief. No doubt as Viviane she had facilitated her theft of the Gwenn Mantle and the Adventurous Sword. Perhaps she had left a chamber door ajar or slyly told Nimue the story of the sword and dropped its location during some innocuous visit, or in Avalon, happenstance over their herb-tending. What other plots had she cultivated to fruition right under his very nose? Maybe she had urged Lady Lile forth from Avalon on the fateful day of her death by telling her the location of Nimue and the sword, securing her own ascension. Viviane had been one of Lile's most trusted advisors. How many times had she surreptitiously led *her* astray?

For that matter, how many times had *he* been manipulated?

She had created for him the mysterious guise of the Queen to hunt and obsess over, distracting him from Viviane. But was the Queen Viviane, or was Viviane the Queen?

He could not help but admire her work. It was masterful in its longevity and execution.

He looked about for Nimue. Had she penetrated the Palace yet? Had she stopped Balin and Garlon?

That was when the first of the stone angels broke away from its housing on the side of the tower like some hatchling emerging from its egg and landed heavily beside him. It struck him with a stone fist that broke one of his ribs and sent him crumpling.

As it bore down on him, its carved, dead-eyed expression placid and thus all the more fearful, he raised a hand and scattered it into gravel.

But a third and fourth hit the roof solidly, then a fifth, and he was forced to roll aside as powerful granite feet stomped down, seeking to pulverize him. He saw others from below rising into the air, spreading their gray stone wings mockingly.

He got up and staggered back, raising both hands to blast them apart, but more and more came.

Viviane ascended over the lip of the roof and touched down lightly behind her stone army, directing them, urging them on the attack. The remains of her samite gown hung in blackened scraps about her, and her flesh was a myriad of crisscrossed cuts, coursing blood. He knew he must not look much better.

The stone angels rose and plummeted, and though he shattered them left and right, the jagged fragments that tumbled down still struck and bloodied him. There were too many for him to concentrate on. There had been thirty-six arranged in all about the towers, and he had barely accounted for nine. Then he saw phalanxes of the little smiling stone cherubs that surrounded the Palace whirling and dipping like flocks of sparrows. He had no idea how many of them there were, but they bolstered the army of granite angels and shot quickly through the ranks to batter him. They were too small, too quick to mark. He was struck hard four times almost before he'd seen them.

He retreated, leaping far free of the grasping stone fingers that tore his robes, and landed atop the central tower, grasping the arm of the golden cross in exhaustion. He barely had time to catch his breath before the stone host leapt as one gray flock into the sky to assail him.

As they reached the top, the four golden seraphim statues encircling the cross turned from their perennial adoration of the cross to repel their besieging comrades. Golden fists struck the heads off granite angels or caught the spiraling cherubim and pitched them down like boulders, smashing into the attackers, breaking them to pieces.

From the two flanking towers, the golden archangels left their pedestals and soared over to Merlin's tower, circling and striking with their lances like glorious wind born cavaliers, turning the rising force of animate stone into a crumbling avalanche of broken rock.

Merlin wiped the blood from his eyes and looked down to see Viviane glaring, eyes full of hate.

BALIN WAS DRIVEN throughout the Palace like a fox. The entire force of the castle had been mobilized against him. Every time he thought he'd chanced upon a free egress, he'd found the passage quickly filled with knights. They came relentless, like a flood of steel, pouring out of every chamber and corridor.

And always there was Pellam, waving his wicked axe and calling for blood.

He fought where he had to. There were weapons aplenty displayed on the walls. He tore mace and morning star, axe and flail, from the walls, and fought madly through tides of men until the weapons broke or they did. Sometimes he met Pellam, and always he came away bleeding. The old king was tireless and immensely strong.

Now he had only a shield he had torn from the grip of one of his pursuers. He set it before him and, ducking low, charged through a wall of knights only to find a single door on the other side, and a long winding staircase leading up behind.

He thought to ascend to some landing and find a window to escape through. He was confident from his previous study of the architecture that he could climb down to a survivable fall onto the stable roof, and there, if God was with him, ride Ironprow or some other horse out into the countryside. If he could but gain the woods beyond, and night fell, he would be free.

The narrow stairwell gave him a slight advantage over his pursuers, rendering their greater number meaningless. He was able to upset their chase and gain ground by catching up a knight and hurling him down the stairs into Pellam and the rest. There was no respite along this course. No landings. The stone stairs wound ever upward, and he knew he must be in that central tower.

His heart hammered in his chest, breath ragged in his lungs. How many times had he wished for his armor during this fight, and yet now he thanked God he had left it packed on the horses, for if he'd been wearing it now, the weight would surely have been the death of him.

Yet he was bleeding badly from a dozen cuts, the majority of them landed by Pellam.

He had also become aware of a mighty storm raging outside the keep. If he could but gain the outside, he felt sure the tempest would aid his escape.

When at last he felt sure he was at his end and prepared to turn and meet Pellam with his bent and battered shield, he rounded the hub and came at last to a short upper landing with a single heavy door.

The door bore markings and emblems, but through the sweat burning his eyes, he paid no attention. If he could get beyond the door, maybe there was something with which to bar it or maybe a much-coveted window lay beyond.

He tried the door, found it locked. He took a few steps back and hurled himself at it. It didn't budge. The clanging and shouting of his hunters grew closer.

NIMUE FLUTTERED ABOUT the central tower, dodging stony debris and deadly little cherubs, their stubby wings buzzing like granite bumblebees. She had chosen the tall stained-glass portrait of the ascending Christ as the most likely place to enter the Palace and head off Balin, but she could not find a way through the dense host of stone angels.

Atop the tower, Merlin leaned against the golden cross as the gleaming six-winged angels defended him. He was covered in his own blood, his tatterdemalion robes hanging from him. He looked even wilder than that first night she had seen him, coming in naked from a storm.

The dark sky still crackled and flashed with intermittent bursts of irrational color, nature fighting to reassert herself over the obscene chaos Merlin and Viviane had unleashed. Purple and emerald thunderheads boiled and collided in the black sky as though solid entities, and where they met red ball lightning flared and dropped to earth. An inky rain like dark blood had begun slashing down, staining the ground.

Below, the attendant buildings of the Palace were aflame, and she saw the horses screaming as they fled in a multicolored line through the outer gate of Carbonek, herded by the brave stable boys, the only servants who had not fled the castle like sea rats. In the village of Lystenoyse, the wailing of the terrified populace could be heard between terrible growls of thunder. A heavy, sulfurous odor permeated everything.

The bells of Carbonek tolled. It was like the very end of the world.

Viviane rose into the air behind her failing army, eyes fixed on Merlin, muttering some new terrible spell.

Still Nimue hung back, waiting for an opening through the thick sky.

As the last of the stone angels crumbled beneath the counter attack of the golden seraphim, she spied her chance, folded her wings, and dove at the glass.

She grew into a fish hawk when one of the treacherous granite cherubim shot up unexpectedly before her. It had been dodging the falling debris of its cohorts and launching one last desperate attack against Merlin. It might have succeeded had it not struck Nimue's beak instead. The resultant collision altered its course so that instead of the back of Merlin's skull, it struck the lance of one of the gold archangels and shattered.

Nimue fell end over end, dazed. She hurtled over the wall of Carbonek, the ground beyond rushing up at her. She did not know if she was yet a bird or had become a woman again.

Then she struck something quite hard, but it broke around her, and she sank into chilly, bubbling waters and knew no more.

MERLIN LET GO of the cross as the last of the stone angels fell away and Viviane rose into his eye line. Once the golden angels lunged at her, and with a dismissive wave of her hand, she melted them all into puddles of gold that ran like candlewax down the tower.

She stepped onto the tower roof and flung herself at him bodily, her hands pulsing with a blue white glow as though she gripped a will-o'-the-wisp in each fist.

He caught her wrists and groaned. They were like ice to touch, and his fingers blistered and burned.

As they struggled back and forth beneath the cross, she hissed at him through split and burned lips. "You're too late…*Melior!*"

One last attempt at mastering him. He grinned in response.

Because she was Viviane, the daughter of Baron Dyonas of Briosque, and while he had known nothing of the Queen of Norgales, he knew something of Viviane. He had visited her home country years ago with his mentor, Blaise. There was a forest lake between two castles there, and the castles, Brion and Charosque, had given the lake its amalgamated name.

There they had met Viviane's old father, so that Blaise could perform the Anointing of the Sick. Baron Dyonas had converted to Christianity for the love of his late wife, and had requested the renowned Blaise to hear his last confession. As part of his reconciliation, he had told them how he had once spared a wounded white hart in the forest, and that it had spoken to him, saying it was the goddess Diane, and would bless his first daughter with unfailing beauty, and that she would bear the name of her divine patroness.

Yet the birth of his daughter had been the death of Baron Dyonas' beloved wife, Vivienne, and so he had felt compelled to honor her memory by, like the two castles of his land, combining the name of her mother and the goddess.

Vivienne and Diane.

Viviane.

But Merlin knew the decree of a goddess was unalterable by man. The Goddess had named Viviane long before she was born, and so touched her with her immortal influence.

In revealing herself to him, there was a possibility she had made a grave mistake. For even if she had been christened Viviane, that was not her true name.

"You're fishing again," Merlin said, still smiling, as with indescribable relish he uttered, "*Diane.*"

The icy glow of Viviane's hands ceased instantly, and she fell to her knees with a shriek of despair and surprise.

"How?" she managed.

"All these years," Merlin snickered, letting the fire that burned in his heart well within him, "trying to find each other's true names… and it was so hard because neither of us even knew them ourselves!"

Viviane screamed as Merlin's hands emitted a soft golden glow, which then turned blue, and then white. She burned in his clutch, the horrible blackness spreading quickly down her upheld harms, down her body, and over her head until she was a gray statue of ash, captured in the midst of a now silent wail, as dead as the angels she had commanded against him.

He released her and admired his work, as though he had sculpted it over a lifetime, which, in a manner of thinking, he had. With great satisfaction, he blew her apart with a puff of his breath.

All she had been scattered on the wind that blew over Lystenoyse.

"Farewell, my dear," he whispered and leaned against the cross once more.

THE LOCK BROKE at Balin's third try and the door sprang open.

Pellam was on his heels, coming around the bend and up the stairs, unstoppable, terrible. Even ahead of his winded Templeise. There was no reasoning with the man. If he begged mercy, he would be slain as soon as his guard was down.

Balin burst into the room. The chamber was bathed in a red glow from the huge stained-glass window on the opposite end of the small chamber.

He had only seconds to take everything in. He was aware of the image of Christ rising into the heavens as his adoring disciples looked on below. It was a thing of beauty, the same window he had seen during his entrance, and he struggled to remember if there was a negotiable drop to the roof beyond or a sheer plummet to the courtyard. Could he grab hold of one of the stone angels and so climb down? He rushed toward it.

There was a stone table before the window. No, not a table, a great marble sarcophagus, the tomb of some august personage. He would have to clamber over it to get at the window.

Pellam came in directly behind him, but instead of swinging his axe, he reached out and grabbed Balin's ankle, pulling him down as he tried to lift himself onto the tomb.

Something clattered and crashed beneath him. He saw a hint of gold, felt liquid splash on his hands. He had overturned a golden cup he hadn't noticed sitting on the tomb.

The knights in the doorway beyond gasped collectively.

Pellam pulled him off the tomb and raised his axe to cleave him.

Balin scrambled to find purchase on the smooth marble. His fingers closed around the haft of an iron-tipped cruciform spear.

He hastily reoriented the crossed lance and drew it back, the butt end smashing the glass window into musical scarlet and white shards behind him, revealing a back and turgid sky beyond, fraught with strange, surreal colors.

As he was pulled toward Pellam, he lunged with the spear. The golden cup went rolling off the sarcophagus and tumbled out the open window.

The lance point pricked Pellam's right thigh and drove easily through, then continued on through his left in a burst of blood, pinning them together. With an anguished cry the old king fell forward, hobbled, taking the lance from Balin's grip.

Balin stumbled.

He was aware of a great impact when the Fisher King fell. He felt it beneath his feet.

Then the floor crumbled away like broken sandstone and he fell into a cacophonous abyss.

Everything was falling.

CHAPTER
NINETEEN

ERLIN FELT THE tower sway beneath his feet, and he leapt into the air, becoming once more the pied raven. He pulled himself ever higher and then wheeled.

Nimue had failed. His sharp eyes espied the cup, the Holy Grail, just a golden glint twinkling as it plummeted down from the heights of the Palace Adventurous. Too far, too fast for even Merlin to catch, had he been able to lay hands on it at all.

It struck the courtyard flags, with a mighty ring that resounded like a booming church bell. Merlin saw a golden halo emit from the point of impact and grow swiftly outward like a ripple in a stone-pierced pond.

Wherever that golden emanation touched, ruin followed.

At its epicenter, The Palace Adventurous and the walls of the surrounding castle of Carbonek crumbled as if a mighty scythe had swept through the foundation of that tremendous structure.

Like the fabled statue of Nebuchadnezzar struck by the boulder, the entire glorious structure collapsed in on itself with a tremendous rumble and crash. The three towers retracted into the earth as though drawn down and disappeared in a cloud of gray debris which rolled in a thick, choking plume all around. The mighty walls dropped.

The golden ring passed on, expanding to encompass the village, the bountiful fields, the forest of Carteloise, and beyond. It stretched in every direction to the furthest horizons, until Merlin lost sight of its progress, but he saw its aftermath.

The fields of Lystenoyse shriveled. The grass browned as if burned away. The leaves blew crackling from the trees, and in the murdered pastures, the cattle and the sheep dropped in their places. The waters shrank, and it was there that he saw Nimue lying crumpled in the mud and made for her.

She was not dead.

"Merlin," she muttered weakly, when he knelt and cradled her in his arms as he had not done in an age. "What has happened?"

Merlin looked all about at the gray land. The strange storms his battle with Viviane had caused were receding, but a gray fog hung low over everything and ash drifted through the air.

"We failed. The Sangreal has been desecrated. Carbonek is fallen. Lystenoyse is no more."

He watched this revelation settle behind her eyes. He saw the burden, that she was partially an instrument of all that had happened settle upon her. She turned her face into his arm in shame and sobbed.

Merlin heard the desolate, lone wail of an infant from the direction of the silent village and then, as if responding to that pitiful cry, the drone of many horse flies buzzing, emerging newborn from their muddy nests, rising blood mad into the air to claim dominion over the wasted land.

THIRD PART:

THE
WASTE
LAND

CHAPTER
ONE

MERLIN LEANED ON his new staff, looking from the beauteous face of Nimue to the Holy Grail, lying on its side in a niche of broken masonry.

It was untouched, undiminished, shining from the gold plating.

Once it had been a simple wooden cup. Some well-meaning adorant of Joseph of Arimathea's coterie had hammered burnished gold to it, to better display its worth. Every chalice on every Christian altar since had followed the model.

Men and their gold. It amused Merlin that some artisan believer had decided he could take a priceless object and improve it. He imagined the man had done so without even a hint of ironic thought to his own hubris.

There was nothing amusing about the devastation the profaning of the Grail had wrought though. The Grail's own light, emanating from the recess in the rubble, was now the brightest thing in sight. All else was gray and dead.

Nimue stooped to retrieve it, but Merlin gripped her by the shoulder.

"Don't touch it!"

She looked at him querulously.

"It is touched by the divine, and our own exposure to magic could cause an unwanted reaction," Merlin explained. "Maybe even a second backlash. Go and find the lance, but do not touch it."

Nimue rose.

"And how are we to retrieve these things if we cannot touch them?"

Merlin straightened and pointed with his staff, to a procession of monks coming from the east.

"They will do it," he said.

"Who are they?" Nimue asked, shrinking behind him unconsciously at the appearance of the strange, robed men.

In spite of all that had happened, Merlin could not help but smile thinly at the wizened, craggy countenance of the bent old monk who led the procession, bearing a rude cross on the head of his staff.

It was Brother Blaise, the man who had been his father, and the human personification of the Christian God to him as a boy. His hair was white and undulant and swept about his head like a bright torch fire. His prophet's beard hung to the rosary around the thin waist of his coarse white mantle. Though his face was aged and half crippled, the bird-bright eyes that looked out were as vital and focused as ever.

Even though he had been a silent newborn nestled in the crook of his mother's arm, Merlin could still clearly remember the younger Blaise standing like the monument of a saint between Vortigern's dour judges and poor Adhan, blinded by the hellish visitation of his incubus father which had deposited him in her womb alongside his sister, Gwendydd. Blaise eloquently denounced their order of execution as his twin sister howled and shook in his mother's other arm. Blaise had sworn before his God that he would raise the Cambion to serve the cause of the Lord, or destroy Merlin himself and then submit to the judgment of the Most High: all to spare the life of a blameless blind woman and her daughter. Blaise was the first Christian Merlin had ever known.

The fiery priest had made quite a strong impression on him. He was the only father Merlin had ever known on earth.

Merlin had begged with Blaise numerous times to retire to the life-prolonging air of Avalon, but the old priest had been content to remain at his hermitage in the wilds of Northumberland, silently contemplating, writing, and praying.

"Father Blaise!" Merlin called and raised his hand in greeting when the monks were near.

"Bless you, my son," said Blaise, in word and action, making the sign of the cross at him as he approached.

"You came quickly."

"The Lord made it known to me that this would happen."

Merlin was surprised to see old Sir Brastias, a knight of Uther's Table who had fought at Bedegraine for Arthur, among Blaise's monks, tonsured and robed. He was one of the knights Merlin had summoned that one shameful May Day long ago.

"Hello, Brastias," Merlin said awkwardly. "How are you?"

Brastias stared impassively at the Grail, as though Merlin had not spoken.

"Brother Brastias took a vow of silence when he joined our order," Blaise explained.

Well, that was likely for the best. No doubt Merlin had earned the old knight's enmity.

How could he ever have explained to Blaise the far-reaching plan he had enacted through their vile deed that day? How could he explain the great service Brastias and the rest had done to Arthur and all Albion? The greater evils they had averted through the one?

Here in this blighted place, it must have seemed to Brastias that nothing he had done had amounted to anything.

Nimue came stumbling over the shifting stone. He had not realized she had left his side.

"I have found the lance. And King Pellam. He is alive."

Blaise waved for Brastias and three other monks to accompany Nimue, while he stooped and retrieved the Grail from the ground.

The old monk's eyes widened at the touch of the holy object but his expression was sad.

Blaise turned to the two remaining monks. From their baggage, they uncovered a simple wooden tabernacle with a pair of carrying straps, and Blaise set the Grail in it, shutting its light from the world.

The old man turned then, and the younger monk strapped the tabernacle to Blaise's hunched back.

"Father, might one of the younger brothers carry that for you?" Merlin asked.

Blaise stared at Merlin and shook his head.

"It is my penance."

Merlin nodded. It was plain that the old man blamed Merlin for what had happened and thus, himself. Had Brastias confessed to him?

Nimue returned, with Brastias and the other monks bearing the pale King Pellam on a bier between them. They chanted lowly, mournfully. The old king's legs were pierced through the thighs, bleeding through linen wrappings. He stared with wide, frightful, faraway eyes at the gray sky and clutched the bloodied Holy Lance of Longinus to his chest. Perhaps it was what had saved him in the end.

Beside the grim procession walked a boy, Pellam's son, Eliazar, with his wailing baby sister in his arms.

"The Queen?" Merlin asked.

Nimue shook her head.

"They are all dead," said Eliazar quietly, between the rattling cries of his sister.

All but one other, thought Merlin.

———

BRASTIAS AND THE procession of chanting monks departed in the opposite direction from Carbonek, bearing King Pellam and the desecrated Lance.

"Where will they take them?" Nimue asked. "The king and the treasures?"

Merlin started to answer, but Blaise spoke.

"Joseph wrote here on the tomb of the traitor, Simeon," the old monk intoned impressively, pointing to the walled cemetery outside the ruins. "*Here shall come a leopard of king's blood, and he shall slay this serpent, and this leopard shall engender a lion, and this lion shall pass all other knights.*" Despite his weak and aged appearance, he still had that way of speaking which made every word a booming proclamation, a divine declarative. "My lady," he said to Nimue, "it is for only the leopard's son to know. Only the lion can heal the king and the land."

"And where will you go, father?" Merlin asked.

"I will see the Sangreal secured and return to my abbey to await the coming of the lion," Blaise said, shrugging.

Merlin eyed the sanctuary on his back. It was a heavy thing for an old man to bear.

Merlin could not hide his anxiety apparently, for Blaise then smiled and said, "Do not worry, Merlin. The journey will be long, and the holy quest even longer in fulfilling, but I will see him."

Then he leaned forward, embracing the enchanter. It was like hugging a skeleton, and Merlin wondered if his old foster father had gone senile. Blaise kissed him, whispering, "You will not, my son."

Then he turned, and to Merlin's surprise, embraced Nimue and held her for a moment, whispering. She nodded, as surprised as he. Then without another word, Blaise broke the embrace and went to catch up with the other monks, going as lightly as if he were a hungry man on the way to a dinner party.

"What did he say to you?" Merlin asked.

"He made me swear not to tell you. Yet," she murmured, watching him go.

Merlin frowned at her. "You do well to abide. He's no magician, and he has no demon's blood, or angel's, so far as I know, but I have never known him to be wrong."

"What happens now?"

Merlin sat upon one of the broken blocks strewn about the ground and turned his palms to the gray sky. "Now, Viviane must die in the eyes of the Avalon priestesses. Merlin must not be seen to kill her, or he will be branded a usurper. You will become Viviane and take her place in Avalon. I will come to you as Nimue, with the remains of the Gwenn Mantle, begging forgiveness. There will be a public reconciliation. Then, slowly, perhaps in a year's time, Viviane will step down, and Nimue will be Lady of The Lake."

"How will you engineer that?" Nimue asked.

"We shall think of something," Merlin said. He had not entirely prognosticated the details, but he had already foreseen the end result. Nimue *would* be the Lady. The how would fill itself in.

"And I am to agree to this arrangement without any protest?"

"Of course," Merlin smiled. "Isn't it what you always wanted, deep down? Before you met your prince, you used to beg me to teach you the secrets of the universe. Won't the duty and the power fill the hole left by the love you lost?"

"What about Balin and the Adventurous Sword?"

Merlin's smile fell. "Yes. You know he lives. Whether it was the destiny of the sword or his contact with the Grail, I do not know. But he lies there, waiting, beneath those stones," Merlin said, looking out over the silent, broken masonry. "Blaise would call it your penance, Nimue. I would call it balance. You gave him the sword, and it cannot be relinquished. Not now. Not except by the way it was foretold. Balin is like a driven animal, and you must be the hunter. I will be the hound that drives him to you. Let it be quick, if you can. You owe him that, at least."

He stood. It was a hard thing, to send a good man to his death, but Merlin had known from the beginning what must be done. Arthur's life was still at stake.

"What will you do, Merlin?" Nimue asked in a low tone.

"I must strangle the love he holds in his heart," Merlin said. "He will follow his hatred to a better, stronger love. Then he will die killing it."

He put his hand to Nimue's soft cheek. She was lovely. "I will see you again in Avalon," he said.

Then her features undulated like the surface of a pond and she was Viviane. For a dreadful moment, Merlin worried that she had been Viviane all along. That Nimue, and Viviane, and the Queen of Norgales, and Morgan, and Morgause, and even his mother Adhan were all faces of one Goddess, a Goddess he had angered through his diplomacy with the crucified god.

Then she was a sparrow, and then she was gone. Merlin picked his way among the broken blocks.

CHAPTER
TWO

BALIN DID NOT know if he was in hell or Purgatory, only that he was not in heaven. Heaven would not be this dark closeness, this heavy burden all about, this tantalizing view of freedom.

The first day, as best as he could reckon time, he thought perhaps he had survived the evident collapse of the Palace, been uncovered by some unguessed party, deemed dead, and laid prematurely in some tomb. All was black and cold.

That thought panicked him. He fought against the stone enclosing him, skinning his fists bloody, and soon succumbed to unreasoning screams.

Then, after who knew how many hours, but at what he guessed was the morning, such as it was, of a second day, a sliver of light appeared to his right, and straining his eyes to see, he perceived only a dull, gray formlessness.

He supposed then that since he had made no final confession and died fighting against Pellam, God's anointed, he had not been granted access to Paradise.

Yet he had not been damned either.

Unless Brother Gallet had been wrong, and hell was not a torture of fire but of cold confinement.

He had never feared fire, but closeness. Once, as a boy, playing at some hiding game with Brulen, he had crawled into their father's old chest and their unwitting mother had set firewood on top of it. She'd been distracted by some visitor, leaving him trapped, too weak to lift the lid. He had remembered the cold sweat of terror, the unreasoning fear that had settled on him like a feasting presence, whispering to him that no one would find him for hours as the air grew hot and his breath short.

His mother and Brulen had heard him scream of course, and released him, but the dread of close confinement had remained all his years.

Maybe every man had his own hell. Maybe Brother Gallet's hell was fire, and Balin's was this internment in stone. To be gripped in a grave for all eternity.

When he heard the grinding of the heavy blocks moving, saw the slim fissure of light widen like a birthing canal, his heart sang and he expected to see Christ or one of his ministering angels beckon him to glory. Instead, it was with a groan that his watery eyes picked out the dark form of Merlin standing over him.

"Merlin!" he rasped, his throat raw from thirst and his previous lamentations. "What's happened?"

"Come and see."

He gladly sat up and eased himself aching from that dark space, but the sunlight did not warm him. It came through heavy clouds and fog, and the ruins around him were as dismal and weird as a disordered graveyard of unmarked tombstones, all heaped upon one another.

He had been freed from one Purgatory only to step into another.

"What is this place?" he whispered, for its silence imposed respect upon him, as though the dead were very near and did not wish to be disturbed.

"Why," said Merlin, gesturing to encompass the foggy ruins with his staff, "this is what remains of the Castle Carbonek and the kingdom of Lystenoyse, which you arrived in only three days ago."

Balin tested his stiff joints and leaned against an upright block. His breath puffed out in clouds. It seemed to add to the stuff that hung all about. "Three days?"

"Three days have passed since you took up the spear of Longinus and struck King Pellam the Dolorous Stroke." Merlin climbed over a pile of stone and pointed down to something jutting from the rubble.

Balin came over and looked. It was the broken door he had burst through to enter the chamber at the top of the tall tower.

He could see the emblems carved onto the door closer now. There a hammer and three long nails, a cross with a cock perched upon the top, a scourge, a long reed and sponge, and a lance very like the one he had wielded before the room had apparently collapsed.

But no, it had not been only the room. He stumbled away from the door and saw the broken head of one of the stone cherubs lying nearby. He picked it up and held it in his hands.

These were the remains of Carbonek. The beautiful Palace Adventurous had been destroyed. The full weight of what he had done settled on him like a descending vulture on his shoulders. In his mad flight, he had burst into the very reliquary and profaned the sacred treasures of Christ Himself. The Holy Grail. The Lance of Longinus. He'd drawn blood with a weapon which had last been turned against Lord Jesus Christ on Golgotha.

He felt sick, and he let the broken carving drop from his fingers. For a terrible instant, he fancied he saw that face recoil in silent terror before it shattered to fragments on the ground.

He pitched forward, legs trembling, and caught himself on a broken block, where his guts heaved and wrung bile from his empty belly in violent surges. He stumbled on, not wanting to believe it, hoping it was some wizardry of Merlin's, hoping he could find the edge of this fog and ruin as he had found the boundary of the Garden of Joy. He could peak through the hedge and find Lorna Maeve again, break through and run to her this time.

He found a place where the ruins gave way to boggy ground and could see the choked river they had crossed over together and laughed to see the boy struck with wet laundry by the washerwoman. There was no joy anywhere in that river. It was only mud and stagnant, fly haunted pools now. The village looked deserted and rundown.

A chill wind blew up from somewhere, pestilent and foul smelling. It parted the fog briefly, allowing him a glimpse of dead trees, dead fields, dead, bloated animals.

His action had done this?

Then he must rectify it. He turned back toward the rubble with a passion and found Merlin standing behind him, impassive.

"Don't bother looking, Balin. The holy treasures are not here. They have gone. And no man knows where."

Balin sought to argue but could not summon the will. He knew the enchanter spoke true.

"What can I do?"

"Here?" said Merlin. "Nothing more." He pointed with his staff. "There is your horse, and your armor, and your precious sword."

Balin looked and saw Ironprow tethered to a gnarled, withered tree. He couldn't remember seeing him there before, but he could have overlooked him in his shock at the change in Lystenoyse. The horse at least, though wet and sullen looking, was alive.

"What about the Fisher King?" Balin murmured.

"Only the Grail can heal him, but it's not for you to find, Balin."

Merlin's robes rustled, and he went alongside Balin and took him by the shoulder, guiding him toward the horse.

Balin stopped rigidly. "Merlin," he said, not daring to ask, knowing he must. He put his heart in the wizard's hands. "There was a nobleman, and a lady with me."

Merlin frowned and sighed. He pointed with his staff, back toward the ruins.

Balin began to sob. He threw off Merlin's arm and ran pell-mell at the ruined castle, turning uncertainly.

"Lorna Maeve! My Lady!" he called.

Merlin stood in the wreckage, looking down at a pile of stone near the edge of the ruin, though Balin had not seen him move.

He looked dourly in Balin's direction and pointed down at his feet with his staff.

Balin stumbled, tripped a few times, dashing his knees and cutting his elbow on the jutting rubble.

He came to where Merlin stood, pointing down at a thick slab of cracked white marble.

Balin whimpered but stooped to attack the stone. He strained to lift it, but it wouldn't budge. He kicked it, clawed at it, struck it with his fists.

Merlin drew him aside.

"Get back," he said and struck the center of the marble a blow with the end of his staff.

A web of cracks burst out from the point of impact, and the stone crumbled, so Balin, digging in his fingernails, could pick the block apart.

His fingers were bleeding by the time he uncovered the pale face of the Lady Lorna Maeve, framed in stone like the carved face of a guardian angel on a tomb.

She was perfect, unmarred, eyes closed, lips parted slightly so that he could see her white teeth. Only unconscious, he thought desperately.

He touched her cold cheek, leaving a streak of his own blood. He cursed that and tried to wipe it away with the edge of his hand.

She did not react.

Balin scrabbled at the stone, praying aloud, though the words were jumbled and made little sense.

Then he began to see, the odd shape of her breast beneath her gown, the stone jutting into her torso.

His prayer became a wail, and a scream.

He got up and staggered, tumbled over a stone and fell to his knees on the earth outside the ruin's edge. He drove his fists into the mud, then ploughed his face into it.

He felt as if a spade had gouged his chest and extricated his heart and buried it here somewhere. He dug at the ground like a dog at a fox den. He lay doubled up there, pulling his hair and howling into the mud and ashes, thinking of her bright, unexpected smile, pining for the feel of that ridiculous hair in his hands, and the precious laughter he had heard once and would never hear again.

It was too much to bear.

"This is the grave of many men and women," Merlin said, compounding Balin's misery just when his rage and sorrow had subsided enough for the stillness to descend once more. "Count Oduin, too, and Pellam's queen."

"God, Merlin," Balin croaked. "What can I do? What can I do to amend? How can I…? I'm lower than Cain. I have slain the world!"

"You have wounded it," Merlin assented. "Grievously."

"Is that all the wisdom you can offer me now?" Balin gasped, sitting up.

Merlin said nothing.

Balin looked out across the stones and wiped the mud from his eyes with his sleeves.

His heart lay beneath Carbonek with Lorna Maeve, and with Oduin, whose son would die in agony now.

Yet still, it beat. Why?

Why had God spared him in the middle of this catastrophe? There had to be a purpose, still. He had become an instrument of the will of God and also a tool of demons, of that there was no doubt. He reflected that he had seen so much of magic and miracles lately. Merlin was the master of that magic.

Who then on earth was the lord of miracles?

For all his esteemed trappings and lineage, for all his stewardship of the sacred Sangreal, it had not been Pellam. He had been but a man in the end, driven to blood and vengeance over the death of as bad a villain as Balin had ever known. He had harbored his murdering, godless brother for decades, hadn't he? Surely, he had known he was a villain as far back as Agrippe's time. Well might his line been, chosen by God as custodians, but he was no better or worse a king than Rience had been in the end.

He was a king, but not God's king. There was still Arthur.

Arthur who had proven his right to rule under God with the sword of Macsen, Arthur who had inspired the very people to rally around him at Caerleon, Arthur who had kept the serpents of Avalon at bay and brought God's justice to the Saxons and Rience at Cameliard, and whose castle now housed the miraculous Round Table.

To undo what he had done would take a miracle. He would have to return to the place where miracles could happen, to Camelot.

"I'll go back to Camelot," Balin mumbled. "I'll tell Arthur what's happened, what I've done. If you have no guidance for me, I can at least inform the king. Maybe I can't reclaim the Grail. Maybe I'm not worthy, but Arthur and the Round Table are."

"Already in Camelot they have begun to feel what has happened here," said Merlin.

Balin rose and walked purposefully toward where Ironprow was tethered.

Merlin walked along behind him. Balin reached Ironprow and stripped off his torn tunic. Merlin seated himself on a stone.

Balin loosed his bundled armor with a clatter and stooped to sift through the components, selected his sabatons.

Merlin watched him strap the armor to his feet.

"The first time we met, Balin, was not the first time I saw you," Merlin said.

Balin paused, then found his greaves and sat down to fit them over his legs. "I know," he said. "Brulen told me. You were there the day our mother died."

"She was a good woman," Merlin said, not denying it, laying aside his staff.

"Not good enough for you to stop her death," Balin said, picking out his cod piece and cuisses.

"Some things are unavoidable, Balin," Merlin said, with an air of regret. "The hook must transfix the worm to bait the trout. The fisherman gives the worm and its loves and hates no thought. He only wants to feed his children and himself. The farmer who buys the fish so that he may have the strength to work his plough and harvest his field gives no thought to the worm, nor does the baker or the king who takes bread at his table. But without the sacrifice of the worm, none of these things can ever happen. And without the doings of baker and farmer, king and fisher, the worm, too, has no sustenance. There is a course to events, Balin. Everything is interwoven, like a tapestry on a loom. Certain things must trigger or desirable events may never come to pass."

Merlin had come over while he spoke and picked up Balin's gambeson. He held the arming doublet open for Balin.

Balin reached out and took the jacket from Merlin and shouldered into it himself. As Balin tied his laces, Merlin's gaze lingered on him a moment. Then he went back to the stone and retrieved his staff.

Balin moved onto his cuirass, dwelling on the notion that his mother was but a worm in Merlin's mind.

"Your brother understood this, I think," Merlin said.

Balin looked at him.

"He told you of me," Merlin said, looking wistfully now across the ruins, "and of May Day, too, I expect. I hated to shoulder him with such a dreadful task. But the line has to be cast, you see, if ever the fish is to be landed and it was Arthur's will. Sometimes a king's foresight surpasses even a wizard's. Oh, but not to worry, my divinations all bore Arthur out. It really was the best thing we could do to correct his indiscretion with Morgause. Brulen did his duty to us admirably."

"With Morgause?" Balin asked, aghast. Morgause was Arthur's sister!

"I had heard that her sister Morgan was an acolyte of the Queen of Norgales, but I dismissed Morgause, as she had no power of her own." Merlin scoffed. "No power? Only the greatest power given to womankind. Morgan distracted me, and I did not see the Queen's plot until it was too late. Morgause visited Arthur at Caer Gai before he knew his own lineage. Before he knew she was his sister. He confessed it to me as soon as he learned, of course. He was young and flattered by her attentions. She conceived a son by him, and he was born on May Day. That alone I could learn from my divinations, but there was no boy baby among her husband Lot's folk in the Orkneys. For a year I searched for him. By some spell of the Queen or of Morgan, he was hidden from me. I had to resort to mundane methods. Baptismal records, noble birth announcements. I narrowed it down to four boy children, born on May Day all about Albion and came to Arthur with my findings."

Four children, Balin thought, stopping short in his work. A cold sweat blossomed on the back of his neck, though he wasn't sure why. It was as if some danger were creeping upon him.

Four children. Four eggs. Four kings.

"Aguysans," he mumbled.

"The King With A Hundred Nights, yes," said Merlin with a heavy sigh. "And King Cradelment of North Wales and King Idres of Cornwall."

"The fourth was…"

"A boy child belonging to Sir Morganore, the captain of Aguysans' Hundred Knights. My suspicions were the strongest about that one," Merlin said, "as Morgause had befriended Morganore in their youth, but I could prove nothing. My powers failed me."

Balin stared at Merlin. The sweat was pouring down his back now. His pulse was racing.

"Arthur…Arthur commanded…"

"Arthur took a page from King Herod, and Pharaoh before him. *Then Herod sent forth, and slew all the children that were in Bethlehem, and in all the coasts thereof, from two years old and under, according to the time which he had diligently inquired of the magi.*"

Balin reeled and had to grip Ironprow's saddle to keep from crashing down in his steel trousers.

"I had taken great pains to formulate some other way," Merlin went on, "thinking to spare his sensibilities, but he had arrived at the natural solution immediately, as a king should."

"You sent my brother to do this thing?" Balin hissed. "Brulen?"

"By Arthur's decree, yes. Brulen, Sir Brastias, Sir Dagonet, and Sir Kay. The most loyal and unquestioning. I sent them out on May Day's eve, each to steal a certain boy child, each one born on May Day, before their first birthdays. Then, in some secret place even I do not know, they were slain and buried."

The magnitude, the vileness of this sin was too great for him to stomach. He fell to his knees and retched, his body trying to reject all memory of what he'd just heard.

That was the deed that Brulen had done for Arthur and Merlin, the task that had driven him forever and rightfully so, from the High King's service.

The murder of three innocent children and the elimination of a bastard son born of incest.

He remembered kneeling at Arthur's feet in the pavilion at Bedegraine and recalled the king's words then.

I have no need for knights who follow unworthy orders without question.

But he had.

He had!

"I see," said Merlin. "Brulen did not tell you everything, then. The boy would have grown to destroy Arthur."

"Is Arthur worth so much?" Balin screamed. "Is he worth the soul of my brother and of three other knights? Is he worth the slaughter of *babies?*"

"As a knight of Camelot, don't you love him best, Balin?" Merlin said.

Balin grabbed the hilt of the Adventurous Sword and tore it from its scabbard with a resounding ring. It quivered, even in both hands, he was shaking so badly.

Merlin stood, eyeing him warily.

"*Love* him?" Balin laughed madly. "I *renounce* him! And *you*, his conniving, damned, half-devil, black *lapdog!*"

Balin charged at Merlin and swung for his head. The blade whistled through the air, but he was blinded by his own tears.

The swing met nothing. It carried him completely around and severed the top of a dead tree with a crack, upsetting only Ironprow.

Merlin stood away, looking as if he hadn't moved. Perhaps he had never been there to begin with, the old trickster.

"Stand still, you murdering hellspawn! I'll take your head like I did your Avalon whore's!"

"As to that," Merlin said, with a dark and easy smile, "I am easy to find, Balin. Not so easy to kill, you will find."

With that, he became once more, mockingly, the pied raven Brych, and his mottled wings carried him into the gray sky.

He soared north, and Balin screamed the whole time he was in sight.

So was Balin's fate finally sealed, Merlin thought, as it had been, from the day that sword had left Avalon.

Merlin had been so busy with the rebellion, he almost hadn't taken note of Nimue and the plot to kill Arthur with the Adventurous Sword. The fathers of the May Day children had come to suspect Arthur for the disappearance of their sons, probably due to the whispers of Morgause in Lot's ear. After he had manipulated King Rience into silencing the three kings and Sir Morganore, Merlin had been about to depart Mount Aravius when he'd seen Nimue. After her offer to Rience, he had known only one knight in all Albion could claim that sword, and so he had gotten Dagonet to solicit Balin's release from Bedegraine's dungeon.

And now, with Balin's love of Arthur expunged from his heart, at last, the king was safe. Another shield of lies to protect the king. Of course, Arthur had had no knowledge of what Merlin had ordered Brulen, Brastias, Dagonet, and Kay to do. The part of the story about Arthur confessing his unwitting incest had been true. The boy had been distraught, ready to relinquish his crown even before he wore it. A good boy, the makings of a great man. Merlin had had to talk him down, tell him they couldn't be sure Morgause had conceived. Her base treachery exposed, even then Arthur couldn't believe her seduction had been knowing and deliberate. He'd just assumed she had been as ignorant as he. He was naïve to the evils of the world. In that way, he was very like Sir Balin. So he, Merlin, had taken it upon himself to keep Arthur's rule free of rumor. It had taken nearly four years to expunge the deed from history at last with the death of Lot. And there was still Morgause and her sister Morgan La Fey to worry about.

It was never ending.

The loss of the Grail had been an unexpected blow, and very likely the true purpose of Viviane's scheme with the sword all along, but as Blaise said, it would be recovered. All would be well, eventually.

Unfortunately, not for Balin. He must pay the price of the worm.

CHAPTER
THREE

BALIN PRAYED. BUT his heart was filled with wrath, and some of it, he could not help but direct at God Himself.

Part of him, the weak part, the part that shied from tight spaces, perhaps, asked why God had stood idly by and allowed him to be so terribly misused, but a voice within him, Gallet's strong, strict voice, struck these mewling cries away as though with a hymnal.

Hadn't he brought all this sin upon himself by taking the Adventurous Sword? Hadn't his pride, as it was written in Proverbs, led him to his fall? He had rationed and reasoned away his need for personal glory and the iniquitous treasure of this cursed sword, even though the maiden had warned him.

Curse Avalon for spawning this thing in its hellfire smithy. Curse Merlin and Arthur and all these maidens who had steered his family to doom from the outset and curse himself for allowing himself to be led.

But no more. Now he would atone. Now he would put this relic of Satan to one final use.

He would turn it on its masters.

He would begin with Merlin in his Garden of Joy and then go to Avalon itself. Arthur had committed the sin of Herod and Pharaoh.

He would cleanse away that sin like Christ flogging the moneylenders from the Temple. But in place of a flail would be this sword. He would cut down these crafty witches who had devoured his mother, first her soul and then her body, in fire.

From there he would go to Camelot and test it against Excalibur. Arthur was *not* God's king. God had no king in Albion.

Brulen had been right. There was no human master worth serving. Perhaps not in all the wide world.

Brulen. Poor, damned Brulen.

He wept anew for his brother and said a prayer that God would let them reconcile ere he died in battle with heaven's enemies.

I am easy to find, the old devil Merlin had said with a villainous smile.

He gripped the blade of the sword and stared hard into its surface, looking past his own myriad sins and glories etched upon it.

"Show me the way to Merlin," he demanded and squeezed the hilt with both hands as though it were the wizard's throat. Above the image of the falling Grail and Lance, Balin saw an image begin to form like fog on glass, the steel writing the future for him upon its now crowded surface.

He saw a forest and a lake. It was no simple, abstract representation. Every detail was specific, from the twist of an oak on the shore to a strange, moss-covered menhir. It was the place they'd made camp the night before riding into Lystenoyse, the little wood at the valley's edge, outside of Carteloise Forest.

After he had finished donning his armor and had mounted Ironprow, he put the sword across his lap and rode.

As he drew further from the ruins of Carbonek, his heart grew colder, and he closed the visor of his helm to hide his shameful tears. He was leaving Lorna Maeve behind. It was all he could think of.

First, he had to pass through Lystenoyse.

The village he had ridden through with Count Oduin and Lorna

Maeve was gone now. The buildings stood, but they were already falling to disrepair, as if a hundred years had passed between then and now.

Clouds of large, insidious flies buzzed everywhere, lighting upon the scrawny villagers he saw, the eldest and youngest of whom seemed to have been cast into the street. The houses were shuttered, perhaps against disease. Perhaps they were empty.

Those that stayed behind were gray and sunken, faces drawn and miserable. The biting flies clustered in the corners of their drooping mouths and glassy eyes, and raised great suppurating welts on their flesh. Merlin must have lied. It could not have been a mere three days. This village was on the verge of death.

He saw a wasted looking woman sitting against a building, staring off into nothing as a bawling, malnourished baby kicked weakly in her arms and tugged at her naked, withered breast. It was only when he had passed that he realized the mother was dead.

When he turned Ironprow about, thinking to retrieve the infant, a group of shuffling villagers in ragged clothes crept out from between the buildings, bearing hoes and staves, wooden pitchforks and rusty hatchets.

They barred his passage to the child and stared up at him.

"What is the matter here? Why do you all look as if you're starving?" Balin asked.

The villagers said nothing, until one old dry lipped woman answered, "When the castle fell, all the food spoiled. The meat was found to be maggot-ridden. The milk curdled and the grains were infested with weevils. The river ran dry and the animals dropped dead. Then the flies came, and they spread a sickness among us."

"Give us your horse and we'll let you pass," said a gaunt man with a mallet.

Balin drew back on his reins, unsure of what to do as they reached out to pull him from the saddle. A clout from his gauntlet would split a skull. He could kill them all.

Ironprow kicked one of the groaning, skeletal men down and, seeing an opening in the crowd, turned and bolted of his own accord. Ironprow did not stop until he had reached the valley's edge.

The little forest was quiet. Mist and mud had taken the place of ground vegetation, and the trees were winter bare. He could see wolves loping alongside the road, watching Ironprow with the same look as the villagers.

He rode on, until at last he came to the stone and the oak beside the lake.

He was surprised to see a knight riding away from the lake and turning up the road to Carteloise. He was as out of place in this strange and wasted wood as a silver platter among a shelf of broken clay dishes.

He rode like a dream of chivalry upon a beautiful white destrier with gaudy, somewhat incongruous leopard skin saddle skirting and wore a suit of splendidly polished, close-fitted armor, unadorned but somehow more resplendent than all the gold and silver chased harnesses Balin had seen on the breasts of kings. A red and white plume flowed luxuriantly from the knight's helm, and he bore a sword at his side and a bright red and white charge: *Argent, three bendlets, gules.*

Balin hailed the knight with a hoarse cry, and the man stopped and looked back. Seeing him, he turned his horse and waited until Ironprow had slogged up the muddy road to face him.

The knight raised his gauntlet. "I am Sir Lancelot du Lac, bound for the court of Camelot," the knight called in a strident, but decidedly young voice, Gallic in accent. "Who goes?"

Du Lac? He knew enough of the Gallic tongue to understand that meant 'of The Lake,' and his heart, inspired by the sight of so pristine and well-armed a warrior in the midst of desperate times, sank back into the mud of despair and enmity and burned there.

He had ridden from the direction of the lake and there was nothing there.

"You say you are bound for Camelot," said Balin. "From wither are you bound? Not Avalon?"

"You are discourteous not to answer with your own name, sir," said Lancelot. "I do ride from Avalon, though my father was King Ban of Benwick. I was raised at Avalon upon his death, by the Lady of The Lake. Now I am bound to meet my cousins, Sir Bors and Sir Lionel. They will vouchsafe me to King Arthur."

"If the Lady of The Lake is your patroness, then you will never get there," said Balin, with hardness in his heart.

"Why do you say so, sir?"

"I say so because I am the enemy of all that is of Avalon, and I will let no man who owes the Lady of The Lake allegiance pass."

"Do you threaten me, sir?"

"No, sir, I slay you!" Balin yelled. He dug his heels into Ironprow and charged.

Here he would land the first stroke of his vengeance against the devils that had driven his family to ruin. This pagan's blood would baptize the Adventurous Sword anew.

He expected the untested knight to break and run before his charge, but instead the boy, to his credit, met him gamely, drawing his own sword and kicking the splendid white destrier into his path.

It was almost a shame to kill so brave a young man.

Balin swept at Lancelot's head, intending to knock it from his shoulders, but to his surprise, the boy slid nimbly from the side of his saddle and hung there, evacuating the arc of the Adventurous Sword and swinging a short, sharp blow that landed on Balin's shield and broke it with a ring.

Balin recovered and turned, dropping his ruined shield and drawing his second sword.

Young Lancelot swung back up onto his horse's back and turned also. It was an admirable display of horsemanship. He was swift in his armor.

"A knight with two swords!" Lancelot exclaimed, and it sounded to Balin as if he might be laughing.

Balin charged again.

They met in the center and traded strikes. Lancelot's weapon caught his armor pauldron and Balin chopped with the Adventurous Sword, managing to strike Lancelot's shield from his hand, severing the straps. He followed with the other sword and smote Lancelot a blow hard enough to dent his cuirass, but the young knight's arm came down and trapped the second sword. He rolled from the saddle, snapping the blade and leaving the hilt in Balin's grasp but landing on his feet.

Balin roared and swung down at Lancelot, shaving his helmet plume. Ironprow joined the fight and struck at Lancelot with his fore-hooves, but Lancelot batted them aside with his gauntlet. This time Balin was certain he heard the boy laughing beneath his helm.

"Your horse has spirit, sir!"

Balin took the Adventurous Sword in both hands and swung low, this time compensating for the dexterous boy's annoying tendency to duck. He caught Lancelot full in the face and the magic blade broke the visor of his helm and sent the whole accoutrement spinning.

At first, he had thought he'd sent the boy's head away with his helm, but there he crouched, exposed, and no longer laughing. He was surpassingly handsome, yellow haired, blue eyed, and beardless, with the sort of milky skin that registered rage and embarrassment in a red flush of the cheeks, precluding all hope of guile.

To Balin's surprise, Lancelot sprang vertically into the air with such strength that he found himself eye level with Balin. He swung his silvery blade and struck Balin such a blow on the vambrace that his fingers popped open and the Adventurous Sword tumbled to the ground.

Then, as he began his return to earth, Lancelot slapped his free hand on the side of Balin's helm and twisted, using his weight and momentum to tip Balin from the saddle and pinwheel him hard to the ground.

Dazed, Balin spluttered as Lancelot was suddenly astride him, sliding the point of his sword through the slit of Balin's helm to threaten his left eye.

"Do you yield?" Lancelot demanded.

Balin, breathless, succumbed to the first honest defeat he had suffered. Also, his last. "I do not yield. Kill me now," he said tiredly.

Lancelot looked confused. "Why would you rather die than yield? We have no audience. No one knows of your defeat. I do not even know your name, so how can I tell anyone?"

Balin chuckled wearily. "This is the caliber of knight Avalon produces."

"What do you mean?"

"I speak of a man's honor, boy. I sought your death, pagan creature that you are. In doing so, I was fully prepared to die. When a man challenges another, he does so at risk of his own honor. It doesn't matter if I am defeated in this secluded forest or in the tiltyard of Camelot with the entire kingdom looking on. God above has witnessed my failure. And by the law of God, I may not live. For no true knight can stand against one who is false."

"Then you are false?"

"I do not know," Balin said truly. "I only know you must kill me. If you call yourself a true knight and yet have no knowledge of honor, then you are a glory seeker who fights to please a crowd, and I do not wish to remain alive in a world where a knight like you is esteemed."

Lancelot looked at him thoughtfully and slid his sword from Balin's visor with a scrape.

"I am a very young knight, yet. I have not even embarked upon my errantry nor sworn to a king. You are obviously a knight of wisdom and honor, and by the state of your armor, many battles. Do you think perhaps, that God granted me this victory over you to teach me humility?"

"How do you stand to learn humility as a victor?" Balin scoffed.

"Through your words I have learned it. I am used to praise and the attention of women for my skill at arms. But you have shown me that a true knight may fight and die without anyone knowing at all. What is your name?"

"I will not give it."

"If I insist?" he said, brandishing his sword.

"Never."

Lancelot shook his head. "You amaze me. You hold your tongue, and your reasons are your own. I respect that," he said. He got to his feet, smiling down at Balin. Then he offered his hand.

Balin looked up at this peerless boy, so like St. Michael himself in form. There was something inspiring about him, which he had to fight to resist.

He slapped away the hand and rose on his own. Maybe the boy was right. But if his victory had taught this pagan a lesson, then what had it taught Balin?

When Balin stood again, the boy had gone off a ways and was now coming back, smiling. "I'm sorry about your sword. Here is the other."

Balin stared. Lancelot was holding the Adventurous Sword out to him. The sword no man had been able to lift but him. He reached out, and for a moment, feared it would pin him to the ground if he tried to hold it, but Lancelot handed it over lightly. He mounted his horse again.

"Will you not ride with me to Camelot, Knight with The Two Swords? I am of Avalon, but if you promise not to hold it against me, I will ask my cousins to present you to King Arthur."

Balin was moved by this boy's offer. More, he was in awe of him. Tears swelled unbidden in his eyes as he remembered Dagonet and Safir and the other knights who had been kind to him in his time. Perhaps this boy was something new. Perhaps…but no. He could not give into the temptation to ride beside this knight back to Camelot, no matter how strong.

"When you see King Arthur, tell him where last you saw the Knight with The Two Swords."

"I will," said Lancelot and with a smile, he raised his hand in farewell and rode off.

Balin watched him go, until he was a bright speck like the pinpoint of a star on the road to Carteloise.

Balin found his broken shield. It was beyond repair, the boar charges forever riven, so he hung it in the oak tree.

Then he took Ironprow by the bridle and gazed at the blade of the Adventurous Sword, matching the engraved image to the lake and the menhir and the tree.

There was something new carved there on the sword.

Two knights fighting on foot. He thought maybe it was Lancelot, but no. Their shields were blank, and the sword was nothing if not accurate. He looked out across the lake.

Merlin had said that every forest led to his Garden of Joy. He had seen Lancelot ride from the direction of this empty body of water. What if every lake led to Avalon?

He waded out into the lake, wetting his ankles, and stood staring across the misty surface for a time. The sun was sinking now, and the red played on the water. It was the bloody Nile of cursed Rameses. The mist had thickened, and the far side could no longer be seen.

He lowered the tip of the sword and let it pierce the water. Immediately he heard the sound of spars groaning, of water lapping. Then he saw a skiff skimming through the mist, making for him.

It was empty, but the poles moved just the same.

CHAPTER
FOUR

BALIN LED IRONPROW onto the skiff and it tottered not at all. As soon as he had stepped aboard, the poles groaned and the skiff departed the shore.

He passed a hand through the space where a ferryman should have stood, but there was no resistance. The skiff proceeded quietly across the water and into a bank of mist so thick Balin could barely see Ironprow's outline.

Though he had seen the diameter of the modest lake, the skiff proceeded for some time. Balin saw the tower of a keep rising ahead. The skiff beached once more, and Balin led Ironprow onto dry land.

This was not the waste land he had left. Here the grass was lush and green. Fireflies pulsed and circled in the dimness like will-o'-the-wisps. He saw a dark castle loom over the tops of an orchard of apple trees. There were soft lights in the windows, and he could hear the sound of gentle music.

He started toward the orchard, when a bobbing torch light appeared, and a woman emerged, all in samite such as he'd seen the Lady of The Lake wear.

"Are you the Lady of The Lake?" Balin growled, gripping his sword.

"Don't you recognize me, Sir Balin?" said a familiar voice. The maiden lowered the brand so that it illuminated her lovely face.

"You are the lady who gave me this sword."

"I am," she whispered. "Come with me, before the Red Knight is alerted." She turned, but he hesitated.

"Is this Avalon?"

"It is. And I am its prisoner, just as you may be if you don't hurry." Then she went off into the gloom.

Balin swallowed, terribly confused. Hadn't he come to the realization that this sword was a thing of evil, and that thus, the lady who had given it him must also be evil? Yet she had given him fair warning hadn't she, that day? Hadn't she entreated him not to claim it?

He followed, aware of the clink of his armor and the heavy breath of Ironprow as they passed through the silent rows of trees.

She led him through a copse that skirted a great field in front of the castle, where maidens strode the grounds in the light of the windows, singing and speaking to each other, and drinking wine. She guided him carefully to the back of the castle to a stable and showed him into an empty pen where he could put Ironprow.

"What is this?" Balin demanded.

She hushed him. "Be quiet, Sir Knight. I beg you! I came to this accursed island by accident, when my homeward bound ship entered a storm and somehow emerged here. I am a prisoner, assailed daily to join the society of these dark maidens, and I may not leave. It is the fate of all women who wander into Avalon. But my sex spares me the harsher fate of hapless men like yourself who find themselves on this shore."

"What do you mean?" he asked.

"Any man discovered on Avalon is forced to face the Red Knight in battle. He is the Devil's own champion, Sir Balin," she said, rapidly crossing herself. "Nine good knights have I seen him lay low in the time I've been here."

Balin gritted his teeth to hear this. The Red Knight. The same black-guard that his mother had spoken of. No doubt part of a triumvirate of evil on this island. The Lady, Merlin, and the Red Knight, standing in direct opposition to the Father, the Son, and the Holy Spirit.

"Show me this Red Knight, that I may slay him for you, my lady."

The maiden smiled and touched his arm. "Oh, Sir Balin, it glad-dens my heart to hear you say that, to think that my emancipation is at hand. I do not doubt your strength, but do not be so bold. You are not at your peak, and you have no shield. Stay here tonight, and in the morning, you and your horse will be fresh, and I will secret you a new shield and armor from the castle's stores."

Balin fidgeted. He didn't like the idea of spending the night in this place. "I do not like to carry any more of this island's arms into battle than I have already. This sword I freed you of has proven a great curse to me. You were right. I should have heeded your warning."

"Yet the Red Knight's arms are all of Avalon, and they will cleave through your harness like paper. Please, Sir Balin. Rest and let me arm you. I will not fail."

"Nor will I, my lady," he said, touching the back of her hand. "Very well."

She thanked him tearfully, blessed him, filled the manger with apples for Ironprow, and shut him in. He did not doff his armor, for fear that some night watchwoman might find him and he might need to fight, whatever his equipment. He piled the straw and sank into it, listening to Ironprow eat.

The air through the stable was cool and clean, and it brought also the weird music of the women which, heard in some benighted hamlet miles away, might have soothed him with its graceful melodies and beauteous feminine voices. But here in the enemy's camp, it sounded like the song of sirens, presaging death and doom.

He could not sleep in his armor, as he remembered the last time he had tried to do so, after slaying Lanceor, and like every man past midnight, the sins of his days washed over him and he trembled in his steel skin to think of what the morning would bring.

If life, it would mean death for the maidens he had seen. It would mean the throats trilling sweet songs this night would be cut in the morning when he raged like fire through their castle.

Yet if the Red Knight proved his better, as already another knight of Avalon had been, then it meant death.

And then what?

If Brother Gallet were to be believed, would it be heavenly sunlight for all eternity? Ministering angels and trumpets? What would he do in heaven all day? It was a thing he had often wondered in his boyhood. Would he be given a duty complementing his station in life? Would it be his lot to kneel before God through eternity and sing praises as he had in church?

And what if the sins of his life outweighed the good? Did his good deeds outweigh his failures? He thought to bring out the Adventurous Sword and mark them, but the light was dim and he dared not kindle any. There was the avenging of his mother, had that been murder because the woman had been unarmed? Was his sin compounded because she had been his aunt unknowing? There was the defeat of Rience, surely an evil soul. The defense of Cameliard and Queen Guinevere, the slaying of Lanceor and by inaction, his lover Colombe. The adventure of the Leprous Lady, in which he had done no great wrong that he could remember, though he had slain two blood drinking creatures, and then of course, the slaying of the murderer Garlon and the loss of the Sangreal.

That last was a very great sin indeed, and it burdened him, made a coward of him. He wanted to steal way from the island and find some priest to absolve him before he undertook this thing, so that if it was his fate to die, he would not go to hell. Why had he not thought of that before?

What if hell did receive him tomorrow? What would it be like? Would he have to conform to its myriad tortures for all eternity or was there some way he could resist and fight his way free? It seemed intolerable to him that he should spend eternity at the mercy of demons. Better to fight and suffer the wounds of battle again and again than be cowed and mistreated.

In the last, he wondered, wherever his soul was bound, would it meet Lorna Maeve's again?

Heaven, hell, or dismal purgatory, each would be markedly better if she were there.

Could he find her? Would she blame him for her demise? Would she hate him in the end as she had that night outside her tent?

He clasped his hands and prayed for victory on the morrow. For all his questions, he would rather fight than know the answers.

CHAPTER
FIVE

B ALIN DID MANAGE to sleep somehow. In the morning, he was awakened by the sound of a summoning drum. There on the straw before him, neatly stacked, he found a suit of fine armor and plain shield, a sturdy lance and great helm, and a basket of apples and bread. The lady had proven true.

He doffed his battered old harness and dressed in the new, his heart hammering the whole time to the sound of the drum, which sounded like an execution march. The food he left where it was. He would not touch anything of this island to his lips. He knelt before he mounted Ironprow, and using the sword for a cross, pressed it to his forehead.

"Heavenly Father, I beseech you…grant me atonement. Let me slay their unholy champion if it means my dying stroke. Then, if it is your will, let me triumph over this undying enemy. Here, where she abides."

It was a new Balin that rode from the stables of Avalon, sure and bright in his gleaming arms and straight lance. He rounded the corner of the large white castle and came to the edge of the field.

Waiting on the other side, upon a black destrier and all bedecked in red armor, with hellish red plumes upon his helm, a red shield, and a red lance, as though he had been dipped in blood, was the champion of Avalon.

His destroyer or his salvation? He looked about and saw that the battlements of the castle were lined with maidens all in blazing white and chief among them, a white haired woman, tall and statuesque, beautiful and villainous.

The woman raised her hand and the drumming ceased.

"Where is the lady who brought me to shelter last night?" Balin demanded before she could speak. His new helm had no visor, and he could not easily remove it, so he had to shout with some force to be heard.

"You will see her only if you live," the Lady of The Lake replied.

"Then ready her to leave this island!" Balin called, "and all you ladies, make ready to depart, if you would keep your lives, for I bring the sword of God to this nest of vipers! Once I am finished here, I will come for you, dread Lady!"

He spurred his horse and charged across the lush green yard.

The Red Knight came, too, silent as a scarlet monolith bearing down, his red plumage flying behind him like fire.

Balin could not help but admire the form and fearlessness of his opponent. Avalon was a cradle of evil, but it was also a wellspring of knights.

As the distance closed, their lances lowered simultaneously. Neither man nor horse veered away but met in the center with a resounding crash that flung them both from their saddles and sent their shields wafting away like autumn leaves.

Balin lay stunned on the ground, staring up at the gently moving clouds in the blue sky.

Who was the Red Knight? Some lost hero of Uther's table, like Segurant, or a child of Avalon itself, raised solely for the purpose of its defense?

He sat up slowly and saw the Red Knight do the same.

They drew their swords. The Red Knight's had a crossguard of burnished red-gold. By its singular gleam, Balin knew it was no ordinary weapon he could break with the Adventurous Sword. They circled and advanced, like detritus being drawn inexorably into a whirlpool.

At the center, their blades met. Each ring of steel on steel was titanic, like the clash of Excalibur on Marmyadose that day in the field before Carhaix. Balin felt the force of their meeting in his upper arms. It was like holding onto lightning.

They were well-matched. Better than in the fight with Segurant, which had been a test of endurance and patience, and better than in the duel with Lancelot, in which he had been sorely outmatched.

This Red Knight was his true equal. Every lunge was parried. Every swing checked and countered and rapidly checked again. It was as though he fought himself.

The last time he had felt so perfectly matched was when he had sparred with Brulen, and for a moment, he was terrified that somehow the silent Red Knight *was* Brulen, bewitched or somehow compelled. But no, this knight's armor was right-handed, and Brulen was called The Sinister for his left-handed blade.

They battered against each other with shoulder, elbow, and fist, and locked together a dozen times, but their swords could not penetrate.

Balin did not know how long they fought. The sun rose to its zenith, and the inside of the armor was stifling, his breath loud and panting in his own ears.

Then the Red Knight's sword slipped and the edge of the Adventurous Sword fell by mere happenstance into the joint between his shoulder and neck, eliciting a pained groan and a burst of blood which disappeared against the crimson steel of his harness.

Surprised at his own fortune, Balin pressed the attack and directed blow after blow at that weakened spot. The Red Knight protected it fiercely though, switching his sword with a flip into his left hand so that he could check the overhand strikes. The right arm hung mostly useless, and when Balin found the wound thus protected, he managed to batter furiously at the Red Knight's cuirass, denting it ever inwards.

He was thrilled. God was with him. He was winning.

Then the Red Knight pivoted unexpectedly and swept upwards with his sword, catching Balin so hard across the helmet that the steel met his face and smashed his nose. He stumbled back, tasting the river of coppery blood that poured down over his mouth.

The Red Knight leapt in, striking at the helm, and when Balin raised his arm to deflect, his opponent stabbed him deeply in the armpit.

Balin retreated, clutching the grievous wound, hearing the blood trickle down his side. He could not raise his left arm higher than his chest.

The Red Knight did not advance, but jammed his sword into the red sprinkled grass and leaned there for a moment, heaving blood into his helm, which drizzled from beneath his chin and down his front. The dents in his breastplate were substantial.

Balin took respite, too, but as soon as he stooped to catch his breath, the Red Knight charged him, raised his sword overhead, and brought it down so hard on the top of Balin's helm that he heard the ladies on the castle roof gasp. Blood immediately covered his right eye and his crown felt hot and exposed. The twisted steel pressed against his face.

He fell to one knee, ears ringing, and thrust savagely at his attacker. He saw the tip of his blade disappear in the Red Knight's side. The Red Knight fell backward and sat down hard, grasping at the fresh wound, blood gushing over his gauntlet.

Balin went to one knee and painfully forced his wounded left arm up, to slide his fingers beneath his dented helm and undo the fastenings. He was half-blinded and could scarcely breathe. He needed to get his helm off.

The Red Knight rose unsteadily, and Balin cursed him under his breath.

Stop, damn you! Stop!

The Red Knight stumbled forward, raising his sword. Balin lifted his blade, his left hand now trapped beneath his helmet.

He jabbed again and again at the Red Knight's wounded side. Twice he was struck aside, but the third time he scored a hit, and as though the rent flesh remembered his blade, this time it welcomed it like an old lover, and the sword sunk in almost to the third engraving from the tip.

The Red Knight cried out and fell once more to his knees. He struck Balin's sword down with his mailed fist. Then he took up his sword stiffly in both hands and began to furiously attack, striking the side of Balin's helm and chopping away at his shoulders.

Stunned, Balin could do no more than shudder under the heavy rain of attacks, but he lifted his sword once more and began to stab persistently at the gory wound in the Red Knight's side.

Again and again they struck each other from the kneeling position, tearing steel, tearing doublets, both screaming in pain and rage, each seeking only the other's immediate death to stop the agony. Blood and flesh flew in the air, and the women atop the castle screamed and turned away. All except the Lady.

When both were spent and exhausted and the pieces of their armor hung half severed and twisted from their torn bodies, they fell against each other. Each heard the ragged, tortured breathing of the other close by.

Balin pushed the Red Knight away, and they both fell on their backs in the grass, which was now a dark red circle around them.

Balin lay until he thought life would slip from him. When it didn't, he propped himself up on his elbows and strained to see his opponent.

The Red Knight turned on his side in the same moment and looked at him. His breastplate was punctured six times and leaked blood from every hole, and his cuisses were broken and hung by scraps of leather.

Balin's own helm was crushed to his skull, so that he had to suck his breaths through the narrow gap of twisted steel. His breastplate flapped open on his bloody chest like a broken cabinet door. In this reposing attitude, they stared at each other for a time.

No higher thought passed through Balin's exhausted mind. He could register only pain and the need to put an end to the source of his agony.

He rolled and pushed himself up. He slipped a few times and clattered into the red-painted grass, but then he found his knee, and then his feet, and then he was standing with his sword in hand.

The Red Knight watched him the entire time, not moving, perhaps not wanting to make the effort himself unless he was sure the fight would continue.

Balin stood and waited. For a moment, he thought the Red Knight had died.

But then he rolled on his stomach, put his sword into the ground again, and pulled himself up trembling by the crossguard, dragged his legs up, and managed to stand, wobbling on the sword like a cane.

The women of Avalon murmured. Some wept.

The Red Knight raised his sword and straightened.

Balin breathed deeply and limped closer. He hefted the Adventurous Sword and brought it in an arc at the Red Knight's head.

The Red Knight could not life his sword past his breast.

The edge of Balin's weapon struck him in the face and he reeled as if from a fist, but recovered. Balin hit him again on the backswing.

The Red Knight stumbled wildly, then recovered his balance and brought his sword in, knocking aside Balin's hanging chest piece and chopping into his left side ribs like a butcher.

Balin groaned, pitched forward, and came up swinging, catching the Red Knight in the helm again, forcing him to look at the sky. The Red Knight wheeled and came back with a thrust that found Balin's exposed shoulder.

Balin hit him in the face again. His helmet was bent out of shape like a clutched fist, and blood poured from the eye slit like tears.

The Red Knight did not withdraw his sword, but twisted it, stirred it in Balin's shoulder socket, grinding the muscle and bone together. Balin screamed and struck his sword arm.

The Red Knight only leaned forward, shoulder moving steadily, ripping apart Balin's muscles. Balin shrieked wildly and with a supreme effort, hacked vigorously at the Red Knight's elbow as if it were firewood.

The Red Knight made no sound, even when with a crack, his forearm separated from his rerebrace and twisted entirely around on a tether of flesh, which Balin then parted with a final, tired swipe. The Red Knight's arm and the offending sword hung from Balin's ruined shoulder for a moment, and he pushed it off in disgust, so that it tumbled into the grass between them.

Balin fell after it. For a time, all was black. Then he heard the weeping of the women again, and a hissing in the grass.

He looked and saw the Red Knight lying nearby. He had a hold of the sheared bone protruding from his own severed arm. It still clutched his sword, and he was pulling it closer through the grass.

Balin moaned and flopped over on his belly.

The Red Knight pulled his own arm over his chest.

Balin took hold of the Red Knight's feet and began to pull himself up the length of the enemy's body. The Red Knight began to pry the fingers of his dead hand open.

Balin pulled himself atop the Red Knight and shimmied up his waist, panting. The Red Knight freed his own sword.

Balin pushed himself up, straddling his chest.

The Red Knight swung his sword up and caught Balin's helm again. Metal tore.

Balin gasped and brought up his sword.

The Red Knight struck him again. The helm rattled loose on his face, half turned. He was looking at the side of his helmet now, totally blind.

Another hit knocked it clean from his head, and he was numbly aware of his own eye tumbling down his right cheek in a surge of white agony, of teeth spilling over his bloody lips.

The Red Knight ceased his attacks.

Balin roared and brought the Adventurous Sword up. He drove the point into the Red Knight's chest, throwing all his weight on it. The ultimate measure, for one final blow.

He sank the sword to the hilt in his enemy's chest, pinning him to the ground underneath.

He lay full upon the Red Knight, spent.

The Red Knight let out a long, haggard rasp and his head fell back against the grass.

Balin lay panting, his ear to the bloody red armor. His battle was over. His life was over. His rampage against Avalon would end where it had begun.

He had failed to destroy the priestesses, failed to end Merlin, failed to punish Arthur for his crimes, but one of the unholy trinity was gone, at least.

The Red Knight, the guardian of Avalon since his father's day, lay dead beneath him.

And then, as he felt his soul begin to seep from his ruined, shuddering body, the Red Knight whispered from the depths of his smashed and bloody helm.

"Balin?"

CHAPTER
SIX

BALIN WANTED ONLY to succumb at last to the death he had earned.

It took him a great deal of time to pry the broken helm from the Red Knight, and when he had pulled it aside and revealed the mangled, bloody face beneath, swollen and slashed, harsh, coppery breath hissing out through a crooked jaw and broken teeth, more than ever he wanted death to come swift and immediate, to spare him from what he saw.

But death didn't come.

And Brulen said his name again.

Balin had poured out the last of his strength on this bloody field, but somehow his body found the wherewithal to shake and tremble as sorrow burst within him like a poison and flooded his fevered brain.

"I didn't know!" was all he could force up from his raw throat through the contracting muscles of his grimace.

"Nor did I," Brulen whispered, and he at least was more peaceful, though tears cut tracks through the blood on his slack face. "It doesn't hurt."

Balin sobbed.

"I came looking for *him*, for Merlin," Brulen said.

Balin clenched what remained of his teeth. "As did I."

"Defeated the last Red Knight," Brulen said with difficulty, "but won only his curse, to defend the Isle until I was killed by the next. Compelled. No choice."

Balin flung off his gauntlet and felt for his brother's fingers, worked his steel from them. They were cold and did not return his grip.

This cursed, cursed Isle. Even victory was defeat.

"Wanted to see him," Brulen said. "That's all. Just…see him."

Brulen's face wrinkled and he closed his eyes.

"Don't talk," Balin said, for he knew it pained him, though truthfully, he did not want him to stop. He wanted Brulen to say everything, anything he could, before Balin would hear his voice no more.

"Wanted to know, why, why he chose his own son," Brulen murmured.

Balin knitted his brow. Was he delirious now? He didn't know what Brulen was talking about. Unless, at the end, faced at last with eternity, he had seen the light of the Lord.

Balin struggled to find the right words. Brother Gallet had once told him that a man of God could open his mouth and the Lord would speak through him, say whatever another man's heart needed to hear, but nothing was coming to him. He was too drained. A few moments ago, he had focused all his hate on the Red Knight, but the Red Knight was his brother, for whom he bore all the love that was left in him.

"Because… He loves us, Brulen," Balin said, repeating something he'd heard Gallet say in a sermon once. "He loves all of us. And He gave His son that we all might live. Who else could He choose, Brulen? Who else was equal to the task?"

Brulen opened his eyes. They were far away now. The sun was setting over the rim of the castle, and a harsh orange light was in his face. Balin raised his trembling hand to shade his brother.

"I didn't do it, Balin," Brulen said rapidly. "In the end. I couldn't. I swore I would, but I just couldn't. We drew straws. Dagonet, Kay, Brastias and I. I was supposed to drown them all in the sea, in a sack, those boys. I found a boat, and I cast them adrift. Maybe they did die. It was stormy that day. One of them looked over the prow at me, and I watched him till he was over the breakers. Such dark eyes. I swear I saw him again later. In Lot's court in Orkney, holding onto his Morgause's finger. It was him. I know it was him. He lived. I don't know if the others survived, but he lived."

He smiled broadly, as though that thought gave him great comfort.

Balin stared. He was speaking of the May Day children now. He hadn't carried out Arthur's order after all. He hadn't had the heart. Balin's heart swelled with pride.

"I just wanted to tell him, Balin. I wanted to tell Merlin that I couldn't do it."

Balin put his forehead to his brother's.

"I love you, Brulen."

Brulen made no answer.

NIMUE APPROACHED THE dark circle of grass in the gathering twilight. None of the other women dared to come near. Seraide, Rossignol, none had the heart to approach the two brothers who had fought each other to the death.

The grass was boggy, marsh-like with blood, and her feet sank past the rim of her shoes and stained the hem of her samite gown red.

They lay beside one another on their backs, embracing, Brulen's head inclined against Balin's shoulder.

She stood over them, weeping softly. She had been the cause of their misery. She had driven them to this.

Balin's one eye opened, glassy and unfocused in the growing dark.

"Lady?"

There was no one to see, so she let slip the guise of white-haired Viviane and knelt beside him.

"I am here," she whispered gently, dripping tears on his ruined breast.

"Why do you linger?" Balin asked weakly. "Fly, before the lady of the castle discovers you. I have slain the Red Knight, don't you see? When I die, there can be no other. I have broken the spell. You are free."

"Thank you," she sobbed, taking his bloody hand and pressing it to her cheek.

"Please tell of my brother and me in Camelot," he whispered.

"I shall tell them all of your deeds," she promised.

"And lay us in a single grave. From one womb we came and to one we return."

She nodded, unable to respond.

He smiled slightly. "You are lovely," he said.

His hand hung limp in her own, and she laid it back on the breast of his brother's, from where she had picked it.

His shining eye reflected the wheel of stars.

THE
ESPLUMOIR

ERLIN STOOD BACK and admired the block of red marble with the Adventurous Sword protruding from the top. He had fitted it with a new pommel, one entirely of solid emerald, in which gold script had been inlaid, reading:

NONE SHALL TAKE ME HENCE BUT HE AT WHOSE
SIDE I AM TO HANG AND HE SHALL BE THE BEST
KNIGHT IN THE WORLD.

It was exactly as he had foreseen it.

He put his foot to the marble and pushed it from the bank, and it floated like a hunk of cork off into the mists. He watched it disappear.

When he turned to go, Nimue was standing there in her samite gown, no longer the tearful, love-struck girl who had played with vengeance and magic, but the Lady of The Lake.

"No more Viviane, eh?" Merlin said.

"She is dead at last," Nimue said. She looked over his shoulder in the direction of the sword in the stone.

"You cannot stop, can you?"

"Stop what?"

"Interfering."

"It's not interference when it's been divined," Merlin said. "I like to think of it as a ratification of Providence."

"More swords in stones? When will you think of something new?"

Merlin shrugged. "Coming into the Garden?" he asked with a hint of playfulness. He had granted her her own means of entry. It was becoming quite serious between them again.

She said nothing but walked along beside him. "You've not been to Avalon since their funeral," she said. "You've not been in the Garden of Joy, lately. Where have you been spending your days?"

In truth, Avalon held no amusement for him. The memory of Balin and Brulen pained him, as he had not ever thought it would. He had thought himself above such things. Nimue had told him all of their final hours. She had not spared him a single gory detail, as though punishing him with the excruciating minutiae of their fate somehow alleviated her own guilt and heaped it upon him. He already ached for them, in ways she could not guess.

He had built their tomb, laid them together, as Balin had requested. He could do no more.

"I wanted to stay out of your way, Lady. I went traveling. After Sir Lancelot set foot in Albion, I had to be about undoing much of what Viviane had done and what Lancelot will do, unwittingly. I've scarcely had a moment's rest."

Lancelot. He would bring more doom to Arthur than ever Balin could have, if he was not stopped. Much of Camelot loved the young knight. Too much, really.

Then, of course, there was young Mordred, the son of Arthur and his aunt Morgause, safely under the protection of Morgan Le Fay. Somehow, he alone had escaped the May Day slaughter.

They passed from the shore into the forest, and soon they were at the spring, and they walked in silence through the sunbeams that pierced the jade roof of his sanctuary. They went ever deeper, until they came to his crystal cave, wherein he had wiled many hours peering into the future, picking through the complex threads of destiny, scowling over inevitabilities, and tweaking potentialities, trying to steer Arthur and the world toward that golden day far along, that day which even the purest heart in the world would mock with a cynic's scoff if Merlin were to tell them of it.

It was his secret joy to tend it. He was like a parent before Christmas, hiding gifts for his loved ones and imagining their delight to come. No, perhaps not like a parent.

"What's the matter?" she asked, seeing his face darken.

"Nothing, my dear," Merlin said.

They came to the edge of the cave, and he smiled at the curtain of ivy hanging down over the entrance.

"I *have* been away awhile," he said, rubbing a green leaf between his two fingers. "Or you've been redecorating."

She smiled sweetly.

"I hope you haven't been reordering my reagents. I have a system." He went inside.

The scintillating hues of the many crystals in which he had gazed for hours beyond the frontiers of many universes, the shelves and stacks of books, the old workbench, all were gone, replaced by blank walls of ugly black iron.

A cold iron box.

Behind him, Nimue had deftly turned the soft earth of the threshold with the toe of her shoe and dropped an iron dagger into the prepared hole beneath.

When he turned, she was kicking dirt over it.

"I'm sorry, Aurelius Ambrosius."

He smiled thinly and stretched his staff across the threshold. When his hand moved over the knife, it was as though he had met solid stone. The staff could leave. He could not.

"So that's my true name," Merlin said. "Bit of a mouthful."

"Blaise named you for the High King he once served," Nimue said. "I'm sorry. You can't be permitted to meddle anymore."

Merlin nodded in agreement and set his staff against the wall. He put his hands in the pockets of his robes. "What will Avalon do?"

"Avalon and the Lady of The Lake will retreat into the mists," said Nimue. "The crucified god has won Albion."

Merlin could only frown. There was no point in voicing disagreement. This was not Lile. Nimue would not be swayed. She had found resolve to match her power.

"You told me that Blaise was always right," Nimue said.

"I know," said Merlin. He looked about the bare chamber. There was a simple bed, nothing more. "Not even my books, eh? How will I pass the time?"

Nimue did not smile.

He touched the iron wall. He could not feel the crystals beyond, and the door with no key which led to Camelot was gone. They must have walled it up during his sojourn to the east. He went to the cot and sat down.

She still stood in the cave mouth. "Farewell, Merlin." Then she raised her hands.

He took it as a parting gesture and lifted his own, but then he saw the great iron shutter slide down slowly, grinding, groaning against its housing.

Then the light was shut out and he was in darkness.

As he had foreseen. He lay on the cot and sighed.

He had told Arthur of course, all about Lancelot and Guinevere, and the great rift it would bring. Once free of Avalon's mists, he had seen all that would come, all that would be undone by the young knight.

Viviane had struck even from beyond death with that one, sly vixen, but he had also seen what would spring from Lancelot, and how the Sangreal could redeem them all.

So he had warned them all, uselessly, but only so they could not later wonder why he had not.

He had warned Balin, too, and his brother, but they were not entirely to blame for their own fates. He had piloted them as sure as he had put them to sea, hadn't he?

They alone were the whole of his regret.

"I'm sorry," he said aloud, and his voice boomed in the iron walled chamber.

It was foolishness. He had done all he could. Arthur's life was his own again.

And he, he would sleep until they needed him again.

He closed his eyes and thought of the summer he had spent as other men, sitting on the rude bench outside the stone cottage at the edge of the forest, bouncing his sons upon his knees as their mother picked wild chives and spignel from the base of the old Roman wall, and dandelion fluff from her red hair.

"And I pray all you that redyth this tale to pray for him that this wrote that God sende hym good deliverance and sone and hastely – Amen."

ABOUT THE AUTHOR

Edward M. Erdelac is the author of twelve novels including Andersonville, Monstrumfuhrer, and The Merkabah Rider series. His fiction has appeared in numerous anthologies and periodicals ranging from Occult Detective Quarterly to Star Wars Insider Magazine. Born in Indiana, educated in Chicago, he resides in the Los Angeles area with his family. News and excerpts from his work can be found at www.emerdelac.wordpress.com

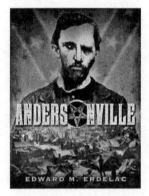

ANDERSONVILLE *(Del Rey-Hydra)*

In 1864 thirty thousand ragged Union soldiers pray for a way out of the disease ridden confines of the South's most notorious prison camp, unaware they are about to become unwitting accomplices in a dark ritual enacted by a madman to turn the tide of the Civil War.

When Mary Todd Lincoln's spiritual advisor has a vision of the nation awash in blood, Union Black Dispatch agent Barclay Lourdes is dispatched to infiltrate Andersonville prison and put a stop to the terrible events about to enfold....

— PRAISE FOR *ANDERSONVILLE* —

"[Edward M.] Erdelac makes a heady brew out of dreadful true events, angel and demon lore, secret societies, and the trappings of Southern gothic novels. This is thoughtful horror at its best, and not at all for the faint of heart."—Publishers Weekly Starred Review

"Andersonville is a raw, groundbreaking supernatural knuckle-punch. Erdelac absolutely owns Civil War and Wild West horror fiction."
—Weston Ochse, bestselling author of SEAL Team 666

"If you took a tale of atmospheric horror by Ambrose Bierce and infused it with the energy of Elmore Leonard, you would come close to what Edward Erdelac has accomplished with Andersonville. But even that combination would sell the novel short. What Erdelac has done is not just splice genres together but create his own voice in telling of the horrors, real and supernatural, inhabiting the most infamous prison camp of the Civil War. This is U.S. history seen through the eyes of the tortured dead, told with amazing skill by an author who knows how to create genre literature with a purpose."
—C. Courtney Joyner, author of Shotgun and Nemo Rising

"Andersonville definitely stands out . . . with its nuanced language, complicated characters, engrossing narrative, and subtle commentary on the past and the present."
—LitReactor

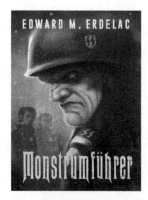

MONSTRUMFUHRER *(Comet Press)*

In 1936 Dr. Josef Mengele discovers the lab journals of Victor Frankenstein and is tasked with replicating his reanimation procedure by the Reich Institute.

In 1945, a Jewish boy uncovers the secrets of Mengele's horrific experiments behind the barbed wire of Auschwitz KZ. He escapes and heads north in search of the only being on earth who can stop the Reich's insidious project – Frankenstein's original creature.

But the Creature has its price....

— PRAISE FOR *MONSTRUMFUHRER* —

"....profound; a wrenching and tragic look at the horrors of war, tortured dynamics of father-and-son relationships, race and ideology, pride, belief, ambition, survival, philosophy, brotherhood, the very nature of humanity and life, and the darkest insights into our collective psyches." —The Horror Fiction Review

"....absolutely devastating." —Cemetery Dance

"Highest possible recommendation." —Confessions of a Reviewer

COYOTE'S TRAIL *(Comet Press)*

In 1886 a bloodied and battered Chiricahua Apache boy drags himself out of the Arizona desert, intent on revenge. He kidnaps a Mexican prostitute and with the help of a sadistic whiskey peddler, uses her as bait to lure the cavalrymen who massacred his family out from the safety of their fort, unaware that the woman is pursuing her own bizarre course of revenge.

— PRAISE FOR *COYOTE'S TRAIL* —

"With *COYOTE'S TRAIL*, Ed Erdelac has created a story as raw as the wound from a bullwhip. His blistering prose, combined with superb use of time, place, and character, gives *COYOTE'S TRAIL* the kind of life that springs off the page and into the reader's consciousness. That's a rare thing these days, and in the world of genre fiction, rarer still. This is a damn hard story about damn hard men, and told damn well."

—C. Courtney Joyner, Author of *SHOTGUN* and *NEMO RISING*

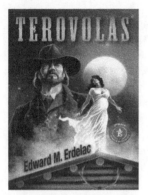

TEROVOLAS *(Journalstone)*

The recovered personal papers of Professor Abraham Van Helsing recount the events which took place immediately following the account of Bram Stoker's DRACULA.

Following the killing of the nefarious count and his vampiric wives, Van Helsing suffers from violent, recurring fantasies and commits himself to Jack Seward's Purfleet Asylum for treatment. Upon his release and seeking a relaxing holiday, Van Helsing volunteers to transport the remains and earthly effects of Quincey P. Morris back to the Morris family ranch in Sorefoot, Texas.

He finds Quincey's brother Cole embroiled in escalating tensions with a neighboring outfit of Norwegian cattle ranchers led by the enigmatic Sig Skoll. When men and animals start turning horrible mutilated, Van Helsing suspects a preternatural culprit, but is a shapechanger really loose on the Texas plains, or are the delusions of his previously disordered mind returning?

— PRAISE FOR *TEROVOLAS* —

"Professor Abraham Van Helsing in the Wild West! What more could one ask for? [Erdelac] melds the stylistic concepts [of Dracula] perfectly with those of the classic western tales."   —The British Fantasy Society

"Erdelac manages to recreate the style of Stoker without lacking originality as one might expect. By staying true to the tradition laid down by Dracula while simultaneously putting his own spin on the story, Erdelac breathes new life into an old tale. The action scenes are crisp, the characters well developed, the plot filled with surprises."

—Brett J. Talley, Stoker award winning author of *That Which Should Not Be*

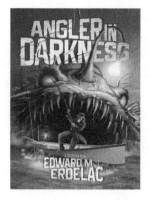

ANGLER IN DARKNESS

A frontiersman of bizarre pedigree is peculiarly suited to tracking down a group of creatures rampaging across the settlements of the Texas Hill Country.…. A great white hunter is shaken to his core by a quarry he cannot conceive of.… A bullied inner city kid finds the power to strike back against his tormentors and finds he can't stop using it.… Outraged plumbing plots its revenge.… Here Blackfoot Indians hunt the undead, the fate of nations is decided by colossal monsters, a salaryman learns the price of abandoning his own life, and even the Angel of Death tells his story.

— PRAISE FOR *ANGLER IN DARKNESS* —

"If you're new to Erdelac's work, *Angler in Darkness* is a fabulous introduction, a bizarre medley of the perverse, sinister, and strange. Erdelac weaves a refreshingly unabashed tapestry, his blunt naturalistic dialogue hitting as hard as the visceral thrills splashing across the pages. Most importantly, his work gives voice to diverse points-of-view, his protagonists arriving from walks of life often overlooked in genre fiction. *Angler in Darkness* is a provocative, compelling, and deliciously devilish anthology from one of the most talented voices in fantasy fiction, and a must read for aficionados of the unusual."
—Cemetery Dance

"Erdelac's first collection of 15 reprints and three previously unpublished stories runs the gamut of monster mayhem and historical weirdness, with plenty of gore to satisfy horror aficionados.… Erdelac has a gift for inspiring fascination with whatever era he chooses to write about, especially the Wild West, where he shines. This entertaining and varied collection, enhanced by the author's story prefaces, will appeal to a wide variety of horror readers."
—Publisher's Weekly

"You'll find history not sanitized and prettied up for modern sensibilities; this is the raw stuff, the gritty stuff, with the ugliness and racism right there alongside the bravery and beauty.

Sometimes, the tales focus on the small-scale, families or individuals, lonely journeys, confrontations with cruel mortality and truth. In others, the fates of nations are at stake. There's variety here, a display of ranges -- temporal, stylistic, genre—and it all serves to reinforce my initial opinion. Whatever the era, Ed Erdelac does historical fiction RIGHT."
—*This Is Horror*

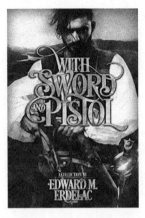

WITH SWORD AND PISTOL *(Crossroads Press)*
Collects four fantasy adventure novellas.

RED SAILS - In 1740 a British marine and a Dominican Blackfriar are captured on the high seas by a blood guzzling pirate captain and turned loose on a cannibal isle to be hunted down for sport under the full moon by his shapeshifting crew.

NIGHT OF THE JIKININKI - In 1737 three disparate men, a casteless bandit, a sadistic samurai sword tester, and a mad, child killing monk band together to fight their way out of a feudal Japanese prison as it fills with the walking dead.

SINBAD AND THE SWORD OF SOLOMON - In 796, Sinbad the Sailor and motley crew undertake a mission from the Caliph of Baghdad to retrieve a magic sword from a demon on an enchanted island.

GULLY GODS - In 2005 a young South Houston gangster learns the horrific secret behind the power behind a seemingly unstoppable clique of Liberian ex-child soldiers taking over a South Chicago neighborhood.

Hundreds of years removed. Thousands of miles apart. They all make their end WITH SWORD AND PISTOL.

MERKABAH RIDER

A Hasidic gunslinger tracks the renegade teacher who betrayed his mystic Jewish order of astral travelers across the demon-haunted American Southwest of 1879.

In this acclaimed first volume, four sequential novellas and one bonus short story chronicle the weird adventures of THE MERKABAH RIDER.

In THE BLOOD LIBEL, The Rider fights to save the last survivors of a frontier Jewish settlement not only from a maddened lynch mob, but from a cult of Molech worshippers hiding in their midst. In THE DUST DEVILS, a border town is held hostage by a band of outlaws in league with a powerful Vodoun sorcerer. In HELL'S HIRED GUN, The Rider faces an ex-Confederate sharpshooter who has pledged his allegiance to Hell itself. In THE NIGHTJAR WOMEN, The Rider drifts into a town where children cannot be born. Here an antediluvian being holds the secret to his fugitive master's insidious plan; a plot that threatens all of Creation. Finally, never before collected, THE SHOMER EXPRESS. On a midnight train crossing the desert, a corpse turns up desecrated. Someone stalking the cars has assumed its shape, and only The Rider can stop it.

— PRAISE FOR *MERKABAH RIDER* —

"The Rider is a fabulous character, in all senses of that word, and Erdelac's a fabulous writer. *High Planes Drifter* contains all the demons, ancient gods, and gunplay a lover of weird westerns could want, but told from an angle no one else has touched before. Where else are you going to find a Jewish Doctor Strange packing heat in the old west? Nowhere, that's where. This is crazily entertaining stuff."

—Daryl Gregory, award-winning author of *Pandemonium* and *Spoonbenders*

"Riding out of the Old West comes the Merkabah Rider, a Hasidic gunfighter who owes his provenance as much to the nasty inhabitants of Elmore Leonard's westerns as he does his piousness to Robert E. Howard's Solomon Kane. This highly original episodic series breathes new life into the overworked western with tight action, inglorious heroes, and unpredictable plots."

—Weston Ochse, award-winning author of *SEAL Team 666* and *Scarecrow Gods*

"I don't have any hesitation in calling *Merkabah Rider: High Planes Drifter* the pinnacle of the Weird West genre, and one that will be hard to surplant."

—*Sci Fi and Fantasy Reviewer*

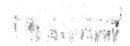

CPSIA information can be obtained
at www.ICGtesting.com
Printed in the USA
LVHW041942250719
625346LV00005B/606/P